PRAISE FOR CHRISTOPHER RICE

Bone Music

"A stellar and gripping opening to the Burning Girl series introduces the tough, smart Trina Pierce, aka Charlotte Rowe, who survived a childhood of murder and exploitation to discover there might be another way to fight back . . . Readers will be eager for the next installment in Rice's science-fiction take on *The Girl with the Dragon Tattoo*."

—*Booklist* (starred review)

"*Bone Music* is a taut and gripping thriller that's as bleak and harsh as the Arizona desert. It never lets up until the final page. Rice has created a great character in Charlotte Rowe."

—Authorlink

"A simply riveting cliff-hanger of a novel, *Bone Music* by Christopher Rice is one of those reads that will linger in the mind and memory long after the book itself has been finished and set back upon the shelf."

—Midwest Book Review

A Density of Souls

"An intriguing, complex story, a hard-nosed, lyrical, teenage take on Peyton Place."

—*Publishers Weekly*

"A chillingly perverse tale in which secrets are buried, then unearthed . . . very earnest plot."

—*USA Today*

"An imaginative, gothic tale."

"Solid debut novel . . . an absorbing tale."

"Tormented families . . . unspeakable secrets . . . a blood-thirsty young man. No, it's not Anne Rice, but her 21-year-old son, Christopher."

"[Rice's] characters speak and act with an ease that proves [him] to be wiser than his years."

"He's learned . . . a storyteller's sense of timing. And he capably brings a gay teen's inner turmoil to life."

The Vines

"His best book yet."

"Does not disappoint and grabs you from the opening chapter straight to the end with plot twists that are dark and thrilling . . . The transitions between modern-day and French colonial slavery are exquisite and leave the reader intrigued throughout the narrative. Rice also creates a beautiful mythology infused with a thriller that gives you many shocks and oh-my-God moments in every chapter."

"As gothic as one could expect from the author (*The Heavens Rise*) and son of Anne Rice, this tale of evil vegetation that feeds on the blood of those seeking revenge for past wrongs is gruesome . . . there are dark thrills for horror fans."

—*Library Journal*

The Heavens Rise

"This is Rice's best book to date, with evocative language, recurring themes, and rich storytelling that will raise the hairs on the back of the neck. It rivals the best of Stephen King at times and sets a standard for psychological horror."

—*Louisville Courier-Journal*

"A masterful coming-of-age novel . . . Rice's characters are complex and real, his dialogue pitch-perfect, and his writing intelligent and strong. He builds suspense beautifully . . . amid enduring philosophical questions about what it means to be human."

—*Publishers Weekly* (starred review)

"Christopher Rice never disappoints with his vivid people and places and masterful prose. He will hold you captive under his spell as his images and emotions become your own."

—Patricia Cornwell, #1 *New York Times* bestselling author

"Christopher Rice is a magician. This brilliant, subtly destabilizing novel inhales wickedness and corruption and exhales delight and enchantment. Rice executes his turns, reversals, and surprises with the pace and timing of a master. *The Heavens Rise* would not let me stop reading it—that's how compelling it is."

—Peter Straub, #1 *New York Times* bestselling author

"Christopher Rice has written an amazing horror novel with more twists and turns than a mountain road. You'll think you know your destination . . . but you'll be wrong."

—Charlaine Harris, #1 *New York Times* bestselling author

BLOOD
VICTORY

OTHER TITLES BY CHRISTOPHER RICE

THRILLERS

Blood Echo: A Burning Girl Thriller
Bone Music: A Burning Girl Thriller
The Vines
The Heavens Rise
The Moonlit Earth
Blind Fall
Light Before Day
The Snow Garden
A Density of Souls

ROMANCE

The Flame: A Desire Exchange Novella
The Surrender Gate: A Desire Exchange Novel
Kiss The Flame: A Desire Exchange Novella
Dance of Desire
Desire & Ice: A MacKenzie Family Novella

WITH ANNE RICE

Ramses the Damned: The Passion of Cleopatra

BLOOD VICTORY

A BURNING GIRL THRILLER

CHRISTOPHER RICE

 THOMAS & MERCER

Published by Thomas & Mercer, Seattle

www.apub.com

Amazon, the Amazon logo, and Thomas & Mercer are trademarks of Amazon.com, Inc., or its affiliates.

ISBN-13: 9781542014724 (hardcover)
ISBN-10: 1542014727 (hardcover)
ISBN-13: 9781542014717 (paperback)
ISBN-10: 1542014719 (paperback)

Cover design by Kirk DouPonce, DogEared Design

Printed in the United States of America

First Edition

*For my aunt, Karen O'Brien, who gave birth to
Charlotte Rowe without realizing it*

I

1

Dallas, Texas

Whenever Cyrus Mattingly sees an automated ticket machine, he thinks of closed factories and good men thrown out of work, of winds whistling through the shuttered prairie towns of his youth, and he feels a combination of rage and despair so acute he usually ends up clenching his fists until the nubs of his filed fingernails make white indentations in his palms. He's never considered himself a political man. His life affords him freedom from politics, along with many other things. But there's no denying that the automation of the world around him and his country's complete disregard for the places where he grew up go hand in hand. Throwing good men out of work circuit by circuit and swipe by swipe.

He avoids swiping now. It's one of Mother's many rules.

Cash only. Nothing traceable in the days leading up to a snatch. That includes his ticket to the 7:15 p.m. showing of *Sister Trip*.

Another rule: wear clothes that hide the bulk of your figure. Nothing so ridiculous as a trench coat and sunglasses. More like light waffle-print coats and baggy hooded sweaters, even when it's a touch too warm out to justify the outfit. The whole world's got cameras now, she constantly reminds them, and your figure can give away as much about you as your face. And she's right. Cameras and automated ticket machines and those QR code things you can read on your phones. It's like humans are trying to get rid of everything that requires effort.

And that's a shame. He's found great peace in his efforts. But he didn't find it alone.

Dressed in a button-front leather coat and a Dallas Cowboys baseball cap, Cyrus walks through the entrance to the AMC NorthPark Center, leaving the cheerful buzz of the shopping mall behind him. The crowd's thick, but it's not quite what he'd hoped. The movie business is also changing. He'd read an article just the other day that said the type of film he'd been using for years now, the "chick flick," they called it, was showing up in theaters less and less. These online companies, the streamers, they called them, were making them so women could just sit at home on their sofas and watch one right after the other. No driving to the theater, no parking. No running into a man like him.

That was all well and good, he guessed, but it made it all that much harder for him to find new seedlings.

Used to be he could hit a multiplex on any given weekend and there'd be at least three or four to choose from. Movies about wedding planners who finally find love. Movies about sisters finding ways to get along that also snag them new boyfriends. Movies where the majority of the audience was women, most of them alone, some in the company of reluctant husbands and boyfriends and, more recently, homo friends, who seemed just as interested in the movie as they were.

But for the past three weeks there's been only one film in wide release that fits the bill. He'd call it meaningless, but it's so packed full of twisted, damaging messages about what it means to be a woman, he can't dismiss it so easily. It's called *Sister Trip*. The plot concerns three sisters who go on a road trip together. At every stop along the way, their inappropriate loudmouth behavior is rewarded with either new friends or degrading sex they pretend to enjoy. In the end, they finally make it to the lookout point where they're supposed to throw their grandmother's ashes off a cliff, but not before disrespecting almost every man they come across and pretty much disrupting the natural order of things everywhere they go.

He'd much rather see a film in which all three sisters came across a man like him out in the dark, a man confident enough to break their spines. But while plenty of women attend those kinds of films, plenty of men do, too, so that's a no go.

A small popcorn and a soda, which he pays for in cash. Then he keeps his head down as he makes his way through the thicket of moviegoers in between him and his theater. It's like the crowd's moving in four different directions. Another second or two and he realizes that's exactly the case; they're all staring at their phones as they walk, most of them completely unaware of where they're headed.

When he arrives at the red velour seat he picked out when he bought the ticket, he sees it's a nice-enough-size crowd inside the screening room. Better yet, it's mostly female, and not too many in groups.

It's a stadium-style theater, with a few rows of seats at floor level and a raked seating area behind. He's second row, close to the center. Not as close as he'd like to be, but that's a casualty of paying cash and not being able to reserve the seat in advance with a credit card.

He tries not to eavesdrop on the chatter all around him. He doesn't want his judgment of anything he overhears to bias his selection.

By now he's familiar with the chain of trailers that precede the film—a superhero saves the world from blowing up, long-dead kings and queens in some foreign country have stupid fights in expensive costumes, something with aliens but he's not really sure because it's really just a teaser, but in that one it looks like the world actually does blow up.

So many damn people in Hollywood want to blow up the world.

Frustrated souls they are. They need a way to channel and focus all that rage so they can survive in the world without twisting it to their own ways. The world has enough dark corridors for men like him to slip into and feed their impulses before returning to daylit roadways, focused and purged. You just need someone like Mother to show you the way.

Once the lights inside the theater go completely dark and the studio's familiar logo fills the screen, Cyrus takes out his phone, turns up the brightness all the way, and begins swiping through a random assortment of web pages on his phone. Right away he feels the ripple of tension go through the women on all sides of him, and it sets off a warm churning in his gut. They shift in their seats; a few of them mutter curses under their breath.

He's willing to bet all of them are debating whether to say something to him about his rudeness.

And that's good.

Because the one who does won't have much longer to live.

2

Lebanon, Kansas

Lightning strikes so close to the end of the airstrip, Cole Graydon's security director makes a sound like he's been kneed in the gut.

The blinking wing lights of the Gulfstream they watched descend out of the stormy sky have vanished, Cole's sure of it. Heart hammering, he waits for a plume of orange on the horizon, proof that he was wrong to ignore his security director's earlier warnings.

Look, I know Noah Turlington could use several pieces of humble pie, but think twice before you send him hurtling headfirst through a tornado.

Cole had pretended to indulge Scott Durham's concerns by leaving the decision whether to land in the hands of the Gulfstream's pilot. But secretly he'd been savoring the image of Noah—beautiful, strong, brilliant, ice-water-in-his-veins Noah, the man who's caused him so much grief for so many years—gripping armrests while trying not to hurl.

There've been several breaks in the rain since Cole and Scott stepped from the Suburban and took shelter under the overhang next to the airstrip. The wind, however, hasn't let up once. Every now and then it drives residual droplets from the overhang's roof into their faces with stinging force.

Cole spots the plane again, wings canted, fighting crosswinds.

It's too close to the ground now to recover if wind shear drives it into the earth like an angry god's fist. That's when he realizes how right Scott is—Noah is incredibly valuable, maybe as valuable an investment as Charlotte Rowe, the test subject his more iron-hearted business partners still call Bluebird. Project Bluebird is the name for their collective effort to harness the powers Noah's drug unleashes in Charlotte's blood. Still, he's worried his business partners have come to view her as more of a lab rat than a person. Noah's drug might be Cole's passport to changing the world, but changing the world becomes more of a challenge in those moments when it seems like he might have to tear Charlotte's life apart to do it. Maybe it's time he extended the same courtesy to Noah, despite their tortured history.

Cole reminds himself that all of Noah's work at the island this past year has been logged, monitored, and backed up and backed up again. His days of conducting rogue scientific experiments on unsuspecting private citizens like Charlotte Rowe are long over. So if the plane does go down, it won't be a total loss.

The truth is, when you operate at the level of Graydon Pharmaceuticals, there's no such thing as a total loss.

A few minutes later, Noah's the first person to step off the parked jet.

A blush in his cheeks, he descends the staircase with steady steps, ignoring the handrail. There's no vomit on his windbreaker, either. The security team filing out behind him is another story. The two guys in the lead grip the staircase rails like they're battling throbbing hangovers, and Cole figures the only reason Noah was able to slip ahead of them is because the terrifying landing has left the men's stomachs in their throats.

Cole's been watching Noah's confident approach so closely he jumps at the sudden *whump* of Scott opening an umbrella over their heads. Head bowed to hide his embarrassment, Cole starts forward,

Scott accompanying him with his customary Secret Service–style attentiveness.

"Well, I knew you wouldn't pull me from the lab for something that wasn't important," Noah says. "I just don't know what could be so important in South Dakota."

"Nothing," Cole tells him. "You're not in South Dakota."

"Nebraska, then."

"Why would you be under the impression that you know where you are?" He directs the question at Noah's security team, but the recovering men don't even flinch at their employer's suggestion they told Noah more than they were supposed to.

"I've got a great sense of direction."

"With blacked-out windows, even?"

"I've got a compass in my head."

"Uh-huh. Welcome to Kansas."

"It was the storm, then. We were doing more up and down than forward, I guess. Threw me off a bit. How are you, Cole? It's good to see you in person for a change."

In their recent past, Noah would have kicked off this type of unexpected meeting with some crude reference to their sexual history designed to embarrass Cole in front of his men. But now that he's back in his labs at Cole's expense, he's been all charm. It's like he's baiting Cole into being the dark shadow in the perpetual sunny day in which he now lives.

"Did you get some sleep like I asked?"

"Some, yes," Noah answers. "I'd like to shower and change if that's OK."

"Of course."

"So, we're going to be up for a while, I take it."

"Possibly, yes."

"More storm chasing?"

9

"You're grounded for now, and the storm's only supposed to last another few hours."

"Pity. I enjoyed that part."

"Did you, though?"

"Absolutely. If only you could have been there." Noah's acidic smile suggests he knows full well Cole played some hand in his flight's terrifying final minutes.

"I was," Cole answers, "in spirit."

"I always knew you had more than you let on."

"More what?"

"Spirit."

"That's very kind of you. Let's go to the house."

"There's a house?" Noah asks, looking in both directions.

Cole smiles and starts for the car. When Scott touches his shoulder, he turns.

Noah hasn't moved an inch. The security team has encircled him. Another moment of this and they'll be reaching for their weapons.

Noah's expression is blank now, no charming smile, no twinkle in his eye.

"What is it, Noah?" Cole asks.

"I'd like to know if she's OK."

"Charley?"

Noah nods.

Cole's startled not just by the question but by the gentle, unaffected tone with which Noah asked it. Once, Noah endangered Charlotte's life by making her an unwitting test subject in an experiment that could have killed her. The result was quite the opposite, and now Cole's company is working to reap the rewards. But Noah's actions then seemed to show a callous disregard for Charley's well-being.

And now he's worried about her? Maybe that makes sense. Whether they like it or not, Noah and Charley are bound by more than just the consequences of Noah's dangerous experiment; years ago, when they were both too young to remember, their mothers were both brutalized and murdered by the same serial killers, a married couple named Daniel and Abigail Banning. So maybe his concern is natural, if it's genuine. And Cole's hoping it is.

"Of course she's OK," Cole says. "She's operational."

"And the operation's in Kansas?"

"Not quite, no."

"Then what am I doing here?"

"I said I would explain at the—"

"I heard you, but first, I have to be driven through the middle of nowhere while I'm hemmed in on all sides by your men with guns. The last time this happened I ended up in an underground cell for a few weeks. Perhaps just a bit more explanation before we—"

"Oh, for Christ's sake, you don't really think I flew you halfway across the world to shoot you and bury you in some mud, do you?"

"I didn't say that, but stranger things have happened in our line of work."

"And you caused most of them."

"And you paid for them."

"If I wanted you dead, I could have just crashed your plane."

"You almost did."

"Come now, that's a bit of an exaggeration, isn't it?"

"Is it?" Noah says to the security team surrounding him, all of whom turn to stone in response. "I mean, I'm not going to say I didn't enjoy myself, but plenty of enjoyable things in the world make you feel like you're about to die."

"Speak for yourself, special ops."

"I am, if the faces of these gentlemen are any indication."

"Get in the car, Dylan," Cole says, then does everything he can to conceal his frustration at having accidentally used Noah's old name. The name he used to call him in bed, before he knew his real one.

Maybe, Cole thinks, *he'll take my use of his chosen name, the name he still wants to be called, as a sign I'm* not *about to have him executed.*

"Kansas," Noah mutters, surveying his vast, empty surroundings. "Huh. Will there be more of it when the sun rises?"

He's right—it's too dark to see the farmhouse on the horizon, and they haven't planted any of the fields. But the airstrip underfoot is new, installed only months before. Surely Noah won't be willing to believe they bought a farm in the middle of nowhere and installed an airstrip just for the purpose of flying him here and killing him.

But there's something else going on with his most important scientist, and it takes Cole a moment to puzzle through it.

Noah actually has a life he loves now, and he doesn't want to be pulled away from it for even a second. His residence on the island is plush, luxurious even. Of course, he lives as a prisoner, his movements constantly monitored, no contact with the outside world—other than Cole—allowed. But remarkably, after a year, he hasn't asked for any. There's nobody from his former life—lives plural, if you want to be technical about it—he wants to speak with. For Noah, the past year has been all work and no play, and he couldn't be happier about it. And so the prospect of spending even a short amount of time in a temporary holding cell has him exhibiting signs of an emotion he almost never displays—fear. The charm with which Noah stepped off the plane was his cover for an emotion so out of character Cole had trouble recognizing it at first.

"Did you have a bad experience in Kansas at some point?" Cole asks.

"No," he says, "but you, good sir, have *no* experience here, and that's what concerns me."

"How so?"

"For God's sake, Cole, you own your own helicopter, and you've never stayed in a hotel room that doesn't look like either Versailles or an Apple Store. Your idea of roughing it is a house where you can hear the laundry room. And now you're on a farm. In Kansas! And so am I, apparently. The whole thing's very out of the ordinary, even for extraordinary men like us."

"Well, it's what she wants," Cole answers.

"Charley?"

Cole nods.

"Does she want me here, too?" Noah asks.

"No. But I do."

"And why's that?"

"I'll explain once we're inside."

This time when Cole starts for the Suburban, he's determined not to stop, even if the men behind him all begin shooting at each other.

Cole thought seeing the inside of the farmhouse might calm Noah down a bit. But given his ramrod-straight posture as they pass through its rooms, decorated in what can only be described as bland western chic, that's not going to be the case. Maybe the absence of personal effects unnerves him. Aboveground, the place looks ready to list on Airbnb.

Still, does Noah really think Cole would have someone blow his head off where his brains might land on a brand-new leather sofa or a vintage hand-drawn map of the Great Plains in a thick gold frame?

The trip down the cellar steps doesn't help, either. That's no surprise. The year before, Cole had Noah thrown in an underground cell for several weeks as punishment for making unauthorized contact with Charlotte.

When they move through the false basement, Noah sucks in a deep breath that sounds more weary than frightened. Just then, the security team lifts a stand-alone shelving unit away from the walls, revealing the vague outline of a hidden door. The cover over the fingerprint reader is camouflaged with the surrounding stone. When the door unlocks with a hiss under Cole's touch, they're all suddenly bathed in a glow Cole finds comforting. Maybe Noah will, too.

As they enter the bunker, Noah's exhalation is just barely audible.

The control room's impressive. The soothing glow comes from the wall of LED screens, the largest of which is a detailed digital map of Dallas, with pulsing red pinpoints indicating the position of Charley, her boyfriend, Luke Prescott, and their target, a long-haul truck driver named Cyrus Mattingly. Right now, the three points are grouped together closely on the grounds of the NorthPark Center Mall, which is identified with blazing red text brighter than the rest of the map. The dimmable lighting installed along the rough-hewn ceiling and floor minimizes eye strain for the techs, but it also makes the bunker feel like a large passenger jet that's leveled off at cruising altitude for a long nighttime flight, which Cole likes—maybe because he always flies first class.

With wide-eyed fascination, Noah takes it all in. His labs are certainly impressive, but he's never been inside one of their command centers. And with good reason. Cole promised Charlotte he never would be.

But that was before.

A short hallway leads to several other cavern-like rooms with closed doors. One's a break room occupied by the idling strike team. Inside, the men have cots to nap on, a drink machine that dispenses ten different forms of caffeine, and a fully stocked snack bar along with a foosball table and some arcade games and a PlayStation or a dudebox or whatever it's called—all of it designed to fill the time until the men deploy in one of the jets that's already gassed up inside the hangar Cole had built over the site of the old stables and barn.

In another of the far rooms sits the young man who's arguably the most important person on site, a man Noah's never met in person even though the two conspired on a hack the year before that almost destroyed Cole's relationship with one of his key business partners.

He'll introduce the two of them in person when he's ready, which won't be anytime soon.

The third room is Cole's private communications center; the fourth, a rest area with bunks for the surveillance techs.

Noah could not care less about the nearby hallway of closed doors. He's too enamored by the mosaic of images on the screens above. The rightmost monitors are taken up with various biometric readings transmitted directly from Charlotte Rowe's bloodstream and brain matter. They refresh every few seconds—everything from her blood pressure to her blood oxygen level to her white and red blood cell counts and more. Noah's got his own version of these devices circulating through his blood. The difference is, his blood trackers are programmed to cause excruciating pain and/or kill him if necessary.

"Which one is she?" Noah asks.

"That's her," Cole says, pointing to a screen that's mostly black except for a smaller screen that appears to be showing a movie. "In the theater."

Transfixed, Noah approaches the backs of the technicians sitting at their stations, who ignore his arrival. It's not the first time he's seen a TruGlass feed, but it's probably the first time he's seen one on a large high-definition screen and not a laptop. It drives home the miracle of a set of contact lenses that can transmit a crystal-clear feed of everything their wearer sees.

Noah points to the screen below. It offers a view of a skybridge that connects the top floor of one of the parking structures with the main shopping mall at NorthPark Center, a view that shifts and bounces with the jerky motions of a restless, bored human.

"Whose eyes are those?"

"Luke's."

Startled, Noah turns to face Cole. "You flew me all the way here to help you spy on Charlotte and Luke's date night?"

"Luke isn't attending the movie, as you can see. He's parked outside the mall."

"What's he doing there?"

"Whatever I tell him to."

"In Dallas," Noah says.

"Yes."

"And we're in Kansas."

"You're really flashing that PhD, aren't you?"

Noah's suddenly so close to him, Cole can feel the man's breath on his lips. A few of the techs turn, startled.

"Your evasions justify my interrogation." It's not a growl, but it's close.

Cole gently raises a hand to push Noah back on his heels. "Easy, tiger. This is my show."

And we're not at a hotel suite at the Montage in Laguna Beach, and I haven't had a glass of merlot.

"Didn't you promise her you'd never include me in an op? You know, given my terrible, horrible, no good very bad betrayal which, oh, by the way, turned her into a superhero."

"Things have changed."

"How?"

"Let's go upstairs, get you that shower you asked for. You smell . . . not up to your usual standards."

Like cedar and baking bread and a hint of pine . . . and oh my God, shut up, you teenager.

With a cocky grin, Noah steps forward into the inch or two of space Cole had just created with one hand. "It's not that bad, is it?"

"She's getting up!" one of the techs barks.

Noah turns back to the screens. Cole brushes past him and takes up a post right behind Shannon Tran. In the past, Shannon's job was coordinating with the extensive ground teams and microdrone surveillance crews that followed Charley during an op. But those have been taken out of the mix now, leaving Shannon focused on Charley's every move.

The command center was quiet to begin with; now you can hear a pin drop.

"Bring up her audio," Cole says.

The raucous sounds of a barroom scene from *Sister Trip* thunder through the control room. They've all watched most of the movie right along with Charlotte three times now, each time in a different theater located in a different part of Dallas. If memory serves, the sisters are hatching a plot to fend off the unwanted advances of a drunk cowboy. When they're done, the entire bar will be caught up in a massive line dance that allows all three of the film's plucky heroines to escape out the bar's back door.

"Could you cut that out?" Charlotte says.

Her voice is loud enough to be heard over the movie. She's standing in the aisle closest to a man in a baseball cap and a leather jacket who's just looked up at her from his iPhone's glowing screen. The other moviegoers looking in her direction must assume she's staring the guy down out of anger. The truth is, she's trying to give everyone in the control room a good long look at him.

Silently and swiftly, Shannon takes a screen cap of the guy's face and drags it onto an adjacent screen where she's already called up Cyrus Mattingly's driver's license photo. Their face ID software goes to work on the fuzzy, shadowed image from the movie theater.

"You're bothering everyone in the movie, all right?"

The women sitting on all sides of Mattingly mutter their agreement. Two of them clap weakly.

Finally, Mattingly puts his phone to sleep and slides it into his jacket pocket. Then he puts his hands up in a gesture of surrender, all without taking his eyes off Charlotte. If Charlotte and Cole's theory holds true, he's actually studying every detail he can discern in the darkness of the theater; that way he'll be able to catch up with her as soon as she leaves.

"Thank you!" Charlotte says to him with nothing that sounds like gratitude. She heads back to her seat, her TruGlass capturing glimpses of grateful-looking women who smile and silently applaud her as she goes.

"Well," Noah finally says, "I'm honored to be part of a multistate operation devoted to improving the moviegoing experience in the Dallas metroplex. Truly."

Ignoring him, Cole asks Shannon how much of the film they have left. "About an hour," she says.

He jabs Noah in the side and gestures for him to follow. "Upstairs," Cole says. "Time for that shower."

3

Dallas, Texas

Hailey Brinkmann is from California, which is why she doesn't have a Texas accent.

Hailey Brinkmann never attended college, and that's good because it means Charlotte didn't have to familiarize herself with some random campus and unfamiliar town before she turned herself into Hailey.

Hailey Brinkmann recently dyed her hair corn-silk blonde because she felt like that's how girls in Texas wear their hair. (Charlotte's black bob, with its single streak of platinum, was about as Texas as a surf shop for vegans, Luke told her.)

Hailey Brinkmann is assertive. She moved cross-country with no clear prospects and no friends in the Dallas area. So, it makes sense that she's also outspoken and determined and *really freakin' hates it* when people text all through the movie.

She is, in essence, exactly the type of woman who will capture the attention of a man like Cyrus Mattingly—provided he continues with the routine he's followed for three nights now.

As Charlotte takes her seat in the fourth row of the theater, she reminds herself of how thoroughly convincing her alter ego's fake ID is. She also reminds herself that the likelihood of her having to share the details of her cover story with anyone else just turned remote. Especially now that she's managed to capture Mattingly's attention.

In the three weeks she's been pretending to move into the tiny little rental house in Richardson, she's only had to share her story once, thanks to an accidental run-in with the next-door neighbor. The poor chain-smoking woman spends most of her time caring for her wheelchair-bound husband and their two service dogs, and as Charlotte shared Hailey's story with her, she seemed both too exhausted and too worried about accidentally blowing smoke in Hailey's face to absorb a single detail.

The props that come along with being Hailey Brinkmann serve one real purpose. They're for Cyrus Mattingly to root through after he abducts her.

As for her little rental house, the name on the lease belongs to a company hiding a company hiding a company. Besides, she doubts Mattingly's the type of guy who'd be willing or able to check.

He's not a hacker. He's a truck driver. And if what they've observed of him over the past few nights can be believed, he's got a particular weakness for women who speak their minds.

Two nights before, at another showing of *Sister Trip*, this one at the Cinemark 17 in Farmers Branch, she watched Mattingly rise from his seat just a few seconds after the woman who'd earlier called him out over his texting walked past him. Instead of hopping into the little Kia Soul in which she drove to the theater, Charlotte stepped into Luke's souped-up Cadillac Escalade, courtesy of Graydon Pharmaceuticals, and they followed Mattingly as he followed his target to a sprawling apartment complex about a fifteen-minute drive from the theater.

They watched as Mattingly's target pulled into a subterranean parking garage, an automated gate rolling shut behind her while Mattingly watched her from behind the wheel of his Econoline van, which he'd parked at the nearest open curb. If Mattingly made a play for the woman, they'd initiate their thwart plan—Luke would find a way to intercept Mattingly before he got to the woman's door, posing as either a concerned citizen or an affable moron who'd made a wrong turn down a dark hallway.

But Mattingly never got out of his van. He didn't even wait around for very long. Instead, he sped away, driving an hour south to his isolated house in Waxahachie, where he promptly turned out the lights and went to bed.

While Luke and Charley got some rest, Kansas Command watched Mattingly through the spyware they'd planted in his devices and the microscopic cameras they'd placed throughout his house. Mattingly did nothing of note.

Until the following evening rolled around.

Then he started all over again.

Once again, he stocked the pouches in the thick Velcro belt wrapped around his stomach with a syringe full of sedative, three pairs of flex-cuffs, and a nine-inch leather billy club with wrist strap. Then, wearing a similar outfit to the one he's got on now, he headed to the movies. This time it was a 6:45 p.m. showing of *Sister Trip* at the AMC Valley View 16. When Mattingly took out his phone at the exact same time, right as the studio logo filled the screen, Charley rose from her seat to say something to him, and that's when the woman sitting right behind him beat her to the punch. Charley thought about saying something to him anyway, just to try to draw his attention. But there was a risk in that. If he chose to follow the first woman who spoke up, her chance of hooking him at a later date would be blown; she'd be exposed.

So, she kept silent, and she watched.

Again, Mattingly followed the woman who'd dared tell him to turn off his phone.

Again, he watched her pull in to her residence, a freestanding ranch-style house.

But this time he lingered. Until another car pulled into the driveway soon after the woman's, and a man, clearly her boyfriend or husband, stepped out, clad in gym gear matted with fresh workout sweat.

Within seconds, Mattingly was back on the road to Waxahachie.

The qualifications for ending up in Mattingly's sights were simple—you had to have the nerve to tell him to turn off his phone during the movie. But for the courtship to continue, you had to have something else—an easily penetrated residence.

Patrice Longman and Melissa Esperanza—Kansas Command kept them under digital surveillance just in case Mattingly decided to make a play for either of them after the fact—were both very lucky women. One lived cheek by jowl with her neighbors in a gated apartment complex; the other had a husband with excellent timing. Of course, Charley and Luke would have found a way to intervene before Mattingly managed to snatch either woman. But still, the potential victims had no idea how close they'd been to a monster.

Let it stay that way, Charlotte thinks, *forever.*

Feeling the first easing of tension she's experienced in three days, Charlotte settles into her seat and pretends to watch the film.

It's a halfway decent flick. She just wishes she didn't have to watch it with a serial killer.

Again.

Luke Prescott's only heard the term *phantom pain* applied to missing limbs, not scars that have recently healed. But there aren't better words to describe the latticework of fiery pinpricks that ignite down the length of his back whenever he's under stress. They follow the patterns of the old burn marks from the box spring he was tied to almost six months ago now, a box spring heated by flames his abductors had planned to lower him into face-first.

His abductors are dead, the brief flowering of evil they brought to his hometown stamped out by Charlotte and her wealthy overlord, Cole Graydon. But the pain often returns. It's not debilitating, but it's humbling. Mainly because it comes on without warning, announcing his body's separation from his thoughts and producing a sense of powerlessness he's come to call, against his will, PTSD.

As he waits outside NorthPark Center, behind the wheel of a matte-black Cadillac Escalade that's been retrofitted to survive a bomb blast and lined with trackers transmitting everything from its location and speed to its interior temperature and CO_2 levels, Luke employs the tactics for curbing his anxiety he's learned over the past six months.

He makes a mental list of the disfiguring injuries he might have suffered had Charley not saved him when she did. He imagines his face gone Freddy Krueger; his torso coated in mottled flesh. Failing that, he can always imagine the slow, horrifying death he might have endured. But he rarely has to go that far.

Gratitude is the best antidote for self-pity.

Stress can be rechristened as excitement; anxiety rebranded as anticipation.

And what is anticipation really but a form of enthusiasm?

The effort needed to flip those coins from one side to the other is sometimes as simple as a few deep breaths.

Or at least that's what the Graydon-approved therapist he's been talking to for half a year now has assured him.

Cole was wise enough to integrate Luke's therapy into an overall training regimen designed to turn Luke into a one-man fighting force and pivotal asset to Charley's ground team. If the therapy starts to make Luke feel broken and crazy, he's almost instantly distracted by a personal training session in hand-to-hand combat or firearms proficiency or a course in drown proofing of the type offered to Navy SEALS. Over the past six months, at various Graydon facilities throughout California, Luke has received training from some of the finest security experts in the world, and the result has, in the opinion of one expert, left him at the threshold of special ops qualifications. To say nothing of the body it's given him. A body about which Charlotte has said plenty, all of it complimentary.

And therein lies another source of healing gratitude.

Preparing for action while his girlfriend lures a human monster into her trap is exactly what Luke's wanted since he started training. It doesn't matter that Cole granted his request out of guilt. (Cole was the one, after all, responsible for the security failures that led to Luke's abduction.) What matters is that Luke's finally part of the team. And if the scars along his back are the evidence of what he needed to go through to gain access, then so be it. He's happy to consider them a brand instead of an injury that's yet to fully heal.

"Hey, bro," the voice in his ear says, "how do you get a nun pregnant?"

Luke's brother, Bailey, isn't telling his favorite joke to amuse; he's sending a signal that Cole is up to something at Kansas Command, something he didn't share with Luke and Charlotte in advance. Jokes, especially the ones so bad they make you cringe, have always been their code, a sign that Bailey's about to impart secret information in the presence of others. When they were kids, it was the location of a stolen pack of cigarettes they didn't want their mother to know about. Today, it's the movements of the mysterious and morally suspect people for which they both work. They'd call them dad jokes, but they never really had a dad.

Luke gives the agreed-upon response. "You're really gross, you know that?"

"You've always had a sensitive stomach for such a big dude."

Translation: Whatever's happening at Kansas Command is suspicious but not major.

Luke says, "Still, can't you ever come up with a joke that I could tell in, like, mixed company?"

This cues up the next code. If Bailey tells the joke about lawyers and dogs—*What's the difference between a dead dog in the road and*

a dead lawyer in the road? There are skid marks in front of the dog—
that's a signal there's someone in the bunker he doesn't recognize,
someone who doesn't seem to have a clear operational purpose.

If, on the other hand, Bailey tells his lawyer and God joke—
What's the difference between a lawyer and God? God doesn't think he's
*a lawyer—*that's a sign that while the bunker's staffing seems ordinary,
Cole's planning something in Luke and Charlotte's immediate field of
play they didn't agree to ahead of time.

Like deploying a strike team in their vicinity after Charley specifically asked him not to.

His brother is silent for a beat, then says, "Honestly, I'm a bigger
fan of doctor jokes than lawyer jokes. But they're all stupid. Know
any good ones?"

"Doctors?"

"No, doctor jokes. Ones that are really funny, not just gross ones
about ball doctors or butt doctors or headshrinkers."

Headshrinkers. None of this is their code; Bailey's improvising.
By not giving their code responses, Bailey's eliminating those pos-
sibilities. No strangers at the bunker, no unplanned field operations.
Instead it's a third option.

Involving doctors.

There's a doctor at the bunker.

A doctor they'd all recognize—Noah Turlington.

Son of a bitch, Luke thinks, but he does his best not to say it, in
case Cole is listening in.

"They're just jokes, dude. Don't freak out. Oh, by the way, it looks
like she's hooked Mattingly, so I'll give you a warning when the movie
starts to wind down."

"Um, hi, that's actually my job," Shannon Tran cuts in.

"We're a team, Shannon, remember?" Bailey responds. "That's
why we spent all last month doing trust falls and making pottery
together."

Luke's pretty sure Bailey and Shannon have done nothing of the kind, and it's no shock that his younger brother, one of the country's most wanted fugitive hackers until Cole Graydon essentially made him disappear off law enforcement's radar screens, is having trouble getting along with his new coworkers. Bailey would have trouble getting along with a Ragdoll cat.

"I'm Luke's primary point of contact with Kansas Command, Bailey. I don't care if you're family."

"Cole said we're allowed to talk," Bailey says.

"You're allowed to chat during downtime, not direct his movements."

"I have nothing to do with my brother's bowels."

Shannon says, "You're being gross and inappropriate *and* you're ignoring the chain of command."

"Uh-huh. Does our chain of command allow you to keep eating my Nutella out of the break room?"

"Um, try the small army down the hall."

"They know who ate it or they ate it?"

"Ask them," Shannon says. "It should be fun for everyone."

"Yeah, smooth move, pinning your compulsive eating on a room full of heavily armed trained mercenaries with nothing to do."

"You bring up your Nutella every ten minutes and I'm the one who's eating compulsively? And you have your own office with a door you can lock, so why are you so afraid of a bunch of Navy SEALs who could kill you with their bare hands?"

"Only a sadist would call what I have here an office."

"When's the first date, guys?" Luke asks.

"Never," Shannon answers. "Bailey, I'm serious. Do not direct Luke's movements."

"I didn't direct his movements. I told him how much of the movie was left. Also, just FYI, I'd rather drown in my urine than call this

26

place Kansas Command. It sounds like a country-western bondage club."

Before his brother can raise the topic of any other unpleasant bodily functions, Luke says, "So we've got a positive ID on Mattingly?"

"We do," Shannon says. "Charley's back in her seat, so now we sit and wait and see if he tails her out of the theater. In the meantime, how about we cool it with the dirty nun jokes?"

"It's not dirty," Bailey protests.

I gave you a chance, Shannon, Luke thinks, *but there you go baiting him again.*

In what sounds like her most derisive imitation of the world's worst man, Shannon says, "How do you get a nun pregnant? Fuck her. *Hu hu hu.*"

"You didn't have to use the f-word, Shannon. And the lawyer ones are better anyway."

"I do not even want to know, so don't bother. Just please . . . be quiet until the movie's over and we have something to do."

A silence falls. Luke watches two parents with several excited toddler-age children emerge from the skybridge that connects the top level of this parking structure to the mall. One of the kids runs ahead, a towheaded little boy no older than four, but the father springs on him the second before he races in back of a parked pickup truck that just started its engine.

"Oof," Bailey says, "that was close."

His words are another reminder that for the time being Luke's eyes are not his own. Whatever he sees is being transmitted through his contact lenses to a satellite, which then bounces it down to the bunker in Kansas. Luke's also reticent to call the place Kansas Command, but for a different reason—it conjures images of old movies about nuclear war that terrified him as a kid.

"For an hour?" Bailey finally says. "I'm supposed to just be quiet for an hour?"

"I don't know, Bailey, go hack something!" Shannon barks, and behind her words Luke hears a burst of raucous music and excited talking from amplified voices. It's got to be the movie playing inside the theater, the one being transmitted through Charley's TruGlass and the audio from her earpiece.

"Oh my God," Bailey whines, "are you actually watching this terrible movie?"

"It's good."

"It's terrible. The oldest sister makes me want to jump out a window."

"Go ahead," Shannon says. "Get a running start."

"We're underground."

"Hence the running start," Luke says.

"The movie's fine," Shannon says. "You're just a dude."

"Yeah, that's me. I'm a regular surfin', drinkin', bikini babe lovin' *dude*."

"Bailey," Luke says, "it's so good to hear you integrating with the team."

Shannon laughs. Bailey doesn't.

"My job is not to integrate. My job is to go where all of you can't. And last time I checked, I go alone."

Shannon has no response to this, and neither does Luke.

Luke's words weren't entirely sarcasm. He actually is relieved to have his brother on the team and not living as a fugitive abroad.

But it's hardly a relief that Noah Turlington, the jackass who pretended to offer Charley therapy under the name Dylan Thorpe, is at the bunker. Is he monitoring their movements and communications along with Cole?

If Charley knew . . . well, she wouldn't want to know right now. Not when she's working, and not when she's worked so hard to create the illusion she's working alone.

As for his own feelings toward the mad scientist who set them all on this path, at some point, Luke fears, they'll have no choice but to abandon their collective anger over how Noah deceived Charlotte into taking her first dose of Zypraxon and neglected to mention the drug had killed every other human who'd taken it.

Zypraxon, and by extension its inventor, Noah Turlington, are what give Charley the power to go after killers like Cyrus Mattingly. And if all goes well tonight, Mattingly will join the other human monsters Charley's taken out of circulation while powered by the awesome strength Noah's drug unleashes in her veins.

There's also the fact that Noah's last-minute intervention to help Charley a year ago is the only thing that saved Luke from being devoured by flames.

The question's simple.

How much longer can they all stay mad at Noah Turlington while they continue to enjoy the fruits of his mad science?

The answer isn't simple at all.

Hopefully, Luke won't have to give one until this operation's over, and neither will Charley.

4

The bedroom where Cole's brought Noah is the only one of the three with heavy steel storm shutters covering its windows. The storm's slacked off, but Cole had the men leave the shutters in place anyway. They're not necessary to prevent Noah's escape—the windows don't open, and the glass is so thick Charley would need several tries to break it even when Zypraxon's triggered an explosion of super-strength inside her veins. And it's not that Cole wants Noah to feel trapped. Exactly.

Rather, he wants Noah to feel directed. *Channeled.* Undistracted by big skies and endless vistas once the sun rises.

If you don't count the security team stationed right outside the bedroom door, this is the first time they've been alone together.

Cole hasn't wasted any time.

Seated on the edge of the bed, elbows on his knees, rubbing his chin in one hand as if he's not sure it's still there, Noah's still absorbing the impact of the bomb Cole dropped as soon as he drew the bedroom door shut.

"Nothing," Noah finally says quietly. "She's got nothing on the ground with her except for . . . her boyfriend." He says the word *boyfriend* like it's *puff pastry.*

"Correct."

"And that's why you're in Kansas and she's in Dallas?"

"Yes. We're close to the geographic center of the continental United States, less than three hours from the farthest coast by plane. But she wanted significant geographical separation between our response forces and the op field."

"And you thought this was a good idea?" Noah asks.

"Oh, no. Not at all," Cole answers.

"And you agreed because?"

"Because our target started escalating before I could think of a better option."

"I'm not following."

"Zypraxon only unleashes paradrenaline into her bloodstream when she's absolutely terrified. Not anxious, not afraid. Terrified. If I've got ground teams all around her and snipers on rooftops, there's nothing in her environment that can frighten her badly enough for the drug to start working. And when it comes to her overall security, if one of her targets is capable of inflicting a fatal blow in a split second, what good is a sniper anyway?"

"Surely there were other—"

"There were not. On her last op, she had to injure herself to trigger. Badly. I don't want her resorting to acts of self-mutilation to try to create the panic and shock she needs to feel before your drug kicks into gear. What if she cuts a nerve to her heart or her lungs before the trigger event heals her? Worse, what if she starts to desensitize to self-inflicted wounds, and then the only way for her to traumatize herself effectively the next time is to hack off one of her limbs? Her fear is the engine that drives this thing . . . for now . . . and that means letting her feel like she's truly alone with these monsters. She has to become the victim; those were her words. And if she tells me there's something that shuts down that process, I've got no choice but to remove it from the field of play."

"You've removed your resources from the field of play. That's dangerous."

"No, their deployment is just delayed. There's a difference."

"It's still dangerous."

"I know."

"Lie to her. Put a team in place and don't tell her it's there."

"How many times do I get away with that? If I lie to her and she realizes a ground team was ready to swoop in and save her the whole time, on the next operation she'll assume I lied again and she won't trigger because her brain's telling her help's just around the corner. If she's not afraid, your drug never triggers in her system, and if she doesn't trigger, she can't overpower these guys, and then we can't swoop in and fake their deaths so that you can have more brains to play with in your labs."

He's getting a lot more than just their brains, and they both know it. But Cole's hoping Noah gets that point here. Giving in to Charley's wishes maintains the pipeline of test subjects for Noah's experiments that Charley doesn't even know about.

Thanks to Cole, two of Charlotte's previous targets are now housed in Noah's island lab. One, a serial killer who skinned his victims, and the other, an aspiring terrorist bomber, live in a state of suspended animation except for when they're awakened within virtual reality environments designed to trigger their homicidal impulses. After six solid months of exhaustive and meticulous work, Noah has managed to generate what may well be the first neuroimage of a psychopath's brain in the midst of a calculated murderous act. With a virtual victim, of course. Some people might consider the two men they've imprisoned against their will and forced to live inside an endless tape loop of their crimes "victims." Cole's not one of those people. If that's the cost of illuminating the biological underpinnings of the sadistic violence that motivates some of humanity's worst crimes, then so be it. The cost that keeps Cole up at night is the financial one. Noah, on the other hand, is more afraid they won't be able to obtain the additional test subjects he needs to confirm his initial results.

"Christ," Noah whispers. "I'm hoping you've given Luke some training in how to deal with at least some of the things that could go terribly wrong."

"Beyond. He's practically special ops certified."

"Speaking as someone who is, it's not that easy."

"It *wasn't* easy," Cole says, "and the men training him had more deployments than you did, so step off. I'm not running an adventure camp here."

"Fine. Luke is a SEAL who's never seen combat."

Cole remembers the combined smell of burnt plastic and burnt human hair and the wire-frame box spring evil men had turned into an implement of torture; he remembers how the horrors visited upon Luke reminded him of the rope that was slipped over his own wrists when he was just a boy, of the agony that came after. Some evidence of these memories must be pulsing in his expression, because Noah studies him closely, his own expression both intent and guarded.

"He saw combat," Cole whispers, "believe me."

"Fine," Noah says. "Clearly, I'm not being consulted on this decision to fall back, since it's already been made. So, at the risk of sounding impolite, what the hell am I doing here?"

"I need you to get inside her head," Cole answers.

"I haven't spoken to Charley in six months."

"Forgive me. I need you to get *me* inside her head. If I can't control her movements on the ground, I have to control her mind while she's out there. Nobody knows her mind better than you. You deceived her for months back in Arizona. She trusted you, let her guard down."

"Much of that assessment is correct."

"Good," Cole says. "Then you're my leash. She made a bad judgment call on the last op. Your job is to tell me if you think she's about to make one again and to tell me how to appeal to her sensitivities if I need to rein her in without the help of a ground team trailing her every move. You can read her better than anyone else can, so tonight I need you reading her constantly and closely."

"Have you consulted your business partners on any of this?" Noah asks.

The question's innocuous enough, but Cole knows from the tension undergirding his jaw that his anger's evident in his expression.

"Why do you ask?"

"I don't know, a lot of this feels . . ."

"Feels like what?" Cole asks.

"Like you're bending over backwards not to hurt Charlotte's feelings when you should be considering the larger implications here."

"Well, the only feeling of Charlotte's you've ever cared about is fear."

"That's a little glib, don't you think?"

"I think you're lecturing me on aspects of this operation that aren't exactly your purview."

"It wasn't a lecture. It was a comment. You need sleep."

"I'm sleeping just fine. What exactly do you mean by larger implications?"

Noah looks stricken, as if he's not quite sure how he's angered Cole, and the possible punishment for doing so has him concerned. It could be an act. He's good at acts.

"The first time Charley took down a killer, she was alone and we were just watching. The second time, you were the only one working with her. Now, you've got three business partners, and they'll want you to consult them. Not just give them orders. Like you're giving me."

"Apparently you have relationships with Stephen, Philip, and Julia I'm not aware of."

"I don't, Cole. I'm just assuming their egos are as big as yours. Don't step on their feet and bring the house down all around us. That's all I'm saying."

"I will take your concern for their feet under advisement."

The truth is, Cole's business partners are already acting like he's stepped on their feet when he's done his best to tiptoe around them, and he'd like to know why. It's why he flew Noah halfway around the world. Sure, he'll appreciate whatever insights into Charlotte's behavior Noah might offer. But the real reason, the one Noah's comment just poked in the center of its gut, is much bigger and harder to wrestle with: Cole's worried his business partners have turned against the idea of Charlotte's field tests altogether and want to stick her in a lab for as long as her blood's of use to them. In the event they take measures to obstruct tonight's operation, Cole needs to know first-hand where Noah's loyalties lie.

Noah's raising the prospect of Cole mishandling his business partners is not a good sign his loyalties lie with Cole.

Right now, his urge is to interrogate Noah, ask him if he's had any contact with the members of what they long ago nicknamed The Consortium. But it's a ridiculous question. The man's under such constant surveillance it would be impossible for him to make contact with anyone while he's in residence at the lab. More importantly, Cole doesn't want to shine too big a spotlight on his suspicions. Because the fact of the matter is, Charlotte's not the only one participating in a field test tonight. So is Noah, even if he doesn't know it. The difference is that Noah's being tested for loyalty, not the ability to tear holes in walls with his bare hands.

"You're not telling her I'm here, I take it," Noah says, referring to Charley.

"No."

"And if she finds out?"

"I'll deal with it. Unless she finds out from you, in which case you'll be on the first plane home."

"That's fair, I guess."

"Fair?" Cole asks. "This isn't a proposal, Noah."

Smirking, Noah rises to his feet and begins unzipping the suitcase resting on the bed behind them. Or maybe he's not smirking.

"Fine, then," he says, pulling out his toiletry bag and unzipping it—probably to make sure the security team didn't remove anything from it. "I accept." He zips the bag and tucks it under one arm, turning to Cole with a confident grin.

There's no point in arguing with Noah about the fact he's accepting a set of directions as if they were an offer, so Cole ignores the bait, confident what he has to say next will get the necessary meaning across.

"You'll come downstairs when I need you and only then. Don't engage with any of the other personnel. Speak only when I speak to you, and speak only to me. Got it?"

"Sure," Noah says. "On one condition."

"There are no conditions, Noah. This isn't a—"

"Shower with me."

He knows what Noah's doing; he's trying to defuse the anger that swelled in Cole when he mentioned Cole's business partners. Another bad sign. If they were only going to be forced together for another hour or two, Cole would ignore this request as a childish head game. But there's no telling how long this operation is going to last. If he doesn't put Noah in check now, who knows how many inane distractions he'll have to put up with.

Once they're nose to nose, Cole grabs Noah's crotch with just enough force to make the man wince. "Careful," he says, "it's been a while. Tastes change. You might be the one who ends up tied to the bed this time."

Confident there's nothing Noah Turlington would like less than losing control, Cole turns and leaves the room.

Scott Durham's waiting for him right outside, standing so close to the door they end up crashing into each other.

"Get me Bailey," he says.

The rain's let up some, but it still comes in infrequent gusts, and every few minutes there's thunder and a flash of lightning on the horizon. Cole walks alone to the airplane hangar under the shelter of an umbrella. The path is sprinkled with the same type of foot-level landscape lighting that lines the front walk of his primary residence in California.

He passes the old windmill, its blades spinning loudly as they slice the cloud-filled sky. It's pastoral, pretty even, but still, he can't make sense of his affection for the thing. Scott was startled when Cole asked them to leave it up during construction, muttered some joke about *The Wizard of Oz*. Cole's never seen the film, so he deflected Scott's suspicions with a line about his gay card being revoked.

But his response was ridiculous, really.

As if Cole's a member of any tribe—gay, straight, or otherwise. He doesn't walk among the normal, the living. Not since his college days at Stanford, and even then, he was considered part of the intermediary elite; not a big enough deal to rub elbows with the children of royalty, but too suspiciously rich to hang with the children of doctors and lawyers. It was the science nerds who ended up taking him in. Maybe because they thought he'd give them jobs someday. Which in some cases he did. But he can't remember the last time he watched anything on television other than cable news, and most of the pop culture references he knows come from the Instagram accounts of the gay porn stars he hires to have sex with him at his glass and steel mansion above La Jolla Bay. On some days, he's not sure if these are the privileges of being a member of the .01% or the costs.

The ordinary world often feels exotic to him, and he guesses that's how to explain his strange affection for the windmill. Every now and then he'll drive to a fast-food restaurant on the outskirts of La Jolla and eat a meal alone, his security detail sitting unobtrusively at a nearby table, as he silently marvels at the speed and ease of the experience, the lack of decisions required. Order, sit, eat, leave. Nothing like the highly choreographed formal dinners of his childhood, or business banquets with as many agendas as courses.

Footsteps approach. As instructed, Scott Durham's escorted Bailey here under the shelter of an umbrella.

It would be easy to blame Bailey's current hairstyle on the stormy weather. In the hands of a professional, Bailey's mop of sandy-blond hair could be something special, but he always wears it brushed forward on his head like he's hiding under it. He's got two fashion styles—bedraggled hitchhiker and parachutist. Tonight, he looks ready to skydive. His long-sleeve shirt and pants are made of the same vaguely shiny coffee-colored material that bags around his small frame, and if the pants have pockets they're well hidden.

Bailey's personal choices usually have one thing in common— ease of movement. Not surprising for a kid who spent years as an international fugitive. Still, the idea that he and manly man Luke came from the same DNA contains as many startling revelations about the human body as Charlotte Rowe.

Once Scott's departed, Cole asks Bailey, "Are you ever going to let me do something with your hair?"

"No."

"Just a brush, maybe."

"I don't let strange men brush my hair."

"I was offering to give you one, not use it on you."

"My hair's cool, thanks."

"Suit yourself. Status report, please."

"Your super-secret ground team in Amarillo is on the ready. Looks like our connection to them's secure, so no sign your business partners are onto us."

"Good work."

"I know. I'm trying to be a good boy for once. Following orders. Not breaking too many federal laws for my own personal pleasure. Basically, I'm not having any more fun at all. Just for you."

"Good."

In the pause that follows, water drips somewhere in the vast hangar in a place they can't see.

"With one tiny exception," Bailey adds.

"Oh, dear."

"I kinda told Luke you brought Noah here."

"That was *really* not what I told you to do."

"I know, but you didn't tell me he was coming, and I'm supposed to be your secret buddy on this operation so I kinda got my feelings hurt, OK? Sorry."

"You have feelings?" Cole asks.

"Don't go seeing devious operators everywhere you look just because you like committing crimes against nature with one."

"Nature is just a collection of easily manipulated chemical reactions."

And I haven't been to bed with that particular devious operator in years.

"Yeah, you should put that on one of your ads," Bailey says.

"We do," Cole says. "We just find different ways of saying it each time."

"Noah sure manipulates your chemical reactions. That's for sure."

"Bailey—"

"Seriously, why'd you bring him here?" Bailey asks.

"I need Noah here to find out who he'll be more loyal to if the shit hits the fan. Me or my business partners."

"That makes sense."

"I'm glad you can see the logic."

"And that was big for you, so . . . thanks."

"I'm sorry, big?"

"Giving a direct answer to a direct question. That's not usually your style, so I just want to give you props. That's all."

"Props. I see."

"What? Why are you pissed?"

"I'm not pissed; I'm just curious."

"About what?"

"They say the Germans have a word for everything, so I'm wondering if they have a word for being condescended to on the topic of personal authenticity by someone who uses aliases to hack other people's personal accounts for fun."

"Sort of fun. The joy's been going out of it ever since I had to do it on the run."

"Did you look at the letter again?" Cole asks, getting back to business.

"I've looked at that letter a billion times since we screen capped it, and I don't have anything new. I'm sorry. We got what we got from it. Maybe that's enough. The postmark was Amarillo. And the date on the top was the date Cyrus Mattingly started trolling movie theaters. The rest could be nonsense."

"It can't be nonsense."

Bailey shakes his head. "Well, it's personal and that's the problem. I ran it through every search engine I could, and there were no connections to symbolic references. If it's a code, it's *their* code, and I don't know enough about either of them to break it. Mattingly barely has a life outside his job, present psychofuckery excepted. And the other person? We've got no clue who they are. Sorry, man, but these two guys are analog killers. They might not know we're watching them, but they think somebody is, and they're off the grid because of it. So how about you just give me credit for noticing the letter in the first place? There was about six million hours of footage on his living room camera."

"You're not in federal prison for the crimes you committed before you met me. That is credit, Bailey."

"The point is I'm a hacker. Not a code breaker."

"You're not a hacker," Cole says.

"Excuse me?"

"You heard me."

"Now you're just being insulting."

"Don't get me wrong. You're very talented, and you can hack with the best of them, but what you do . . . it isn't just hacking. It's something else."

"There's a more politically correct term I'm not aware of?" Bailey asks.

"For as long as I've run this company, I've had some of the best cybersecurity specialists on my payroll, and not one of them could hop in and out of a giant telecom company on a moment's notice. Somehow you do it all the time. Because you're not hacking them. You're going through doors that have been left open for you. You know where they are because someone's told you where they are. And that, my friend, is why you work for me now."

Bailey sticks his lip out like a pouting baby. "You don't care about me. You just care about my friends."

"I care about both, but your friends scare me."

"Why?"

"Because they're completely invisible, and no one's invisible to someone as rich as me. No one."

"Well," Bailey says after an uncharacteristically thoughtful pause, "they support everything we're doing."

"Good. Then let's support each other by not telling Luke our secrets."

"Fine."

"Except for one."

Bailey's eyes light up. The only thing he loves more than discovering secrets on hard drives is sharing them, apparently.

"At your first *organic* opportunity, I want you to find a way to tell Luke that we think the end destination's Amarillo," Cole says.

"Organic?"

"All our communications tonight are being monitored by The Consortium, and Julia Crispin's paying especially close attention because you hacked her network last year and I still haven't fired you over it."

"You haven't fired me because I'm really good."

"Be that as it may, I don't want her knowing we've got Amarillo in our sights, either, but I want Luke to have fair warning. So if it looks like the operation's moving in that direction, find a way to tell him without broadcasting it to the entire team."

"On one condition."

"Could the people who work for me please stop acting like I'm a used car salesman? These are orders, Bailey!"

"Bring Noah in on this."

"That's insane."

"You need him. If he's your ally, make him one."

"Noah Turlington jeopardized my entire company by conducting a rogue experiment on an unsuspecting private citizen."

"A year ago and now that poor, unsuspecting citizen is getting ready to throttle another serial killer's ass. Let bygones be bygones already. The dude's a genius."

"And he has no conscience or loyalty to anyone besides himself."

"He made Zypraxon so the weak could defend themselves."

"He made Zypraxon because his mother was murdered by a serial killer and he's still not over it. Why are you on Team Noah all of a sudden?"

"My brother's alive because of him."

Bailey doesn't have to polish the flip side of that coin to make it visible: Luke's alive because Noah took action after a massive security oversight on Cole's part put Luke in danger, and Bailey helped Noah do it.

"I'm not telling him about this. He needs to earn it."

"You know, Cole. You dress nice but you're pretty weird."

"How so?"

"Well, I mean here you are, this like shadow government, secret billionaire type, making morally questionable decisions like it's nothing. Then Noah Turlington walks in and you act like you're a nun getting pawed by a werewolf."

"Two orders of business here. One, less caffeine. Two, less focus on my personal relationships."

"You need him, Cole," Bailey says with a surprising lack of sarcasm. "You do. You're running a secret wing of this operation because you're afraid your business partners are setting Charley up to fail. And I've never heard you say a kind word about your own mother, and she's the only family you have. And honestly, I can't take the pressure of being your only friend. This little face-to-face has already been more human contact than I usually do in a month."

"We're not friends."

"Good, 'cause I was starting to worry."

"And if things escalate we can't meet outside again," Cole says. "Keep updating me on the Amarillo team, but text my phone and go to the bathroom."

"You just want me to pee all over the floor or on my phone?"

"*Meet* me in the bathroom, you little cretin. Whatever the update is, write it down on something I can tear up."

Bailey gives him a thumbs-up and heads back toward the house, seemingly relieved to be freed of direct human contact. For the time being.

Cole's relieved, that's for sure.

Footsteps approach again, and for a second, Cole thinks Scott must have been eavesdropping. But instead, he walks right up to Cole and says, "Video call."

"How much time left in the movie?" Cole asks.

"Twenty minutes."

"I don't have time for a call right now. Who is it?"

"It's them."

The Consortium. Cole tries not to grimace. He fails.

"Which one?"

"All of them," Scott says.

This is not good, Cole thinks, *not good at all.*

A few minutes later Cole's sitting at the head of his eight-top glass conference table in the office-slash-conference room underneath the main house. It will only take a swipe of one finger across the control panel next to him to put the faces of his three business partners on the flat screen hanging on the far wall. But his finger's frozen above the touch pad.

"God help me," he whispers, longing for that simpler time when the prospect of not being able to put The Consortium back together kept him awake at night. The adage *be careful what you wish for* is popular for a reason. But he's come up with his own version—*be careful of what you say you can't live without.*

And there they are.

At bottom left, Julia Crispin, with her never-a-hair-out-of-place silver bob, whose idea of casual at-home wear is a pearlescent silk blouse and several gold bracelets. She makes cameras and surveillance devices that are mostly invisible to the naked eye. Maybe that's why she always dresses as if she's got an audience.

Just to her right, Philip Strahan, former marine, six-term US senator, now the CEO of Force Bolt, one of the largest private security contractors in the world. He wears his baldness like a shiny crown, and there are so many antlers in the frame it's impossible to tell how many animal skulls are hanging on the wall behind his desk. Cole's only paid one visit to the man's sprawling ranch in Whitefish, Montana. What he remembers most is how the living room furniture looked like it might be pretty tasty after a few minutes of being turned over an open flame.

Stephen Drucker fills the top half of the screen thanks to some random decision made by their videoconferencing program. As usual, he's staring suspiciously at his laptop's camera as if it's his first videoconference. When you take into account that his company develops weapons that use the latest technology to kill people as quickly and cleanly as possible, it's possible Cole's the one being stared at suspiciously during these calls and not Stephen's computer. Stephen's the group's only international member, as evidenced by his paisley-patterned silk bathrobe and mussed salt-and-pepper hair. It's late in London.

Over the past year, it's become a game of Russian roulette to see which one of his newly reinstalled business partners is going to be the biggest pain in the ass. For a while, it was just him and Julia. Which seemed fitting. They've known each other the longest, thanks to the allegedly passionate affair Julia had with Cole's late father. Now it's the four of them again, the same group Cole abruptly dissolved when their first experiments with Zypraxon killed all the test subjects. They were all traumatized by the initial tests; it's why Cole shut them down so abruptly and also why it was a struggle to get The Consortium back together even after he'd circulated mind-blowing footage of Charlotte's early accomplishments—one original member refused to return for a second round. But now that the band's back together, Stephen and Philip have been acting like Charlotte's latest field test is some unacceptable security risk and not their reason for existence. It's not just infuriating; it's downright suspicious.

"As I'm sure you can see on your feeds, we're underway here, folks," Cole says. "Can we make this quick?"

"Of course. I only have one question," Stephen says. "How is it possible that with all of our resources we have no bloody idea where Cyrus Mattingly plans to go with that truck?"

One question with several answers I'm not about to give.

"The purpose of the report was to address that question," Cole says.

Philip Strahan guffaws and slaps the side of his desk.

The report is over two hundred pages long. For the most part, it's a raft of details about the planned operation, sent two hours ago and for one reason—to give the illusion of transparency while distracting them with irrelevancies. He'd hoped they'd brush it aside with a groan and just be content to watch the action unfold. They'd already objected when Cole promised them after-action reports and demanded instead to be cut in on the live feeds. He'd conceded, figuring it would buy him some operational latitude. But no such luck, apparently.

"The purpose of the report," Philip manages once he catches his breath, "was to drown us in bullshit while you maintained a distinctly *go it alone* attitude on this, my friend."

"Not that I disagree," Stephen cuts in, "but my question stands . . ."

"The answer's in the report," Cole says, "and I worry about insulting your intelligence by repeating it now."

"Indulge me," Stephen says.

"Every internet map search he's done since we began surveillance has been for an official run he's made on behalf of a licensed cargo company. No searches that can't be explained by legitimate business. In other words, he hasn't tried to figure out where he's going tonight, because he already knows, and he's known for some time. He's probably been there before, a lot. It's the only logical explanation. All that said, the fact that we may be on the verge of stopping a serial predator potentially responsible for scores of unexplained disappearances in the state of Texas is a cause for celebration, my friends."

Julia Crispin breaks the silence, sounding more thoughtful than he expected. "And those other runs, those were in trucks he doesn't own, right? Then all of a sudden he bought a box truck for himself using cash, and that's what you cite here as the escalation that justified greater surveillance."

That and the letter, but I'm not telling you about it until I'm convinced you're not trying to sabotage this operation with bureaucratic nonsense. And maybe not even then.

"*Constant* surveillance," Cole adds. "For four solid months, yes."

"You included his 'regular' mail in that surveillance?" Philip asks, sounding like the term makes him nostalgic for a bygone era.

Cole feels a prickle under his skin; thankfully it's on the back of his neck. Although he doubts it would be visible to the callers even if it were on his cheeks.

"We did. He's got a combined internet and cable package that saves him a bit every month, if anyone's curious."

Don't steer them off the topic of his paper mail, he thinks. *That will look too obvious. Let them get bored with it and move on.*

"All right, these truckers, they talk on the CB all the time, right?" Philip asks. "I mean, is that still a thing? Did you guys monitor all that? Maybe when he was out on those official runs he was using that as cover to coordinate with accomplices in code or something."

"We did and found nothing of note," Cole lies.

"Well, color me impressed," Philip says, "if it's true."

"It is," Cole lies again.

Sounding as if he thinks he's being ignored, Stephen says, "And meanwhile this guy's outfitting his own truck into a traveling horror show, but he's not talking to anyone about where he plans to take it or the person he's presumably going to put in it."

"That's correct, Stephen. In my experience, serial killers can be very tight-lipped."

The door to the conference room opens so quietly Cole doesn't hear it. Doesn't notice a freshly showered Noah until he sees him scooting along the wall, taking care to stay out of the camera's view as he makes his way to the far corner out of the room. The room's designed to let people enter and exit undetected during a videoconference, so there's no reacting to Noah without making this already tense call even worse.

Cole's not sure what angers him more: Noah's arrival, or the casual manner in which he's arrived, all wide-eyed curiosity as he studies the faces on-screen. Like he was invited to attend and will later be asked to share his insights on the participants.

"If he even *is* a serial killer," Stephen says.

Cole summons enough appropriate self-righteousness before he says, "You've seen what's in the cargo bay of that truck. If that's your idea of a fun road trip, remind me never to travel with you. And we didn't pick him at random. He's one of a select group of people who buys the chemicals you need to completely dispose of a human body, more than once a year. And he lacks any legitimate professional reason to do so."

Stephen's messing with him. He's heard the qualifications that land an individual on the Hunt List countless times, and he also knows that the more frequent the purchases, the higher up on the list they appear. The top fifteen names Bailey Prescott's extensive hacks have uncovered now occupy what they've come to call the Red Tier; Mattingly's currently number six.

To say nothing of Mattingly's personal history. No living family members, no close friends. A loner from a home so broken he'd landed at a boy's ranch outside Lubbock when he was a teenager, a ranch that later closed amid widespread accusations of abuse. He's also a fan of such violent pornography Cole directed his tech team to investigate whether some of the more upsetting images they found on Mattingly's hard drive had been made with consenting models. So far, they'd only matched three of seven images to a known porn company.

Stephen chews his bottom lip, like he's debating whether to defend himself. When he takes in the silence from his other business partners, he seems to decide against it.

"Why aren't you giving her the first dose remotely? You say in here the blood trackers are equipped to re-dose her remotely if her abduction period takes her outside the trigger window. Give her the first dose remotely. What's she doing out there carrying around one of these pills in her back pocket?"

"It's tradition."

"Tradition?" Stephen snaps. "You've done this *twice*."

Julia waggles one hand and says, "*Once* when we were actually involved and not just watching. The first time was ... highly improvised."

"Hence, my question," Stephen continues. "What's the tradition here? She's literally states away from you. What happens if she loses the pill or someone tries to take it from her?"

"Luke Prescott is trained to respond to a dozen worst-case scenarios. And no one knows she has the pill, so how is that a risk?"

"But what's the point?" Stephen whines. "I mean, why give up control over the first dose?"

"It's part of my understanding with her."

"I see. So not a contract, but an understanding," Stephen says.

"Yeah, because we're swimming in contracts and lawyers with this operation, Stephen. Come on. I allow her to start the process so she can feel a certain sense of control right before she gives up all of it for the sake of our research. How's that?"

"So, you're setting our drug loose in the world like a feather on the wind because of a social justice issue. Well, that's just ... *quaint*."

At the words *our drug*, Noah, Zypraxon's inventor, bows his head suddenly, which tells Cole the man almost talked back to the screen.

"There are risks to remote dosing," Cole tries, even though he knows it's a weak argument. "If she's still inside the trigger window and we remote dose her by mistake, the results could be catastrophic."

Waving his hand at the screen, Stephen says, "We've got trackers in her bloodstream telling us when it's full of paradrenaline. There's no risk of overdose unless someone on your end sits on the remote dosing button by mistake."

"It would be quite a mistake. I can show you the picture of what happened to the animal test subjects we dosed when their bloodstreams were already full of—"

Julia says, "Gentlemen, I'd like to point out that Cole's time does appear to be limited, which is probably why he's being more unpleasant than usual."

Bitch.

"Thank you, Julia. Allow me to add that remote dosing is physically unpleasant and accompanied by nausea and dizziness, so we reserve it as a backup plan only."

There's a brief silence as they all stare at him.

Stephen finally says, "She can tear the arms off serial killers and she's going to complain about a bit of the spins?"

The comment's innocuous enough, but Cole can feel his anger boiling. The fire under it is the fact that *Stephen*'s being the most difficult one here.

So far, he's the only one to derive any personal benefit from their research. What initially looked like a seismic victory for the lab in Iceland—the ability of paradrenaline to wipe out cancer cells—took a dramatic left turn when a catastrophically more virulent strain of the same cancer appeared in the test subjects two days later, a strain that condensed the devastating months-long progression of the disease into a horrifying two hours that practically liquefied the subjects.

The development was so disappointing that both Cole and Kelley Chen, the director of the Iceland lab, took to their beds for days. As soon as The Consortium was reactivated, however, Stephen immediately saw the weapons potential in the supercharged cancer strain that had been created by exposing cancer cells to paradrenaline, and now his people were hard at work mining this by-product, which they've nicknamed "paradron."

Handing over this newly created poison to Stephen was Cole's obligation under the agreement that binds The Consortium. By collectively funding the operation at levels that won't raise red flags on their company's books, each member is allowed to reap those individual benefits that contribute to their specific industry.

To date, Stephen's poison is the only significant advance Project Bluebird 2.0 has been able to make. Injecting samples of stable paradrenaline, the miracle chemical Zypraxon unleashes in Charlotte's bloodstream, into animal subjects has yielded mixed to befuddling results, far less reliable than simply dosing the animals with Zypraxon directly and triggering them the old-fashioned way—by scaring the crap out of them. As for Charlotte, they're no closer to determining why she is the only human test subject who hasn't torn her own head off minutes after Zypraxon unleashes paradrenaline in her bloodstream.

If Charlotte's body continues to yield no clues as to why the drug works so successfully in her and her alone, they'll have to consider the terrifying scenario of testing Zypraxon on more human subjects who might die horrible, gruesome, self-inflicted deaths.

That said, the idea that Stephen might be trying to dial down the entire operation after reaping the only new benefit to date is too infuriating for Cole to contemplate in this moment.

"What can I say, Stephen?" Cole finally says. "I'm a good boss. Now if I may, I need to get to work."

Stephen waves his hand dismissively at the screen. Philip is already pushing back from his desk, and as usual, Julia is shaking her head slightly, as if Cole's a perpetually disappointing toddler. He knows not to expect a more respectful series of goodbyes from his business partners, so he ends the call with a swipe of his control pad.

Now he's only got Noah to deal with.

"What are you doing here?" Cole asks.

"You flew me here."

"What are you doing *downstairs*? I said only come downstairs when I need you."

And he'd meant to tell Scott to keep Noah in his bedroom, but the call from The Consortium distracted him before he could give the order.

"Well, they're just lovely," Noah finally says.

"Don't just walk in on my videoconferences."

"Why didn't you lock the door?"

"Because I forgot you're a cross between a sociopath and a curious seven-year-old."

"I do love your sharp tongue. Wish you'd used it on me in the shower."

"Noah, instead of trying to throw me off-balance with a bad web-cam routine, why don't you just ask me what you want to know so I can explain why I'm not telling you?"

"Mattingly does all this prep work and there's no digital footprint for any of it? That's weird, Cole. I see truck, abduction, I think human traf-ficking. And if I'm your business partner, I think we're sending Charley into the middle of a dangerous operation with only her boyfriend as a backup. You're sure surveillance didn't miss anything?" Noah asks.

"Absolutely sure," Cole answers because the two words, by them-selves, are the truth. They didn't miss anything. "Want to know what else I'm sure of?"

"All ears."

"You have one job tonight, and it's not this. Get inside her head, stay there. Leave the rest of it to me."

Orders like these are usually a perfect opportunity for Noah to mouth off, but something about Cole's tone this time has chased the mirth from him. He doesn't just look serious; he looks wary. As if the prospect of being back in Charlotte's head after all he's done to her frightens him.

Cole studies Noah's expression for as long as he can, then looks away.

It's not that he feels guilty about lying to Noah.

Or lying to The Consortium.

He just gets nervous when the number of people he has to lie to suddenly goes up unexpectedly. Even by one.

Scott Durham doesn't knock before entering. When he sees Noah sitting at the conference table as if he belongs there, he goes rigid. Cole gives a wave of his hand to indicate all's well, and Scott says, "She's leav-ing the theater. Mattingly's following her. Looks like she's hooked him."

5

Dallas, Texas

If she takes her time, it might look suspicious.

If she moves too quickly, he might lose her. Then she'd have to slow down again—also suspicious.

Given how easily Cyrus Mattingly was scared off by a gated apartment complex and the sudden arrival of an unexpected husband, Charlotte's willing to bet he'd be just as wary of a target who started moving erratically. Worse, at this hour most of the mall's stores are in the process of closing, so there's not much for her to stop and study if she needs to let him catch up. It seems like the only people in the mall, aside from the clerks locking storefront doors and pulling down guard gates, are the other moviegoers leaving the theater. They're walking in sparse clumps, their laughter echoing off the stone floors.

It's an upscale mall, and this particular section is lined with strange towering sculptures. Walking in between them now, she realizes they're silhouettes of giant faceless men. Each one repeatedly brings a hammer down in one hand on a stone they're holding in the other. They remind her of oil derricks. With the whole place emptying out, the slow up-and-down swings of each hammer seem ghostly and threatening.

If Mattingly is following her and he sees her look back, he might assume the sight of him, familiar now from their brief encounter in the theater, would put her too on guard for whatever snatch he's planning. With this in mind, she walks as slowly as she can without appearing drunk, keeping her gaze dead ahead.

Kansas Command has said nothing through her earpiece since she confronted Mattingly in the theater. They're falling back, allowing her to maintain the illusion she's on her own with a killer. That's good. It means Cole's respecting her wishes. That said, she's pretty sure if Mattingly wasn't following her, they would let her know so she and Luke could regroup. Instead, there's silence in her right ear. The earpiece is tiny and perfectly matched to her skin tone. It's also capable of transmitting audio back to the command center. Like all the other gifts and gadgets Cole's given them, it probably costs a small fortune.

But she's pretty sure they've also hacked into the mall's security cameras to watch her now, which is how they'd be able to warn her if Mattingly wasn't on her tail.

Correction. *Bailey's* hacked into the mall security cameras on their behalf.

How did Cole put it? Bailey Prescott sees a world without walls, and he's willing to go anywhere within it he desires. Combined with the raw computing power Cole provides him, Bailey's unstoppable. Allegedly.

Careful, she chastises herself. Thinking too much about Bailey might be a sly way of reminding herself that her boyfriend's waiting outside.

He's just one man, she tells herself, *one man sitting inside a retrofitted SUV that could probably survive a four-story drop, with who knows what kind of high-tech weapons buried inside of it. Still, that shouldn't be enough to kill the fear.*

She needs her fear. Needs it ready and waiting, coiled like a cobra in a clay jar. But she doesn't need it quite yet. They've got no idea where Mattingly's planning to take her, and she's determined to make the entire trip. The longer she can go without triggering, the better. It means she won't have to pretend to be rag-doll limp as he loads her into that truck. There might come a moment when she has to block all thoughts of Luke in order to trigger, but she'll know it when she gets there.

And in that moment, she'll send her mind to the place where she's learned to find pure, undiluted, and immediate terror. It's not technically a memory, more like a construction of her mother's last tortured bit of life—a compendium of horrifying facts about the final hours endured not just by her mother, but by each one of Abigail and Daniel Bannings' victims.

Calling it all to mind at once feels like reaching one hand into a planter where the top layer is all the jagged rock of her desire for revenge and then, underneath, a cold, sickeningly soft soil, the touch of which fills her with the same suffocating sense of dread her mother must have felt during her final hours. Her memory rapidly assembles every photo she's ever seen of the root cellar online—of its clawed earthen walls and dirt floor and wooden double doors reinforced with metal panels on the insides, reinforcements put into place after toddler-age Charlotte overheard the screams of one of the women inside. The handcuffs and the duct tape and the constant dread of Daniel Banning's return and another brutal violation. A moment when she feels closest to a mother she can't remember because she was killed when Charlotte was just an infant . . .

For now, she'll hold those memories at bay by thinking of Luke, by remembering the tender way he kissed her neck just the other night. The way he whispered "I wish I could be the one to heal you again and again" while she swayed against him. "Maybe you are," she'd answered. Meanwhile, "Angel of the Morning" played gently on the little Bluetooth speaker Luke had connected to his phone. The song was her mother's favorite, so they'd decided to play it like a gentle anthem as they hunted a killer of women like the ones who had struck her down. But in that moment, it became a kind of love song.

Even though they had only another hour of downtime before they needed to track Mattingly again, Luke led her to one of the twin beds in his motel room—a room where he'd been staying alone while she went to bed each night as Hailey Brinkmann in her new rental house in Richardson. He made love to her urgently and thoroughly. He may have been the one sporting a new armor of muscle, but she was the soldier being loved goodbye in the desperate hours before another combat deployment.

Cyrus Mattingly is behind her.

The glass exit doors are just a yard or two ahead of her. She can see his reflection in them. He's far enough away that he can tail her with a confident stride without looking too suspicious. Just like he followed the other two women. She feels his stare. It sends pinpricks up the back of her neck, across her scalp, coils tension across her shoulder blades, and constricts her chest. Her cheeks flush, too.

Fear.

Not yet, she tells herself. *Not all of it, not yet.*

She pushes the door open and steps out into the crisp fall night.

She walks past Luke's Escalade without looking in his direction.

The car's covered in some special type of paint that barely gives off any reflection. Luke totally geeked out when he described how it worked. It was cute at the time. Right now the mysteries of her own blood, of the drug that's already coursing through her veins, have her full attention.

As she starts the car, she runs through the salient factors of her identity again.

Hi, I'm Hailey, and I'll be your victim this evening. I moved here from California. I worked reception at a car dealership in San Jose, and maybe I'll do that again but who knows because I'm young and life seems wide open right now. I moved because my engagement fell apart. I had an aunt who lived here when I was younger. She's dead now, but I used to visit her a bunch when I was young, so I know Dallas pretty well.

Please don't hurt me, Mr. Mattingly. Please just drive me to wherever you've committed all your crimes so I can kick your goddamn teeth out and make sure you never commit another one again, you twisted fuck.

By the time she's finished this little speech in her head, she's pulled away from the parking structure. On the drive down the ramp to street level, she caught more than one glimpse of Mattingly's headlights behind her.

Excellent, she thinks.

As he follows his potential seedling across town, the soothing near silence of swift travel across traffic-free streets envelops Cyrus with a sense of gentle calm. Save for this whisk of tires over asphalt, it's not quite the same sound as the one that welcomes him to open highways, but it's close, a reminder of that eternal quiet some people call the presence of God but that he prefers to call "the enduring."

He feels a little sheepish about the name. He's never shared it with anyone. Maybe he told Mother once, but he's not sure. If he did, she probably gave him one of her indulgent half smiles. More importantly, she long ago gave him the confidence to be free of any need to justify his sense of purpose to others. True, he does offer some explanation to his seedlings during their special journey. But he doesn't do it to get validation. A man like him doesn't need the world's validation or approval. The great understandings he's come to about the immutable nature of the universe, arrived at mostly during long cross-country drives, can remain his and his alone.

The enduring isn't silence, and it isn't really quiet, either. It's filled by the shuddering of his truck's containers in strong winds and the occasional impatient rush of passing vehicles. Fundamentally, it's wordlessness, and that's a more urgent and truthful thing. Only a fool would think silence the true nature of the universe. The stillness of an open field, the predawn hush—these are transitory moments soon disrupted by the first crack of thunder or the branch-tossing intrusions of strong winds. The wordlessness that connects him to the underlying fabric of the universe is actually a collection of low sounds, some man-made, but all of them indicating a constant forward motion. It's the inventions of man and God in perfect unison, without the yakking intrusion of human chatter and all its petty, fleeting concerns.

Wordlessness . . .

This is also the gift he gives his seedlings.

In the beginning, he saw it as their punishment. And that's how Mother described it. The voices of his cargo needed to be removed from them because they'd used them for disruption and abuse. One of the world's greatest lies, she'd taught him, was that volume was strength. Volume was only strength when it emanated from volcanoes and thunderstorms. For humans to try to assert strength through volume alone was to try to arrogantly steal the language of gods. Like Prometheus stealing the fire from Olympus, it was an effort that doomed one to ruin. Women, Mother had taught him, fell into this trap more often than men, because they lacked the physical strength of men and were therefore more prone to desperation and error when they betrayed their true nature by trying to frighten others into submission. Women could achieve dominance, but not by turning shouts and screams into cudgels, as so many of them tried to do.

But now that he's been paying special visits to Mother for years, Cyrus realizes he's not just meting out a punishment on his women; he's giving them a gift. In the dazed, glassy-eyed expressions of his seedlings after their long journey with him is through, he sees more than just a human doll. He sees the liberation of their tortured souls, a return to a state of innocence, and the place of a woman's true power—to enchant with silence and a use of other softer arts.

Whether she knew it or not, this desire to be set free was positively emanating from that bitch back in the movie theater. In her quaking self-righteous anger as she told him to darken his phone, he could feel a desperate need to be released from her ego and the prison of her constant demands. Demands she no doubt placed on everyone in her life, especially the men—if there were any, and he doubted there were. No doubt she's driven them away by constantly pelting them with a dozen different buzzwords the self-help frauds of the age try to sell as mental health cures—*needs, boundaries, communication, listening*. Between his lessons from Mother and the years of work he's been doing on various seedlings, he's become convinced of one thing.

The women of the world were terribly unhappy. The ones who'd freed themselves from essential male attachments were miserable wanderers, congratulating themselves on their so-called independence while stewing in a constant pool of anxiety and dissatisfaction.

They weren't free of anything.

To be truly free, they had to go on the kind of journey he offered them.

Charlotte has Hailey do everything a woman traveling alone at night shouldn't do. But no other woman in the world right now has been dosed with the drug currently sitting dormant inside her veins.

She deliberately parks in shadow.

As she approaches her front door, she watches her phone so intently it probably looks like she's streaming something on Amazon Prime. Then, at the door, she lingers, right under the porch light she removed the bulb from the night before.

There's mail in the mailbox, all of it addressed to RESIDENT or the former tenant, a guy named Tim Johnson. Good thing she caught it. If Mattingly decides to go through her mailbox, the sight of a man's name might scare him off. She tucks the envelopes under one armpit and unlocks the front door as if the keys are covered in syrup.

The whole time she wants to look over her shoulder, but she knows she shouldn't. Same rule as the mall. Maybe Mattingly's not skittish; maybe he's just particular. Either way, he, like many a serial killer, prefers to travel the path of least resistance.

Inside, cardboard boxes are pushed against the walls. They're filled with clothes about her size, but they've all been through a washing machine several times and given other little handmade marks of wear and tear, even though she's willing to bet they were bought just for this operation.

It's the framed photographs Cole's team has filled the house with that really impress her. They line the mantel and the open shelves separating the kitchen and breakfast nook. They give her a completely fake life that she appears to have thoroughly enjoyed in the company of stock photo models she's never met. The Photoshop work is so good she's even embracing some of the models.

She's come up with a piece of backstory to go with each one.

Here's Hailey's ex-boyfriend Josh, who dumped her right before she met Fred. Josh was a former college football player felled by a shoulder injury his sophomore year who never quite found his way in life after. Fred, on the other hand, is two pictures over; he's the red-head in the Hawaiian shirt, the guy she's hugging in front of a tropical background. Fred's family owns a Cadillac dealership where Fred will probably work until he dies. That's where he got her a job in reception so she could save money for veterinary school. But then he broke off their engagement and there went her job, so here she is, pursuing a fresh start in East Texas with the money she saved up.

After weeks of inspection by a skeptical stranger, these stories, along with the photos, might reveal inconsistencies she can't see in this moment. But they're a great cover for now. The prep team was wise enough not to use any pictures from when she was young enough to be recognizable to most of the country as Burning Girl, the captive child of serial killers who tried to raise her as their own.

She left all the curtains open before she left for the theater. Now she goes from room to room, turning on the lights and pausing now and then to stretch and yawn in a manner that makes her appear relaxed, confident. Oblivious.

Then she does what women in horror movies have always done to the consternation of audiences the world over, the difference being that she actually wants to draw a monster in from the shadows.

She takes a shower.

6

Lebanon, Kansas

"What do we think he's waiting for?" Luke Prescott asks in Cole's ear.

"Not sure," Cole answers.

It's been an hour and thirty since Charlotte stepped from the shower.

Mattingly's Econoline is still parked in the nearest bed of shadow to the little one-story rental house. The cameras planted inside reveal an almost motionless figure, watching Charlotte's rental house like a faceless hawk in a Dallas Cowboys baseball cap. Any cop on a stakeout would aspire to this man's level of meditative calm, Cole thinks.

Off to Cole's left, the digital map of Dallas still shows Charley's, Mattingly's, and Luke's locations in gently pulsing red dots. Just above the map's top border is the local time, same as theirs in Kansas: 11:45 p.m.

The rest of the surveillance screens offer various views inside Charley's—*Hailey Brinkmann's*, he corrects himself—rental house, along with repeatedly alternating exterior views of the backyard, side alley, and surrounding streets. It's a flat, tree-filled suburban neighborhood, but Julia Crispin's upgraded their camera technology to night vision without any of the customary flare. He can see insects flittering around the streetlamps. Over the past hour, he's been able to track the lights winking out in the front rooms of the neighboring houses.

It's a nice setup, but Cole still misses his microdrones, tiny little eyes in the skies he could sweep almost silently over any area. They weren't much good after dark if you weren't chasing a specific light source, but still—they gave him a sense of almost godlike power. Despite their individual resolution, the angles on the surveillance screens feel fragmented, too interior. His brain's already tired from constantly assembling them into a complete picture of the scene in his head—another consequence of Charley's new rule that they fall back.

"Seriously, what's he waiting for?" Tim Zadan asks. Cole realizes another twenty minutes have gone by since Luke asked the same question through his earpiece.

Zadan is baby-faced, blond, and blue-eyed; not Cole's type, but cute enough that Cole has to constantly catch himself to make sure he doesn't treat him with unearned deference. The camera tech is seated at one of the monitoring stations in front of where Cole's been slowly pacing since Charley walked inside the house. Zadan's usually tight-lipped, but without flocks of microdrone camera feeds to monitor, he, like Shannon, has a lot less to do.

The only one who seems as intent as always is Paul Hynman, the med tech in charge of monitoring Charley's vitals. Her blood tracker stats are displayed on a constantly refreshing screen to the extreme right of the monitor bank above their heads. The neuro panel is brand new. After some work, they've made it so it can detect the actual presence of paradrenaline in her brain. In the past, Charley's blood trackers identified trigger events solely on the basis of the impossible blood pressure and blood oxygen levels they produced. No more.

All told, Paul is the only tech who now has more responsibility, not less. Right now, it shows. Bald and wiry, with a constantly skeptical expression, he's relying on the computer monitor in front of him instead of the display screen filled with the same information overhead. It looks like he expects Charlotte's heart to stop at any second.

"I don't know," Cole answers. Then he touches his earpiece and asks Luke, "How you holding up out there?"

"What can I say," Luke answers, "the Caddy's comfy."

On one of the displays overhead, Luke looks right into the camera implanted in the Escalade's dashboard and gives them a broad smile and a thumbs-up.

It's also damn near invisible, Cole thinks, *and thank God, because Mattingly's sure had a lot of time to study the street from behind the wheel of his van.*

"She's still got a light on, right?" Luke asks. "I think I can see a light."

"He can't see her feed?" Noah asks from behind Cole.

Cole spins in place. When Noah sees his expression, he bows his head and mutters a soft apology. It's doubtful Luke heard him through Cole's earpiece, but still, orders are orders. Maybe he should give Noah a little credit, though. For the past hour he's been sitting in a chair against the back wall, quiet and erect as a statue, studying the uneventful progression of events on the monitors with the fierce intensity of a student trying to impress the teacher.

Making sure the connection to Luke isn't open, Cole says, "We don't think it would be possible for Luke to maintain an effective tail while also being treated to the sight of some sicko trying to dismember his girlfriend."

"We?" Shannon Tran says. "Nobody asked my opinion."

"Did you have one?" Cole asks.

"No."

"But you wanted me to ask you anyway?"

"No, you just said *we* so I thought I should point out . . . Look, it's been slow, OK. I'm just bored. I didn't mean anything by it."

Over the internal channel, Bailey Prescott says, "Ask her about my Nutella."

"Shut up, Bailey," Cole and Shannon say at the same time.

Then, to Shannon, Cole says, "See. We're more of a *we* than you thought."

For some reason, the longer they all sit down here together in tense silence, the sillier Cole's gag order on Noah seems. Cole moves to him, then takes out his earpiece and clamps it in one hand.

"I don't think he's up to it yet," Cole says quietly.

"Who?" Noah asks.

"Luke."

"What's he doing out there, then?"

"He's not up to watching her feed during an op. That's what I meant. He's got a history of emotionality, and it'll be a while before I'm comfortable."

"Makes sense," Noah says in almost a whisper. "Have the control room act as a filter, telling him only what he needs to know. It's how I would have done it."

It's chilly down here under the ground, but Cole feels suddenly warm. He's worried it's pure attraction, triggered by Noah's nearness. But it's not. He feels less alone. For the first time in years, it actually feels like he and Noah are working toward the same objective and not just on the same secret project.

Or Bailey's intrusive advice got into his head.

Cole moves back to the monitoring stations, wondering if he's made a mistake.

A little while later, Noah breaks the silence. "Two a.m.," he says.

"Excuse me?" Cole asks.

"If he's done his homework, he's going to wait until two a.m."

"Why?" Shannon asks.

"The Night Stalker was about home invasions, and that's how he did it. He figured out the majority of people obeying a normal sleep schedule entered REM sleep by two in the morning, so it was easier to break into their house without waking them up first. That way he could surprise them in bed."

The room takes in this information like a family trying to process a relative's explicit account of surgery during Thanksgiving dinner.

"He also stopped smoking crack so he could be a better serial killer," Shannon says. "That's one fact I wish I could get out of my head."

Tim says, "I think he's going to try to lure her outside. Maybe take her in the yard. Who wants to bet?"

"We are not *betting* on the actions of a serial killer," Cole says. "You want to play games, go back to Trivial Pursuit, Night Stalker Edition."

"Sorry," Tim mumbles.

"Which one was the Night Stalker?" Shannon asks.

"Richard Ramirez," Paul Hynman says without looking up from his computer. Everyone's startled by his sudden contribution.

"Was that the Golden State guy?" Tim asks.

"No," Noah answers. "The Golden State Killer was the *original* Night Stalker. But he went so long without being caught they gave the title to somebody else who also liked breaking into people's houses in the middle of the night and raping and sometimes killing them."

"California's a competitive place," Shannon says. "He started out as the East Area Rapist."

"Who's the East Area Rapist now?" Paul asks.

"That's enough. I understand the need to let off a little steam while we kill time," Cole says, "but I don't want us to get tunnel vision here. We can't be one hundred percent sure he's going to go for a break-in, so let's keep our eyes open so we can advise Luke accordingly."

They answer with silence, which he figures is about as much obedience as he's going to get. And he understands. The worst part is the waiting, and Mattingly is making them wait a long time. But is it really Mattingly making them wait?

He looks to the monitor showing Charley's TruGlass feed. The pages of a novel are gently drifting past the frame. She's actually

66

reading the damn thing, as she might do on any normal night before bed.

"What is she doing?" Shannon asks.

"Getting in character, trying to forget we're there," Noah says.

Cole doesn't disagree, so he doesn't say a word.

"Maybe we could tell her it's time to turn out the light," Paul mumbles.

"That would be about *our* comfort," Cole answers, "not hers. We only speak to her if it's critical. That's the deal."

"That's not why," Noah says.

"Not why what?" Cole asks him.

Noah's next to him so abruptly, Cole actually jumps. Then Noah points to one of the views of the neighborhood on-screen overhead. The light in one of the back rooms of the house next door to Charley's is still on, just a few yards away from where her bedroom drapes haven't been drawn all the way closed.

"She's waiting for them to go to bed," Noah says. "She doesn't want the neighbors to scare him off."

Nobody says anything for a while. Then the neighbor's back room light clicks off.

A few minutes go by, then a few more, and then, as if sleep has overtaken her, Charley closes the book she's been reading, reaches over, and turns off the lamp next to her bed.

7

Dallas, Texas

Charlotte pretends to sleep.

First on her back, then on one side, facing the bedroom window so she can see any shadows that might dart past the crack in the curtains. At what feels like regular intervals, she opens her eyes slightly to check the time on the nightstand's digital clock. After a short while, she's able to predict the passage of fifteen minutes with a fairly impressive success rate.

Then, sometime around 1:00 a.m., she hears a sound that probably wouldn't have awakened her if she'd actually been asleep—the sound of the lock on the back door being picked. It helps that she'd left all the doors between her and the kitchen partly open. But still, if it's really Mattingly and he's doing what she thinks he's doing, he's incredibly skilled.

Then silence returns.

A cool breath of air moves across her throat, then her face. She knows it has to be coming from outside because it smells faintly of the confederate jasmine growing on a trellis in the neighbor's yard. Mattingly opened the door so quietly she didn't hear the lock click.

She can hear her pulse in her ears.

Not good. It's too much, too soon. She doesn't want to trigger yet, so she tries to imagine the room her earpiece connects her to, even though the connection's been silent for hours. She's never seen a command center, but no doubt the space is dominated by Cole Graydon in his usual dark slacks and one of his perfectly pressed dress shirts pacing in front of a bank of computer monitors that reveal multiple views inside the house she's in now. Visualizing this remote space is helpful, but the surrounding shadows and her pose, prone in bed in pajamas, are triggering fear receptors no sense of connection to something larger and more powerful can keep dormant.

And Luke is outside, ready to kiss your neck in all the right places when all of this is done.

"Thread the needle" is a mantra she typically uses once she's triggered, a way of focusing her actions and reducing her strength so that she can do everyday movements without pulling off doorknobs or breaking keys in half. Right now, it applies to the delicate dance she's doing between fear and confidence, isolation and connection. She can't let go of her fear entirely. She needs it close, but still coiled.

Cobra in a jar, she thinks. *That one'll work because I'm not all that afraid of snakes.*

Her breaths are short and shallow, nothing like sleep. She forces herself to breathe deeply. Loudly, creating something close to a snore. It helps. Slowing her heartbeat, dropping the temperature of her body some. She's so focused on her breaths she misses the first few footsteps he's taken into her bedroom. He's not a spry or slender man, but he's moving like someone at home in shadows. *How many bedrooms, how many women? If I'm bound for the truck on his property, who knows how many unexplained missing persons cases he's behind?* If it's as many as it is purchases that landed him on the Hunt List, there's no way she's letting this go wrong.

Her eyes slits, she continues breathing deeply even as he stands over her nightstand.

There's a soft squirt. She groans slightly, turns onto her side, facing the nightstand, figuring it would be more suspicious not to react to the sound at all, given how close it is. She feels movement in the air above her, but she's more taken by the sight on the nightstand, which she sees while trying not to visibly squint. A tiny tendril of pale, viscous fluid is drifting through the water in the glass she brought to bed with her. The squirt must have come from the syringe he loaded onto his tool belt earlier that night. Instead of piercing her flesh with it, he's used it to spike her water glass.

The tendril falls, dances slightly, like a tiny spirit trying to gain corporeal form. Then it's gone.

Poison? she wonders. *All this trouble just to poison a woman in bed?*

She doubts it, but maybe she's being too optimistic. A rash of poisonings throughout the Dallas area would have come up during Cole's investigation into Mattingly. The bastard's been Dallas-based for twenty years. No, that can't be it.

When she's dosed with Zypraxon, a potentially fatal injury can trigger the drug, releasing the paradrenaline needed to heal the injury. But there's always the possibility that some instantly fatal injury might be able to sneak through the tiny gap between injury and release— severing a nerve related to heartbeat or respiration so quickly the trigger event will come too late to heal. The chances of this aren't substantial, but they exist, and it's been a constant source of anxiety during their lab tests this past year. Cole calls it the *trigger gap*. Poison raises a host of other issues, ones they haven't tested. Not all poisons are sudden, jarring injuries that immediately traumatize the body and the brain; some of them are creeping monsters in the blood, damaging the inside with slow, silent persistence. How much cumulative damage could a poison do before she feels the kind of sharp pain or traumatic injury that triggers Zypraxon? The drug doesn't respond to actual physical damage; it responds to the conscious awareness of it and the terror that results.

Once triggered, sedatives of any kind, ranging from alcohol to medical-grade anesthesia, don't work on her. But they've got no research to prove that Zypraxon can stave off a deadly poison prior to a trigger event.

Triggering now could blow half the game. If Mattingly plans to carry her out of here—which she's ninety percent sure he will—he might figure out that her limbs aren't bending quite the way they should, that she's not really out cold. She hasn't verbalized this to anyone, but throughout the run-up to this operation, she's harbored hope that a man who goes to this much trouble to whisk victims off in his truck might be keeping some of them alive somewhere, and then she'd have the chance to set them free. According to Cole, they've intercepted no communications at all about Mattingly's destination, not even a map search. That means he knows exactly where he's going. And since he's made no recent visits to his destination, there could be an accomplice there, possibly an unsuspecting one, holding down the fort while Mattingly arranges deliveries.

Any attempt to overpower Mattingly before they reach the evidence of his crimes throws off Cole's endgame. In a perfect scenario, tonight will end with Cole's ground team drugging Mattingly and leaving him surrounded by the evidence of his killings. They don't just want Mattingly to go down for his awful crimes; they want him to be a babbling lunatic by the time the authorities arrive, raving about the woman who overpowered him in the language of drug-induced madness.

Mattingly's no longer standing over her, she realizes.

The next sound she hears is so strange she can't place it at first, a light spray accompanied by a tiny metallic rattle. A breath of cool air fires across her nose and lips. The coughs are instantaneous. Violent enough that they would have awakened her from a dead sleep had she been in one. At first, she thinks he might have gassed her, but the coughs are dry and irritating, and she smells a strange combination of noxious scents—a hint of bleach and pepper and other smells that don't belong together and that make the back of her throat burn.

When she starts sneezing, she sits up. Against her will, her eyes open. Mattingly has dropped down out of sight, probably pressed to the floor on the other side of her bed.

Oh, I get it, she thinks, amazed to have such neutral thoughts about the workings of a serial killer.

Charlotte does what any person in her situation would do. She reaches for the glass of water on her nightstand, the same one Mattingly just spiked.

One swallow, two swallows, then three.

Only once she's nestled back into the covers does she realize the implications of surrendering to his little trick. She's allowed him to drug her before she's triggered. And that means darkness will be on her soon. A part of her resists this, but she needs to stave off a trigger event. So she tries banishing the images that might bring her closer to it—her mother's face, a wild collage of a dozen different photos used for her MISSING posters after the Bannings abducted them—and reaches for the ones that will delay it. *Luke. Kissing my neck. Singing along—badly, but who cares?—with "Angel of the Morning." That goofy smile he makes when he pulls so hard on the jar lid it snaps off unexpectedly and he spills artichokes or tomatoes or who knows what else on the kitchen floor because he's just so goddamn strong after all the training they've given him.*

She's still thinking of Luke when she feels the weight of a heavy, unnatural sleep descending on her, and before it takes her completely, she thinks, *All right, Mr. Mattingly. Let's hit the road.*

Charlotte is sixteen years old and holding the gift from Uncle Marty on her lap. She's still known as Trina then—she only changed her name after her grandmother's death—and she's only been free of her father for several weeks. Her brand-new bedroom, the one her grandmother made for her out of the house's old sewing room, is immaculate but

mostly bare. It's waiting to be filled with knickknacks and curios and posters, the stamps of an ordinary teenage life she hasn't been allowed until now. The sunlight here in California seems so much clearer than the light back in Georgia, cutting through the part in the bedroom's ruffly sky-blue curtains with cleansing power.

Does Uncle Marty know how special this gift is? Does her grand-mother? She visited them a few times over the years, but always strictly under her father's supervision. Do they know she's never had a computer of her own and never been allowed to use the internet unsupervised? Now she has her very own laptop, her very own connection to the world.

It makes her head spin.

Given who she was, given what she's been through, her father believed letting her surf the net by herself was the same as letting her walk alone through a bad neighborhood at night. Several times, they'd been hacked by true-crime conspiracy theorists convinced that little Trina Pierce had played more of a role in the Bannings' crimes than she'd let on and that there was proof of this on her father's hard drive. The truth was, her father's insistence that she keep performing for hor-ror movie fans all over the country placed her in more danger than any Google searches.

But what does that matter now? She's free of him, free of those speaking engagements he'd always schedule to coincide with the release of a new installment in that ridiculous horror movie franchise that claimed to be based on her life.

She can hear her grandmother and Uncle Marty out on the front deck, talking to the few lingering guests. The party was for her, to wel-come her to Altamira, California, the little town at the foot of Big Sur where her grandmother reinvented herself after almost drinking her life away while grieving her only daughter and granddaughter.

The guests were her grandmother's other AA friends, all bright-eyed and rosy cheeked no matter their age. Each one of them seemed to be guzzling a caffeinated beverage, their eyes alert for any new food item that might appear from the kitchen at a moment's notice. Sober folks needed their parties to have food, Marty assured her. It's how they made up for the sugar intake they lost when they got off the sauce. They're not married, Marty and her grandmother, but they're girlfriend and boyfriend, even though that seems like a silly way to describe two grown-ups in their fifties.

In addition to the computer, the other gifts were all things her father didn't allow her. All sorts of novels, both youthful and grown-up, scary and romantic. DVDs of popular movies for her new disc player. Nothing filtered, nothing censored. Magnifying glasses. Ant farms. Elegant leather-bound diaries. A buffet of things that might pique her interest, since no one, not even she, was quite sure of what those interests were.

Only now that she's free of him does she realize the extent to which her father managed her life. She's always thought the erratic blend of tutors, homeschooling, and therapists was simply about maintaining the grueling travel schedule they had to meet to keep up with all the appearances, a schedule that intensified whenever a new Savage Woods film was released. But recently, she's started to understand her father had a different agenda. When she saw how quick he was to send her to her grandmother's once she refused to appear with him onstage again, it was impossible not to believe that what mattered to him most was the money he could make off her. So, when she looks back on his protective-ness, she doesn't see a dad trying to protect his little girl's feelings. She sees him trying to keep her on script. He shielded her as best he could from depictions of other teenagers' lives, of other normal families. Of kids who went to school and made friends, kids whose lives were not constant therapy and constant touring around the country and some-times the world.

But that's over now.

In another week or two, once she's had a chance to settle in, she will go to a normal school. Go to normal classes. Try to make normal friends.

Now, she has her very own computer.

She can go anywhere online. Read anything. Watch anything.

But once she opens the Google web page, her fingers type the words automatically. Simultaneously, she feels a sudden weight pressing against her upper back. She figures she'll just find pictures she's never seen before, that's all. But that's a cover story for a need she's too afraid to identify. She wants to know more, the things she's sure her father never shared.

She wants to know what she went through.

Fingers trembling, she lifts her hands to the keyboard and types her mother's name.

"Hailey?"

Not her name.

Someone else's.

The voice is smooth and confident, the tone reserved. He's measuring every word because he's convinced his words have as much power as the restraints he put her in while she was out cold. Charlotte knows better than to mistake his tone for humility; it's quiet, dangerous arrogance.

She blinks, unsurprised by all of it. The gag in her mouth, the fabric hood plastering her hair to the crown of her skull, the pressure on her wrists and ankles, and the hard, unyielding surface under her back. For another woman, an unprepared woman, these would be implements of terror, no doubt. And they should be. But she's visited hells like these before.

There's a bright light shining on her face that prevents her from seeing anything beyond the dark shadow of her captor sitting next to whatever she's tied to. When he leans forward, she sees his trimmed salt-and-pepper mustache, his deeply set puppy-dog eyes under heavy dark brows. He's still wearing the baseball cap he wore to the movie theater. It's Cyrus Mattingly, for sure.

Behind him, she can just make out a patch of flat concrete wall. Are they on his property in Waxahachie? Cole and his team know it backward and forward, but she insisted they not share any of the details with her. She's willing to bet this is some sort of storm cellar. How long does he plan to hold her here?

He reaches forward and gingerly tugs at the straps of her gag. It's all for show. The thing's firmly in place, but he's demonstrating that the ball gag inside her mouth is attached to a more extensive contraption that covers the lower half of her face, even wrapping her nose, save for two slits that allow her nostrils to take in air. She's not sure but she thinks it might be leather. The sedatives are wearing off in stages. Now she can feel her hair bunched up and smashed to the top of her head, covered by the top half of whatever this bizarre face mask is. It's meant to do more than silence. Only her eyes and forehead are exposed. Her ears are covered by the sides of the hood, but the fabric's not so thick that she can't hear through it.

"Can you hear me? Blink once if you can hear me." His tone's so casual he could be asking her for directions to the nearest grocery store.

She blinks once.

"Good," he says, but he sounds distracted. "I'd like to tell you a few things about what you're wearing. It was made just for this so it probably feels strange. Does it feel strange?"

Your wording's also strange, she thinks. *It was made just for this, not I made it for this.*

She blinks once. He nods, tightens a strap against the side of her head.

"I need you to understand something, OK?" Again, that unnervingly calm tone. Like he's bringing her in on a secret that will benefit them both. "There's something you need to do here. It'll make all this better, promise. It'll make *you* better, too. I know that might be hard to believe, but it's the truth. You're not going to have to wear this thing much longer, but I can't take it off you just yet. So, while you've got it on, let's agree to some things, OK?"

She blinks once. But she's busy taking in details. The deadness in his eyes, the fidgety but consistent way he keeps securing the mask's various straps. There's also what he doesn't do: he doesn't caress her. He doesn't kiss her. His manner suggests she's not some sexual plaything he's brought here for his twisted delight. For now, he remains invested in her submission to the strange implement designed to silence her. The sedatives are wearing off in stages like they did with the last two monsters who drugged her. For the first time, she feels a slight tickle against the back of her throat. At first, she thinks it might just be saliva or postnasal drip. But it's not. It's solid. And with a jolt of fear, she realizes there's some sort of rubbery extension attached to the gag's solid rubber ball and it's lying against the back of her throat like a sleeping snake.

Gooseflesh sweeps her reawakened skin. For a second, she's sure she triggered. But when she goes to ball up her fists, the plastic flex-cuffs on her wrists don't break.

She's running the lyrics for "Angel of the Morning" through her head and it calms her some, but Mattingly noticed her jolt of fear, and now he's studying her with a patience and reserve that suggest supreme confidence.

"Hailey? Blink once if you're listening to me."

She blinks once.

"The thing in the back of your throat—you can feel it now, I can tell. You need to be very careful of it, OK? I don't want it to hurt you. I really don't. But if you scream, something bad will happen." He sounds as if some godlike force is inflicting these indignities upon her, and not him, not Cyrus Mattingly. "If you scream, you'll probably throw up and I won't be able to get back in time to get the thing off you before you choke. And I don't want that to happen and you shouldn't, either. Now, a lot's going to happen tonight that you might not understand. Not right away anyway. For now, I need you to embrace your silence. Can you do that for me, Hailey? Can you just breathe? Can you just stay silent? It'll be good practice for the rest of the night. 'Cause we're going to spend a lot of time together."

She's not surprised when he places a gloved palm against her exposed forehead. He is, however. He's surprised she didn't flinch, and for a moment, some look passes through his otherwise dead eyes, some vague suspicion that it seems like he's trying to put words to but can't.

Shit, she thinks. It's too late to flinch now. It'd be obvious she's faking it. So, she puts as much fear as she can into her wide eyes, blinks madly as she tries to see him through the light. He leans forward, blocking out whatever light source is blinding her, staring into her eyes without any trace of evident emotion. His breath still smells like popcorn; she's grateful for this marker of the passage of time, however sour.

When his gloved fingers caress her exposed throat, gently but without any tenderness, she does flinch, and he nods as if this was confirmation he needed. She prepares herself for some mad, lunatic speech intended to enflame her fear, but all he says is, "Your silence is your strength, Hailey Brinkmann. Forget everyone who's ever told you otherwise."

She blinks once.

He nods and pats the side of her cheek gently.

Then he's gone, and she's alone with the blinding light.

A few seconds later, she hears what sounds like double storm doors creaking open directly overhead, but she can't see anything past the lamp's fierce white blaze. Then she notices a strange feeling in the last place she wants to feel anything right now. An intrusion in her most sensitive parts, which makes no sense, given that she's not naked. But it's clear he had no trouble sliding off and then replacing her pajama pants.

There's something else, she can feel. She's right at the edge of triggering. Closer than she's been all night. She was stupid to assume the fact that he didn't caress her face or try to kiss her meant his madness had no sexual tint to it. Clearly he violated her while she was unconscious with some sick implement like the one currently lodged in her throat. And if Cole managed to get cameras inside this storm cellar, too, then everyone in the command center watched while Mattingly worked on her.

Not the same, a rational voice that sounds like her grandmother's whispers. *Calm down, honey. They don't feel the same.* Luanne's ghost is right. Whatever's been placed inside of her down there is smaller, plastic. Not as intrusive. It doesn't seem designed to immobilize and humiliate.

It's a catheter, she realizes.

At first, this realization seems comforting. Until she realizes that no matter how basic and utilitarian this device, it means Cyrus Mattingly plans to keep her confined like this for a very long time.

8

Tulsa, Oklahoma

When Zoey Long tosses her keys on the console table, Boris the Destroyer leaps off her sofa and streaks down the apartment's single hallway, an orange blur across the cream-colored carpet.

Her cat's frenzied escape doesn't surprise her. Zoey's too startled by how good her apartment smells, the best it's smelled in days.

Maybe enough time's gone by since Boris got into those nachos she stupidly left on the kitchen counter, or maybe her decision to move the cat's litter box out onto her tiny patio was a wise one. Whatever the case, she can once more smell the little glass bowls of spiced apple and cinnamon potpourri she's placed every few feet.

If she weren't so stressed out from her fight with Jerald, she'd track the cat down and make him sit with her on the sofa. But right now, she doesn't have the energy. He'll come out after a bit, she's sure. Probably just in time to rub against her legs and purr during all the best parts of whatever she decides to watch on TV.

Unless, of course, Jerald calls, in which case her cat will end up interrupting one of the most uncomfortable conversations of her entire life.

But Jerald isn't going to call. Zoey's sure of it. Not now, not ever.

It's over.

It has to be.

She's never spoken to him that way before. Never spoken to anyone that way, really. And she'll need a dozen phone calls to her sister and her girlfriends before she'll be one hundred percent convinced he deserved it.

Her sister, Rachel, will say he did. She's never liked Jerald, not since he showed up to her birthday dinner at Prhyme Steakhouse in a T-shirt and shorts before dominating the conversation with talk of how much cash one of his ex-girlfriends was making as an Instagram influencer.

Zoey Long has never considered herself the angry type.

In Zoey's view, anger was arrogance, plain and simple. Angry people, she would have said if pressed, were childish and spoiled and masking those truths with aggression. She wouldn't have used the words *childish* and *spoiled*, of course, because she wouldn't want to make the person she was talking to angry. But as far as Zoey was concerned, if you stomped your feet and slammed doors, it didn't matter how old you were—you were throwing a tantrum, plain and simple.

And Zoey didn't throw tantrums.

But she wasn't exactly the sweetest of girls, either. Her friends thought she was a good listener, but her friends also knew that on most days she preferred books to people. She was different from her sister, or so she thought. Rachel could be a ferocious loudmouth when the situation called for it. Just the other day, in fact, over drinks at the little dive bar down the street from the dental office where they both work, her big sis had implied that Zoey's lack of anger might be a weakness. That wasn't the extent of what Rachel said, of course, but that was the part that kept ringing in Zoey's ears afterward.

How had Rachel worded it exactly?

Zoey had recently accomplished something "pretty f'in' monumental" and she wasn't celebrating herself enough. Worse, she was probably staying fairly quiet for one reason. If she spoke up about her new success as an author, it would draw attention to the fact that her boyfriend of one whole year was staying pretty damn quiet about it, too.

If only she could call Rachel right now—she'd be *so* proud of her—but Rachel's on a flight over the Atlantic with her husband, an anniversary trip to Paris. So, for now Zoey's best option is quality time with her thoughts, awaiting the emergence of her jittery cat, and wondering whether she had a right to read her boyfriend for filth because he insulted the realization of one of her lifelong dreams.

Sex books, Zoey fumes, bracing herself against the doorframe because the memory of Jerald's words is that powerful. *Just don't talk about your sex books in front of my mom next week.*

A year of seeing each other exclusively, the first ever visit to his parents, and his main concern was that she stayed quiet about the first major accomplishment of her adult life. They weren't *sex books*, for Christ's sake. They were romance novels. And while she hadn't expected Jerald to become a Harlequin junkie just because she'd made some Amazon bestseller lists, she'd expected him to give her a little more credit for all the time and hard work she'd put into them.

True, he'd thanked her for the new laptop she'd bought him with some of the royalties, but that was about it.

She'd spent ten years of her life outlining the backstories of the Roark sisters, plotting out various versions of the ancient legend that was the source of their shared supernatural abilities. She'd drawn dozens of maps of Fog Harbor, the picturesque town on the Oregon Coast that was home to their compound, written three different books in the series, all of which were rejected by a slew of New York agents for reasons ranging from the condescending to the cutting. Then one day, her online author friends in her various Facebook groups encouraged her to "go indie," as they put it. She'd scraped together the money for editors and a cover designer, and then the miraculous happened.

Not long after she released all three books, people started reading them. And liking them. And reviewing them. Some people were nasty, of course, the internet being the internet. But only one of the one-star reviews managed to really stick in her craw. It was from Bored Reader, and the headline read, Hopefully this writer can be good at other things because it's not writing stuff. The review's grammatically incorrect headline was just the tip of the iceberg. The review itself didn't have any specifics about the book. Just a string of book review clichés that could have easily been cut and pasted from another romance novel's sales page.

But it didn't seem to matter what any of the negative reviews said—the damn things kept selling, and the checks kept coming.

And while Rachel was right, Zoey hadn't exactly gone around crowing about it, she hadn't kept any of it a secret from her boyfriend, either. But now that she thought about it, his insulting words that night at dinner—if a last-minute trip to the food court at the Woodland Hills Mall because "I could fucking rape some chicken tenders right now, babe" could be considered *dinner*—were the most he'd ever uttered about her literary accomplishments.

As she sinks into the sofa, she's remembering the stunned expression on Jerald's face when he saw the wounded look on hers. The speed with which his expression turned to a smirk, and then a dismissive snarl. Her next words had come tumbling out so fast, she still can't remember all of them. But they weren't furious. Not yet. They were specific.

It was a speech she'd rehearsed ever since Rachel had suggested she might be hiding her light under a bushel to avoid causing a fire in her relationship. She explained to Jerald the time it had taken, the effort she'd put in, the rejection letters she'd received over the years and how much they'd hurt. And the whole time, Jerald's snarl just got more severe, as if she had no right to be boring him with any of these details and oh my God why was she still talking?

And, of course, she knew it wasn't about the books. Their relationship was a hot mess, had been for months now, and now that fact was bubbling to the surface like magma, ready to melt everything in its path. In the beginning, he'd said all the things he thought he needed to say to land the deal; then, as soon as they decided to go exclusive, he merged with her sofa. It's where he spent most of his time whenever he came over, and the steady stream of criticism he gave her seemed designed to derail any decision she might make that would require him to get up off it.

Maybe they could have recovered, sought higher ground. But what Jerald said next was even worse than his opening line. "That's fine and all, babe, but I honestly don't think you'd *need* the books if you felt better about your body."

She spoke her words as she thought them. For her, that was rare. "Did you just say I only wrote my novels because I'm fat?"

"I didn't say you were fat. *You* said you were fat. I said you don't feel good about your body, and when you don't feel good about your body you have to do all these other things to feel better about yourself. Just be you, is what I'm saying."

"I *am* being me. The books *are* me. All my life I've wanted to be a writer."

"Yeah, well all my life I've wanted to date a supermodel but . . ." He realized his mistake too late and went quiet and still, as if she might not have realized it was a mistake.

"But you're just dating me? Who's fat, but not fat, apparently. I just feel bad about my body. I'm sorry. What are we even talking about right now?"

"Stop yelling."

She'd barely raised her voice, but the next thing she heard herself say was, "I'm sorry, Jerald, but I really don't understand what you're trying to say."

"I just . . . wish it was something else, OK? I just wish you'd found something else to do other than those books. They're weird and they're hard to explain to people and I mean, I know you're not crazy about working at Dr. Keables's office, but you're good at other things, Zoey. You are. You *can* be good at other things."

Of course, she recognized the phrasing, but it was his tone that gave him away. He sounded like he was continuing a conversation they'd been having for months instead of just a few tense, awful minutes. And that was it—he *had* been having the conversation for months, just not with her. He'd been having it with himself, and along the way it had taken the form of a one-star review.

"Oh my God," she whispered, "that was you."

"What?"

"Bored Reader. You're Bored Reader!"

Anyone who'd never used the moniker Bored Reader on the internet before would have reared back in shock or simply shaken his head in confusion. Instead, Jerald went really still and tried not to chew his lower lip.

"'Hopefully this writer can be good at other things because it's not writing stuff' . . . That was you. You wrote that review."

Jerald's sneer had been replaced by a deer-in-the-headlights-of-an-eighteen-wheeler look. This should have satisfied her on some level, but it didn't. Instead, her stomach felt like it was coated in ice. Her face, on the other hand, felt like it was made of melting wax that was about to smack to the table in front of her, exposing the visage of a rageful she-demon.

"You son of a bitch!"

Her voice went off like a gunshot in the sparsely crowded food court, and she saw the reactions to it as if through fogged glass. A few tables away, a mother let out a small offended yelp and tapped the table in front of the child sitting across from her, as if to remind Zoey there were young, impressionable minds present. A man in a baseball cap and a dark waffle-print coat who'd been walking slowly past their table slowed his steps even further and turned. Clearly he thought a fight was about to break out and didn't want to miss the fireworks. The dude was right, whoever he was.

Her volume rocked Jerald back in his chair, and he ended up with palms flat on the table on either side of his food tray, as if he was afraid the sheer force of her anger would send his chair flying out from under him. Then, just like that, he was gone.

And, scene, as Rachel likes to say.

Only it wasn't the whole scene.

The whole scene included those moments she'd sat alone afterward, enduring the stares of other food court visitors, as the adrenaline rush of anger gave way to the crippling, bone-deep ache of regret, knowing she'd have to get an Uber home because he'd probably left her there. She hadn't just said too much, gone too far. She'd lost something—the delusion that inside she was all sunshine and roses while her girlfriends were the tough, hard-edged bitches. She'd lost a certain sense of superiority to any woman who'd ever had to resort to raising her voice to be heard, to be seen.

And now, alone on her sofa, awaiting the return of her no-longer-quite-so-smelly cat, she wonders if there's ever going to be a time in her life when she doesn't feel like a negative emotion is an indulgence she can't afford, a passport to places inside herself she'd rather not visit.

In the meantime, where the hell is Boris?

When it comes to her cat's movements, Zoey has an internal clock, complete with little alarms that go off when the cat does something off schedule. Even amid her painful reliving of her breakup, one of those bells is ringing now. He should have come out by now. She gets to her feet, counts off her steps down the hallway, an old trick she'd learned to center herself. It almost works. Every third step or so she's back in that food court, suffering through the gallery of Jerald's dismissive facial expressions.

Cold air hits her when she reaches her second bedroom, the one with the elliptical machine she never uses and the work space she managed to assemble by clearing a space out of all the old boxes full of paperbacks she keeps telling herself she'll donate someday but can't bring herself to part with. The little sliding door to the tiny patio where Boris's litter box has been sitting for two days is still open, but there's no sign of the cat anywhere near it. And only now does it occur to her that leaving the sliding door open like this isn't exactly safe. The patio's got a high stone wall around it, over six feet high, but still, it's not too high for a determined burglar to scale. The last two nights she was home before dark, but tonight's impromptu trip to the food court kept her out late for the first time since Boris's cheesy feast, and she hadn't pulled the patio door shut for fear Boris would need to use the bathroom while she was gone. Funny how one visceral fear—the fear of cat doo-doo in your bedroom—can override another, the fear of a robber sneaking into your house.

She's about to laugh at this thought when suddenly her forehead is singing with pain. Somehow she tripped so badly she managed to cross the entire room in no time at all. It feels like the floor itself rose up under her feet and threw her. Her first thought is earthquake. They've had a bunch in Oklahoma over the last several years. Or maybe she just tripped on one of the boxes. She's still trying to tell up from down, realizing she's actually fallen to her knees against the wall, when a vise-like grip around the back of her neck draws her backward and slams her head into the wall again. Every muscle in her body reacts to this terrible awareness that the forces suddenly controlling her limbs are not the miniature chaos of a freak accident. They're organized, *human.*

The pain throbbing in her skull sweeps down her spine, almost strong enough to mask the more focused sensation of a pinprick in the side of her neck. Then she feels a kind of timelessness that reminds her of waking up from surgery.

She's lying flat now, and there's a weight in the back of her throat.

She's blinking against the force of a bright light. For a second, she assumes it's the overhead fixture in her guest bedroom, but it's too bright. If it's not the guest bedroom ceiling, where is it? Someplace with a very hard floor, because whatever surface is under her back is not the soft carpeting of her guest bedroom. And that means the weight on her jaw isn't the result of books spilled from boxes knocked over by her fall.

Not a fall, a rational voice reminds her, *a throw. You were* thrown.

Falls don't pull you back and slam you against the wall a second time. Falls don't make a pinprick in the side of your neck.

Something is on my face, she thinks with a dullness that suggests the pinprick she felt earlier released some sort of drug into her system, a drug that's slowly wearing off. *Something is on my face and it feels wrong.* Then she tries to swallow and feels something lodged against the back of her throat. At first she thinks its phlegm, but the way it only slightly bucks at the force of her swallow sends fear jolting through her. The thing in her throat isn't natural. It isn't flesh. It didn't come from her. And it's very hard.

It was *put* there.

When a man leans forward into the light's blinding glare, she recognizes him instantly. He's the guy in the waffle-print coat and baseball cap who stopped to stare at her right as she exploded at her boyfriend in the middle of the food court, and he's caressing her face. He's got light stubble and eyes like knife slashes on either side of his big, broken-looking nose. At first, she thinks he's whispering something to her, then she thinks he's trying to soothe her, then she realizes that he's shushing her with a gentle, sustained hissing sound.

"Easy," the man says quietly. "Easy, Zoey Long. Your silence is your strength. Forget everyone who's ever told you otherwise."

II

9

The first time she used the catheter felt like an unacceptable surrender; the second, the hazard of doing business with serial killers. She's never had a nervous bladder, so unless her system's been aggravated by whatever Mattingly drugged her with back in Richardson, both events suggest she's been in this cellar almost a full day.

Charlotte's still astonished she managed to sleep, but after he left and the blinding lamp shut off, plunging her into darkness, it seemed less like a choice and more like she'd been gassed. Maybe it really was the latter, but she doubts it. She'd feel groggier and out of sorts, not just thirsty and hungry.

The darkness is impenetrable. Whatever structure is sitting above the storm cellar is windowless, or the storm doors she heard open earlier are sealed down to the last centimeter. Not even a thread of light has appeared during the hours she's been down here, not a single sound from the outside world has reached her ears.

Over the course of two operations, she's never been confined for this long. She's been tied up, held down, treated like a piece of meat, drugged. But she's never been left in total darkness for what feels like hours on end. Throughout, she's kept her mind occupied by trying to puzzle out what this phase of the process means when it comes to Mattingly's modus operandi.

So far, she's been able to stave off panic by reminding herself she's not truly alone. Aboveground and close by, Luke is sitting in his armored Cadillac, awaiting a signal from Kansas Command. Much farther away but in a similar predicament to hers, Cole and his team are also underground, waiting for Mattingly to do something other than store her like cargo. Hell, for all she knows, Cole might have some technology that can brighten the images coming from her TruGlass.

It doesn't matter. What matters is that she's not alone.

She's not her mother. Not yet.

Based on how far away the storm doors sounded when Mattingly opened them earlier, Charlotte figures the cell must be about ten or twelve feet deep. It also sounded like he climbed a ladder on his way out. If the cellar's as deep as she thinks it is, she can't imagine him carrying her down that ladder all by himself. Maybe he's got an accomplice here, but nothing about Mattingly's speech suggested as much. He seemed possessive of her and inordinately proud of the face mask and gag he's placed her in. More importantly, mentioning accomplices, if there were any, would have been a great way to frighten her into silence, and her silence seems especially important to him for reasons ranging from the practical to the pathological.

These questions, however difficult they are to answer in this moment, keep imaginings of her mother's final hours in the Bannings' root cellar from doing anything more than knocking at the door to her mind.

The wood beneath her starts to shake, a steady quiver. Some sort of machine or engine has shuddered to life close by.

A vague pulse of light divides the blackness overhead, providing answers to one of the questions that's circled in her head for hours. Yes, they are in fact a set of double storm doors, and no, they're not perfectly sealed. The illumination isn't daylight. It's red. It has to be coming from the taillights of a vehicle—probably the truck he bought that started all of this. The fact that no pulse of daylight preceded its approach suggests the structure above has no windows at all. Or it's night again.

The double doors make the same sound they made earlier when Mattingly left her. In the vague illumination given off by the taillights of the truck parked overhead, Charlotte can see her surroundings for the first time. A narrow concrete-walled storm cellar, accessible by a ladder attached to one wall, a ladder Cyrus Mattingly is descending in a different outfit from the one he wore to her abduction. He smells conventional and clean, like Old Spice mixed with Irish Spring, and somehow this sickens her worse than her confines. There's something on the wall closest to her feet. At first she thinks it's another ladder, but before she can be sure Mattingly is standing over her, blocking her view.

He places one palm against her exposed cheek, then her forehead. Again, she notes the absence of any sort of perverted desire in his touch. He seems like he's just checking her temperature.

When he sees her eyes are open, he unfolds the bunched-up edge of the fabric hood covering her skull, turning the extra fabric into a blindfold. Then she hears him mounting the ladder again.

A low, droning whine echoes up the concrete walls, a sharper, more high-pitched sound than the idling truck's engine. She's rising slowly into the air. That's what she glimpsed on the wall a moment before, a track for some sort of automated platform underneath her. There has to be another track on the wall behind her head given how smoothly and evenly she's traveling toward the open storm doors above.

Blinded, rising toward diesel fumes, she has the sudden, over-whelming fear that he's going to back the truck over her once she's level with the garage floor. It's irrational, but so is everything else about this situation and this place and this horrible man. But still, it makes no sense that he'd go to all this trouble to take delight in crushing her with giant tires. She's cargo, not roadkill. Maybe in his twisted mind she's a wretched mix of both, but still, if he does try crushing her and he starts with her legs, she'd trigger for sure and be able to tear the tire off the damn truck. But if he starts with her head . . .

The cloth blindfold isn't blackout material, so she can tell her surroundings are changing. She can see the truck's taillights as she rises past them. Then she's pulled sideways suddenly. The platform lifted her until she was level with the truck's open cargo door. She hears a screech just underneath her, then a vaguely familiar rumble: wheels meeting a metal floor. The wheels confirm her initial suspicion: this is a gurney he's tied her to, but the mattress pad has been removed, turning its hard surface into a subtle form of torture. He's pushing her toward the truck now. Someone else, someone without her strange history, might be assaulted in this moment by upsetting memories of hospital visits with dying relatives. But the last time Charlotte was tied to a gurney by a psychopath, the psychopath ended up with multiple broken bones; the guy's on death row now, clinging to sanity as he babbles incoherently to a host of prison psychiatrists about the "angel of darkness" who redeemed his soul.

Organ harvesting, she thinks. *Is that what this shit's about?*

She doubts it. Cyrus Mattingly's strange rituals—from his masks and gags to his startlingly petty method for selecting his victims—don't suggest something so clinical and cold.

"I need to remove your gag."

Again, she notes the distinct absence of emotion in his voice. He either lacks the deranged convictions of the last two killers she took down—one of them fatally—or he's a devoted practitioner of his own maxim: silence equals strength.

To signal consent—as if such a concept can exist in this moment—she opens her mouth so wide she feels air on her gums, hoping he can see her teeth clenched around the gag. Without touching her lips or face, he grabs the gag and tugs. It's a smooth, practiced gesture, but her throat still spasms when the tendril-like extension leaves. Hot saliva slicks her bottom lip and those few parts of her chin that aren't covered by the mask's leather straps. Her coughs are so strong they cause her to buck against the restraints that tie her to the gurney. Once they stop and she relaxes again, she feels him carefully wiping the spit from her jaw.

She's rehearsed this part. She just thought she'd have to do it sooner.

"Please," she whispers, "please . . . my parents have money."

"Your parents don't have money." He sounds bored.

"They do, promise. I . . . *please*, I won't say anything. You can just let me go and I won't tell anyone. It's true. I won't tell, I won't." When her tears dampen the cloth covering her eyes, she realizes her performance is so good she's convinced herself. "Just tell me what you want."

He grabs her jaw with sudden force unlike any he's shown so far. "Your *silence*," he growls. "What I *want* is your *silence*."

He releases her jaw. Then she assumes he's rooting through a pile of tools, but the sounds he's making are a plastic-sounding clatter—not the clinking of metal on metal you'd expect. A few seconds later, he grabs her chin, squeezing until she opens her mouth. Braced for the nausea-inducing violation of another gag, the first thing she notices is the different taste—less like pungent rubber, more like bland plastic. It's forcing her mouth open wider than before, but when it stops short of the back of her throat, relief washes through her, holding Zypraxon at bay once more.

She's surprised when he starts to untie her wrists from the leather straps that have secured them to the gurney during her confinement. But just as quickly, he ties each one to something else, and whatever cable or rope he's using puts tension on both wrists. When he's done, she realizes the taut cables suspend her wrists at her waist, but about two feet off the gurney.

"Don't move," he says quietly, but he sounds distracted. Maybe because he's still working. There's another plastic clatter similar to the first, this one accompanied by what sounds like small wheels, smaller than the gurney's, rolling across the cargo bay's metal floor. *He's putting something into place*, she realizes. The plastic tube inside of her mouth starts to wiggle. The top end of it is being repositioned. Then the tube goes suddenly still, indicating it's been fitted inside something above her head.

"It's time to take your blindfold off," he says. "No matter what you see, no matter what happens, you have to stay quiet. And you can't move. I'll explain why, but first I need you to agree by grunting once."

She grunts once, and he pushes the hood's fabric up onto her forehead again.

The truck's cargo bay is illuminated by those soft blue lights you stick on walls and press once to make them light up like cracked glow sticks. It gives a vaguely nightclub-style glow to what he's done to her, maybe because the contraption she's been attached to is made almost entirely of transparent Lucite. The tube wedged inside her mouth extends up into a large transparent cube about three feet above her head. The cube is supported by metal legs that extend to the floor on either side of the gurney. The cords on her wrists are secured above her head to a Lucite panel that divides the cube horizontally and extends out from either side. After a few seconds of blinking madly, she can see the horizontal divider is actually two pieces that fit snugly around the open end of the tube, creating two spaces inside the cube: a top half that's exposed to the tube's open end and a bottom half that's shielded from it. Finally, the cables make sense. If she moves her hands in the slightest, she might pull the divider inside the container apart, exposing the tube's open end to the lower compartment.

It's not just a cube, she realizes, *it's some sort of container, and it's empty. For now.*

This isn't just about silencing her. It's just as she feared. The ride itself is going to be a form of torture.

Cyrus Mattingly stares down at her dispassionately. He's lost his baseball cap, and his hair's a thick mane brushed back from his broad forehead. She stares back, hoping Kansas Command is devouring and analyzing every image her TruGlass lenses are capturing of this monster. So occupied is she by this hope, she's afraid for a moment that she forgot to affect the necessary level of quivering fear.

"Whatever's in here," Mattingly says, tapping the side of the empty container, "you don't want to get in here"—he taps the side of the tube extending into her mouth. "You do that in two ways. You stay quiet, and you stay still. Whatever you do, don't move these." He taps one of her wrists.

Rage keeps the panic at bay. Rage for all the other women, and maybe some men, who endured these cold instructions and the terror of finding themselves trapped in this instrument of transparent torture.

"Your anger doesn't make you strong, Hailey Brinkmann. You don't know what bravery is. Not yet. But you'll learn tonight. So long as you look deep within yourself and find whatever it takes to stay very quiet and very still."

An accordion room divider cuts off this section of the cargo bay from the rest of the truck. Other than the gurney and the terrible contraption she's attached to, there's not much else here. When he turns his back to her, for the first time she sees three wooden crates stacked against the wall a few feet away. They're lined with air holes along the tops of the sides facing her.

Mattingly removes the lid from the Lucite container, sticks a rubber plug in the tube's opening, then unties the top of the cable attached to her right wrist from where it's secured to the divider. He lays the lax cable across her lap so he can slide one half of the divider free from the cube. If she were an ordinary victim, this would be the time to fight back, even at the risk of choking herself on the tube. But for her, it's not time to fight back. Not yet. Not until they've reached their destination. If she takes him down now, he's just a kidnapper with a fetish for Lucite. When they reach his kill site, she'll have the chance to overpower him, leaving him half-alive and surrounded by the evidence of his other murders before law enforcement arrives.

Mattingly turns to the stack of ventilated crates and picks up the top one by its handle. He tilts one end down into the Lucite container, then pulls up on a vertical gate. The crate's inhabitants stream down into the Lucite container in such a frenzied rush, it's hard to tell what they are. They're gray and they're panicked—that's all she can see at first. He sets the crate aside, then slides the divider back into the container so both halves are firmly enclosing the tube's shaft again, trapping the wriggling creatures in the bottom half. Then he reties the cable around her right wrist to the divider. He removes the plug from the tube's mouth in the top half, snaps the container's lid back into place, and gives her time to stare up at the writhing mass of rats, some of which might come crawling down the tube and into her mouth if she panics or makes the wrong move or does anything to disrupt the construction of his hideous invention.

He looks at her only briefly. He's not savoring the sight of her terror. Not in this particular moment, at least. He's a sadist, for sure. But for now, this seems like just another procedure in his workday.

Because it's preparatory, she realizes. *Awful as it is, this isn't the main event.*

Then she sees the tiny black camera affixed to the truck's wall. Maybe he'll savor the sight of her fear in private. Or maybe he just wants to keep an eye on her while he drives.

He steps behind the accordion divider and pulls it closed, separating the scene of her degradation from whatever else is inside this box truck. Leaving her alone with her racing heartbeat, alone with the lyrics of "Angel of the Morning," alone with the rats writhing in the center of her vision. The creatures have settled into something that looks like a contained, gently swelling sea. While somewhat less frenzied, it still pulses with a collective desire to break free.

She closes her eyes and sucks the deepest breath she can through her nostrils.

Then the truck starts moving beneath her, and she realizes they're finally on their way.

10

Eighteen hours. That's how long Mattingly kept Charlotte in that damned storm cellar.

Everything following her placement in the truck has been a horror show, for sure. But the long wait for some beam of light to pierce the endless dark coming through Charley's TruGlass was its own special agony, and as crazy as it would sound to someone who hasn't seen the things he has these past few years, Cole's relieved they're finally moving on to the next phase of this nightmare.

When the surveillance cameras showed the bastard actually going to bed, Cole tried to do the same. That's when he had Scott Durham break the news to Noah that he was to be placed under armed guard in his bedroom whenever Cole tried to get some rest. And, no, it didn't matter if he wasn't tired. The not-so-good doctor accepted the arrangement with an eye roll, but that was it. Meanwhile in the bunker below them, the techs rotated monitoring shifts, which gave Luke the chance to catch as much shut-eye as he could inside the cozy confines of his armored Cadillac.

Then, right at the moment when Mattingly started his truck and descended into the storm cellar for the first time since he'd left Charlotte there, Durham called everyone at Kansas Command back on deck and sent word to The Consortium.

When Cole looks over his shoulder now, he sees Noah's sitting forward in his chair, staring at the screen, a slight dimple in his chin, the muscles flexing in his jaw, eyes bright and unblinking—it's the expression he'd get after another early test subject tore themselves to pieces. It's what he looks like when his battle against real fear is partially successful.

And that makes sense, doesn't it? Charley's mother, Noah's mother; they're different women, but they both died in the same dark cellar at the hands of Daniel and Abigail Banning. It has to be getting to him. Still, Noah's never experienced a disturbing emotion he couldn't swiftly exorcise by way of a diabolical conspiracy. But there's something in the man's expression Cole can't quite read. A muffled form of pain, he's sure of it.

"Too much?" Cole tries for parental sympathy, but the question sounds condescending nonetheless.

"I'm sorry?" Noah asks, looking straight at him now, his nostrils flaring.

"Watching this part. Is it too much for you . . . Your mother?"

"You knew all this was in the truck?" he asks.

No insult or smart remark, Cole notes. *That's as good as an admission.*

"I did, and she didn't want to know. She wanted to experience the truck *organically*. Those were her exact words."

"I can't decide if all this means the ride is more important than the destination or vice versa."

"Focus on Charlotte, not Mattingly."

"As long as she's in that truck, it's the same thing. That . . . *thing* is designed to break her, and since we've got no idea how long she'll be in it, I'm afraid he might succeed."

"Nobody can break Charlotte Rowe."

"I'm talking about her *mind*, Cole."

"Rats weren't one of the phobias she listed during her intake."

"Forget the rats. The device isn't working in isolation. He prepped her with fourteen hours in that storm cellar. In that . . . *darkness*. You asked me for my analysis of her, so take it. If there's one thing that haunts her every waking moment, it's the amount of time her mother spent in that root cellar on the Bannings' farm."

"So, she triggers before they reach their destination," Cole responds. "Then she and Luke take the guy down roadside and we collect the pieces. Not optimal, but we'll manage."

"That isn't the worst that could happen."

"OK. What's the worst that could—"

"She's headed into the middle of some sort of operation we don't understand, and all she's got with her is her boyfriend in some fancy car."

"I told you, we can get anywhere she is in three hours, max."

"A lot can go wrong in three hours."

"Maybe, but in the presence of a suitable trigger event, Zypraxon has never failed us."

Scott Durham's standing directly under a screen transmitting an angle on everything that's piled on the other side of the accordion panel from where Charley's been confined.

"Thoughts, Mr. Durham?" Cole asks.

"Is he going to make deliveries?" Scott asks. "While he's got her back there? I mean, there's a flat screen. Bags of books. Clothes still in department store bags, it looks like."

"None of it's sorted or packaged," Noah says. "The guy's not doing business while he's got Charley tied up in back. And why would he buy his own truck for that?"

"He makes the deliveries once he's done with her?" Durham says, sounding suddenly less sure of himself. "I don't know. Maybe it's black market stuff."

"He's selling black market items and he hasn't corresponded with anyone about drop-off and delivery before now?" Noah asks.

"He bought all that stuff himself, guys," Cole says. "We have records."

On an exterior cam angled at Mattingly's property, Cole can see the barn doors opening, allowing the box truck's headlights to cut twin swaths across the flat lawns leading to the nearest road. The local time in Dallas is 8:00 p.m.

"Make sure Luke's ready to tail," Cole says.

"Already did," Shannon Tran responds.

"OK. Mattingly's hit the road at exactly eight p.m. Based on that, we're going to assume he wants most of this drive to take place while Texas sleeps. What I need is for someone to animate a map for me that basically highlights the entire ground area he could reasonably cover before sunrise. In any direction. I need it to take in time changes if he suddenly tacks east or west, and I need the highlighted area to move with him as he moves. Tell me *now* if I need to explain that again."

"You don't," Tim Zadan says. "I'm on it."

Cole's pretty sure he knows exactly where they're headed, thanks to the Amarillo postmark on Mattingly's letter. He feels guiltier about creating the extra work for Tim than he does for keeping the letter a secret from his business partners, which says a lot about his feelings toward The Consortium at present.

Noah's next to him so suddenly, Cole jumps, which makes Noah smile. "This is fun. You should bring me in on these things more often."

Bullshit, Cole thinks. *Don't distract me with a smile, Mr. Turlington. It won't work.*

Noah's still rattled by the hours Charley's spending in confinement, for sure, and that's good. Even though Cole's managing several different agendas this evening, finding out if Noah has a heart is one of the more important ones.

11

Highway 287

The traffic's thinned out, leaving Luke all by his lonesome while he follows Mattingly's truck in the highway's northwest-bound lanes.

With a press of a button on the center console, he transforms his view of the road ahead into something resembling a vast undersea landscape. The transition's so jarring, an untrained driver might careen nose-first into the nearest guardrail. But after months of practice, Dark Mode, as the techs call it, has become Luke's favorite special feature on an SUV with many.

Personally, Luke prefers to call it Cloak Mode since the process blacks out all of the Escalade's windows with previously hidden tinting that blooms ink-blot style if you're watching the process unfold from outside. Which you shouldn't be. The feature's only designed to be used at night and during a close pursuit. On the inside, the windshield and windows transform into opaque computer screens transmitting hyperbrilliant views of the surrounding landscape streamed from exterior night vision cameras lining the Escalade's exterior. Guardrails, other vehicles, the occasional tufts of brush beside the flat prairie highway—they're all defined by a seemingly infinite spectrum of blues and greens that give them a dazzling texture. Even lane markers, which typically require reflected light to be seen, are clearly visible.

Simultaneously, every light source inside the SUV dims to nearly imperceptible levels so as not to reflect off any of the critical displays. That means no using the GPS screen manually, which is fine because he's only supposed to use this mode when he's trying to follow someone closely. The system works in conjunction with the reflection-deterrent paint covering the Escalade's exterior; paint so gritty it feels almost like shark's skin to the touch, but that's how it reduces the amount of light that can bounce off it.

In other words, with the press of a button, Luke can turn his SUV into something that can be hard to spot on city streets after dark and nearly impossible to make out on a vast stretch of empty highway at night. Which is exactly where he is now.

But processing all of this new visual information, not being startled by an animal's watching eyes from the brush beside the road or a dozen other potential distractions he might never see with his naked eye, required extensive training.

In the event of distraction, electronic sensors give off soft chimes if Luke veers too close to any sort of obstruction. Learning how to drive by those took practice as well. His eyes still need time to adjust to the windshield change, and during just that brief period, he has to drive by sound, not sight. This part seemed simple enough when they first explained it; then he took a spin in the thing and realized the extent to which his reflexive reactions behind the wheel were inextricably tied to his eyes, not his ears.

Yet another potential hazard addressed in training, the Dark Mode screens are so detailed and realistic that after an extended period of time, the driver can lose touch with their immediate physical surroundings and start to feel like they're floating through the dark untethered. Every few minutes or so, Luke's supposed to touch his own nose, then grip the gear shift for thirty seconds to fight this sensory-deprivation effect.

When the techs first explained the whole system to him, chests bursting with pride, Luke was pretty sure he'd identified its Achilles' heel before they finished their pitch. "What about oncoming head-lights?" he'd asked. "If the thing's that sensitive, they'll blind me and wash everything out, right?" Apparently not. The program's designed to recognize the fierce intensity of approaching headlights and dim them until they look like candle flames behind a pane of smudged glass. And that was when Luke had yet another moment of shak-ing his head and wondering just how much goddamn money these people had.

Mattingly's truck is a bright-green rectangle speeding down the highway ahead of him, the occasional rattles of its carriage visible in the windshield's new hyperbrilliance. Charley insisted Cole not tell her what was waiting for her inside, but Luke, they all made clear, wouldn't have been given the info even if they had shared it with Charley. No gory details for him. Not yet. It'll be a while before they're confident he can handle whatever Charley endures at the hands of these monsters before she kicks the shit out of them.

But with this particular psycho, the goal's the destination.

Surrounded by all this technology, the item hanging around his neck feels ironic. It's a stopwatch, the kind gym coaches wear, and he'll set it for three hours the minute he gets word Charley's been triggered.

"Hey," his brother's voice says quietly in his ear.

Maybe Bailey's on edge, but there's a hint of hesitation there. Luke immediately assumes something awful's happened to Charley and Bailey's trying to figure out how to break the news. Why anyone who's spent longer than five minutes with his little brother would pick him to break bad news of any kind is beyond Luke's ability to comprehend.

"How's it looking out there?" Bailey asks.

"You tell me," Luke says before he can stop himself.

"Uh, that's a no-go, guys," Shannon cuts in, a reminder that he and his brother don't have a private line of communication.

"I'm not allowed to ask my brother how he's doing?" Bailey asks, sounding genuinely pissed. Not just pissed, Luke notes, stressed.

"Actually, you asked him how things were *looking*. Which is a different question."

"Let me guess, Shannon. When the teacher at school forgot it was Friday and said I'll see you kids tomorrow, you were the first to raise your hand and say, 'Nah-uh, Ms. Parker. You're not going to see us tomorrow because tomorrow's *Saaaaaaturday*.'"

"I'm just saying maybe being more direct with your brother might improve your relationship," she answers. "I've heard it's had its moments."

"You could also try leaving us alone," Bailey says.

Shannon says, "The question Bailey meant to ask, Luke, is how are you *feeling*?"

"Well, annoyed, to be frank, now that this comedy routine's lighting up my right ear."

"I figured it was time for some jokes," Bailey says. "I mean, how else are we going to pass the time?"

There it is, Luke thinks. The hesitancy in his brother's tone. Bailey's about to start speaking in code.

"Sure thing, brother. It's not like I'm jamming out to satellite radio out here."

Luke never calls Bailey "brother" or even "bro," so he hopes this deviation from their usual pattern will tell Bailey he got the message and he's listening closely.

"How many Texans does it take to eat an armadillo?" he asks.

"No idea."

"Three. One to eat it, and two to watch for headlights."

"Ha."

"Seen any out there?"

"Nope."

"Well, watch out. Armadillo shells are hard as hell. Might take out one or two tires on that thing and leave your grille looking a little different. Probably two, I'm guessing."

"I doubt that. This thing's pretty souped up."

"Still, an armadillo should stop you in your tracks. Not sure you'd have to stop for one blowout. But for *two*, definitely. Even in that thing."

Armadillo, armadillo. In the past minute, Bailey's said the strange word more than he probably ever has in his life. Impossible not to think that's the basis of whatever code he's trying to project. What else has he said? The number two.

Not sure you'd have to stop for one . . . but for two, definitely.

Armadillo.

Stop.

Two.

Leave your grille looking different.

He's not telling Luke to stop right now. He's telling him he might have to stop in the future if he encounters whatever an armadillo is code for in this instance.

He's telling us where we're headed.

Headed, direction. Maps. Naturally, since they're being listened to, Bailey wouldn't be able to give place-names or points on a compass with his coded directions.

There's something in the number two . . .

Luke can't use the GPS screen in Cloak Mode, but Lord knows he's studied enough detailed maps of Texas, Louisiana, Oklahoma, Arkansas, and even New Mexico as prep for this operation. He visualizes them in his mind. If they stay on their current course, the next big town they'll hit will be Wichita Falls and then . . .

Boom.

He has to stop himself from crying out.

Amarillo, Texas.

He can see it on the map in his head, all by itself at the top of the Texas Panhandle, just about due north of Lubbock.

It's *armadillo* with two letters knocked out, not two tires. And the different-looking grille must be the *r* you have to add to get it.

Now, how does he signal he read the code?

"Appreciate the warning, brother. I'll be sure to brake for the ugly little sons of bitches if I see one."

"Sure thing."

"Got any better jokes? That one wasn't actually very funny?"

"Yeah, I think that well's gone dry for the time being."

No more code. Is that really all Bailey knows about their destination? Just a city?

"I don't know. Shannon? You got any gut busters about famous math problems you want to chime in with?"

"Shannon's gonna bust your gut with her foot if you don't knock it off," she answers casually, as if the threat took no effort at all.

"You see how they treat me around here?" Bailey asks.

Better than the feds would have treated you if they'd ever caught you, Luke thinks. But he keeps that joke to himself.

Silence falls, leaving Luke to consider the information just shared.

Charley never asked for their destination to be withheld from her. Just the method of Mattingly's madness, specifically the contents of his truck. If Bailey's telling him now, does that mean Bailey knows and Cole doesn't? Or does it mean Cole's been keeping it a secret from Bailey and Bailey just now managed to find out?

If so, why keep the information from Charley?

Trying to get the answers to these questions through coded conversation would either result in preposterous confusion or detection by their multiple monitors, so Luke decides to take the only option available, even though it's far from being the easiest one.

Shut up and drive.

12

Joyce Pierce.

Sixteen years old, safe in her new bedroom at her grandmother's house with no one peering over her shoulder, typing her mother's full name into her new computer feels like the most rebellious act Charlotte's ever committed.

As Charlotte, still Trina then, pages through the search results yielded by her mother's name, her heart starts to race, fingers of tension pressing against the back of her neck.

There is information she's never heard before; details that have been hidden from her. Somehow the therapists, the tutors, the press agents, the network of staff her father constantly encircled her with all kept these pieces of the story from her. Maybe for a very simple reason. Their job wasn't to sell Joyce Pierce's narrative; it was to sell Trina's. That was the sales pitch. That by having spent seven years as the child of serial killers, Trina Pierce possessed intimate knowledge of how such predators concealed themselves.

It was a lie.

She'd had no idea that Abigail and Daniel Banning weren't her real parents, not until a SWAT team exploded from the woods one day, the result of a deliveryman recognizing Trina from an age-progression photo he'd seen on a true crime show.

Her father had built a story for her that didn't exist.

Worse, that narrative didn't even fit with his own suspicions about his daughter.

He sometimes worried aloud about the effect Trina's experience might have had on her young mind. Once, as a teenager, when she'd complained about yet another series of speaking events, he'd snapped and said, "We keep doing this so you'll never forget who they really were."

And what would have been so bad about forgetting the Bannings and what they had done?

In that moment, she didn't have the courage to ask. Later, she'd come to suspect that her father believed if he didn't drag his daughter constantly through the mud of her past, she might turn into a literal heir to the Bannings' evil ways. Did he actually think he was competing with those monsters for the care and feeding of his daughter's soul?

The search results reveal details about her mother's final hours she's never heard before—first reported by the Washington Post *right after her rescue and the arrest of the Bannings, then repeated in countless other articles. She realizes that her mother's death is something she's never truly experienced or grieved.*

Now she experiences it as a body blow.

Her ears are ringing; her cheeks hot.

The exhumation of her mother's body from where the Bannings had crudely buried her revealed that she'd broken four fingers on her right hand during her captivity. The manner of the breaks suggested she'd done it trying to claw open the doors to the root cellar in which Abigail and Daniel Banning confined her. Abigail confirmed it in interviews. Four fingers, all but her pinky on her right hand. Worse, the pathologist believed she broke one after the other, which meant she kept up her efforts even after the first bone snapped. Maybe it was pure panic. Or maybe it was something else.

The root cellar was dug out of the side of a gently sloping hill. Charley can remember the mound it made between the trees. Many of the victims scratched messages into the stones in the walls with their fingernails or tiny rocks. They weren't messages for other victims; they were

messages for the Bannings, and the most famous one read **U CAN'T
RAPE MY HATE AWAY.**

*Several families of the victims believed their loved one had written
it, but there was no telling, really. There was another message, though,
that had most certainly been left by her mother; Abigail confirmed it.*

LET ME HOLD HER PLEASE.

*Impossible not to believe that Joyce Pierce had broken her fingers
not just to escape the root cellar but to get to her baby girl, who she
wanted to believe was somewhere alive on that farm. Did she find out
she was right before she died? Abigail says no. It was not Abigail's job
to visit the victims during her confinement; that was the time her husband spent alone with them. On the third day, Abigail would cut their
throats, but not before whispering in their ears, "You are now nothing."*

*No interviewer had ever mentioned this message to Charley. When
she was first rescued, she was a little girl, appearing only briefly on
camera, seated mostly on her father's lap and answering basic, insipid
questions about whether she was OK. Those interviews were like proof
of life for television watchers everywhere.*

*Then, once her father was able to put the money-making machine
in place, he did the interviews, and she appeared onstage to read the
agreed-upon script. Maybe she should be grateful now that the horror
movie fans who flooded their events had enough restraint not to ask
about her mother's last, anguished request.*

*But now, sitting in her brand-new bedroom, free to Google and free
to roam the countryside surrounding her new hometown, she is also
free to experience the leveling pain of her mother's loss for the first time.
It's their first goodbye, really, and it's composed of broken bones and a
desperate plea scratched in stone.*

LET ME HOLD HER PLEASE.

*She can't remember falling off the bed. She must have, though,
because the next thing she remembers is being on all fours, staring at
the laptop, which landed on the back of its screen and then snapped*

closed. Then she's listening to the loud footsteps of her grandmother and her boyfriend as they run toward the sound of her hysterical sobs years in the making.

A familiar tingling spreads through her body.

She knows this sensation.

She's even named it.

Bone music . . .

Charlotte's tempted to think memory's the cause. The cloying scent of her grandmother's carpet powder rising up to meet her as she sobbed on all fours; the feel of Uncle Marty's powerful arm as he looped it under her stomach so he could lift her up and onto the bed; the sight of her grandmother going still and silent when she saw what Charlotte was studying on her new computer's screen. LET ME HOLD HER PLEASE. If these things were powerful enough to unleash Zypraxon's power within her veins, that would be a breakthrough, for sure. Memories, mental images, have never been enough to trigger her before. Lord knows they've tried in the lab. But she'd be fooling herself if she said that was the cause now.

The truth is, Mattingly has worn her down. The hours in the storm cellar, the thick leather straps pinning her body to the gurney, the interminable invasion of the Lucite tube wedged inside her mouth. It's an endurance test, and she's about to fail it. By her standards, not his. Would this be the moment a normal victim lost her mind, tried to claw her way free of the trap, and ended up opening the tube's entrance to the confined, restless swarm of rats overhead?

The truck bounces over a bump in the road, carriage shuddering. For the past few hours, her arms have sung with pain from the rigid pose she's held them in to keep from parting the container's divider.

Too late, she notices the pain is gone.

That means she's fully triggered.

And that means she didn't exert enough effort to keep her arms still.

A fat-bottomed rat is already wiggling upward through the newly opened space in the divider.

Once it enters the tube, she loses a clear view of it, can see only the press of its fur-covered back. But it's headed straight for her open mouth, convinced it's the escape it's craved now for hours.

This doesn't have to be the end of it, she tells herself. Now that she's triggered there's little the rats can do to her other than gross her out. Their bites will instantly heal; whatever diseases they might communicate will have trouble taking root in her system because her cells will rebound from any alteration. If she can just endure the pure horror of this, she can keep going, get closer to Mattingly's endgame.

But when she feels the rat's nose brushing against the tip of the tongue she's pressed to the bottom of her mouth, those thoughts feel like theory.

Her stomach lurches. She coughs with enough Zypraxon-infused force to frighten the rat out of her mouth. From what she can see of its fur pressing against the tube, the little creature looks like it's trying to turn around.

Another rat squeezes through the new opening above. Followed by another. It won't matter, she realizes now, if the first rat senses there's something large and potentially dangerous blocking its escape. The pressure of its comrades streaming down after it might trap it and push it forward.

And here they come. A tide of gray filling the tube, so thick it's impossible to tell where one rodent ends and the other begins.

Fur clogs her mouth suddenly. The first rat's pinned, unable to escape.

It's the taste that does it—a taste that reminds her of turned mushrooms and the smell of sour milk.

When she feels the head strap slide away, she realizes she jerked her head before she could stop herself. Did Mattingly see it on that little black camera of his? He'll spot the broken strap eventually, but he doesn't have to know how she broke it. Not yet.

With the smallest motion she can muster, she jerks her hand free of the cable attached to the divider, but she still pulls one half of the divider free from the cube and sends it slamming to the floor. She reaches up, pulls the tube from her mouth, and rolls her head to one side. When she spits the rat out of her mouth, the force of her supercharged breath sends the thing hurtling into the stack of crates nearby with a loud crack before it slaps to the floor with deadweight.

Oops.

But by then she's feeling the brush, brush, brush of the other rats landing on her shoulder and streaming down her body, hears them hitting the container's metal floor with similar thuds, heading out in a dozen different directions. If she yanks her other hand free of the cable with a single tug, that will reveal her powers for sure, so instead, she rolls to the side facing away from the camera until the strap across her stomach gives way with a soft pop of leather.

The gurney slams to the floor with a thundering crash, kicking one leg out from the Lucite contraption and toppling it. The impact would have knocked the wind out of a normal victim, but she's fine, more concerned with keeping her fetal position so she can make it look like the straps around each ankle snapped when the gurney turned over and not because she's gently pressing upward on each one.

She's free. Slowly, she rises to all fours, coughing with great drama, pretending to be stunned.

"Showtime," Shannon's voice says in Luke's ear.

"Already?"

"Yeah," she answers curtly.

Shannon's job isn't to assess the situation, but she sounds disappointed, and he wonders if it's a feeling shared inside Kansas Command. More importantly, he wonders what horrors inside that damn truck triggered Charlotte this soon in the process.

These are wonders for a later hour.

His only order of business now is to pull the stopwatch hanging around his neck from inside of his shirt and hit one of the two tiny buttons on top.

"Son of a bitch," Cyrus whispers.

Sure, he's got backup straps, a whole box of them, but in all his years of doing this a seedling's never gotten free during a ride. It's always been a possibility, of course, and he's rehearsed responses countless times on his own.

The ride is not without some risk. It's not supposed to be. It requires practice and calculation. That's the point. Mother invented this challenge to keep their minds sharp, their appetites focused, so their impulses would be effectively purged by the end of it.

Eyes flitting back and forth between the monitor mounted on his dash and the empty roadway in front of him, Cyrus eases his foot off the gas. He's driven this route enough to know where all the exits are. If the shit has to hit the fan, this isn't the worst spot to pull over and clean the blades. Mostly vast farmland with isolated back roads and some hard-packed earth. Not a lot of brush or cover, so he might stick out like a sore thumb during the day. But that's just one more reason they all ride at night.

Cyrus finds the exit. Once his speed drops to thirty on the offramp, he gives another look at the monitor. In compliance with Mother's rules—nothing that uses Wi-Fi—the camera's hardwired to the monitor. If he ever gets pulled over for any reason, he can just unplug the thing and drop it into the space behind the passenger seat. But he's never been pulled over. And technically, he isn't being pulled over now. There's just been a little accident. That's all.

As for the Head Slayer, their collective nickname for the Lucite device designed to slowly erode a seedling's hard outer shell, well, they're easy enough to reassemble. That's part of their beauty. And he's got plenty of sedatives to knock the ungrateful little bitch out with again.

This is an annoyance, that's all.

An accident and annoyance.

He should relax. Which means he should stop whispering both words under his breath in a singsongy mantra.

And look at her, he thinks, down on all fours, coughing like the tube was down her throat when it wasn't really because it doesn't go that far. She's a mess. Looks like the Head Slayer's done at least part of the work. She may not be all the way there yet, not quite as broken as Mother would like, but she's pretty damn close. Hopefully this strange turn of events hasn't emboldened her. Hopefully for her sake. The fate of those who reach Mother's threshold with their egos intact is far worse than what awaits the already broken ones.

The truck starts to rattle as he enters a rough, isolated road heading into empty fields.

Quickly, he turns off the road, wheels bouncing over the rutted dirt. He'd rather keep driving, but he could have trouble getting the truck free if the ground under the tires turns hostile.

He stops.

Relieved to be able to keep his eyes on the monitor now, he reaches into the glove compartment and removes his Taser, the strongest weapon he's allowed to use on a noncompliant seedling. Another one of Mother's rules. Fear is, of course, the strongest weapon of all, she reminds them, but if a seedling arrives with grievous physical injuries, then there are consequences for them all.

That won't be necessary, he assures himself now.

The stupid bitch still can't manage to stand up. If she had any real brains left, she'd be frantically searching for an exit. Then he sees she's gripping the sides of the crates intended for phases two and three of their little road trip. Is she peering inside? Can't tell. She's still heaving with desperate breaths, another sign she's barely sane.

The divider's locked from the other side, but she hasn't even tried it, and that's what tells him he's already managed to do a lot of damage to her, the kind Mother wants.

But when he steps from the parked truck, he wishes Mother would revisit, or maybe relax a little, her rules about internet usage. It annoys him to lose sight of his seedling for even the few seconds it takes him to reach the container's cargo door. If he had one of those wireless security cameras, he could keep an eye on her through his phone. But then he imagines the sight of her—down on all fours, surrounded by scattering rats—streaming through the servers of some massive company and suddenly Mother's rule seems very wise.

Taser in one hand, he unlatches and opens the cargo door, then pulls it shut behind him quickly so that the dim security lights inside don't spill out into the dark field for more than a few seconds.

Ridiculous that the hairs are standing up on the back of his neck, but it's reflex, he guesses. Just the result of not being able to see what's on the other side of the divider. But he knows what's there. One stunned and traumatized woman who still has an opportunity to be freed of her delusions.

He unlocks the divider. He's barely opened it a few inches when suddenly a snake comes nosing through the opening.

When did the snakes get free? The serpent—charcoal colored and about three feet long—doubles back, recoiling from the heat of Cyrus's legs. He saw her peering in the crate, but she didn't open any of them, and they were both standing and still in good shape even after the gurney went over. The retreating snake slides past the body of one of its brothers. Cyrus expects the second snake to start moving away, too. But it doesn't.

Because it's been torn in half.

And that's the only word to describe it. *Torn.* Like all the others in the crate, it's a rat snake, about four feet long, dark. Cyrus's first thought is maybe some of the rats ganged up and tore it to shreds, but that's absurd. Even if all the rats somehow worked in concert, they'd have trouble doing damage like this in the minute or two it took him to round the back of the truck. And rat snakes eat rats. Not the other way around.

Torn. The word keeps pulsing in his brain, bringing with it a cold wash of fear in the pit of his stomach and tension all along his shoulders.

There is something in here that can tear a snake in half.

Suddenly afraid to push the divider back any farther, Cyrus raises the Taser at the narrow sliver of pale-blue light before him.

What happens next happens so quickly he can barely give it a chronology. His instincts assume some vehicle has struck the truck from behind and the entire thing is now sliding through the field. But when he slams face-first into one of the container's hard metal walls, he realizes the truck's not moving at all. But he sure as hell is. Then, as if on a delay, he hears the divider being violently pushed all the way open. That happened first, he realizes, but he was too shocked to process it at the time.

Now he's on all fours, his head throbbing with pain so total it feels like a helmet. Then he's yanked backward and up at the same time. Now he's sure something really did happen to the truck because there's no other explanation for the impossibly powerful force that's taken control of his body.

His back slams down onto something hard. The metallic rattles are familiar sounding but louder than they've ever been before. The gurney. Something's slamming him down onto the gurney. It's been righted and he's somehow landed on it and now he's feeling something that seems startlingly normal and almost soothing given the jarring movements that brought him to this position. She's binding his hands with the leather straps he left dangling from the sides of the gurney after he attached the cables to her wrists.

There she is, standing over him; his little seedling, Hailey Brinkmann. Not coughing. Seemingly unafraid, working with a focus and precision that says he hasn't managed to send even the slightest of cracks through her mind.

A wail escapes him before he can stop it. She looks into his eyes with a coldness and determination he's never seen in one of his seedlings, a look that suggests divine judgment and many other things he's never believed in. But all she says as she holds his jaw in a firm grip is, "Shut the fuck up, Cyrus."

13

After releasing his jaw, Charlotte checks Mattingly's restraints. The light testing tugs she'd like to give each strap might snap them in two, so she settles for running her fingers over each one. He had a box of extra straps nearby, which tells her she's not the first victim to get free. Or at least temporarily free. But now he's bound just like she was when he first loaded her into the truck; there are thick leather straps around his wrists, ankles, and head and a big, fat one just above the waistline of his jeans. She returns her attention to his contorted, gasping grimace, his wide-eyed terror. But she's not just enjoying his fear. She's looking for evidence of something specific in his crazed eyes.

Has he sensed the unnatural extent of her strength? Or is he convincing himself she just caught him off guard and somehow gained the upper hand?

The dumb shock in his expression suggests it could be the former, but it's anyone's guess until he finds his voice.

It's a gratifying sight, of course, seeing him strapped down like this, but the last time she paused to inflame a target's terror, the bastard didn't survive. Memories of Richard Davies, broken and bleeding to death on the snowy hunting range where he tried to confine her, have proved both stubborn and vivid in the six months since. They don't inspire guilt. After all, the man fashioned wallets and belts from the skin of his victims. But if he were alive and in prison, she doubts she'd think about him so clearly every night before bed.

But Cole's order that she blindfold her targets as soon as possible has nothing to do with her memories, good, bad, or otherwise, and everything to do with keeping her incredible strength secret. They've added business partners since last time, people who've helped finance everything from Luke's magical SUV to every last physical and digital detail of Hailey Brinkmann's fake life. She's pretty sure this new rule comes from them. She's also pretty sure they're watching everything she does now, so she's got no plans to defy them.

The headpiece with its grotesque throat attachment—she's not sure what else to call the thing—rests on a pull-down utility shelf attached to the container's wall, looking like a hellish beached jellyfish that floated up from the depths. Gently, she tears the fabric hood from the leather mask that covered most of her face while she was confined in the storm cellar, letting the mask fall to the floor. It's taken her hours of practice in the lab to execute small, everyday moments while triggered without using mantras or deep breathing techniques to keep her from pulling doorknobs out of doors and cracking cell phone screens when she doesn't mean to. She's not perfect, but she's getting better.

The leather tongue hits the metal with a loud, satisfying thwack; then she tugs the fabric down over Mattingly's head, covering his eyes just as he did her own hours before.

"Sending Luke in." Cole's voice through the earpiece startles her so badly she almost jumps. His is the first voice other than Mattingly's she's heard in over a day.

"Afraid a woman can't handle it on her own?"

"Can we minimize chitchat in front of our new captive?"

In a near whisper, she says, "Yeah, I forget. You're a big fan of one-way conversations."

"Letting off steam, I get it. It's been a night. You're allowed. I hate snakes, too."

Charlotte turns her back on the now blindfolded Cyrus Mattingly, moves to the open divider. "I actually don't mind them, but that one struck at me when I opened the crate, and I wasn't in the mood." She glances back, sees Mattingly jerking against his restraints to see who she's talking to. Voice low, she says, "Just want to point out there's not enough here."

"You think if we notify the authorities there won't be enough to implicate him?"

She almost laughs at the ease with which Cole used the term *authorities*, as if the man answers to any higher power at all.

"Not without me, no," she answers.

"Well, you're absolutely not talking to the cops."

"Also, I shredded the headpiece to make the blindfold so that's one piece of evidence that's been tampered with."

"Yeah, it was covered in your DNA, so that would have been out, too."

"You reposition surveillance satellites at your will. I bet you can tamper with a little DNA evidence."

"Perhaps. But I prefer to tamper with it before it's discovered, not after. What are you really proposing here, Charlotte?"

He doesn't sound annoyed, or even put off. More like he's leading her to say something he's afraid to say himself. She's never been quite sure what value Cole Graydon places on the lives of these killers. He didn't shed a tear when he broke the news to her that the target of their last operation didn't survive it. But she knows this: after inserting himself in her very first hunt, he managed to talk her out of her rage before she broke her target's neck. And by doing so, he gave the families of the man's victims a level of closure she hadn't thought to consider when she'd been poised to snap the fucker like kindling. Zypraxon doesn't steal her common sense; the opportunity to exact revenge with her bare hands does.

Sometimes.

And Cole, shadowy as he is, can be a pretty good voice of reason. Sometimes.

In this moment, she doubts he's worried she might flip her lid and kill the guy. His concerns, as always, are driven by a multitude of agendas, often of unknown origin.

"We need a kill site and it's not this truck," she whispers. "This is just . . . prologue. Nothing here's designed to actually kill, and I don't see anything that connects to other possible victims."

In the silence that follows, she wonders if Cole's fighting a desire to agree with her. "We identified the snakes as nonvenomous, but if one of them went down the tube—"

"No snake's going to crawl into a person's open mouth. I doubt they'd even leave the container unless you coaxed them with food. The purpose of the device is *fear*. But that can't be his only game."

"So, what are you suggesting? An interrogation?"

"Something like that, yeah."

"OK. Let's see how it goes. But his blindfold stays on. And keep it verbal."

Don't hurt him, she thinks, *got it. I'm sure the new ethically fluid billionaires we're working with really hate strategic bone breaking.*

But the blindfold part makes sense on several levels.

If Mattingly is going to seem sufficiently bonkers when the authorities find him, they shouldn't give him a prolonged look at how she functions when she's triggered. They'll have no trouble altering her physical appearance and breaking apart all evidence of Hailey Brinkmann's life. For all she knows, Cole's teams are already clearing out the rental house in Richardson and altering the security footage of their mutual exit from the NorthPark Mall. Various apprehended serial killers giving consistent accounts of her impossible actions might spell trouble for Project Bluebird 2.0.

The fewer details Mattingly can share, the better.

There's a knock against the back of the truck.

"Boyfriend alert," Cole says.

Even though it requires her to lose sight of her captive, Charlotte heads for the cargo door, takes a deep breath, and uses two fingers only to pop the latch. Luke jumps back, raising his gun at two rats that shoot out of the cargo door the minute it's open. He didn't know to expect them, a reminder that he hasn't had access to any of the camera feeds from inside the truck.

She's known this moment was coming for a year; the man she loves standing before her and ready to help amid the kind of horrors she used to face alone. But she's not prepared for how much she wants to throw her arms around him, even at the risk of snapping every bone in his body. Just some comfort from his heat, his familiar smell. Although, after the hours he's spent in that Cadillac, his familiar smell has probably turned a little sour. But still, she craves it badly. It must be the terrible duration of this operation, the prolonged isolation, that's made her this unexpectedly needy.

Then she sees his expression: bright-eyed, breathless. *Excited.* He's a part of this now, something he's wanted for a year. Can she be excited about this, too, or will his nearness now trick her into believing they're at home together and not inside a serial killer's truck?

"You OK?" Luke hoists himself inside by his free hand, Glock raised in the other.

"We've been ordered to keep chatter to a minimum."

"Question stands," he whispers.

"I wish I could say I've been through worse, but this one's . . . special."

"What are the rats about?"

"Like I said, he's special. Also . . . snakes."

Luke pales. She's always thought snakes were languid, elegant things that just wanted to be left alone, the perpetual sunbathers of the natural world. But as a boy Luke used to run sprints along the wooded trails above their town and lived in so much fear of stepping on a rattler that he's come to view them as animate bear traps with an appetite for ankle flesh.

"Where are they?" he asks.

"Hiding, and they're not venomous."

She starts for the gurney compartment, gesturing for him to follow.

He doesn't even pause when he sees Mattingly strapped down. He's witnessed Charlotte do much worse while triggered. Instead, he zeroes in on Mattingly's Lucite contraption, sinks down next to it, studying the tube's length with what looks like barely concealed disgust. All told, the thing survived its fall pretty well. There are some cracks on one side of the container, and the leg that hit the floor first is badly warped. Funny how innocuous it looks now without its former inhabitants, like a cat tree missing its padding.

Luke looks up at her for an explanation.

Charlotte opens her mouth and points inside of it, indicating where the other end of the tube went. For a long moment, Luke stares at her, jaw tensing, nostrils flaring. She raises one hand, genuinely afraid he's about to pump six bullets into Mattingly's torso. The old Luke might have, and if the urge is still there, she's wondering where Luke's going to send it to keep from giving in to it. His new muscles are designed to act, not repress.

Is there any training that can prepare you for this moment, being face-to-face with a human monster, a man who seems to glide placidly through the everyday world in a baseball cap, smelling of Old Spice while concealing a gallery of horrors beneath his garage, in the back of his truck, inside his mind?

God knows, the only training she's had has been of the on-the-job variety.

"Search the cab, see if you can find any marked-up maps or anything," Charley says.

Luke stands, moves closer to her, whispers in her ear, "Didn't surveillance already search?"

"They did," Cole says in her ear, and when Luke flinches, too, she realizes their boss just addressed both of them.

Ignoring Cole, Charley tells Luke, "See if they missed anything. It's been a busy night. Then come back here and search the rest of the truck."

"What are you going to do?" Luke whispers.

"Chat," she whispers back.

Luke nods, gives one last look at Mattingly, as if afraid to leave them alone together. Then he departs.

Charlotte takes a moment to breathe, a moment to recognize that it's her feet resting on the container's floor now and not Cyrus Mattingly's. A moment to see where the few remaining snakes have coiled up into the corners of the compartment.

"Let's talk, Cyrus."

He says nothing.

She's tempted to draw the blindfold back, see if he's screwed his eyes shut. His lips look slightly pursed, almost ready for a pout.

"I see, so now you're the silent one. Well, that's fitting, isn't it?"

Nothing.

Keep it verbal, she reminds herself.

"How?" he finally asks, sounding winded.

"How what?"

"How did you get free?"

"What does it matter? You think you're going to refine your process? You're never doing this again, Cyrus. Ever."

He absorbs this announcement without flinching.

"How many?" she asks.

Silence.

"All women, or do you snatch a dude every now and then?"

Silence.

"What was supposed to happen? You know, when I tried to pull the tube out of my mouth before those things could get down it? Is that when you were gonna switch from rats to snakes?"

"I want a lawyer," he whispers.

Charlotte's startled by the sound of her own laughter. She didn't intend to cackle like a mad witch, but that's just how she sounds. It's the tension release she needed, this pathetic, clichéd request from a man who has no idea what's ensnared him. Before she thinks to stop herself, she pats him on the stomach. Too hard. He flinches and wheezes; she almost knocked the breath out of him.

She crouches down next to his head, whispering into his ear.

"What do you think I am? A federal agent? Dallas PD? You really think I let you keep me in that storm cellar for a day because I was trying to build a case against you?"

Cyrus Mattingly's only response to this is a visible tremor in his jaw and several snotty inhales through his nose.

"What's so damn important about keeping me quiet anyway? Why not just keep me in the back at your house? You could have had your way with me there just fine. Why take me on the road?"

Nothing.

"Where were you taking me, Cyrus?"

"I want a lawyer," he whispers again.

His Adam's apple bops nervously. Gently, she places one hand over it, covering his throat with fingers capable of tearing his voice box out.

"You know what I should do, Cyrus? I should break your neck right now and spare the world your sniveling jailhouse interviews where you whine and point the finger at your mom or mean girls or porn and blame them all for the fact that you're a human monster while some journalist sits there scribbling it all on his pad like you're a magnificent enigma, when the truth is anyone who's seen you the way I have knows exactly what you are. A junkie for other people's pain who can't control his urges."

"You c-can't . . ." Cyrus stammers, reconsidering his words, or maybe trying to draw back the pathetic whiny tone with which he just spoke. "You can't do this to me."

When she hears Cole's voice say her name quietly in her ear, she realizes she's clutching Mattingly's throat just a little too hard. She withdraws her hand, but slowly, more interested in making Cole comfortable than Mattingly.

"I can do things to you that you won't be able to comprehend even as they're making you scream. I'm something you will never understand and never have a name for, Cyrus Mattingly. And most important of all, I know what you really are, and I am not afraid. I'm not even all that impressed. The only value you have to me are your answers to my questions. So, start answering them or I will knock you sideways into hell."

Mattingly whispers something.

"Louder."

"Not women," he whispers.

"You didn't just take women? You took men, too?"

A traditional interrogator would probably speak of Mattingly's actions in the present tense, getting him to talk by distracting him from how screwed he is. But she just got done telling him she's not a traditional investigator, so she's free to use dread as a tactic. She'll keep it verbal, per Cole's orders, but the weapon she needs isn't just fear; it's Mattingly's absolute terror.

"They're . . . not women after I take them."

"What are they?"

His lips part, as if the answer is on the tip of his tongue. But instead of giving voice to whatever it is, he turns his head in her direction as much as he can under the strap, which isn't much. "Seedlings," he says with a leer. "They're my seedlings."

Even though she'd like to break his collarbone with a single crushing blow, Charlotte instead crouches down, bringing her lips to his ear.

"Seedlings gets planted," she says quietly. "Where were you planning to plant me?"

Luke appears next to the open divider, gives a small shake of his head to indicate he found nothing of note.

"It's what you are," Mattingly whispers.

"What?"

"You told me I'd never come up with a name for what you are, but I've already got one. You're my seedling, and you always will be because no matter how this ends, you'll never forget what it was like to be under my command."

"Oh, Cyrus, you just can't see it, can you?" she says. "Did you really think I was under your command? I put myself here, silly. I followed *you*. First, the Cinemark 17 in Farmers Branch. Then the AMC Valley View. Both times I had to tail you after the movie because I didn't get your attention in time. And I was there both times you cut and run. You think I'm really going to believe you can stand up to me now when you turned tail at the first locked gate or the first big, strong man coming home at the wrong time?"

Amazing, she thinks, that after overpowering him, tying him down, and threatening him to the extent she has, it's the names of two suburban movie theaters that have brought him to the edge of sanity. The intermittent jaw tremor is now a steady quiver, and his mouth looks like it's trying to form words that are being ripped backward down his throat at the last second. Maybe, as with this terrible trap, she's simply worn him down. But she suspects it's something else. She suspects the knowledge that he was being followed all that time has pushed him to the brink. It's possible this is the weakness of all human monsters; they can't accept the revelation that they were never truly alone during their moments of chosen solitude, moments when they managed to convince themselves they were some of the most powerful apex predators in the world.

"Do whatever you want to me." His voice sounds thick with tears. "You'll never stop the others, you fucking cunt."

The lurch she feels inside at these words is mirrored by Luke's response to them. He raises the Glock in both hands instinctively before he stops himself. Their eyes meet, and she sees him nod. He heard it, too; not the slur, the word that came just before. *Others.*

"What did you say?" she asks Mattingly.

His lips are pursed again, his chest rising and falling.

"Others? What others?"

But her mind's already answering the question. Other trucks just like this one, other psychos like him, only the victims at their mercy don't have her power, her support. Each with a tortured seedling within. What can that all mean? They traffic women and then impregnate them?

Mattingly is whispering something under his breath. She leans in, realizes he's actually singing softly, lyrics that seem familiar, lyrics of a classic song her grandmother used to play while she cooked in the kitchen, "The Sound of Silence." To hear them from the mouth of this monster poisons their gentle metaphors.

Others being lectured by madmen to stay silent, others being subjected to devices like the one she managed to get free of. Others crossing night roads right this minute, unable to break free.

"What others?" she asks again.

But he just keeps singing softly.

"That's enough silence," she says; then she brings the side of one hand down on his forearm with just enough force to snap the bone within. But the sound of the bone breaking is instantly devoured by Mattingly's screams. They're high, barking things that emit as much terrible surprise as pain.

She expects Cole to start protesting in her ear, but she hears nothing except Mattingly's screams turning to gasps turning to a string of hissing profanity between clenched teeth.

"What others?" she asks again.

Tears have dampened the hood's fabric, and he's sucking rapid breaths through his grimacing mouth, but no answer comes. She'd love to snap his bones one after the other, but that's only proved effective when the answer she's looking for is one or two words. This answer, she's sure, is much more complex, and she has to hear every word of it.

"Charley?" Cole says. "You want to fill me in on the plan here?"

Charlotte steps past Luke through the divider, dropping her voice as she moves toward the truck's cargo door.

"You first," she says. "Did you have any indication there were other trucks?"

"None, and we still don't."

"He just said there were others. Didn't you hear him?"

"Yes, I heard him. And we've got no idea what he means."

"I'm going to find out," she says.

"How?" Cole asks. "Breaking his other arm?"

"I don't have time for pain."

"What's time got to do with it?" he asks.

"Everything up until now has been rehearsed and practiced and coordinated. He just said I'll never stop the others. That means he thinks it's too late because I'm too busy here with him."

"What are you asking for, Charley?"

"The thing that just broke him was telling him I'd followed him to all those movie theaters, watched him for nights in a row without him realizing it. That's when he freaked out and slipped up and told us about the others. Pain's not going to get us what we want out of this guy. Fear of what he doesn't understand will."

She lets this sit. When Cole doesn't rush to ask her to elaborate, she figures he's got some sense of where she's headed.

Knowing her words will probably be audible to Cole's business partners, she says, "I'm asking for permission to take his blindfold off and show him what I'm capable of."

"I see," Cole says after a long pause.

Maybe she's imagining it because she's been listening for it, but she's pretty sure she can hear other voices, even some movement in the background when Cole speaks.

"Well," Cole finally says, "this is a question that will require consultation on my end, apparently."

She takes his "apparently" as a sign his business partners are listening in just as she suspected, maybe trying to get Cole's attention even now. That might explain the scuffling sounds on his end. Are they actually present at Kansas Command?

"I see," she says. "Well, I'll be waiting, and so will the others."

14

Lebanon, Kansas

Goddammit, Charley, Cole thinks, *why did you have to ask? Just do it and let me clean up the mess.*

But who is he to judge? He's as sidelined by Cyrus Mattingly's announcement as she is. Cole's withheld plenty of truths since this operation began; concealing knowledge there might be more trucks isn't one of them. As soon as their target snarled the word *others*, Cole had to grip the back of the chair nearest him to stay standing, and he didn't come out of his daze until Scott signaled The Consortium was already calling in.

All that was before Charley made her request.

How long has Noah been right next to them, literally breathing down his neck?

"You'll agree, of course," he whispers.

"It's not my decision," Cole answers.

"What does that mean?"

"Tell you what," Cole whispers, "this time you get to watch the call. With my permission."

Cole studies Noah's reaction, which tells him next to nothing about how Noah feels about this invite. He reminds himself it's damn near impossible for Noah to have corresponded with either Stephen, Philip, or Julia during the past year. Still, Cole's taking a risk. Inviting Noah to watch this meeting will either expose him to the bullshit The

Consortium's been subjecting Cole to for months now, or it will add another voice to the team that's been ganging up on him.

"Do I have permission to speak?" Noah asks.

Depends on what you'll speak out against, Cole thinks.

"Nope. Stand right where you did last time and don't say a word."

Cole's more than halfway to the conference room when he looks back. Noah's right on his heels. Once they're inside, the not-so-good doctor makes a childish show of scooting down the wall like a Scooby-Doo character trying to escape detection by a bad guy. And, of course, he stops just short of where he stood last time. Cole gestures for him to keep moving, then feels like an idiot when he realizes they're both being silent for no reason. He hasn't picked up the conference call yet. Noah moves another foot or two down the wall.

"Right there," Cole says, confident Dr. Feelbad's finally out of camera range.

Noah looks to the screen, even though it's dark; maybe because it's the only way he can keep from shooting Cole the bird.

With a swipe of his touch pad, Cole picks up the call. The expressions on the faces of his business partners seem remarkably unchanged from a day ago, despite what they've all borne witness to since. Cole's surprised by how much this disappoints him, wonders if he's reading too much into it. He'd figured even cold-hearted masters of the universe like Stephen and Philip would be softened some by a firsthand view of what the victims of a beast like Cyrus Mattingly endure. Maybe he hadn't figured this so much as hoped for it, and that's the problem. When it comes to The Consortium, he should keep his hopes to a minimum.

"I assume everyone's been watching the feeds," Cole says.

All three of them nod.

"All right, well, before we address the question before us, let's do a brief review of the facts as they—"

"With all due respect," Stephen says, "I don't think a review is quite necessary in this moment. Bluebird's question is just a by-product of a larger unresolved question we've avoided answering for far too long now, and I feel it's my duty to point out the time has come to have a serious, frank discussion about it. Hopefully, we can keep it divorced from the emotion that usually seems to bedevil this topic."

It chaps Cole's ass that Stephen insists on calling Charley by her code name no matter the circumstances. Even Philip will sometimes refer to her as Ms. Rowe when they're discussing an issue that might have a grave impact on her life, or her sanity.

Cole's poised to ask Stephen about this so-called larger question when the man launches into a speech that doesn't just sound practiced; it sounds scripted.

"We must now make a decision about what it is we actually seek to accomplish with an operation like this. Are we a vigilante organization? Are we an investigative body? Do we fancy ourselves some highly secret arm of international law enforcement? Obviously, we have the power to be any of these things, but what we are capable of and what we *should* be doing are sharply different things. At present it seems like we're drifting back and forth between all the various missions I just mentioned without rhyme or reason. And this drift, if you will, seems to happen entirely at the behest of our test subject's emotional whims."

Stephen Drucker, I am going to find out why you have become such a pain in my ass, and I am going to drag your nose through it while your children watch.

Instead of voicing these thoughts, Cole says, "I hear and I understand your misgivings, Stephen. But in this particular moment, time is of the essence—"

"No," Stephen says. "No, I'm sorry, but I refuse to accept that. I refuse to allow this young woman to simply inject urgency into the proceedings whenever she wants to send this operation in another direction."

"Inject urgency?" Cole asks. "This is not a simulation, Stephen."

"Indeed, it isn't," he responds. "It's a compulsive revenge fantasy based in her traumatic past. And it's expensive. And risky. She's currently traveling across one of the largest states in the US with the fruits of our research flowing through her veins."

"She's in an empty field in the middle of nowhere waiting on our instructions."

"Gentlemen," Julia Crispin says quickly, "this has obviously been a very intense and stressful twenty-four hours for everyone, specifically Charlotte Rowe, who has, I should say, made this request of us directly and candidly. And we should give her credit for that as we—"

"I'm sorry," Stephen says. "I need to clarify something, Julia. Are you saying we should be *impressed* that our test subject didn't simply take it upon herself to tear open the man's jugular vein with her bare hands without asking first?"

"I am. Because unlike you, apparently, I've actually paid attention to what that monster's done to her, and unlike you, I'm having trouble referring to him as a *man*."

"And here we are again!" Stephen barks, holding up his hands in a mock gesture of surrender. "Swimming in this . . . sentiment, and every time we do we lose sight of the most important question. Are we field-testing Zypraxon so we can harvest paradrenaline from her blood, or are we funding reckless vigilante missions? But any such discussion becomes impossible as soon as you all start speaking of our test subject as if she's a superhero and a martyr in one."

"It's also difficult when you mischaracterize the nature of her request."

Noah's voice is greeted by silence.

Reacting to his contribution would only make it more disruptive, so Cole stares at the conference table before him, trying not to clench his fists. Noah steps forward until the faces on-screen stop looking for him, appearing to lock on his position. In the end, there's no reason for Cole's business partners to be all that surprised their head scientist is at Kansas Command, only that Cole didn't make clear he was on the call.

It's not the first time The Consortium's laid eyes on the mad genius who's caused them all so much wonder and grief. But the blend of wariness and reverence with which they seem to view him has never changed. Even Stephen looks like he's afraid Noah might get the jump on him if he looks away.

"Charlotte hasn't asked for permission to tear open Cyrus Mattingly's jugular vein. She's asked for permission to show him the extent of her abilities as a means of frightening him into sharing what he knows of these 'others.'"

"And then what?" Stephen asks. "We fan out all over the country looking for them?"

"Cole brought me in on this operation so I could assess Charlotte's actions and mind-set. It would be inappropriate for me to speak to the logistics of the operation at this time. But if we are going to parse the specifics of her behavior, I feel it's my duty to respond."

"I apologize for mischaracterizing *Bluebird's* request," Stephen says. "Allow me to clarify."

Julia cuts in. "Before Stephen launches into another lecture, I'd just like to say I'm in favor of granting her request as she actually made it. So I vote aye. Or whatever it is we're going to do in this instance."

"Noted," Cole says.

As if neither of them has spoken, Stephen continues. "She's asking to escalate the interrogation to a level where she might lose control of it. That can't be tolerated."

"She can control iron with her bare hands," Cole says.

"I'm not speaking of physical objects. I'm referring to her instincts, Cole. That's why I vote for denying her request. I propose we order her to stand down on the assurance we'll interrogate Cyrus Mattingly at Kansas Command. A plan, I should point out, that gives us sterling cover as we add Mattingly to the test subjects in Dr. Turlington's laboratory. We simply tell Bluebird and her boyfriend that Mattingly died in custody, or we talk sense to them for once and explain that dropping him back into the general population after he bore witness to all of our capabilities would have been insane. Maybe then, once we stop mollycoddling her, she'll actually take some time to reflect on the insanity of her request."

"What about the others?" Cole asks.

"The other test subjects?" Stephen asks.

"The other *victims*. Mattingly made it sound as if there's a window of time for them and it's closing. If it didn't close already during this . . . *discussion*."

For the first time since the call began, Philip Strahan speaks up, head bowed, voice a low grumble suggesting he's uncomfortable with what he's about to say. "We don't know if there are other victims. It could just be a boast. Or a tactic."

"How would it be a tactic?" Cole asks.

"If Charley gave me that speech, I'd be pretty sure she was good and ready to off me as soon as I answered her question. I'd be trying to buy time."

Former senator Philip Strahan, serial killer whisperer, Cole thinks. *Sure, whatever, dude.*

"Stephen, do you agree?" Cole asks.

"I've cast my vote," Stephen says. "What's being asked of me here?"

"Are you also willing to run the risk of other women dying tonight at the hands of men like Cyrus Mattingly?"

"Yes."

"Well, that's just . . ." Cole stops himself, but it feels like his entire face is flushed and beating.

"What?" Stephen says, leaning toward his camera. "It's *what*, Cole? Focused? Professional? Necessary? More clear-eyed than you have ever been on these matters? I'll take any of the above. There are madmen all over the world, and in this very moment some of them are plotting acts of violence and terror that will kill more people in an instant than these serial killers with which you're so obsessed will claim in their lifetimes. The *right* use of Zypraxon and paradrenaline could give the world the armor and weaponry needed to wipe those men off the planet or stop them in the very moment they try to act. Charlotte Rowe can't do that."

Noah says, "With all due respect, until we find another human in which Zypraxon actually works, she's the only one who can."

"Well, sounds like that's an agenda item for future discussion, then. My vote stands."

"Philip?" Cole asks.

Without any of Stephen's pomposity, Philip answers, "The risk of her losing control of the interrogation is too great. I vote no."

"You realize she didn't actually kill Richard Davies? We just let her think she did."

"I do," Philip says calmly. "And that's just it. If that sick fuck does manage to get the upper hand, I'm afraid she'll blink before she breaks his neck. And Prescott's too new in the field to be trusted to bring him down. Then the fuckhead's out in the world talking about everything she can do. My vote's no. Sorry, Cole."

"Very well, then," Cole says. "It's decided."

With a swipe of one finger, Cole ends the call.

Noah's advancing on him before the screen's even dark. "*What?* Decided? What about your vote?"

"I don't have a vote," Cole responds.

"What does that mean?"

"It means our fifth member wasn't interested in a second run. Since it's just the four of us, Stephen and Philip thought Julia and I would vote against them every time and there'd be nobody to break the tie. So, for the time being, I have no vote."

Cole's never seen anyone literally try to tear their hair out. Zypraxon's first test subjects came close. But when they raised their hands to their heads, it was usually to rip open their own skulls. Right now, Noah looks ready to pull out two clumps of his jet-black cap by the roots. When he realizes this, he brings his fists to his mouth, shakes his head, then turns back to the screen as if The Consortium's still on it and he might be able to plead with them.

Painful as it is, Cole reminds himself this is a good thing. He's getting the reaction he sought in flying Noah halfway across the world.

"This can't . . ." It's the first time Cole can remember Noah being rendered speechless.

"*This* is exactly what you asked for when you showed up on my doorstep out of nowhere after years and said 'activate The Consortium' like you were suggesting I turn on the burglar alarm at my house."

"You *cannot* agree to this, Cole."

"You're not listening. I didn't agree, because I don't have the option to disagree. And that's how I got your labs back. I can't fund this on my own, Noah. I've already hidden all I can from my board."

"Yeah, but you've got something they don't and never will."

"What?"

"Charlotte!"

"Don't overstate my hold on her. We've got a mutually beneficial relationship. That's all."

"I didn't say you were best friends. I'm saying you've built something with her and if you order her to stand down now, you'll destroy it in an instant."

"Got it, thanks."

Cole goes for the door, a deliberate tactic that he's pretty sure will garner some sort of revealing response from Noah. But he's not prepared for how swift and severe that response is.

Noah grabs his shoulder so hard Cole's jerked backward. No one's touched Cole with this kind of anger for years, not since he was a child and several young men dragged him into a woodshed, violating him with a viciousness and hate that had nothing to do with actual sexual desire. There have been times when Cole invited Noah to treat his body with force, but those moments were negotiated, almost scripted, two consenting adults choreographing a dance that drew a strange heat from Cole's old wounds without pulling the scabs away. The word that comes from Cole's mouth now sounds like a yelp. "Don't!" Pathetic, childlike. Not a counterattack, but a plea.

Noah's so shocked by Cole's reaction, a new set of emotions muddy the anger in his expression. He doesn't know what Cole suffered that long-ago summer afternoon. True, he's always suspected, sometimes with brazen, insensitive language, that some past trauma has shaped the outer contours of Cole's sexual desires in ways that occasionally spike his desire with bits of shame. But very few people know about the abuse he suffered, or how his father responded to it.

Charlotte knows.

Charlotte knows things about Cole the man across from him doesn't.

And that only serves to prove Noah's point. Cole shares a connection with her that might be holding this project together.

But in this moment, despite all that's taking place around them, his focus isn't Charley.

It's Noah.

He realizes he's done it; part of it anyway. Coaxed a version of Noah out of hiding. A version that cares about Charlotte in a way that transcends the end goals of this operation. Noah, always so damn composed, always so vain, looks downright desperate. And if this

Noah is truly authentic, he will be more loyal to Cole than to The Consortium, no matter what lies ahead.

"I'm trying to do what you asked me to do," Noah says.

"How?"

"This is what I learned about her in Arizona. Every moment of her life—every waking moment, Cole—her mind goes back to that root cellar on the Bannings' farm, to what she imagines it was like for her mom. Do you know she carved a message on the wall?"

"Her mother?"

"*Let me hold her please.* That's what it said. When Charlotte got away from her father and went to live with her grandmother, they gave her a computer for the first time and she Googled her mom's name. And she found that story. From that moment on, she's never been the same. The trauma of discovering that was worse than anything else she went through before then. Her every thought, Cole. Whenever her mind's at rest. No matter what happiness she's experiencing, her mind goes back to that cellar. It goes back to her mother's final hours. When I learned that about her, I knew, I knew, that eventually she would open up to what my drug could do for her, for the world."

And yet you tricked her into taking it.

But there's a sheen in Noah's eyes that might be tears, so Cole measures his next words carefully. What Noah just said might not be accurate, but he's pretty sure Noah believes it. He's also pretty damn sure Noah's so disconnected from his grief for his own mother that he can only access it by using Charlotte as a kind of proxy. Also good to know.

Cole says, "You can't stand here and tell me you picked Charlotte for this back in Arizona. Not for what this has turned into, at least."

"Of course not. She's the one who chose to go after men like Cyrus Mattingly. For this very reason. Because she wants to save women like her mother, and if you deny her the chance to do that now . . ."

"What? What are you afraid of?"

"I'm afraid she'll run."

"We'll find her."

"I'm sure, and I'm afraid of what will happen when you do, and I'm afraid that whatever comes after will be nothing like what this is now."

Cole agrees but isn't about to say so.

He can see Stephen's plan already—Charlotte tied down in a lab, horrifying simulations forcing her to trigger while her paradrenaline-filled bloodstream is milked like a cow's udder.

He hates his urge to linger here, to study the specifics of the pain on Noah's handsome face, the foreignness and all the dangerous invitations it offers. This feels like the first moment in years when Noah's been something more than an oppositional force in his life or a reminder of awful memories.

"I will take your opinion under advisement," Cole says, trying to sound more resolute than he feels.

When Noah flinches as if he's been slapped, Cole steps from the room, leaving the door open behind him. It takes effort not to look back.

15

Off Highway 287

The Thunder Derm, as Luke calls it, makes a sound that reminds Charlotte of a tennis ball cannon, and when Luke fired the device into her arm, it startled Cyrus Mattingly so badly she could hear him let out a yelp on the other side of the divider. The device looks like a bulky, handheld ray gun out of a fifties sci-fi movie, only the central chamber is composed of a fat, transparent vial designed to quickly extract her paradrenaline-charged blood.

Luke's already withdrawn five vials of her blood. Just one more to go.

He's practiced with the thing a bunch in the lab, using Graydon-generated materials that somehow mimic the approximate tensile strength of her flesh during a trigger event. To hear him tell it, the real danger's to himself, apparently. The gun's pretty unwieldy, thanks to the amount of force that needs to be packed behind its artery-piercing needle, and a misfire into his own leg could kill him.

On the night they first met, Cole ordered a terrified lab tech to draw Charley's paradrenaline-filled blood with a large but fairly standard hypodermic needle. The tech later confessed that due to her capacity for rapid healing while triggered, he strained his wrist driving the needle in, and worse, when they got to the lab, they discovered he'd barely managed to fill the vials. The fact that she and Cole can now laugh about this story is a testament to how far they've come and how much they've learned about each other in just a year.

But she's not laughing now.

The wait's taking too long, and the word *others* is pulsing through her mind.

Charlotte watches the device fill, sucking blood directly from an artery with a speed and force that would kill a normal person within minutes. That's why the Thunder Derm is housed inside a titanium case and locked by a code only Luke knows. Only now does she realize she's not sure if that's actually the thing's technical name or just a nickname Luke thought up for it while playing around in Graydon's labs.

Luke would be the first one to admit that much of his training feels like play. He comes home from most of his stints at Graydon bright-eyed and talking a mile a minute about all the cool things he did there. Even now, he's got an energy she rarely saw in him before Cole officially brought him into the fold.

"You good?" she asks him.

He nods, but he's still focused on the task at hand. The blood-filled chamber is now sealed and ready for removal. Luke pops it out and tucks it into the foam-lined case.

"You sure?" she asks.

"Of course. I mean, what did I have to do other than drive?" He gives her a sincere-looking smile.

"At least you had people to talk to," she says.

He looks her dead in the eye, smile fading. "That I did."

She knows that look; it's the one Luke makes when he's biting his tongue, but it's not always accompanied by this kind of steady eye contact, and that's what really gets her attention. He wants to tell her something, but he can't, and whatever it is has to do with whoever he talked to during their drive. That's a very short list of people, and Bailey's probably close to the top. If both of them removed their earpieces and TruGlass lenses, they could discuss it. But that would incur Cole's anger, for sure. Another reminder that everything they're doing, everything they're saying, even everything they're looking at is being constantly monitored, in some cases by people they've never met and probably never will.

"Could you do me a favor?" he asks. "When you have a moment, of course."

"What is it?"

"Could you get those snakes out of here? I know they're not venomous, but I have a feeling they won't fuck with you after what you did to their friend."

"As soon as I have a moment, sure."

She changes out of Hailey Brinkmann's pajamas and into the black T-shirt Luke brought her along with a pair of Charlotte Rowe's favorite jeans.

"Charley . . ."

Luke reacts to the voice, too. Cole's addressing them both.

"I'm here," she says, rising to her feet.

"I apologize for the delay."

"OK."

"Charley, we've discussed your request in detail and given it the utmost consideration, I can assure you. After weighing all of the implications, we have two possibilities we can pursue in this moment. One, you continue the interrogation verbally, with his blindfold on. Or you let us take him into custody so we can ascertain what the meaning of his last statement was."

"We don't have time," she says.

"We don't know that, Charley."

"Others. He said others. Other drivers like him, other victims like me. What else could it mean?"

"I'm not disputing that, but we don't have proof they're all heading to the same place."

"It doesn't matter where they're headed. What matters is that it's happening right now."

"Again, we don't know that, Charley. He could be talking about abductions that are next week or next month or next year."

"Then why would he be so sure we couldn't stop them? If the *others* don't start their sick shit until next week or the week after, why would he be sure we can't stop them by then? What he's really saying is he thinks we're too late, and that's got to mean it's *already* in motion."

"Charley . . ." There's a note of fear in his voice that silences her. "We know things about each other, you and I. Personal things . . ." He pauses suddenly. Is he inviting her to disagree? Is he just nervous about what he wants to say next? She's got no idea, so she says nothing. "I don't invoke the memory of my father very often. I don't know, maybe it's because he left me with big shoes to fill and I don't want to remind everyone how big. But I know this isn't what you wanted to hear. So, I'm asking you to remember the story I told you six months ago. About what happened to me when I was a boy . . ."

Charlotte's so startled by this turn, she looks to Luke to see if she's hearing correctly. Luke shakes his head. He, too, knows the story Cole's referring to; half of it anyway. And like her, he seems to have no idea why their boss is bringing it up now. Cole also doesn't sound like himself. Not the version she's used to working with, at least. The Cole speaking to her now is the same one who takes to the stage in front of the press to make a dazzling pitch for a new stomach drug that's not much of an improvement over the old one despite its snazzy marketing campaign.

"Please, I implore you. Remember what my father did when he found out. Remember what he *didn't* do. He didn't give in to his desire for revenge. He forgave those boys, Charley. You can find forgiveness, too, I'm sure of it."

Luke's still holding the Thunder Derm in one hand, but he seems like he's forgotten about it altogether. She realizes that by looking at him, she's revealing his facial expressions to Kansas Command, so she turns abruptly to one side. He does the same.

She knows what she has to do.

There are dozens of good reasons to hesitate but only one that matters, and it's Luke. If she proceeds along this path and she's wrong, she could jeopardize their relationship to Graydon Pharmaceuticals forever. And Graydon has given her boyfriend more than just a sense of belonging. It's sped him past the trauma he endured in the mountains above their town six months ago. If he loses his connection to it, will nightmares plague him and a sense of constant dread return?

And was that part of Cole's plan all along? Tie Luke more closely to their operations so he might turn against Charlotte the moment she chose to defy Cole's authority?

But there's something else here. A kind of code Cole's speaking in that's taking its time to sink in.

You can find forgiveness, too . . .

She knows the real story of what Cole's father did, and he didn't find anything close to forgiveness.

Why would he tell her such a transparent lie unless he was trying to send her a message? And what's the message? Don't listen? Or at the very least, the people monitoring us, the people who might be solely responsible for this order, can't be trusted?

She knows it could be wishful thinking, knows she's looking for any excuse not to quit. She's never met Cole's business partners. Doesn't even know their names, and she prefers it that way, so long as they let her hunt men like Mattingly. But right now, Cole's frightened, too. Too frightened to speak openly with her on a line of communication his business partners are monitoring. And so, at its most basic level, his code can only mean one thing: *Don't listen to me. Something's very wrong here.*

But if she proceeds with what she's planning, she's got more to fear than the wrath of Cole's partners. She and Luke will lose all contact with Cole's immense resources. In the past, Bailey's been able to work miracles for them when they're in the field, but for the first time he's laced into the center of Cole's operations, and now he's presumably being monitored by the same people monitoring Cole.

Typically, when you're faced with this many fears at once, it's hard to decide which one should guide your next steps.

This time it isn't. There's something she fears more than squadrons of pursuing helicopters and harsh discipline from her corporate overlords.

She's afraid of letting someone die a horrible death at the hands of a man like Cyrus Mattingly.

Without another word or some gesture of defiance, she removes both TruGlass lenses and drops them on the floor. Then she takes out her earpiece and sets it next to them. She gently crushes millions of dollars of technology under one bare foot.

With a strength Zypraxon can never give her, she lifts her gaze to Luke.

If he's surprised, he's managing to hide it, but for an awful moment, he doesn't move, and she's afraid he'll either refuse to join her or suggest they part ways, a delaying tactic for the former.

Then, with a small, satisfied smile that can only mean he's impressed by her bravery, Luke removes his lenses and his earpiece and hands them to her.

"You really are something, Charley Rowe."

16

Lebanon, Kansas

In the minute after Charlotte and Luke's TruGlass feeds went dark, things got so quiet inside Kansas Command that Cole was sure he could hear little shifts in the walls of earth surrounding the bunker. Then came a jarring sound that reminded him of the noise Cyrus Mattingly's wicked device made as it toppled. Only much louder and right behind him.

When Noah picks up the folding chair a second time and slams it into the wall again, Cole is stunned silent. He didn't think the man capable of such a tantrum.

Before Cole can say a word, Scott Durham and several members of the security team are racing toward Noah like Black Friday shoppers through the just opened entrance to a Best Buy.

Noah's expecting them, hands up, unwilling to fight. But Cole doubts his anger's been purged entirely.

"Take him to his room and keep him there," Cole says.

"On it," Scott answers.

When the men seize him, Noah makes eye contact with Cole. "Coward!" he shouts as he's led away. *"Coward!"*

With a dismissive wave, Cole turns his back.

He expected Noah to indict his character over this, but chair throwing—that's new.

Noah's loss.

Noah's the one who just deprived himself of the opportunity to see what Cole plans to do now. Or what he doesn't plan to do.

17

Off Highway 287

Luke's right.

If they're going to talk strategy, they have to leave the truck, even if it means losing sight and sound on Mattingly for a minute. They've got no idea how many cameras and microphones Cole's people have planted inside of the thing, and trying to find them all, if they can even be found, would eat up precious time.

After she checks their captive's restraints again, Charlotte follows Luke out the cargo door he left open. She tries for a ginger little jump, but she still lands with enough force to punch holes deep into the dirt with her bare feet. Luke leads her into the shadows far from the truck and a good distance from where he parked the Escalade. If Kansas Command can hear them this far from the SUV and the truck, then there's no hope of secrecy and their only choice is to work against the clock.

"What do you think their response time is?" he asks.

"Depends on if they kept their word and didn't have a team following us. Did you see anyone?"

"No one, but they could be good. I don't know."

"What's the flight time between here and Kansas Command?" she asks.

"Maybe two hours by Black Hawk, two and a half."

"How much time do we need?" she asks.

Luke pulls the stopwatch from inside of his shirt, shows her the screen.

Two hours, thirty-six minutes left on the clock.

"It's not enough," Luke says after she's taken the number in.

"Not enough what?"

"To get to Amarillo."

"What's in Amarillo?" she asks.

"It's where Mattingly was headed, according to Bailey."

So that explains the look he gave her when she asked him if he'd talked to anyone during his drive.

"And how does Bailey know this?" she asks.

"He was speaking in code, and it's not like I can ask him now, no offense."

"There was no other way."

"Not objecting, promise. Just pointing out that if this does take us to Amarillo, we might be out of the trigger window by the time we get there, and whatever we do, we'll have to do it without Zypraxon."

"There's a first time for everything," she says, "and it might not come to that."

"How?"

"Cole might remote dose me."

The last time Luke just stared at her like this was when she suggested they might be able to repaint the entire living room in just an afternoon. Without Zypraxon.

"Seriously?" he finally asks.

"Well, he won't want me to die. I'm still the only test subject he has."

"Or he might try to intercept us, especially if he knows where the truck was going."

"But we don't know that. We just know Bailey knows where Mattingly was headed."

"Maybe. Also, you've got trackers in your blood, remember."

"Maybe your brother will throw them off-line again."

"I don't know. He and Cole are pretty tight these days. Kind of one of those if you can't beat 'em, join 'em things."

"Your brother's not a joiner."

"I'm talking about Cole," Luke says.

"Yeah, well, maybe they'll work together and give us some time."

Luke says, "Babe, honestly. I'm not following. I'm pretty sure we just pissed them off. Royally. Why would they help us get to Amarillo?"

"Because Cole lied."

"Yeah, he lies all the time."

"No. He lied to the people who were listening in just now, not to me."

"About what?" he asks.

"The story about his father and what happened to him as a kid. You only know the first half, but I know the whole thing."

"OK..."

"Cole's father didn't forgive those boys. He poisoned them."

Luke just stares at her. When it comes to mere shock value, she assumed this piece of news would have a hard time competing with the crates of snakes and rats and the madman inside the truck. But at the end of this night, hopefully, they can leave those things behind. Cole they're stuck with for the foreseeable future, and with him, this dark secret from his past. She gives Luke the moment he needs to take that fact on board.

"Woah," he finally says.

"Yeah."

"So he's telling us to keep going. That's good."

"Sort of. But the code thing means he's either working against his business partners, or they're working against him."

Luke swallows this like an intact gumball. The only thing more fearsome than Cole Graydon are the people he does business with;

men and women they've never met, for whom Charley is little more than a lab rat. Men and women with a vested interest in keeping their funding of this operation a secret and stopping it before it darkens their doors. Men and women to whom the potential victims of Mattingly's so-called others might be little more than an inconvenience, easily forgotten, easily swept aside.

She has to save those women.

"Let's get to work," she says.

18

Cyrus Mattingly is no stranger to pain. He learned how to endure it when he was a kid, back when his father sent him to the ranch. His third day there, some dickhead counselor—Floyd Hickins, a real hayseed asshole who used to go around with a piece of straw in his damn teeth like he was on the cover of a Zane Grey novel—knocked him off his horse because Cyrus gave him lip. There'd been a dizzying moment of realizing he'd left the saddle. Then the thundering agony of his leg snapping as it broke his fall. Determined not to cry, he forced himself to squint up at the guy's big silver belt buckle, sure he could focus the tears away just by trying to make sense of the designs stamped on it even as the bright sun overhead turned the man into an imposing backlit shadow. Cyrus was right, and it was a lesson he never forgot.

That was before Mother got to him and made the ranch a better place. But it was one of his earliest and best lessons on how you could throw your mind past pain, keeping it just so far ahead that it sometimes had trouble catching up. That's part of what he tries to teach his seedlings. Your mind is more powerful than your nerves.

But he'll never have that chance again, according to the evil bitch who's turned this night into a royal clusterfuck.

Should he believe her? They all lie. Mother's taught him this. If law enforcement gets you for any reason, don't say a word, because everything they say back is an attempt to trick you into confirming what they already believe.

That was one of her many lessons, but most of what Mother's given them are rules. Very strict rules. And he knows damn well he's followed most of them down to the last detail. When it comes to their family reunions, at least. Which begs the question, how in the Sam Hill did this bitch get him?

There've been no emails, no phone calls. Not even burner phones. Just a single piece of paper, typed by Mother, which he shredded to bits as soon as he read it. Mother mailed it to him three months ago; a few sentences in a code only her boys could recognize. The code was just filler, a greeting of sorts. The only important detail was the date at the top. The countdown notification.

It was never a huge surprise when the letter arrived. Mother typically picked the same time of year: early fall, when the summer thunderstorms weren't quite so frequent, before the roads iced up in winter.

She'd used the same system for years now. The next run always took place on the first weekend three months from the date at the top of the letter. Upon receipt, his first two orders of business were to clear his schedule for two weeks starting on the run date and to start looking for an affordable truck that could be disposed of when he was done. In the beginning, truck prep would take longer. But they've been at this for so many years now, that part's become a cinch. And now most of the months leading up to the run he spends in delicious anticipation of what lies ahead, their annual ritual. Their family reunion.

There'd be no further communication until they were well on their way. Once they were within hours of her place with a seedling in tow, they were to call from a pay phone, if they could find one. Or any sort of landline. She liked to lecture them that only dyed-in-the-wool city folk thought pay phones a thing of the past. True, they weren't on every corner anymore, but they could still be found throughout remote areas likes the ones they were all crossing tonight, places where cell phone coverage was spotty. In her retirement, Mother subsisted off a steady diet of true crime shows and podcasts; a master class in how to protect her boys, she called them. They'd rendered her constantly afraid of digital surveillance in this new age, so afraid that Cyrus was pretty sure if one of them ever dared to show up at her place with a cell phone anywhere on his person, she might coldcock him worse than Floyd did him all those years ago.

But nobody, nobody had seen that damn letter except for him. They would have literally had to be standing over his shoulder when he opened it.

Kind of like this bitch was when you were at those movie theaters . . .

The effort needed to banish this thought allows the pain of his broken arm to punch through his consciousness. And with it, an even worse thought.

What if they got to Mother first?

But if that's the case, how come the bitch is so desperate to find out where he was headed? Is she just trying to get a confession out of him?

She's got to be law enforcement. Maybe a fed or something more than a local cop, and that was why she felt comfortable making those crazy threats against him, going on and on about how he didn't know what she really was. And now she's falling back a little and talking with her partner because she knows she went too far by breaking his arm.

Who knows? Maybe that'll get everything against him thrown out, and he'll even come out of this a richer man after his big lawsuit against . . . against . . . the FBI?

"How's your arm?"

She pulls the blindfold free. He blinks a few times, sees her standing at the foot of the gurney. And she doesn't look remotely remorseful about breaking his arm.

"You're real stupid, you know that?" he says.

"How's that?"

"You *abused* me. I'm going to have your badge."

"I have a badge?"

The question sounds rhetorical.

Then Cyrus is thrown upward. He expected his arm to cry out in pain and his limbs to spread as he fell. But he's still strapped to the gurney, and technically that's what was just thrown toward the ceiling, not him. When it drops, some force grabs it in what can only be a confident grip. Then he's ascending again, with a few jerks here and there before he levels out. The word he wants to apply to what he's feeling seems downright inappropriate, impossible even. But there's no other way to describe it. He's being *held*. Not just held, carried. Somehow that bitch threw the gurney's plank and his entire body weight up into the air as if they both weighed nothing, and now she's carrying him in both hands over her head.

He's staring up at the truck's rusted ceiling when cool night air washes his body. The cargo door's open, and they're getting close to it. Panic flares. She'll have to lower him before she steps out from the back. There's no way she can . . .

A pathetic-sounding yelp escapes him as he drops down into the night. *Impossible,* he thinks, *fucking impossible.*

She just jumped from the back of the truck while holding him and the plank high above her head like they had the combined weight of a basket of feathers. She didn't even pause to use the drop step on the bumper, and her arms didn't even recoil slightly from the impact with the ground.

"Wait a minute, wait a minute . . ." He assumed he was just thinking these words; then he realizes he's saying them aloud, and he sounds both dazed and pathetic. But the woman doesn't stop; she's carrying him sideways, away from the cargo door as a shadow, possibly belonging to her partner, lowers the door. With the truck's engine cut and the taillights dark, the field will descend into almost total darkness as soon as that door's closed. Somehow that thought frightens him more than being trapped in the truck with these two fuckers.

The gurney's lowered, then tilts so suddenly his stomach knots. His eyes haven't adjusted yet, but he's gone vertical now and the woman's as close as a lover. Her breath grazes his neck. But that's the only part of her touching him. He hears a low crackle at his feet. It sounds almost like flame, but it's too quiet and there's no light. It's the sound of earth splitting from constant, steady pressure. That's when he realizes she's driving the foot of the gurney's plank down into the earth itself.

Impossible . . .

He's thought the word countless times and spoken it aloud even more than that. But never with this much fear, never with his heart roaring like this.

Then she steps away, leaving him standing upright like a stake, and there's another sound. Footsteps. But they're loud. Too loud, it seems, to be human, crunching dirt like it's broken glass.

It's stress, he tells himself. His mind's playing tricks. Hell, maybe he's had a psychotic break.

But the fierce beam of light that suddenly pierces the dark before him doesn't have the quality of a hallucination. The bright halo of a flashlight hits the dirt a few feet from him, and that's when he sees little craters in the dirt. Not craters. Footprints. Footsteps made by something impossibly heavy but the size of a human.

The connections his mind is making are worse than the pain of his broken arm. Because the footsteps make him think of the way she lifted him in a two-handed grip, of the power with which she wedged the gurney plank into the dirt, of the sudden, impossible speed with which she yanked him through the divider and strapped him to the gurney.

Whoever's holding the flashlight, probably the woman's partner, wants Cyrus to see what he's been denying now for too long. The woman who left those footprints isn't impossibly heavy; she's impossibly strong, and she ground those footsteps into the earth on purpose.

When the flashlight beam finds her, she's standing at the back of the truck. The sound that happens next doesn't belong in nature, and it turns most of his skin to gooseflesh. He's heard giant pieces of metal shredded by fast and furious winds or split-second collisions, but he's never heard them emit this kind of low protest as they're torn from something by a powerful force that's just taking its sweet damn time. In the flashlight beam, he sees Hailey Brinkmann rip the entire length of the drop step bumper from the back of the truck. The metal doesn't screech; it whines, the tops of the four vertical support beams popping free like fence stakes as she tears the bumper off like a Band-Aid.

Then she drops it to the dirt with a sound like a giant tuning fork.

"I need you to answer my questions, Cyrus."

Before he can say anything, she places a hand at the bottom of one of the vertical support beams and pulls it free as if it's made of taffy.

"Are you ready?" she asks.

Some stubborn instinct tries to make him protest, but the sound that comes out of him is so phlegmy and incoherent he thinks he might be having a stroke.

The evil bitch shakes her head as if she's disappointed.

Then the broken crossbar is suddenly flying through the air toward him, so fast the flashlight beam can't keep up. When it vanishes into darkness midflight, Cyrus emits a yowl that sounds animallike, braces to be pierced through his center like the lizards he used to torture as a kid. Then there's a crackling impact. Cyrus winces. The flashlight beam finds the crossbar, speared in the dirt a short distance away. Another few feet and it would have pierced him straight through.

"Are you ready, Cyrus?" the woman who shouldn't exist asks.

But Cyrus doesn't answer because he's realizing the wet heat down his leg means one thing: he's pissed himself for the first time in his life. And that's when the pain from his broken arm finally makes him cry.

When another spear hits the dirt a few feet away, he loses control of all the sounds coming from him just like he lost control of his bladder. He hears his wrenching sobs as if from a distance and knows he's crying out for help from gods he's never believed in and a host of others. Even thinks, for a moment, that he's looking down on himself from above and wonders if he's died from the shock of it all.

But then he feels hot breath on his face, blinks, and sees the impossibly strong woman is standing inches away, her nose practically touching his. That's when he realizes he's still very much alive, and his hysterical words revealed something that has brought her close.

"Who's Mother?" she asks.

III

19

Marjorie Payne wishes her father was the one driving the Plymouth GTX and the two of them were on another one of their excursions into the vast, empty fields that surround their town. The kind of night when they'd sit together on the hood of the car, drinking Dr Peppers and eating moon pies and trying to spot the satellite that'd been put into space that year, all while her daddy spoke of the stars overhead as if they were a vast, unknowable ocean and the plains of West Texas its only coast.

But it's her mother behind the wheel, and the woman's pelting Daddy with a dozen frantic questions about the accident that's rendered him unable to drive. The same one that had him limping to the nearest service station to call for their help. He's in too much pain to answer them, but of course, that doesn't stop her shrill, insistent mother, and once again, Marjorie finds herself stuck in a back seat, gazing out a window and remembering that the curse of being a teenager is knowing how your momma can be a better wife and not being able to tell her because she just won't listen.

Daddy had been crisscrossing Texas for days on another work trip, and they'd expected him later that evening, so when the call came, Momma had been in the middle of preparing his usual welcome home dinner—chicken-fried steak with bacon gravy and Frito casserole, his favorites. Of course, once they all sat down to eat, her mother would give them her usual lecture on how Frito casserole was technically an entrée, not a side dish, but just this once she'd yield to her husband's expansive appetite. The same lecture, every damn time. It was a wonder her father still came home.

She listened to KLLL whenever she cooked, so she was singing along with Loretta Lynn when the DJ cut in with a newsbreak about how the Plains Rapist had got another woman up in Plainview. She'd cried out and killed the radio as if the damn thing had bit her. Ironing her hair in her room, Marjorie was so startled by her mother's outburst she almost knocked the iron from the board. The damn newspaper article the other day certainly hadn't helped. They'd run a drawing of a victim's description of the stocking cap, which apparently had star designs around its eyeholes and silver thread around the mouth like fading lipstick, and now her mother's anxiety was even worse.

When the phone rang just a few minutes later, her mother cried out again. Further proof, Marjorie had thought, that Momma was a silly woman who brought needless fear everywhere she went. Like a rapist would telephone first.

Marjorie could tell from her mother's tone that it was her father on the other end of the line, and he was in some kind of trouble.

She followed Momma next door to Uncle Clem's even though her mother had told her to stay put in case Daddy called again. The Plymouth was apparently all right—banged up but drivable, her mother said with an authority that made it sound like she was directly quoting her husband—but her daddy was not. The story came out of her mother in a frantic rush as she stood on Clem's back porch and he listened through the screen door he was holding open with one hand, one arm already punched through the jacket of his janitor's uniform. He was on his way to the overnight shift at the municipal auditorium and in no mood for this nonsense and wanted to know how his sister's husband could have been stupid enough to get out of his car and check on an injured animal like that, even if he was the one who hit it. Her mother had fired back that pronghorn antelopes weren't known to play dead like opossums, and it wasn't her husband's fault the damn thing had kicked him in the gut, and the point was she needed a ride, not a discussion of roadkill ethics.

The three of them squeezed onto the bench seat of Clem's Studebaker pickup while Marjorie tried to draw comfort from the stars. But all the sniping going on right next to her—Clem didn't have time to follow them back into town because it wasn't on his way, so Beatty had better be damn sure the car's actually drivable—was coming close to draining the magic from the big starry skies she loved so much. In the end, that wasn't possible; she was sure of it. She'd always be just like her daddy, comforted by open spaces and strengthened by silence.

They found her father a few minutes past the service station's lone island of light, standing beside the Plymouth, its angled headlights shooting across the empty field. When he started toward them at the sign of their approach, Marjorie saw how badly injured he was. She'd figured the term "kicked in the gut" had just been an expression, but her daddy held his stomach in both arms, as if he was afraid it might burst. The closer he got to the Studebaker, the more visible the blood under his arms became. Despite her mother's protests, Marjorie hopped from the truck before it had come to a full stop. When she ran to him, the instinct to hug her made him flinch. Either he didn't want to get blood on her or just didn't want to reveal how badly he was injured.

"You need to get to the hospital, Beatty," Clem shouted without anything that sounded like compassion.

"Go on now," her daddy said. "Danielle will bring me home."

"You're banged up worse than the car. You need to—"

"Go on now, Clem."

"It's fine, Clem. I got 'im." But Momma didn't sound like she thought Clem was wrong; more like she just wanted to prevent a fight between her husband and her brother. She even sounded a little frightened of *being alone in the vast dark with only an injured husband and a teen-age daughter.*

When her uncle Clem's eyes landed on her, Marjorie realized she'd been glaring at him too confidently because she thought she stood in darkness. But some of the headlights' reflected glow must have been falling on her face, and that's why Clem's attention caught on her look like a hooked trout. She couldn't help it.

Why did he always talk to Daddy like he was the big screwup in the family?

Daddy drove all over the great state of Texas selling insurance while Clem pushed a mop bucket at the coliseum, cleaning up other people's spilled beer after basketball games. While Clem got drunk and picked fights with Hispanics because he blamed them for his problems, her daddy spent evenings with his happy family, watching the brand-new television he bought them in a house he's already paid for. Clem's also one of the many men who's started looking at her differently since she became a teenager, his wariness implying the changes in her body make him think thoughts he doesn't like and he believes she's to blame for them.

She didn't care how badly Daddy was hurt; she was glad Clem left.

If Daddy needed a hospital, he'd tell her mother to drive him there. What he needed was rest, a good meal, and for the people in his life to stop treating him like a child just because he had compassion for some poor, dumb antelope.

As Clem's truck pulled a U-turn, Marjorie watched with relief as the taillights vanished into the endless dark. Behind her there were whispers.

Her mother tended to drop her voice whenever she needed to tell her daddy something he might not like, probably to shield herself from Marjorie's opinions.

When she started whispering, Marjorie moved closer, trying to eavesdrop, while pretending to watch Clem's vanishing truck. Her mother was asking for a boatload of details, and her father sounded tired, so very tired.

Why'd her Daddy walk all the way to the service station to make the call and then back to the Plymouth again? He didn't, of course. He got an employee from the service station to drive him back to the car as soon as he knew she was on her way.

Then how come he didn't ask her to meet him at the service station? It was foolish of him to wait for them alone out here in the dark when he was this badly injured. He responded by saying he wasn't that badly injured. But Marjorie could hear something in her mother's voice, something beyond irritation and fear. Her mother just couldn't wrap her head around the fact that her father had been so determined not to leave the Plymouth alone for any length of time.

Marjorie had to admit, if only to herself, it was a pretty good question.

Was Daddy afraid the Plymouth would get stolen out here in the middle of nowhere? Maybe plowed off the side of the road by a truck that didn't see it in time? She could see how her father might have been able to prevent the former—he never went anywhere without his gun—but in his current state, there would have been precious little he could have done about the latter.

Even though she was afraid it might silence them, Marjorie looked in the direction of her parents, saw her mother try to grip her father's shoulders. He tried to step back, and the attempt caused wince-inducing pain.

"Gosh dang it, Beatty, your rib's broke!"

"Nothing's broke. I'm just scratched up is all. Now get in the car and let's go."

Her mother gave her a look, and Marjorie saw disappointment in it. Like she wished she had an ally in this moment, someone else who recognized the strangeness of her husband's behavior, but she knew she'd never find one in her daughter.

"We should get him home so he can rest," Marjorie said.

"Should we?" Like so many of the questions her mother asked her of late, it was both rhetorical and sarcastic.

When Marjorie reached the passenger-side door, her father managed to pop the passenger seat forward with twice the usual effort so she could squeeze into the back seat.

"Hey, baby girl."

"Pronghorn get you, Daddy?"

"Sure did. No sense in trying to do right by a wild creature."

"Guess a hug'll hurt, then?"

"It will, baby girl. But maybe later after I've had a beer."

"Deal."

He made a kissing sound, gently pinched her cheek.

It was so dark out and the leather in the back seat so black, it felt like she was settling into a void until she heard the familiar creaking underneath her as she readjusted.

Now they're charging through the dark toward Lubbock's halo on the horizon. The Plymouth's powerful V-8 engine feels familiar, comfortable. And finally, her mother's stopped with all the damn questions.

But she's driving like a bat out of hell, which isn't like her. Does she think the Plains Rapist has wings?

"Oh, no." It sounds like a groan her mother hastily attached two words to at the last possible second.

Maybe they have a flat, or the car's banged up worse than her daddy thought and some warning light's gone on in the dash.

"What, Danielle?" her father asks.

Her mother points to a dark smear on the windshield close to the passenger side. It's backlit by the glow of the four headlights, and it's dark. If it's making her mother queasy, it can only be one thing. Her father already told them he struck the pronghorn so hard, it flipped up onto the windshield and then over the roof of the car. It must have left some blood smears along the way. And if there's one thing her mother hates more than the dark, it's blood.

"Can you reach it?" she asks.

"No, I can't reach it. You crazy?"

"You can't just wipe it off?"

"Woman, just drive the damn car and don't look at it."

"I can't, Beatty. I can't with it like that. You know how I am."

Amazing, Marjorie thinks, that one fear can overpower another so quickly. Her mother's so determined to get rid of that bloodstain, she's pulling over in the middle of nowhere despite her fear of the endless night. Her father's letting out a stream of curses, but in no time, she's rounding the hood, standing next to the passenger side, leaning in to see how big the bloodstain is, when her father says, "Well, don't ruin your dress over it, Danielle!"

"I'm not."

Marjorie studies her father, the way he's rocking back and forth, still gripping his stomach. He's hurt bad. There's no denying it. He's not a man to avoid doctors when he's got the flu or even a sore arm that won't go away. And right now, he's badly injured—bleeding, even—and all he wants to do is go straight home. There's got to be some good explanation. He'll share it in time.

With her, at least. And that's just the way she likes it.

She's been watching him so closely she's got no idea what prompted his suddenly wild jostling in his seat. She's worried he's having some sort of seizure; then she realizes that in his weakened state his wrestling efforts to get the seat belt off are so ungainly they look like an epileptic fit. He's also trying to kick the door open with one foot, but it's too heavy and he's in too much pain to accomplish both things at once. When Marjorie hears the familiar creak of the trunk opening, she realizes it's her mother's actions that have freaked him out. She's rooting around inside the trunk, and that's caused her father to convulse with sudden panic.

The seat belt off, the door half-open, her father's managed to turn in his seat. He's looking past Marjorie to where the rear window's blocked by the open trunk. His eyes meet hers. There's a blend of pain—physical and emotional—and resignation in them that she knows she will remember for the rest of her life. A sense that something he's slowly built with his only daughter over time is about to be either irreparably damaged or forever lost.

Then the trunk pops shut, and her mother's striding around to the front of the car and the expression on her father's face seems like it was all for nothing, even though it's left Marjorie with a single, clear thought that keeps repeating itself.

There's something in that trunk Daddy doesn't want anybody to see.

But if there is, then her mother's missed it somehow. She's found some kind of rag, and she's using it to wipe the antelope's blood off the windshield.

But Daddy's frozen solid, staring dead ahead again, watching her mother's every move.

Marjorie sees it before her mother does.

The thing she's using to wipe the windshield isn't just a rag. It's black. The material's thick and not absorbent enough to wipe the blood away. And on the side she's pressed to the windshield, Marjorie can see a familiar starburst design. When her mother retracts it slightly from the glass to ball more of it inside her hand, light winks through the center of the star, and she realizes it's an eyehole.

For Marjorie, there's only one way to make sense of what she's seeing.

If her father's a monster, then it means monsters aren't what the world thinks they are.

Her mother's wiping slower now, as if she's realizing the thing she's found in the trunk won't get the job done. She pulls it away from the windshield, holding it in two fingers like you might a dead rodent by its tail. Uplit by the headlights at her waist, her face looks ghostly, her expression unreadable.

For a moment that slows Marjorie's heart, she's convinced her mother is quietly experiencing the same revelation she just came to. Yes, the stocking cap can only mean one thing. It means her father has done terrible things. But his reasons for them must be complicated. They know who Beatty Payne is. They know who he is at dinner and while he watches television and when he comes through the front door calling out to them as if just saying their names aloud soothes him. And so together, quietly, the three of them will discuss what this discovery really means.

Just the three of them. As a family.

Thank God they're out here alone, free from others' eyes, judgments, and definitions. Maybe her mother will finally see what vast open plains can bring you—the space needed for essential secrecy, the kind of secrecy that can help a family survive anything.

Her mother realizes none of these things.

Instead, she lets out a scream so powerful it sounds loud enough to be heard all the way back in Lubbock. And when Marjorie sees the pickup that just flew past them slam on its brakes and pull a U-turn in their direction, she realizes her mother has destroyed their family with a single, unending cry.

20

Amarillo, Texas

Her mother's scream is playing on a longer tape loop than usual in her dreams, and for a second or two, Marjorie thinks the wind chimes along the porch are to blame. Then she realizes it's the ringing phone. If it's one of the calls she's expecting, they won't hang up no matter how long it takes her to answer. She'd disconnected the machine a few days ago; the only messages she needs this weekend are from her boys, and she'll receive those herself, thank you very much.

Rising from her recliner tightens little bolts of pain in her right hip, but the voice of one of her boys will make the effort worth it, she's sure. She picks up the pump-action shotgun she'll be keeping within easy reach all weekend and walks through the darkness to the jangling phone.

She dozed off just after dusk, and so the only illumination in the house is coming from the oven light in the kitchen, like a lantern that's been left on in the recesses of a cave. It's dark out, but the expansive, dry land around her house looks darker than usual. A few days ago, she got up on a ladder and unscrewed the bulbs from the security lights ringing the roof of a barn that hasn't seen a horse in years. Dangerous work for a woman of her age but essential preparation for what's to come, and worth the risk because it's for her boys. Even though they didn't wake her, the wind chimes along the house's broad front porch are playing a vaguely harmonious concert. It's a sound that's always filled her with confidence and focus, a reminder that the breath of the universe is something that can be played to your advantage.

She answers with a clipped greeting, and a familiar male voice says, "Good evening, ma'am. Is Sheryl there?"

It's Wally, the gentlest of her boys. The first time she's heard him in months, and the soft sound of it relaxes the tension in her shoulders and has her smiling faintly as she rests her forehead against the wall next to the phone. His little eyes always make him look a little sleepy, and he usually sounds it, too. But not right now. Right now, he sounds cheerful and confident, which means his ride's gone well so far. If he'd asked for Susan, that would mean he's being followed. Samantha, and the seedling somehow escaped. The latter could mean a daytime delivery if he lost time to catch up with the little bitch, and daytime deliveries are a last resort.

"I'm sorry, did you say Sheryl?" Marjorie asks, doing her best to sound like a daffy old lady who isn't quite sure who lives with her.

"That's correct, ma'am. Sheryl Peterson. She gave me this number."

Peterson. Another good sign. If he'd said Sheryl Murphy, that would mean his seedling had a hard outer shell and the Head Slayer hadn't been able to crack it.

And if he'd asked for Sheryl Wilcox, that meant the seedling was already dead. Not their plan, but sometimes it happened. So long as there was proof afterward that her boys hadn't simply gotten carried away and released their urges too soon, it was a forgivable mistake.

"Well, that's odd—there's no Sheryl here. Could you read me the number?"

"Sure."

She grabs a pen that's sitting by the phone and writes it down. Including the area code, the first three and last two digits are the same as her number. But the five in between have been changed to the seedling's height and weight, as they're listed on her driver's license. 5′6″,

210. A big one, for sure. No doubt the woman's mouthy to distract from the fact that she doesn't take good care of herself. Well, good. It's about time she learns her lesson, then.

"Sorry, son, but sounds like Sheryl gave you the wrong number."

"Ah, well. Thanks for your patience, ma'am."

"Sure thing. 'Night, now."

When he hangs up, a burst of wind turns the wind chimes into piano keys. She feels as alert now as if she'd just guzzled a mug of coffee.

They're coming. Her boys are coming.

Maybe she's too cautious when it comes to the phone calls, but she knows right where the junction box for the landline comes onto her property, and she checks it regularly for anything that looks like a bug. They've been doing this for over a decade now, once a year. Even better, not a single one of their seedlings' disappearances has been linked with any of the others. Just more women who vanished without a trace. But even her method for obtaining that information is defined by secrecy and compartmentalization; her boys can use the internet to keep tabs on the investigations into the disappearances of their brothers' seedlings but not their own. So far, the whole thing's been pretty damn foolproof, and it's kept her boys coming back year after year.

Men like her boys aren't brought down by the things they do in the moment; they're brought down by the things they leave behind.

Every year her boys return, bearing gifts.

Every year they stay for a while, their urges purged, their true selves revealed and honored, and once again, she's able to enjoy her family. Her real family. The one she built.

The wind dies, the chimes going silent, and in the sudden quiet, she hears a sound she shouldn't. A sound that would seem ordinary in town but way out here on her property is as out of place as a subway announcement.

A car door closing.

Could it possibly be one of her boys?

No way. For starters, they wouldn't just show up without calling, and they've never arrived in a plain old car.

Without turning on any of the lights around her, Marjorie Payne picks up her shotgun and steps out into the night.

21

Seiling, Oklahoma

They've stopped somewhere along the road to hell. Maybe so he can relieve himself; Zoey's got no idea. She wouldn't be surprised if the monster pissed fire. The visual makes it easier somehow. Not as effective a coping skill as imagining herself Paris bound with her sister in some softly lit airplane cabin. But ironically, imagining her captor wreathed in supernatural abilities puts a kind of soft focus on the awful nightmare he's managed to assemble with basic, everyday implements.

He's gone now, outside the truck, she's sure. But she can't be sure, really, because a divider separates her from the rest of the cargo container, and the straps keep her from turning her head.

She can just see that tiny camera mounted on the wall that probably allows him to watch her while he drives.

She's in silence again.

Someday, someone may learn of the horrors that were visited upon her this night. On the TV specials about her murder they will play music that's more scary than sad while the camera pushes in on photos of her from happier times. But by then she'll be a name, a statistic, a face in a collage, because surely this predator has killed others. Over drinks after work, groups of women across the country will talk in serious tones about what happened to her and the other faces in the collage. But what they'll really be talking about is him, the killer, the monster. They'll try to find just the smallest ways in which she was to blame for her own abduction. Did she let her guard down too far? Did she trust a suspicious stranger? She can already hear the narrator for *20/20* or *Dateline* or *48 Hours* describing in vaguely disapproving tones how she left the deck door open so her beloved cat could reach the litter box and that's how the monster got in. But deep down, the world will only remember her to the extent that they can convince themselves they'll never end up like her. They will say her name only as long as it takes to convince themselves they can outsmart or outwit her fate should the monster ever come for them.

She won't be there to defend herself, of course. Won't be there to tell them that when evil like this comes for you, you never see it coming until it feels like the ground underneath you has suddenly thrown you upward. You will be too busy ending a relationship, coping with the pain of speaking up for yourself for the first time, or maybe just unloading the groceries or sliding into your car in a lonely, empty parking lot. The point is, you will be too busy living life to notice the approach of someone who only wants to take it, and only those whose lives have been taken know this.

Rachel would have known, she thinks, *Rachel would have seen him coming.*

Just like her big sister realized something was wrong with that security guard who approached them outside the mall when they were little girls. She'd been six, Rachel ten. They'd been standing outside the mall waiting for their mother when he'd approached, all gentle and solicitous, bent over and whispering, like there was something he had to say that might embarrass them and he was trying to be kind about it because they were so fragile and young. He told them their mother had had a problem trying to pay for something and they needed to come with him so there wouldn't be any more problems. Later, Rachel would tell everyone that it was the patch that did it. This guy's shirt was the same color, but the patch was in the wrong place.

She'd seen some mall security guards earlier, and their patches had been on their shoulders, not their lapels.

That's why Rachel responded to the man's strange whispered story with a single question. "Who are you?"

And the man had said back, "I'm security, young lady, and your mother's in trouble and I'm sorry but you need to come with me right now or she's going to be very upset with you."

Again, Rachel had said, "Yeah, but who *are* you?"

Later she would realize it wasn't just her sister's defiance that angered the man. It was her confidence. He reached out and grabbed Rachel's wrist, and Zoey's eyes filled with tears in that moment because it was all so confusing. It was confusing because Zoey, too, could sense there was something very wrong with the man, but she thought it didn't matter. She thought they had no choice but to go with him and by being sassy Rachel would only make the man's wrongness turn more wrong.

And the man gave voice to these thoughts when he said, "Now, listen here, missy, I'm a grown-up, and that means you have to do what I say." His tense jaw revealed a roil of darker emotions beneath his words. He wanted something and he wanted it now, the same way Zoey sometimes wanted her mother's chocolate chip cookies before they were done cooling on the tray.

"Liar!" Rachel screamed. And when Zoey felt a firm grip on her wrist, she realized the man hadn't grabbed her. Her sister had. She was dragging Zoey back toward the mall and screaming, "Run, run, run!" And then they were inside again where there was music and frosty air-conditioning and people staring at them because they were running so fast and then suddenly they crashed into their mother, whose arms were full of bags, and the story came rushing out of Rachel so fast she started crying, too. And the dawning fear on their mother's face, the way she dropped her bags and hit her knees and took Rachel's face in her hands as if she needed to touch her daughter to absorb the impact of her words—all of it made Zoey feel better because her mother's reaction meant that another grown-up knew something was very wrong with the man who'd tried to make them go somewhere. Blinking back tears, Zoey looked behind them and saw the man hadn't followed them, and that's when she knew for sure, Rachel was right, the man was a liar.

The cops came and asked them to tell the story again and again, and everyone searched the mall looking for the man, and all of this made Zoey feel better because the world of grown-ups was doing things around her that felt right and normal again. They even ran a sketch of the guy on the local news, but they never found him. And Rachel was praised as a hero, a young woman with good instincts, who knew the number one rule of growing up—never go anywhere with strangers.

Meanwhile, Zoey lived with the dreaded knowledge that she would have gone. That she would have never thought to question the man's authority.

"You were six, Zoey," Rachel said the last time she brought it up. True, she'd had too much wine and they'd been tearfully sharing memories of their mother, gone several years now, but still. The memory of what had passed through her mind that day had stuck with Zoey in ways she didn't want to recognize when she was sober. But Rachel was steadfast as always; there was, she insisted, a massive gulf in experience and wisdom between the ages of six and ten, and so it had been her responsibility to rescue them both from who knows what fate that wolf in security guard's clothing would have delivered unto them both.

But Zoey's still haunted by the fact that she can't be sure how things would have gone if their roles had been reversed.

Look at how silent she's been since this nightmare began.

The truck creaks. She hears the cargo door opening. She could scream, but it would be a pathetic, muffled, phlegmy thing thanks to the gag sitting against the back of her throat. He's standing over her now, the man with the big broken-looking nose and the knife slashes for eyes.

"I spoke to Mother," he says. "She's excited to meet you, Zoey Long."

He likes whatever he sees in her eyes. Maybe it's brokenness, or despair. She feels too exhausted for fear. And he seems to take pleasure in saying her full name, a reminder that he rooted through her personal belongings and probably left none of them behind. So that when her absence is finally noticed, people will think she willingly got into someone's car, carrying her own purse.

How can I be this exhausted, she thinks, *when I've barely made a sound?*

When he starts unlatching the mask's straps, she realizes he's probably going to put the tube back in, which means she'll have only a few seconds to be someone other than that terrified six-year-old who was too afraid to say no to an adult even as he radiated malice.

Maybe the truck's soundproof, or at the least, he stopped somewhere no one would hear a struggle.

Either way, the time to decide is now.

Gently, he pulls the mask free from her head, starts slowly sliding the gag free from her throat. When its rubber passes her lips, he gives her a small smile, as if he's done her a kindness.

That's when Zoey spits in his face.

22

In the end, justice—real justice, not the kind trumpeted by braggart cops and disingenuous newspaper reporters—comes from the heavens above on a late spring evening almost a year to the day after her father's accident. But the weeks and months between contain a series of degradations so constant and severe Marjorie Payne can endure them with only silence and her teeth clenched so tightly she'll end up suffering persistent jaw aches well into adulthood.

In the beginning, no one can believe an injured animal brought down the Plains Rapist. The cops are sure Beatty Payne's undoing has to be the work of a potential victim who managed to escape into the night and was still too afraid to come forward.

But when they search for evidence of her, all they find is a dead pronghorn antelope a few yards from where her father claimed he'd struck one and, stuck to its forehooves, tufts of fabric matching the blue-and-white plaid shirt he'd worn that night. One of the cops later tells a reporter that if they'd actually paused to consider the extent of the injuries that had left the Plains Rapist handcuffed to his hospital bed— two broken ribs, a bruised lung, and a broken collarbone—they'd have realized no woman could have done it. No ordinary woman anyway. Unless she'd had a shovel.

In the weeks following her father's arrest, Marjorie's family, or what's left of it, sit around the kitchen table each night while her mother stares absently into space, sometimes lighting a second and third cigarette because she's forgotten about the one already smoldering in the ashtray. All that's left of their dad's kin is her near-senile grandfather and an older aunt who does more beer drinking than working, and they're hunkered down in their trailer in Galveston as if prepared for a bomb blast. But her mother's sister, Aunt Tanya, and Tanya's husband, Earl, drive up from San Antonio as soon as they hear news of her father's arrest. Occasionally, they bring Danielle a sandwich and a cold drink, sometimes pausing to gather Marjorie's hair back off her shoulders when she's forgotten to brush it, but for the most part they hover silently.

Shortly after their arrival, Marjorie's roused from a nap by sounds she can't name. A few minutes later she emerges from her room to find they've removed every photo of Beatty from the walls and surfaces of the house.

But aside from that determined effort to erase her father's existence, each evening they say nothing as Uncle Clem rants and raves about the terrible judgment all of Lubbock is poised to rain down upon their family. People are already talking. Not just about Beatty but about them. They want to know how much Danielle knew and when she knew it. Marjorie will be next. Everyone knows she's a daddy's girl. Well, look at who her daddy turned out to be!

Marjorie endures these insults for as many nights as she can stand until she levels a gaze on her uncle that appears to freeze his blood.

She's always hated Clem's eyes—they're big and bulgy and often rendered bloodshot by the previous night's whiskey. In that moment she imagines picking up one of the butter knives from the dirty dishes no one can bring themselves to clear and driving it into his right eyeball. But in a manner that is both slow and methodical. Maybe while holding his head in place with one hand on the top of his skull so she can really get in there and make a mess of his brains. It's the first time she can remember imagining an act of violence in this much detail, and it sends a pleasurable flush through her that's similar to the feelings she gets when she rubs her private parts against a bed pillow.

But the vision seems to have power outside of her as well. Clem flinches, as if her contempt for him is a solid thing that takes up space.

"You hate me because you can't stop looking at my breasts, and that makes you ashamed," she says quietly.

If her mother possessed the energy, she might have reached out and slapped the back of Marjorie's head. Face slaps had ended for good after Marjorie shoved back one night, around the time she turned fourteen. But this evening, all Danielle Payne can do is regard her only child with a vacant, dazed look, as if she thinks the girl even more of a stranger now that her father has been revealed to be a rapist.

Clem's so outraged he shoves back from the table and storms out, bellowing something about he wouldn't be around to help the family if they treated him with this kind of disrespect. And that's fine, Marjorie thinks. Since Clem's rarely any help to anyone at all.

But pointing that out would ruin the moment. Because something truly special has just happened. Marjorie can feel it.

Even though her words were sharper edged than anything she'd ever heard him say, she's just spoken them with her father's clarity and elegance. She's channeled his quietly powerful tone right there in the kitchen he no longer occupies, in a house he'll probably never visit again. In a house they might lose to the bank because it's in his name.

She's done more than just channel him, she realizes. His voice is hers now, because from the moment the drivers of that pickup truck had wrestled him to the side of the road, holding him there until the cops came, her father hasn't said a word. Not a single word; he's gone as silent as the prairie on a windless night.

And Clem, it turns out, is wrong.

Suspicion does not fall on Marjorie and her mother.

Instead, her mother becomes a hero.

The story of how her piercing scream had ended a rapist's reign of terror is reprinted in papers around the country. The town is in agreement that if that driver hadn't been passing them at just the right moment and if Beatty Payne hadn't been quite so injured, Marjorie and her mother might have ended up in shallow graves so the Plains Rapist could keep his secret. And the cops had found a lot more in his trunk than the restraints he'd used. In a canvas bag they'd found necklaces, bracelets, rings. Tokens he'd stolen from his victims in what the papers called "a final insult intended to compound the degradation." Beatty's unwillingness to toss the bag aside in an empty field the minute he realized how injured he was is taken by everyone as evidence of the pure evil inside him. He wasn't willing to leave the car by the side of the road because he feared discovery, but he couldn't bring himself to part with the physical reminders of his brutal crimes, even temporarily, because he was truly depraved.

Her father adds nothing to the story.

He does not say a word to the police. He does not request a lawyer and says nothing to the public defender appointed to him. He puts up no fight as the charges are brought against him. All take this as evidence of his guilt, and he does nothing to persuade them it isn't the case. After a psychiatric evaluation, he's deemed competent to stand trial. He isn't catatonic, hasn't gone numb to the stimuli around him. He smiles at things he thinks are funny and nods and shakes his head in response to simple, everyday requests. Because of this, the judge brands his silence an act of defiance, not madness. And because his public defender can't establish alibis for any of the crimes or determine a remotely reasonable explanation for why the restraints, the mask, and the tokens stolen from the victims were in his trunk, everyone is spared the indignity of a long trial.

Even though he refuses to see her, Marjorie's sure her daddy's silence is his gift to her, his way of ensuring their last real communication will be that doleful look he gave her in the car once he realized what her mother was about to discover. For his only child, he speaks no words that might give more life to the horrors that divided their family.

What else can he do?

His wife has deprived him of the chance to explain himself to the two people who mattered to him most. For all they know, his so-called victims are all liars. Maybe his worst sin is infidelity, and given what a shrill and terrible woman her mother is, how can Marjorie blame him? It isn't like those sobbing, self-pitying women have been murdered.

None of it's fair, and it's Marjorie's first instruction in how one person's voice can steal another's without interrupting them.

She wishes her mother would start drinking. She wants her to make a spectacle of herself, tarnish her newfound heroine's reputation with some explosion of anger or grief. But Danielle Payne does nothing of the kind. She holds her head high, becomes more active in her church, does everything she can to make amends to the victims even while she publicly states it's arrogant of her to assume she can. In the end, her church passes baskets, which allows her to keep the bank from taking their house, and when there's money left over, she distributes it evenly among her husband's victims. The model wife of a convicted serial rapist.

Marjorie knows it's all an act. A cowardly one.

A truly brave woman would have allowed her husband to open up to them on that road. To explain why he'd done the things he'd done. A brave woman engages the darkness within the man she loves. Learns where it ends and begins and learns how together they can learn the dance steps needed to keep it in submission. And Marjorie would have helped, would have shouldered the entire burden herself if her mother had allowed.

If you can't be loyal and true to your family, you can't be loyal to anyone or anything.

But you can't count on your friends, apparently. Marjorie learns that lesson a year after her father goes to jail, thanks to Brenda White.

Sammy Jo Peyton, Clara Diamond, Daisy Hufstedler—they all hang in with her for a while, but eventually they give up because Marjorie doesn't want to go for cheeseburgers and talk to boys anymore because everyone still looks at her funny, even if they do fall all over themselves treating her like a victim and not the guilty party.

But Brenda stays true for a little longer, mainly because she loves the movies as much as Marjorie does. Especially the westerns. And so, when it turns out the only thing left that brings Marjorie any joy is buying double- and triple-bill tickets at the local picture show and disappearing into the fantasy on-screen, Brenda's content to sit next to her, even while her mind is far away. It makes sense, really. Brenda's always been a quiet girl, as quiet as Marjorie has become after her father's arrest. Together they go on long walks and kick rocks and watch sunsets. They have the occasional conversation about strange things, like whether snakes have dreams when they sleep during the winter, but for the most part they don't have to dress it all up with a bunch of words.

Maybe that's why she tells Brenda more than she should. Tells her that she's saving up money for bus fare to visit her daddy in Huntsville. There are no big prisons in West Texas in those days, so it's a trip across the state, but she's determined to make it. Alone. Brenda nods as if she understands, but apparently she doesn't, because on the day Lubbock changes forever, Marjorie arrives home from an evening spent in the library to find her mother red-faced and pacing in the living room, demanding every last penny her daughter has saved up to visit her father in jail.

She is never to see her father again, her mother tells her, not even with her own money. Her father has refused to see her, and if Marjorie insists on going against that God-given blessing, then she's courting darkness. That's how she puts it. Courting darkness. Marjorie is to give her mother the money until this crazy instinct passes, and her mother will give it back once she's confident her daughter's head is back to rights.

The weather outside has turned downright malevolent; Marjorie had run the last few blocks home with her hand shielding her face from the leaves and dirt turned to shrapnel in the wind. Now, the walls of the house shake in a way that echoes the building rage in both women's souls. The fusillade of hail pelting the roof tells Marjorie she and her mother will be trapped together for the duration of this moment of reckoning, however long it takes to play out.

When Marjorie refuses to hand over a dime, her mother whacks her so hard across the face, she loses her balance and stumbles into the edge of the kitchen table. It's not the strike of an angry parent. It's not a blow caused by lost patience. It's the kind of violence you unleash in a panic against an intruder, containing the force reserved for an insect or a rodent you've found in the kitchen.

Marjorie's face sings with multi-octave pain, her vision blurs. There's no hysterical apology. Instead, her mother unleashes a torrent of accusations to rival the sound of hail pounding against the roof, and that's when Marjorie knows this moment might be the end for whatever still holds them together.

And maybe, she thinks through the pain, that's not such a bad thing.

23

Amarillo, Texas

Marjorie can tell they're tweakers when she's within a few paces of the barn.

Sure, they've used bolt cutters to snap the padlock from the door, but the car they've parked a few feet away is a shitbird on wheels, a decades-old El Dorado beat to hell by both time and bad maintenance. Some old gearhead might be able to restore it to something worth parading at a vintage car show, but only after they spend days scraping the barnacles of rust from its doors.

Tweakers, for sure. High and stupid and messy as all hell. Any thieves worth their salt would at least keep their mouths shut as they rooted through the barn's contents, but from outside the half-open door, she can hear the little bastards whispering up a storm, giggling now and then like mad hyenas.

She hasn't seen the car around town, and she's a good thirty-minute drive from anything you might call civilization. Marjorie doubts they've gone to the trouble of actually casing the place. Probably just cruising the dry open country outside Amarillo looking for a place to tweak and do strange sex things and God knows what else.

Since she'd fallen asleep with most of the lights off, who knows if they could even make out the house at all?

She kicks the door open with one foot, sees the two flashlight beams inside do a jiggly dance in response, beams bouncing over the expanse of tarp and plywood she and the boys placed over the pits they dug last year. Marjorie slides the pump on her shotgun, emitting that telltale sign capable of freezing anyone's blood, she's sure.

One of them—a boy, it sounds like—lets out a frightened cry. She steps inside. There's an electric lantern right inside the door. Without lowering the gun, she reaches down, flicks it on. When the kids before her see the massive shotgun in her dual grip, their hands go up and they start shaking their heads with mad energy. She was right. Tweakers, for sure, as filthy as if they'd clawed their way up and out of the mud lining the creek bed a little ways behind the barn. But they're young. Much younger than she expected, and this gives her a bit of pause. Teenagers at the most.

But another few minutes and they might have assumed the plank flooring covered up something truly valuable, or they might have started messing with the concrete mixer and the coil of the pump's tube resting in the corner like a sleeping anaconda. There's nothing for them to steal, and they should have realized that right away, but they stuck around and that was stupid. Real stupid.

One of them—the girl—starts to panic, blubbering, raised hands trembling. Marjorie's sure the girl's trying to muster a defense of herself, but her brains are so scrambled she can't quite make words. She sounds like a mewling bird.

Kids, Marjorie thinks, *just kids, both of them. The car's way older than they are, which means it's stolen.*

She was a kid once. Before her father was so cruelly taken from her.

But even amid that terrible loss, she never allowed herself to become a broken-down thing like this. She kept her focus. Made choices. Determined her fate. Read the signs and took the opportunities presented her.

When the boy starts talking, he sounds just as bad as the girl, but the words are starting to make sense, like the lyrics of a familiar song being played just far enough from you that when in the first minute after you notice it, all you can hear is the bass line.

"Please let us go . . . please, please . . . let us go. Please let us go. Please."

24

The words come ripping out of Marjorie, powered by a year's worth of repression, further fueled by the remorseless anger on her mother's face.

Words like "loyalty" and "betrayal" and a dozen other descriptions of the real crimes that destroyed their family, crimes her mother committed against her father. A part of Marjorie had hoped that if she ever did get the chance to say these things—and she never thought she would, but her mother hit her so damn hard there was just no keeping her mouth shut—they would overpower Momma, fill her with shame, break down her arrogance and false fealty to Christ and leave behind a woman desperate for Marjorie's guidance and instruction. A moment similar to that night right after her father's arrest, when the truth, spoken plain and simple, had shamed Uncle Clem out of the house.

But there's no shame in her mother's blazing eyes, only rage. For a split second it feels like each of them assumes the unholy wail suddenly filling the kitchen is coming from the other woman. Has she broken her mother like she hoped? But her momma's staring at the living room window as if the madly rattling frame is the source of the awful sound.

She's looking toward downtown, Marjorie realizes, which is where the storm sirens are located.

The sounds of the weather outside have changed in tone. They're less chaotic, less like dozens of holes being torn open in the sky and more like a gargantuan locomotive roaring toward them across the open plains.

It's the combination of all these things that seems to finally do her mother in—her boiling hatred of her daughter, the terrible sirens, and the approach of a massive house-eating predator are just too much for Danielle Payne to bear. She erupts into hysterical tears, hands going to her mouth.

In her mother's emotional collapse, Marjorie sees an opportunity.

She races through the kitchen, throws open the back door. The fierce wind and its stinging curtain of horizontal rain slam the door against the side of the house, holding it wide open like a giant palm. As she crosses the backyard, it feels like her hair's going to be ripped sideways off her head along with most of her scalp. The door to the storm cellar, the one her father dug when Marjorie was a little girl and their house was shiny and new, rattles in its diagonal frame. She heaves it open with both hands, steps inside. At first it seems like her mother hasn't followed, but when she turns to pull the heavy door shut behind her, there she is, blonde hair raging around her head like a Gorgon's snakes. She grips one side of the doorframe with a hand to steady herself so she can step through, and that's when Marjorie pulls the door shut with both hands.

She slides the bolt in place, backs away into the cellar's dark. For a few moments, her mother's pounding and pleas are audible above the raging storm; then the scream that destroyed her family is consumed by the sounds of fencing tearing from the ground, tree branches snapping and being shed of their leaves, the serpentine protests of power lines ripping free of their poles, followed by the whumps of transformers exploding.

It's all lined up so perfectly. Brenda's betrayal, the fight with her mother, the tornado's approach. The heavens and their earthly compatriots have conspired to deliver the judgment that has eluded her mother for too long.

25

Amarillo, Texas

There's blood all over the blue tarps covering part of the barn's floor, and the plain fact of the matter is she's too damn old to drag the bodies of these kids anywhere. Shotgunning them would have been a mistake if her boys hadn't been on their way. But they are, and so they'll clean up this mess when they get here. Dispose of the bodies the way they dispose of broken seedlings.

It's not like she didn't try. Even managed to drag the boy's body some distance from the edge of the covered pits, just because it felt like too much of an indignity to leave him lying right in the middle of where they'll begin the planting in a few hours. But the effort drained her, reminded her she's aged into being a woman whose real power comes from her shotgun and her willingness to use it. And her boys.

She shot the girl first because she thought maybe, just maybe, some protective instinct in the boy might keep him from running. No such luck; no such loyalty. Hysterical in the wake of the thundering blast, he'd run for the door as soon as he'd found himself splashed in his girlfriend's blood. The blast that brought him down filled Marjorie's already ringing ears with a veritable scream that reminded her of her mother's dying one.

She set the shotgun down a few moments ago, but her hands are still shaking.

She tells herself it's just the aftermath of the recoil, not nerves. No one's going to come looking for this human trash anytime soon. She's thirty minutes from the nearest neighbor and anyone else who might have heard the shot. But maybe that's not her worry. She's an old woman now, and the older she gets, the more room there is for error. These past few years she's wanted the boys to stay longer. Wanted them to visit during other parts of the year, too, not just their annual reunion. But that would be a betrayal of them, she knows. A betrayal on par with her mother's betrayal of her father. None of them will be served by her clinging to them like some little simp.

She's built many things of which she can be proud. This family most of all. A family based on understanding and truth.

But right now, she needs a bit of rest.

Whenever she feels fatigue or some form of doubt, she calls to mind the sight that greeted her when she emerged from the storm cellar after one of the worst tornadoes in West Texas history tore through downtown Lubbock and reduced her neighborhood to splinters. At first, she thought her mother was floating high above the earth, suspended by an invisible force, her body eerily lit by the explosions of blue sparks from the battered power pole nearby.

Another few flashes from the transformer and Marjorie saw that her mother had been speared by a dozen leaf-stripped branches of the cedar elm tree. Like Saint Sebastian and his arrows. And one of those branches had been run straight through her mother's throat, a sight that almost sent Marjorie to her knees. But prayer, she realized, was not the language of the god who had sent her this vision. This god taught you how to channel the darkness of men and storms for your own benefit, and he had used both of those things to set Marjorie free. This god spoke in thunder alone.

He'd silenced her mother, and in this was the key to Marjorie Payne's liberation.

The phone is ringing. Tinny and distant, coming from the house.

The lure of talking to another one of her boys is so strong she's halfway back to the house before she becomes aware of the pain in her hip. But even as she hurries through the dark house, it feels like the exhaustion of killing the two tweakers has been pumped from her system. Then she gets to the phone and finds herself breathless again.

"Good evening, ma'am. Is Sheryl there?"

It's Jonah, the handsomest of her boys. If Cyrus is the smarty-pants and Wally the sweetheart, Jonah's the soulful one, the one prone to fits of darkness and too much self-reflection and, in her opinion, too much book reading. Jonah, out of all of them, is the one who struggles mightily with the gifts of focus and direction she's provided them for most of their adult lives. It's because he's the handsomest and therefore perpetually distracted and deceived by the women who desire him sexually. For him, the added benefit of a planting is that it will purge him of natural urges he might accidentally unleash on the women he insists on sleeping with. She's explained this to him many times, and each time he seems to get it. Then, a year later, he's mired in the same self-doubt. Given the demons that haunt his mind, she's always most relieved by his call.

"I'm sorry, did you say Sheryl?"

"That's correct, ma'am. Sheryl Peterson. She gave me this number."

Peterson. Good. Everything's going well on his end.

"Well, that's odd. Could you read me the number, because there's no Sheryl here?"

"Sure."

She grabs a pen that's sitting by the phone and writes it down. As with Wally a little while earlier, the first three and last two numbers are the same as hers—the middle five are the seedling's height and weight. This one's 5'9" and 180 pounds.

"Sorry, son, but sounds like Sheryl gave you the wrong number."

"Ah, well. Thanks for your patience, ma'am."

"Sure thing. 'Night, now."

She hangs up. The call with Jonah has restored her some, even if the boy did sound as exhausted as she currently feels.

26

Charlotte should be long past the point of being amazed by the technology available to Cole Graydon and his business partners, but by the time she discovers the third camera hidden inside the cargo area of Mattingly's truck, she can't help but shake her head and exhale in a long, slow hiss.

It's not a camera so much as a patch of translucent gel-like material. The tiny swirl of milk-colored wiring inside only became visible when she pressed the lens of Luke's halogen flashlight almost flush with the metal wall and began moving the beam in slow sweeps over it. There's no lens she can see, so it's probably less of a camera and more of a motion detector that uses vibrations to send some sort of digital image back to Kansas Command.

However it works, it doesn't belong here and sure as hell isn't Cyrus Mattingly's.

Instead of trying to peel it from the wall, she punches it, leaving a fist-size crater in the wall.

Bound to the gurney, Mattingly yelps and sucks snot through his nose.

If she's already enraged Cole's business partners by defying their order to stand down, no doubt they're currently screaming bloody murder over her casual destruction of another several million dollars' worth of their secret technology.

As if he's an obstacle on par with an ottoman in a crowded living room, she pushes Mattingly's gurney to one wall, then starts raking the ceiling of the cargo compartment with the flashlight's beam. She spots another faint glimmer of tiny, nearly invisible wires that could easily be mistaken for a patch of lint and drags one of the crates over—the one he didn't use on her; the one filled with spiders—so she can stand on it gently before punching through one, two, then three cameras adhered to the ceiling.

"You have to let me call," he says meekly. "If I don't call, she'll . . ."

"She'll what?"

"It's a code. I'll just give her a code and then—"

"Yeah, see, that's just it, Cyrus. How do I know you're going to give her the right code? You might warn her I'm coming, and that wouldn't be good for anyone. Especially you."

"Please . . ."

"Please what, Cyrus?"

"She's my *mother*," he wails with more despair than anger.

"But she's not, though. Your real mother died when you were a baby, and you didn't meet this lovely lady until you got sent to some reform school. Isn't that what you just told us?"

Along with a lot of other seriously crazy shit, she thinks. *Seriously crazy shit that was also devoid of full names, addresses, and locations.*

She's staring at him now, but after pouring his guts out in the form of the strangest, most laudatory tale of twisted familial bonding she's ever heard, Cyrus Mattingly can't bring himself to look directly at her. She doesn't mind. What she minds is that he hasn't been able to bring himself to provide the name and location of the woman he calls Mother, and her kill site.

Mattingly falls silent.

They need to get going. They were only supposed to pull over long enough to buy some burner phones, then get a little ways down the highway from anything that looked like civilization so Luke could make the phone call they'd discussed and she could interrogate Mattingly. Maybe Luke's making the call now, but she can't hear him outside. That's a good thing, though. She doesn't want Mattingly to hear Luke, either.

"Tell me more about your mother, Cyrus."

"Let me call her and I will."

A phone number, she thinks. Without internet access, they can't use just a phone number to pinpoint Mother's location. The road between here and Amarillo isn't exactly lined with cybercafés, and their own devices are all being monitored by the same business partners who somehow frightened Cole into sending coded messages.

"When I can see your mother, literally, like with my own two eyes, then you can talk to her. How's that?"

"If I tell you where she is, you'll kill me."

"I won't."

"Liar."

"I'm not like you, Cyrus."

"That's for fucking sure," he barks, then cackles like a mad dog. "If I could do what you could do, I'd . . ." He seems to remember himself suddenly, but it's too late to stop her from bending down over him and resting a hand atop a chest she could crush with a gentle press.

"You'd do what?" She didn't mean to growl, but that's how it came out. "Rescue kids from a burning building? Or break some poor woman's legs so she couldn't get away from you?"

What's worse, she wonders, the malevolent sanctimony of the speeches he gave her when he first tied her up or his pathetic tears of defeat now? Maybe he's nothing without his mother's love. Which gives her an idea.

"What do you want?" he wails.

"I want the other two women your mother's holding captive in that factory."

"It's not a *factory*. It's a ra . . ."

Too late, Mattingly realizes he fell victim to a classic trick, instinctively correcting wrong information and revealing something in the process.

A ranch, she thinks. *It's not a factory, it's a ranch.* Charlotte makes a point to list all the additional easy-to-overlook facts this information reveals. Ranches are isolated. Ranches often have several structures on the property, barns or otherwise. Earlier, Mattingly bawled up a storm at the mention of Amarillo, which as good as confirmed that Luke interpreted Bailey's coded message correctly. So they're looking for an isolated property on the outskirts of Amarillo where no one would bat an eye at the late-night arrival of three large box trucks, and there's no one close by to hear the screams that would result from the gruesome rituals Mattingly described to them as if he were recounting the baptisms of the saints.

It doesn't narrow things down as much as she'd like. Amarillo's surrounded by a lot of vast, open country.

Still, her idea might just work. And more importantly, it might get them back on the road again.

Mattingly sucks snot back from his nostrils, clears his throat with a few coughs, and says, "If I don't call her, that's as good as warning her."

"Not really. Just means you ran into trouble somewhere on the road. But if I run the risk of letting you tip her off, then she knows *she's* in trouble, not just you, and she might kill those women and run."

"She's not going to fucking run," he says with trembling defiance.

And why not? she thinks. *Is it because this place, this ranch, is her actual home?*

She keeps this to herself.

"What's she going to do, load her guns and prepare for battle? Well, I'm just fine with that. I mean, look at me, Cyrus. Do I seem like the type of woman who needs a gun to solve problems?"

I won't be for another hour or two, at least, she thinks, hoping Mattingly can't detect this nagging worry in her expression. But he's wide-eyed and gasping, as if every few minutes he needs to remind himself of the fact that she really does exist and can really do impossible things.

She could waste all night trying to get Mother's name and address out of this psycho, but they're not just racing against whatever Mother's clock is.

They're racing against the response team Cole's business partners have probably insisted Cole send after them, most likely with orders to put an immediate stop to her defiance. And since Cole's playing both sides of the field, no doubt he had no choice but to send one. She'd love to know who the teams answer to, but up until now, that question seemed above her pay grade. In the past, before he involved new business partners, Cole's commanded all the small armies of fence-hopping, shadow-crawling mercenaries she's worked with. If that's still the case, then it doesn't seem foolish to hope he hasn't ordered them to stop her in her tracks. Just to make sure she doesn't vanish into thin air once the operation is through.

In essence, she's trying to avoid two potential nightmares.

One, allowing Mattingly to give his beloved Mother a warning that would allow her to slip off into the vast Texas night with two innocent women in trucks just like this. And two, sharing Mother's name and location with Cole's business partners, who've made it clear they're far more invested in stopping Charlotte from reaching her destination than saving the women being held captive there. If Bailey, and possibly Cole, had really managed to keep Amarillo a secret from the partners, she and Luke would lose their only real advantage over the response team if they gave away that information now.

She's got a compromise that will allow her and Luke to get back on the road and figure out Mother's location when the time's right.

"Tell you what," she says. "You can call your momma when we get to Amarillo."

"Liar," he says, but there's childlike hope in his desperate tone.

"I guess we'll have to see when we get there."

She bangs lightly on the cargo area door so Luke can push it open for her.

This time she doesn't jump from the truck. She sinks to a seated position, drops one leg to the dirt and then the other. There are no searchlights filling the night sky. If Cole's been pressured into sending an airborne battalion in pursuit, it's not on their tail yet. They left the SUV, along with the vials of her blood, in the field where Mattingly first pulled off the highway. It broke Luke's heart to say goodbye to his favorite car, but between all of its top-secret technology, as well as the paradrenaline-filled vials resting on the front seat, they figured the response team would either stop to collect it first or divert some of its members for the effort. In either scenario, maybe it would buy them a little more time. The skies are empty save for stars and wisps of high-altitude clouds. And she figures the cars whizzing by on the highway are bound for ordinary homes where ordinary people live, most of whom go to bed each night believing monsters like her captive don't exist outside fiction.

Her eyes focus on the stopwatch dangling around Luke's neck, counting down what remains of her trigger window. He probably forgot he's wearing it outside of his shirt, a sign that he's been nervously checking it every few minutes.

"How'd it go?" she asks Luke.

"Not good. They said they'd get back to me. I tried to make it sound like I had more facts than I did, but if I just started spewing the crazy shit he told us, I'd tip them off that I was fishing."

Up until a year ago, Luke had worked as a deputy for the sheriff's department in Altamira, California, so they'd decided to let him pretend like he was back in his old job so he could call the Amarillo Police Department.

"They had no idea who you were talking about?" she asks.

"I said we were trying to close a cold case in the area that might be connected to the Plains Rapist who'd worked in the Texas Panhandle in the late sixties. I said we had someone in custody who was bragging about all the bad shit he'd done with the guy back in the day, but we thought it might be lies and so we wanted to see if the daughter could confirm some of her dad's movements during that period so we could see if our guy was bullshitting. I even tried to throw in the fact that the daughter might want to talk to us because maybe our guy was responsible for some of what her father went down for."

"It didn't work?"

"He had no idea what I was talking about, wanted to know why I was calling so late, and was starting to get curious about why I didn't have more names. I even threw in the part about the woman's mother getting killed in a tornado, and that's when Deputy Dawg started acting like I was on meth. I tried, Charley. I'm sorry."

"Doesn't matter. Let's get going."

They're wasting time, but she's not surprised Luke isn't rushing to get behind the wheel of the truck again. Given the type of cameras Cole's men planted on the truck, any audio-only recording devices are probably damn near invisible to the naked eye. Trying to debug the truck's cab could take all night. Once they're inside again, it'll have to be radio silence between them or any information they discuss might get transmitted back to Kansas Command.

"Charley, we don't know where we're going," Luke says.

"We're going to Amarillo. It's where your brother told us to go."

"Yeah, but after that. I mean . . ."

"What?" she asks.

"We could always just start breaking his bones."

"You drive, I torture?"

Luke nods, then goes silent as he considers the idea. Terrifying Mattingly into revealing his twisted origin story was one thing. Extracting information from him through pure pain is another.

"If it comes to that . . ." But even she sounds unsure.

"If it comes to that," Luke says, as if trying to encourage her.

But he sounds pretty damn unsure, too.

As Luke starts the truck's engine, she watches Mattingly on the same little flat-screen monitor he used to watch her. It should be gratifying, but it isn't. Not with two other women hell bound somewhere on these vast plains, not with the filthy residue of Mattingly's twisted tale still clinging to her skin.

27

Lebanon, Kansas

Charley and Luke haven't said more than a few words for a while now, and the audio feed from the Black Hawk trying to catch up with them is a bore, so Cole removes his earpiece, stretches his neck from one side to the other. Tries for a deep breath that ends up sounding like a growl.

Are there yoga poses recommended for someone whose business venture is coming apart? He should really look that up before they do this again.

If they ever do this again.

His tablet's split between two feeds. On the right, he's got a view from the chopper's nose cam as it fires through night darkness in pursuit of Charley and Luke. On the left, the feed from inside Mattingly's truck. He's amazed by Charley's apparent calm, unsurprised by Luke's loyalty, and, though he hates to admit it, envious of the simple bond between them.

If he minimizes both screens, he can watch the digital map tracking the Black Hawk's flight path and the ground path of Mattingly's commandeered truck. But the map's misleading. On-screen, the distance between the two flashing points seems deceptively small.

In the bottom right corner of the map, a constantly fluctuating number provides Cole with more uncertainty than enlightenment. Using speed readings from the Black Hawk and Mattingly's truck, the figure gives him an estimate of how long it will take the chopper to catch up with Charley and Luke. But it doesn't factor in the drop-off of two men at the sight of the abandoned SUV and the paradrenaline vials within. Cole assured the pilot before he left that even though they had new orders and more distance to travel, retrieving the vials was paramount and he should take as much time as he and his crew needed to safely land and take off in the unfamiliar field in which they'd been left. In short, he'd tried to buy Charley and Luke as much additional time as possible without making his business partners even more suspicious.

On the opposite side of the screen and at the top is the time remaining in Charley's trigger window, a bright-red number counting down like a stopwatch.

0:58:32.

Remote dosing her shouldn't be an issue. He can justify it later—if there is a later—by saying she was too valuable as a test subject to face down whoever these monsters were with just a gun in hand. And the only one who might realize he's dosed her in the moment is Julia, since her team's been given access to the network so they can monitor Bailey.

So there's nothing he can do for the time being. He's dealt with every factor he can.

With one minor exception.

He's alone in the main house's ground-floor kitchen, feeling as out of place as all the shiny, untouched implements and utensils. There's a coffee maker that still looks brand new because it's never been used. The drawers, he knows, are full of untouched flatware. There's even a framed photograph hanging beside the window above the sink—a sepia-toned black-and-white shot of open prairie that by day roughly mirrors the view. The window's even got curtains. Hunter green with a gold stripe along the bottom. Plain, tasteful. The kind a semicloseted gay guy would buy for his dorm room and say his mom picked out. There's a veritable commissary attached to the bunker below that's actually designed to feed everyone on staff. This kitchen is just for show.

Now that he thinks about it, he's not sure why they went to such trouble to create a false ground floor for the house. It's not like he has meetings with civilians here, and the chance of someone wandering in by mistake is almost nil. Electrified fencing blanketed by motion-activated security cameras rings the entire property, and armed guards walk the perimeter twenty-four hours a day.

As long as I can afford them, they do.

If Stephen and Philip pull out, he might be forced to secure this place by locking the front door and pulling some furniture over the basement entrance to the bunker.

He could kill time just as easily belowground, but there's a task waiting up here. And even though he's near to it, he's avoided it now for just a little too long.

The guards flanking the door to Noah's room straighten as he approaches. He waves his hand and they part.

Inside, Noah's seated on the bed, back resting vertically against a mountain he's made of the pillows, his elbows resting on his bent knees, staring into space with an expression somewhere between defiant and exhausted. He's changed into a pair of heather-gray pajama pants and a V-neck white T-shirt. The outfit's designed to send a message, Cole's sure. *I don't expect to be let out of this room anytime soon, so enjoy trying not to look at the outline of my ball sack while you discipline me.*

Noah's eyes track Cole's every movement as he takes a seat in the chair across from the bed, but Noah doesn't move a muscle otherwise. For a long time, neither man says anything, and after a while the sounds of their intermittent breathing starts to annoy Cole.

"I'm not a coward," he finally says.

"Have they caught her yet?"

"No."

"What happens when they do?"

"I'm not a coward, Noah. A coward never would have gone to first base with you."

"First base. You mean, like, kissing?"

"That's not the part of our relationship I meant."

"Which part did you mean?"

"The mad scientist part."

"Don't confuse angry with insane. Not right now."

"Sane people throw chairs. Got it."

"I apologize for letting my outburst get physical," Noah says.

"Thank you."

"Now tell me what happens when they catch her."

"Both teams are mine; they answer to me. They have orders to assist her and then bring her back. That way I can give her what she wants and make The Consortium think I actually reacted to her going rogue."

"I'm talking about after."

"There're some things I haven't told you."

"Of course there are."

"Oh, what does that mean? Like you're so transparent?"

"Six months. Six months, Cole. I've worked in your lab for half a year now under constant surveillance, cut off from the world. This is the first time I've left, and I didn't request the trip. I have been the best little boy at Graydon Pharmaceuticals, and the whole time you still haven't given me access to a single vial of stable paradrenaline."

"Kelley Chen and her lab are doing good work on the paradrenaline studies."

"Obviously not or there'd be progress."

"We've manufactured a poison. A very effective one."

Noah is startled silent by this update. Truth be told, it's not really an update. The news is a little over half a year old; he just hasn't told

Noah about it until now, partly because Noah was on probation for a big chunk of that time, but largely because, in Cole's opinion, it's never been very good news. Noah wasn't expecting it, that's clear.

"A poison?" he asks.

"We used a paradrenaline sample to wipe out cancer cells. The catch was, the cancer returned a short while later. A supercharged version of it that could kill tissue samples within minutes. Paradrenaline plus cancer equals instant death, apparently. Congratulations. It's our first success, other than, you know, Charlotte. Stephen's thrilled."

Although, given his current behavior, you'd have trouble telling.

Noah's stunned expression contorts into a grimace.

"A poison," he whispers, as if it's a dirty word.

"It's not what we were shooting for initially, but it's something."

"Well, give me back my breakthrough and I'll give you a lot more than something."

"It's not a breakthrough."

"Excuse me?"

"Electricity was not a breakthrough until they figured out how to use it without setting the world on fire. You made a drug that works in one person, Noah. One. And the by-product is not exactly rolling out the way we thought it would."

"It works. That was the breakthrough. I'll give you more when you stop punishing me."

"This was supposed to be the beginning of that."

"Oh, I see. And now that I threw a chair the sanctions are going to stay in place?"

"I didn't say that."

"There's a lot you haven't said, apparently."

"Because I don't know if I can trust you yet."

"What's it going to take?"

"Calling me a coward in front of my staff isn't a good start."

"Don't be petty."

"OK. Then maybe it's because you almost killed Charlotte Rowe."

"Oh, for fuck's sake. No. Uh-huh. No way."

"I'm sorry, what?"

"I'm not relitigating Arizona. Put me on a plane. Throw me in a cell again. I don't give a shit. Enough, already. You've made far more questionable calls than I did with her. And we both know good and well you're not still pissed because of what I did to Charlotte at that wellness center. You're pissed about what I did before. To you."

"Enlighten me, then."

"I left."

"I stopped giving what you wanted, you stopped sleeping with me."

"I left *you*."

"Yes, you did."

He's fully prepared for Noah to sneer, to turn away, to do any manner of things that would suggest he finds Cole's resentment tedious and pedestrian and beneath the worthy glare of his attention. But Noah stares into his eyes with an intensity that shortens Cole's breath.

"See, that's just it, Cole. That's where we're different."

"How?"

"You drew this big separation between what we did in the bedroom and what we were doing in the lab. But for me, it was all one and the same. It was ours. It was *us*. And when you shut down the project without a word of warning, you dropped an ax on all of it. On me. I had to find out from the security director because I requested a flight to a lab that wasn't operational anymore. And then, when I saw you again, you treated me like I'd jilted you at prom, when you were the one who took our dream and shattered it into a million pieces. I wasn't your high school boyfriend. I was the man you were going to change the world with."

"You showed up out of nowhere after years demanding I throw together the funding for this on a moment's notice. I wasn't treating you like an ex-boyfriend."

"What, then?"

"I was treating you like a whore because you were acting like one."

"I didn't offer to fuck you again. I offered you Charlotte Rowe."

"She wasn't yours to give."

"Apparently she was because here we all are. And I've slept with your whores. With you. And they give you a fraction of what I can."

Maybe it's the wording, but Cole can't control his laughter. Noah looks away quickly, turns his back to Cole as he swings his legs to the floor and moves to the side of the bed. Is he trying to hide anger or amusement? Cole's not sure. Then he sees Noah's back is shaking, and he realizes the man's laughing as well. Maybe it's the hypocritical judgment in the word *whore*. As if either of them has the right to judge the world's oldest profession given how many people they've killed.

After a while, he says, "I'm not a whore."

"*Sex worker* is the more appropriate term."

"I'm not that, either."

"And I'm not a coward," Cole says. "I didn't build this place because I'm a coward."

"OK. That's a fair trade, I guess."

"I'm glad you agree."

As the anger leaves the room, it unveils softer, more frightening emotions Cole fears he won't be able to control.

"Charley's always said that if you'd told her what Zypraxon could really do, she would have let you test it on her."

"So we are going to relitigate Arizona?"

"No. I just . . . Bear with me, I'm headed somewhere with this."

"Charley's wrong."

"You think she's lying?"

"No, I just think she's wrong. No one can know how they would have reacted after the fact."

"Guess there's no point in asking, then."

"Asking what?" Noah asks.

Cole has stared down killers, made decisions that have cost lives. But in this moment, he's beset by a fear and anxiety so total he can feel sweat along his spine and a deep chill in his bones. Noah's intense stare worsens both sensations.

"If I'd discussed it with you first, shutting down our first go at this, I mean, would you have stayed?"

When the silence between them becomes too long for Cole to bear, he says, "I get it. No one can know how they would have reacted after the fact."

"Something like that," Noah says quietly.

It's not the answer to the question that fills Cole with shame; it's that he had to ask it in the first place. And that, he realizes, is the real curse of having spent time in Noah's arms. For years, he'd convinced himself he was above all the conventional models of relationships that bedeviled straight people. Told himself that being gay liberated him from the expectation to marry, to raise kids, to compromise his professional obligations to a biological clock. But the truth was darker and more painful, and until Noah he'd been able to ignore it. Deep down, he'd convinced himself that what happened to him as a boy had so damaged him he was incapable of needing someone in a romantic sense. That sex for him could never connect to intimacy, only transitory pleasure. Then along came Noah, and when he realized there was a man in the world who could fuse both things for him, Cole was afflicted by the terrible realization that he's capable not just of needing someone, but of hungering for them. Obsessing about them.

He'd reacted by searching for a dozen ways to blame Noah for the effects he had on him. To depict Noah as a drug and he the hapless addict. He leaped on the man's every flaw as if it were an epic moral failing and in the process became such a shrieking hypocrite, someone with the fragile people skills of Bailey Prescott had ended up calling him on it.

In the end, it all feels like yet another reason to avoid romantic entanglements altogether.

But that's easier to do when he's got Noah confined to an island half a world away.

"You were going to tell me something, something you hadn't told me before." Noah's studying him, maybe the way he studied Charlotte back when he was pretending to be her therapist. "Is it about the boys?" he asks. Cole is genuinely confused, and it must be showing on his face because Noah adds, "The last thing you said to Charley. About your father. How he forgave some boys who did something to you when you were young. I thought maybe . . ."

Cole's face is hot, and he's afraid his cheeks just turned a telling shade of red. It's not the memory that's doing it but the idea that Noah would invite him to share that secret with him, that Noah believes they're capable of sharing secrets from which they can't reap scientific glory or a massive financial reward.

"I know where they're going," Cole says. "I've known for months. I've got a secret ground team waiting for them. Nobody knows about it except for Bailey and my security director."

"That's good." A new light is coming into Noah's eyes. "This is good, Cole."

"I'm glad you're impressed."

"You have an address?"

"A town, but it's not a very big one. Amarillo, Texas. They're headed in that direction now, so it looks like we were right."

"How'd you get it?"

"A letter we intercepted. In a manner of speaking. Surveillance cams caught Mattingly opening it, and we were able to zoom in and screen cap it. He tore it up a few minutes later, but he wasn't as thorough with the envelope. We pulled the pieces, and we were able to put the postmark together. We were already taking the mail out of his trash every day. This was the first thing he tried to destroy."

Approval emanates from Noah, and even though Cole is trying with all his might to ignore it, he's savoring it.

"And why'd you keep it a secret?" he asks.

"I think The Consortium's conspiring against me. Maybe not Julia. I wasn't sure about her until tonight. But I think Stephen and Philip are in cahoots, and I think tonight was about forcing Charley to defy them so they'd have pretext to confine her in a lab and end the field operations."

"That's why you wanted me to see the second call," he says.

Cole nods. "Everything changed after paradron."

"The poison?"

"I gave it to Stephen. It's his now. Since then, I think he's lost his taste for the rest of this."

"You just gave it to him?"

"That's how The Consortium works, Noah. A breakthrough becomes the property of whoever's business relates to that specific area. Stephen's in weapons, so he gets poisons. It's the only way to justify all of us contributing substantially to the funding."

"Fine, but I'm having trouble believing Stephen would suddenly need to start messing with everything just because you guys made one little poison. There's a huge potential here for everyone if we all keep working, and if he's trying to dial this down, there's got to be some bigger agenda at work. And what about the killers? We don't get any more to study if Charley stops going after them."

"Maybe he thinks we have enough."

"We have *two*. That's not enough of a sample for anything."

"I'm just saying, since we gave him paradron, he's been a nightmare. Nothing's right. Nothing's safe enough. He wants nine planning meetings about every move, and he doesn't spend them giving any actual ideas, just picking stuff apart. It's like he's done."

"Done with what, though?" Noah asks.

"Operations like this."

"It's his first one."

"I know, and I think he wants it to be the last," Cole says.

"So, he was trying to turn Charley against you so she'd act out and become too dangerous to let run around in the world."

"Yes, which, given our difficult history, isn't the tallest order."

"But what does he get out of that?"

"Well, for one, with Charley locked in a lab, we're all spending a lot less money, and we're not exposed to the security risks of her driving halfway across Texas on a whim while triggered. Honestly, I think he's trying to reduce his investment in this now that he's got paradron, and for some reason, he feels like we don't need to make Charley happy anymore to get paradrenaline out of her blood. And that scares me."

"Philip, though. How does he get Philip to go along with him? Philip's private security. He's about people power. He's going to be invested in science that increases human capabilities. He doesn't give a shit about poison. I certainly can't see him joining a thwart plan over it."

"I don't know. Philip's never liked me very much."

"This isn't that."

"Isn't what?"

"It's not personality driven, Cole. There's something else here. It's bigger."

Noah's irritated, for sure, but it's not the anger of earlier, and it doesn't seem to be directed at Cole. He rises to his feet, crosses to the window, and stares through it, even though all he's looking at is a lowered metal storm shudder on the other side of the glass. He's seeing his own thoughts, and apparently, they're as vast as the hidden view outside.

"What?" Cole finally asks.

"These men, they're masters of the universe. If Stephen's hoping to harvest weapons from all this, he's got to be looking at the psychos I've got in my lab and thinking their brains could yield something pretty damn effective. I've spent the past year generating never-before-seen neural maps of the brain structures that lead to sadistic, remorseless violence. I'd like to use those to treat violent psychopaths, but a guy like Stephen, it makes sense he'd start asking how to mimic those neurological systems to create super soldiers who can kill in battle without hesitation or remorse. Instead, with weapons potential all over the place in our studies, he suddenly decides to screw with Charley's ability to feed that pipeline."

"It's the security risks," Cole says, but he's repeating himself and believing the explanation less and less each time. "He's just worried she'll do something out in the world that will draw attention to his involvement."

"I don't believe that. There's almost nothing you guys can't cover up. That can't be why. And for Philip there's no why at all."

"Noah, if you've got a theory, then share it."

The challenge gets his attention. He turns, his expression focused.

Shit, Cole thinks, *he really does have a theory.*

"I think you don't know what you gave them," he says.

"Meaning?"

Noah turns from the window, sinks down onto the foot of the bed, studying Cole as if he's not sure Cole will be able to handle the impact of what he's about to say. "I think paradron is a lot more than just a poison. And when Stephen took a good look at it on his end, he realized that and for some reason decided he doesn't need Charley at all. Or us."

"Just Philip?"

"Maybe."

Cole wants to protest, but it's just defiance. There's an elegance to Noah's theory that's impossible to ignore.

Memories of his own behavior are coming back to him with vicious force; he's thinking of how heavily he sugarcoated paradron's origin story when he related it to Noah just a few moments ago. They didn't generate a poison; they ended up with one by mistake, and it came as a terrible defeat. They weren't trying to turn cancer into a more effective poison; they were trying to cure it. Had their emotions blinded them? Had he and Kelley Chen been so stung by their sense of failure they'd offloaded the samples to Stephen too quickly and without enough analysis? If that was the case, then he was partly to blame.

The last time he'd been blinded by emotion and ego, Luke Prescott had almost died. Now the same weakness could have endangered not just Charley but everything they'd built.

"Cole?"

He's on his feet without remembering having stood. The concern in Noah's voice behind him sounds unguarded, genuine. But in a strange mental twist, even though it only feels like something's sitting on his chest, he turns his back to Noah as if he might be able to see the invisible source of whatever's causing him pain, and for some reason that would be terribly embarrassing. He tells himself he's still unexpectedly raw from their discussion of their own history. That's why he's a strange, unfamiliar blend of nauseated, dizzy, and breathless.

Is he having a heart attack? Is this what one feels like?

A sound comes from far away, a faint thud. He feels wood underneath his palms, realizes what he just heard were his own hands grabbing the windowsill to keep himself upright.

"Cole?"

Not just concern in Noah's voice now. Outright alarm.

Has he been poisoned? Is that it?

He blinks, stares at the shuttered window before him. If it were a poison this sudden, it would be accelerating. But even amid the other symptoms, there remains a strange sense of being grounded. It's as if some invader inside of him is trying to decide which body part to turn against him, and it's tuning up everything as it prepares to make a choice—his head, his stomach, his chest. He's dizzy, but his head isn't throbbing. He can't draw a deep breath, but he isn't suffocating. There's pain in his chest, but it's not the thundering fire of a heart attack. He feels like he's outside of his body, yet he knows exactly where he is.

"Cole!"

His knees go weak. The pressure against his stomach is Noah's arm. The man's righted him. Not just that, he's holding Cole to keep him from crumpling to the floor.

This isn't me, he tells himself. *I don't have feelings like this.*

But on some deep intuitive level he can't ignore, he knows what's happening to him.

He's having a panic attack. Full on, like the kind you see in the commercials for the drugs he sells but refuses to take. Because Noah's right. He missed something. And again, it was big. And it's a reminder that he's a fraud. A spoiled little fraud playing at being a master of the universe with daddy's fortune, with his company.

It's an embrace now, what Noah's giving him. Cole's hands, which felt limp and lifeless a second before, are resting against Noah's solid chest. Slowly, Noah cups one side of Cole's face. Maybe he's gazing into Cole's eyes to see if he's lost his mind. And maybe it's calculated, manipulative tenderness, the way he's gently cupping the side of Cole's jaw in one hand. But Cole can't bring himself to care. Not right now. Not when he's this panicked. He needs his touch. Noah's touch. Dylan's touch. It doesn't matter which one he is in this moment, because when they're in each other's arms, he's both.

"Cole?" It's a whisper now, but still a question.

"I can't do this alone."

Noah doesn't gloat, just strokes Cole's cheek gently as he gazes into his eyes. Maybe that's what gives Cole the courage to say what he has to say next, even though he's never been more terrified by anything he's had to say in his life.

"I need you."

At first, neither one of them reacts to the pounding against the door.

When it's Noah who pulls away first, Cole realizes he's still having trouble breathing, still feels like he's moving through molasses. But relief is spreading through him, no doubt brought by just having said those last few words. By the time Noah opens the bedroom door to reveal Scott Durham on the other side, Cole's walking toward his security director as if nothing's amiss.

"There's a problem," Scott says. Given he's had no reaction to the fact that Noah opened the door, Cole knows it must be serious.

"Charley?"

"Bailey," Scott answers.

28

"Babe?"

Charlotte's still seeing the road sign they passed a few minutes earlier.

Amarillo 60 miles.

At their current speed, they'll be there in less than an hour.

Then one of them will have to hop in the back of the truck and start working Mattingly again. Will it be her? Maybe. If Cole remote doses her.

"Babe?" Luke says again.

"I'm listening."

"Fifteen minutes."

She knows exactly what he's referring to, but she looks at him anyway. Sees he's holding the stopwatch in the hand that's not on the steering wheel.

"No judgments if . . ."

"If what?" she asks.

"If you want to bail. I mean, it's not bailing, but you know what I mean. We might have other options."

"Yeah, like we slow down, let them drop out of the sky and load Mattingly into some chopper, and a few weeks later Cole gives us a pat on the head, says it's all been taken care of and I shouldn't worry because his business partners got the best of him after all. But he never gives us Mother's name, so we can't be sure."

"Not to play devil's advocate here, but last time Cole really did take care of it. Like hard-core took care of it."

"It's not Cole I'm worried about it. It's his billionaire buddies."

"I know, but maybe Cole can do a better job of protecting us from them if we fall back."

"Give in, you mean."

"I'm not for it. I just don't want you to think I'm against it if it's what you need."

"All that would require *stopping*, and if Cole's under pressure to take Mattingly all the way back to Kansas to interrogate him, the other women might get tortured to death in the interim. If the best we can do is bring whoever he's sent after us right to the doorstep of these assholes, then let's do it."

Luke nods, watches the road. "I just don't want you to feel like you can't change your mind."

"Thank you."

"And I sat here for about an hour trying to find a way to say that that didn't make it sound like I was trying to make you change your mind, but I couldn't come up with one so I just said it."

"No judgments," she says, hoping her repurposing of his phrase will lighten the mood.

It does.

For about ten seconds.

But the closer they get to the end of the window, the more she realizes how confident she's been that Cole will remote dose her. Only now is she starting to think about what the hours ahead will be like if he doesn't.

29

Kansas Command

The cavern from which Bailey Prescott travels cyberspace and protects their communications is so cramped with server towers and computers there's barely anywhere for Cole, Noah, and Scott to stand.

Bailey doesn't look up from the screen in front of him as they enter.

Sweat threads the sides of his face as he types and mouse-clicks like a speed freak. Thanks to all the heat coming off the surrounding equipment, the room's air-conditioned to a constant winter chill. If Bailey's sweating, that means whatever this is, it's serious.

"You rang?" Cole says.

Holding up one hand, Bailey says, "This is how this needs to work. Nobody talks except to answer my direct questions. I am *incredibly busy* here."

Nobody says anything. Maybe because there wasn't a direct question.

"How many people know about the remote dosing system?" Bailey asks.

"Everyone in this room and the members of The Consortium," Cole answers.

"Does anyone else have the log-in credentials?"

"No, just you and me."

"OK. Well, someone's trying to get them."

"What?"

"Don't ask *me* questions; that's not how this works."

Noah grips Cole's shoulder. "Explain what this means, please. Computers aren't my thing."

"No talking!" Bailey shouts.

Noah repeats the exact same question in a whisper.

"Whispering counts!"

Cole steps out into the hallway. Noah and Scott follow.

"The remote dosing system's password protected," Cole says. "Only Bailey and I know the password, and only I'm supposed to actually use it."

"Yes, thank you, I got that part," Noah says.

"Someone else is trying to hack the system to get it," Scott says. "Do they want to lock us out?"

"Or they want to dose her before we do," Cole says.

"That *cannot* happen." Noah's eyes blaze with anger, as if the idea of injecting another dose of Zypraxon into Charlotte's blood was Cole's idea. "In every animal test when we added a dose to a triggered subject's bloodstream, their brains literally came out of their eyes. As in the actual definition of literally."

"That's never happened in a human," Cole says.

"We've never tested it on one, and we sure as hell shouldn't now."

"I'm not planning on it. Maybe a little quieter, please."

"I'll quiet down as soon as you tell Bailey not to dose her preemptively to fend off this hack."

Cole throws the door open. "Bailey!"

"No talk—"

"Shut up! You work for me. Listen, do not dose her preemptively just to fend these people off."

Bailey's eyes leave the screen. "Then we might not be able to dose her at all."

Shit, Cole thinks, *he was about to do it. Good thinking, Noah.*

"That's preferable to blowing up her brain."

"Her *brain*, what?" Bailey cries. "Oh my God!"

"How much time do we have?"

"Less than ten minutes."

"Hold them off until her trigger window closes, then wait thirty seconds and no longer and dose her."

"Her *brain*? What are you talking—"

"Focus!"

Noah and Scott are standing so close to the door Cole bumps into both of them when he emerges from the room. So, Bailey's never seen the photos of animal test subjects, their eyeballs missing and their eye sockets run through with tentacles of mangled, glistening brain matter. If they get through this, he'll have to give Bailey a better education in the potential perils of a double dose. Cole closes the door behind him.

"How big is the suspect pool here?" Noah asks.

"I can count on one hand the number of people who know about the system," Cole answers. "But only one of them's already in the network."

"Who?" Scott asks.

"Julia. It was her condition for letting us use Bailey after what he did to her last year."

"You think she's behind this?" Scott asks.

"Not after the way she acted earlier, no."

They all fall silent as they mull the implications.

"How long do we have?" Noah finally asks.

"Less than ten minutes," Scott answers.

"And we're counting on Bailey to hold them off," Noah says. It sounds less like a question and more like a warning.

"Yes," Cole says.

"But we don't know exactly what we're holding off. I mean, whoever this is, they could either be trying to make sure Charley can't retrigger or they're trying . . ."

"To kill her. I'm calling Julia."

"You think it's her?"

"No, I think this whole thing's in Bailey's hands, and calling Julia's the only thing I can think of to do right now and I should have done it before. Like months before."

A second later, the three of them are in the conference room.

When Julia Crispin's face fills in the screen, he sees familiar signs of worry around her nose and mouth.

"I was expecting to hear from you sooner," she says.

"This hasn't been my favorite night."

"That makes two of us." Her tone is strained but not accusatory. A positive sign.

"Good. I could use a friend. We have a problem, Julia."

"We have many."

"This one's urgent."

"And you're only notifying me?" She sounds curious.

"You're in our network, as per our agreement."

"That's correct."

"Seen anybody else in there with you?"

"My team hasn't notified me of anything. Why?"

"So it's not you that's trying to access the remote dosing system?"

Julia's brow furrows, and she actually leans toward her computer as if she didn't hear most of what he just said. She's got a great poker face, but she's not an ace at manufacturing emotional displays. Cole's pretty sure this one's genuine.

"I've given no such orders, no," she answers.

"Can you instruct your monitoring team to help Bailey fend this off, whatever it is?"

"You think it's Stephen and Philip, don't you?"

"I don't mean to be rude, but I need an answer. Time's running out."

"Her trigger window . . ." Julia seems to put it all together in a flash. And she pales.

"Julia?"

Julia nods, reaches for her mobile, and begins texting frantically.

"Done," she says.

"Thank you."

"I was wondering when you were going to reach out," she says.

"The hack's only minutes old."

"I'm not talking about the hack," she says. "I know what your father really did to those boys, Cole, and there wasn't a lot of forgiveness to it. I'm assuming Charley does, too."

She doesn't seem to care one whit she's just spilled a dark family secret in front of Noah and Scott. In the end, Cole shouldn't be all that surprised his father confessed a decade-old murder to his mistress. Their affair lasted for years. In the end, it was his father's secret to share. The part that included murder, at least.

"I should probably hop on the phone with my cyberteam," Julia says. "My voice seems to scare them into action."

"Julia?"

"Yes."

"This problem we have. It's very big."

"I know."

"Can we fix it together? When it's time?"

He wasn't expecting anything like an unqualified yes. She's too savvy an operator to grant anyone unconditional compliance. Still, she's staring at the camera for what feels like an eternity. She moistens her lips with the tip of her tongue, looks to the ceiling, and clears her throat. It was her efforts that helped put The Consortium back together, but she did it at Cole's insistence. Now he's asking her to turn against business partners who may or may not have turned against them. But she's also had a front row seat to how Stephen and Philip have acted since Project Bluebird 2.0 commenced, so it's not like the request's coming out of nowhere. Still, maybe it's the kind of ask you make over a quiet, private dinner and not at the end of a frantic phone call. But right now, he's not very hungry and they're in different parts of the country.

"When this is over, we can certainly discuss the road ahead. Just the two of us. In confidence."

With that she ends the call, and Cole takes what feels like his first deep breath in days.

"I'm open to thoughts," Cole finally says.

Noah and Scott exchange a befuddled look. It's like Cole just spoke four words of a foreign language.

Christ almighty, Cole thinks, *am I that bad at taking advice?*

"Thoughts?" Scott asks.

"What's your opinion of Julia's behavior? Do we think she's behind the hack?"

"No," Noah answers. "But you know her better than I do."

"I'm with Dr. Turlington," Scott says.

"Well, my father knew her better than I did, that's for sure."

"Indeed," Noah says. "It sounds like he told her a great deal about your past."

Cole's silent.

"It sounds like your father didn't actually forgive those boys, did he?" Noah asks.

"He did not."

"And Charley knows the real story?" Noah asks.

"She does."

Noah nods, getting it. Scott, however, is still staring at his feet as if he's trying to decipher fading text written on the floor.

"So since the last thing you said to Charley was a lie, and she knew it was a lie," Scott says, "you were basically ordering her to defy you."

"Correct."

"It was more than that," Noah says. "You ordered her to kill whoever Cyrus Mattingly's working with."

"I'm not sure it was an order. More like a . . . vague allusion."

He can't tell if Scott's judging him. He can never tell if Scott's judging him.

Noah, on the other hand, is smiling and nodding. "Works for me," he finally says.

"How much time do we have?" Cole asks Scott.

Scott checks his phone. "Five minutes."

Another silence.

"They're not going to overdose her," Noah says. "They just want to stop her. They don't want to kill her."

"Killing her would stop her," Cole says. "It would also stop Luke, who's heavily armed with some of our technology." Just the thought of being confined in a moving vehicle right next to someone undergoing the cascade of grotesqueries that visits animal subjects when overdosed makes Cole nauseated.

"You want me to get an update from Bailey?" Scott asks.

"No. Let him work."

"Is this really all we can do?" Noah asks. "Wait for Bailey?"

"Well, if you believe in God, you could always pray," Cole says.

"I am," Scott answers, "silently."

Noah seems to consider this for a moment.

"I'm on the fence," Noah answers. "I think I'll just try positive thinking."

30

Highway 287

"Three minutes," Luke says.

Charlotte nods, stares out the passenger-side window, acting like she's searching for a CLEAN RESTROOMS sign and not trying to silence a storm of thoughts in her head.

Thoughts is a generous word for what's plaguing her.

It's more like a quick, angry inventory of what she'll be and what she won't be if she doesn't get dosed again.

Basic firearms training, check.

Hand-to-hand combat training, nope. Cole's been understandably reticent about letting her take martial arts classes when a single strike from her right hand during a trigger window is capable of almost taking someone's head off.

Ability to fight her way free of a reasonably strong captor. Half check. Maybe.

Experience fighting for her life in real-world situations without paradrenaline flowing through her veins. Giant red X mark indicating a value lower than zero.

If they don't dose her, she'll be in a position she's never been in before.

Relying on Luke for her personal safety.

Luke's special, but relying on a man isn't her favorite thing.

Her father forever warped the concept of what protection means. He exposed her to constant risk from dangerous stalkers rather than endanger the cash flow generated by their public appearances, all while claiming he was shielding her from a world that would never truly understand what happened to her. Her grandmother's boyfriend, Uncle Marty, is probably the closest she's ever had to a male protector, before and after her grandmother's sudden death. When she was a teenager, he and some of his friends escorted a particularly frightening stalker to the edge of town when the guy showed up on her grandmother's doorstep. But that was a group effort, and there'd been some women in the crew.

It's not about relying on a man, she realizes. *It's about relying on the man I love.*

She saved Luke's life, and under the right circumstances, she could do it again with ease. It's a unique foundation their relationship's rested on comfortably for a year. But it's the reverse of most of the relationships she's seen, the straight ones anyway. When she and Luke both hear a strange noise in the middle of the night, their feet hit the floor at the same time. Then Charley remembers she doesn't take Zypraxon every day, and although there's an emergency reserve of pills close to her hometown, it's not exactly in her bedside drawer, and the conditions under which she's allowed to access it are strict. But still, she's not the girl who grabs her man's arm when she's startled or afraid. Maybe because her experience of bringing down hideous predators with her bare hands has rewired her brain to the point that she's less skittish and afraid even when she's not triggered.

For a while now, she's felt like an asset instead of a need. After being treated like a burden and a head case by her father, a possible infant serial killer by vast swaths of the internet, and a freak show oddity by large auditoriums full of horror movie fans pretending to care about her case, Charlotte stopped being a burden shrouded in darkness several years ago.

But now, in just a few short minutes, she might become that burden again; a woman who doesn't know when to quit, being patiently indulged by her gun-toting boyfriend.

In the eyes of who, though? Who would judge her like this?

Someone who doesn't care enough about the women who might die tonight, she thinks, *and who gives a damn what they think?*

"One minute," Luke says.

She tells herself not to get nervous if she doesn't feel the symptoms of a remote dose right away. Re-dosing her during a trigger window apparently entails some risks, even though Cole's never told her what they are. He'll probably wait a beat. She's tempted to share this with Luke. But that might reveal Cole's actions to his business partners, and she's guessing he'd like to keep them covert.

"Thirty seconds," he says.

"Babe?"

"Yeah?"

"I'm good without the countdowns. We can just wait for the beep."

"Sure."

As soon as they fall silent, she feels a sudden lurch in her stomach she assumes is fear.

31

"Thirty seconds," Scott says.

Cole can't bring himself to watch the feed from the truck. Scott's assumed that duty. He's standing a few paces away from where Cole and Noah are practically resting their bowed heads against the door to Bailey's lair, like parents eavesdropping on their child.

They'd look ridiculous if anyone was looking at them, but the ground team's long gone, leaving their break room empty, and none of the monitoring techs have dared to leave their stations since Noah threw a chair. The last time Cole checked, they were hunched over their desks like kids in detention.

When Bailey yelps, Cole jumps.

Noah looks into his eyes. They're both trying to decipher the sound, both realizing the other's expression isn't going to help with that endeavor. The sound from the man who holds Charley's fate in his typing fingers could have been joy or terror, no telling unless they throw open the door and ask him. And Cole's not about to do that. Not in this moment, when Bailey's the equivalent of a surgeon with his scalpel pressed to his patient's brain matter.

He can't even bring himself to look at Scott for some indication of whether something went wrong on the feed.

"Cole?" Noah whispers.

"Yes."

"If they kill her . . ."

"We'll deal with them," Cole answers.

Noah looks into his eyes again, and Cole realizes he's satisfied by the answer in part but searching for more.

"Together," Cole whispers.

"You mean you'll deal with Stephen and Philip together or . . ."

"You and I will deal with Stephen and Philip together," Cole whispers.

Noah's smile looks so sincere, Cole's distracted from the other thing he's doing with his body. He's raised one fist in front of him. It's an invitation. It feels childish and silly, but he'd rather feel both of those things in this moment than the stark terror that's defined the last twenty minutes.

He makes a fist of his right hand, bumps it lightly against Noah's. As soon as he does, Noah takes his hand in his and grips it, interlacing their fingers and holding on tight.

A second later, Cole realizes they're both resting their heads against the door and breathing like tired dogs.

32

Highway 287

It's a quieter sound than she expected. Three quick little beeps. Easy to miss over the rush of the truck's tires if she hadn't been waiting for them. Three quick beeps that could mean the end of so many different things at once.

She reaches out, presses one hand gently against the glove compartment, feels its normal give. Presses harder, igniting the sort of achy pain in her wrist any human could expect to feel during such an effort. The glove compartment doesn't warp or crack or give any sounds of audible protest over the truck's engine.

She keeps pressing.

Her persistence must look a little manic to Luke, but he doesn't say anything, knows better than to try to police her reactions in this moment. A minute goes by, then another. And when she feels none of the telltale unpleasant symptoms of a remote dose, she's surprised by what comes next.

Tears, a sudden, hot sheen of them, but enough for her to blink away before they spill. Tears of anger and frustration. Because she wasn't prepared for how this was actually going to feel—a reminder that this power isn't really hers, that it can be taken away at a moment's notice by forces she doesn't always understand and often fears. Worse, a trigger window's never closed on her in the heat of battle like this, with the job left undone. All her discussions of what they might do after this moment seem theoretical now. Empty. Boastful, even.

Now she's just another woman who can easily be killed no matter how much she wants to help other women. She can't save Luke. She can't save anyone.

"Hey," Luke says quietly.

He reaches out. When she takes his hand and squeezes it back, he's got his confirmation that the window's closed, and for the time being it's not reopening.

"It's taking too long," she says.

"What?"

"They should've . . ." *Done it by now,* she wants to say, *done it by now.* She tries to cough the sound of tears from her throat, but it makes her hack, and that makes Luke squeeze her hand even tighter.

Their names. We don't even know their names. How are we going to stop them if Mattingly never gives us their names?

"I'm sorry. I really thought they'd dose me again."

"Well, maybe they will."

"It's taking too long."

He doesn't argue with her.

"I feel like a fraud."

"What?" Luke sounds genuinely astonished. "Why would you say that about yourself?"

"I just didn't expect . . . When the window closed, I didn't expect to freak out like this. I'm sorry. It's just . . . It's not done, Luke. We're not done."

"I know, I know, and we don't have to quit, Charley. We don't. I'm sorry if I said it the wrong way earlier. I just didn't want you to feel like you didn't have a choice."

"I don't." It feels like a painful admission, and maybe that's why she says it with a sob. "I don't have a choice."

"Then we keep going, baby." He brings her hand to his mouth, kisses her fingers. "And we do whatever we can with what we have."

She gives in to every repressed urge she's had since she first laid eyes on him again, squeezes up against him, embraces him as tightly as she can without pulling his arms from the steering wheel. A few minutes before the effort would have crushed him. But now she's doing what she can with what she's got, just like he said.

Just then she feels a sudden piercing headache that turns into blurred vision and a dizzy feeling. Then it gives way to a flush of heat down the back of her neck and along both arms.

33

Kansas Command

"*I* am the *Prince* of *Awesome!*" Bailey Prescott cries.

"There's no such thing," Cole responds. "Get off that chair."

Bailey ceases his strange jig, which has made him look like a leprechaun crashing a hip-hop music video, and steps to the floor.

"Oh, by the way," Bailey says, "we no longer have a remote dosing system. It was a 'destroy the village in order to save it' kinda thing."

"Nothing like a Vietnam reference to inspire confidence during a combat situation," Noah says. "So we can't dose her again?"

"Moot point," Cole answers. "Remote dosing's a one-shot deal. There's only so many nanobots I'm willing to inject into her blood at one time. Bailey, next order of business. Boot Stephen and Philip from the system. Pull their feeds, block their access. I don't care what it takes. Throw them out and keep them out."

Scott says, "And if they ask why?"

"Tell them we've had a massive security breach and it's for the protection of everyone."

"And if they say it wasn't them?" Scott asks.

"I'm not saying it's them. Yet. Right now we're doing this to keep their hands clean. That's the official story."

Scott nods.

Bailey says, "Can I at least have a Nutella break?"

"Charley and Luke are forty-five minutes from Amarillo. Pull Stephen and Philip out of our network right now. When this is over, I'll provide you with a bathtub full of Nutella at the posh resort of your choice. Got it?"

"The bathtub part sounds a little dangerous, but the resort part I'm—"

"Bailey, now!"

"You know, you really yell a lot for a guy who always wears shiny shoes."

Noah clears his throat and steps toward Bailey. "Bailey, good job. You are a bright light in the darkest corners of cyberspace." He pats Bailey on the crown of his head. "You are to be commended for your good work, young sir."

Grinning, Bailey sinks into his chair.

Noah turns to Cole with a cocked eyebrow, as if to suggest people skills aren't that hard if Cole would just try. If that's what Noah thinks, he should try working with Bailey year-round.

"Thank you, Dr. Turlington," Bailey says. "It's nice to be appreciated."

"Yeah, I know, Dad's so mean and never understands." Cole gestures for Noah and Scott to follow him into the hallway.

Once they're out of Bailey's lair, Cole says, "We're not staying here."

"You want to evacuate Kansas Command?" Scott asks.

"No. The three of *us* are not staying here. We're going to Amarillo. In my helicopter. But first . . ."

Cole looks to Noah, who's trying to hide his excitement and failing, then to his security director. "Arm him," Cole tells Scott.

Both men stare at him silently, expressionlessly. They all know a line is being crossed here, and no one's quite sure what comes after, but neither of them seems eager to hold that line in place. Not even his security director.

A few minutes later, Noah's emerging from the guest bedroom having donned his windbreaker. It hides the gun holster at the small of his back. The guards flanking him aren't sure of whether to treat him as a prisoner or an asset, and their confusion is evident in their jittery poses.

Cole can't blame them. It's all happening pretty fast.

By the time Cole, Noah, and Scott step out onto the front porch, he can hear the familiar chop of his helicopter's rotary blades starting up inside the pen behind the hangar.

What he's not prepared for are the three people waiting for them on the front porch. Shannon Tran, Tim Zadan, and Paul Hynman have all left their stations. They're standing off to the side of the front door. Because they're not exactly blocking Cole's path, their poses don't seem hostile. But still, after recent events, it's impossible not to assume this is part of some conspiracy or plot to thwart what remains of this operation.

Shannon steps forward, and he notices she seems on the verge of tears. "Please," she says, "please just make sure she gets through this OK."

The concern in her voice seems to resonate in Tim's and Paul's facial expressions. Cole's so startled by this display that at first he can't come up with a response. Given how much they know, it's amazing how quickly these three people seem to vanish from his thoughts the minute he looks in another direction. Given what they have access to, they're under as much surveillance as Charlotte. But maybe it's not just fear of professional repercussions that ensures their secrecy. It's what he's seeing right now.

They care about Charlotte Rowe and believe in what she does. Deeply.

Cole opens his mouth to give the most appropriate and simplest response he can think of. *I will.* Then he thinks better of it.

"We will," he says.

Shannon bows her head and takes a step back. She looks exhausted. Maybe it's the last few weeks catching up with her, or maybe this small, simple act required all the bravery she has.

Then he and Noah and Scott are hurrying toward the helicopter pen behind the hangar, into the blast of wind from its spinning rotary blades and toward the very real fact that he just made a sincere promise he might not be able to keep.

34

Marjorie's wondering if she should have put a third Pyrex dish of Frito casserole into the oven—her boys always arrive hungry—when she hears a familiar, comforting rumble drifting toward her across the fields outside. She wipes her hands on her apron, picks up the shotgun from where she's rested it against the wall next to the oven, and moves to the sink and the window above it.

She's turned only a few of the lights on inside the house in case someone does coming looking for those shitass kids, but she doubts any of her boys will take that as a sign of trouble. And her hopes are confirmed when she sees the twin headlights of a large truck mount the gentle crest in the road leading toward the barn. The truck continues on its practiced path, around the barn's northern side before it parks in back, hidden from the county road and just up from the slope to the wooded creek bed. The landscape's got some low and gentle folds, but save for the little ravine cut by the creek, it's mostly flat prairie, surrounded by lots of arid property nobody would want for anything besides privacy and space.

There's a skip in her step as she leaves the house. The boys purchase used trucks each year so they can be easily disposed of after the planting's through, so there's no telling who made it first just from the sight of what they're driving. That means she's always pleasantly surprised by the first arrival. There's usually no rhyme or reason to it from year to year, no pattern that might illuminate the character, or at least driving skills, of her boys. Some years it's Cyrus, others it's Wally, then Jonah for a stretch.

But when the cargo area door of this particular truck rises with a familiar rumble, the surprise comes when the man inside doesn't jump to the dirt and throw his arms around her. Instead, Jonah Polk turns his back to her and sinks to a seat atop some plastic crates she knows are housing whatever gifts he's brought her. Besides the seedling.

"Jonah?"

Her handsomest boy looks crestfallen, staring into space. For a second, she thinks he might not have snagged a seedling at all. Which means his heads-up call would have been all lies. Then she sees the divider door is open and there's a pair of slender bare feet strapped to the gurney in back. They're still.

She scans his Wrangler jeans and red-and-black plaid shirt for signs of a struggle but doesn't see any. He's got a haircut now that reminds her of bankers; a neatly combed side part that seems to be well in place.

"Jonah." This time it's not a question. He recognizes the sound of a command. It looks like he's aged more in the past year than most of the years prior. But there's no getting up into his truck without help, and when she waves one hand at him, he jumps to the dirt, wraps an arm around her waist, and half hoists her inside by letting her rest most of her left side against him as she pulls herself up with her right arm.

Their little dance seems like a great prelude to an overdue hug, but no such luck.

She has to remind herself he doesn't shrink away from her when he's angry; he does it when he's ashamed.

Marjorie's enormously proud of the Head Slayer every time she sees one assembled. It's a marvelously simple invention, and durable to boot. And it's her design. They've only had to replace one of them twice since they've started.

Did something go wrong with this one?

It looks like the seedling tried to get free by jerking her head upward and that somehow jammed the insertion tube farther down her throat than it should be able to go. The results were predictably disgusting. Even the rats still clumped in the cargo area above have moved to one side and gone still, as if huddling together will protect them from the stench of vomit that's surely wafting up the tube. The same vomit that apparently choked the woman to death.

Technically it's not a violation, and so technically, Marjorie shouldn't withhold her affection from Jonah, which after so many years of almost perfect obedience is the only punishment she'd consider meting out in this moment. What the boys aren't allowed to do is get unnecessarily rough with their seedlings or use them as sexual playthings along the way. A planting is designed to purge dark instincts, but not by letting them run wild. It marries them to structure and purpose. It's an extraction, not masturbation, as she's said on more than one occasion, provoking boyish giggles every time.

So technically, this is the seedling's fault, and it's because she refused to heed the lesson the Head Slayer's designed to teach. Silence is strength; screams are not.

"I should've watched closer," Jonah says. "I got distracted."

"By what?"

"Music. I was playing music."

"Well, that's not against the rules."

Marjorie slaps the side of the woman's face, feels a satisfying absence of response. Her head jerks slightly to one side, but it's the tight strap across her forehead that makes the move feel reflexive and quick. A living person would be trying to spit out the tube or cough away the vomit. The seedling's scrawny, with sharp, visible cheekbones, a high forehead, and a loose tumble of bottle blonde hair studded with dark roots.

"She's not a hooker, is she?" Marjorie asks.

"No, ma'am."

"'Cause hookers *are* against the rules."

"I know, too easy."

"How'd you get her, then?" Marjorie's hoping a bit of small talk will pull Jonah out of his funk. Nothing seems to calm a man down like asking him to explain a complex, mostly physical process. Especially if he thinks he's in control of it.

"She was mouthing off to a cashier at a gas station outside town. Claiming she got overcharged for cigarettes."

"Smoking's bad for you."

"I know, ma'am."

"Well, she doesn't have to worry about that now, does she?"

"I'm sorry, Mother."

Shame on her for wanting to draw this out. Maybe it's shooting the little tweakers that's done it; made her feel older, weaker, needier. The yearlong wait between plantings, even though it's served them well for so long, is getting too long for her old heart and her old bones. And now she's desperate to exert some small measure of control over one of her boys.

And what she said a moment ago is still true.

Technically Jonah didn't violate any of the rules. Sure, he should have watched the seedling more closely, but he's never had one die on him before a planting. That particular distinction belongs to Wally. He's lost two. But that's because he goes for the real fighters, the real screamers. For a while there, Wally's seedlings had such tough outer shells, the group thought he was abducting them from the middle of literal, screaming bar fights. Two of them he beat to death because they just wouldn't quit trying to escape. Of course, both times, Cyrus and Jonah ribbed him, calling BS on Wally's weary accounts. In both instances, the footage from the cameras they all used to monitor their seedlings while driving revealed Wally was telling the truth. Oh, how her boys had whistled and clucked their teeth over the aggressiveness those seedlings had displayed before Wally bashed their heads in.

But for a while there, Marjorie was concerned they were part of a larger trend.

Was Wally turning self-destructive? Worse, would the other boys be encouraged to compete with his recklessness?

It doesn't seem to have been the case.

The planting's better with three, but it can work with two just fine. Three's better, though. A trio makes a nice, satisfying harmony.

"Come here," she says.

Head bowed like he's sixteen again, he moves to her, steps into her embrace, and then returns it.

"Show me what else you brought," she says.

A moment later, they've closed the divider door so he can present the gifts he brought her without distraction. A new police scanner—that's a nice surprise; the old one's been busted for a few months now—and a framed watercolor of Lake Coeur d'Alene; she and her daddy went there on a road trip once when she was little, before her mother destroyed their family. It's so dear Jonah remembered her affection for the place. She's only mentioned it a few times. The problem is, she hates watercolors in general. Why make everything look so messy and vague when a good artist can re-create pretty much anything with a pencil? She doesn't say any of this to Jonah, of course. He already feels bad enough about the seedling. And it's a thoughtful gift. And he's her boy. Her beautiful boy.

He's answering questions about a music box he bought her at a garage sale when they both hear a sound like muted thunder. A few minutes later another large pair of headlights swings around the northern wall of the barn. It's a truck of similar size and make to Jonah's, maybe a little rustier and more battered, and it's headed straight for them.

35

How could Zoey have thought this was a victory?

So she didn't panic during the last stretch of the ride, didn't scream, didn't cause that hideous device to send a thick black snake sliding down the tube wedged into her mouth. But she's still a captive, and the last steps that brought her out of the truck and to this cold place included a blindfold and the kind of harness you put on a difficult dog. Using a cord attached to the harness's back, they lowered her into what must be some sort of pit, then they lassoed her to a thick column of wood.

There were whispers and other sets of footsteps besides her abductor's. So she's outnumbered now. But the scariest change of all is the one that seemed like a relief at first. She's not gagged. There's not even anything covering her mouth. But that can only mean one thing. There's no one to hear her scream. No one who can help anyway.

The blindfold's pulled from her eyes.

Relief floods her before she can think better of it.

A woman's backing away from her, a stout woman with deep lines in her face and sensitive-looking blue eyes complementing a patient expression. Her gray ponytail is long and thick and pulled forward over one shoulder as if she wants the world to see how much time it took her to braid it. Zoey sags against the giant wooden post they've tied her to in a cruel parody of a romantic embrace. The words pour from her; she can't stop them. She's explaining the whole thing like a hyperactive child trying to recount her first day of kindergarten to her parents. Only there's no kindness and excitement in the tale, just misery and pain and degradation, and she needs someone else to know about it. She's not sure why that's her instinct in this moment, but it is. Because if this woman's here to rescue her, Zoey should tell her everything because she's a woman and a woman will under—

Zoey's forehead explodes with pain. The woman's done it, grabbed the back of Zoey's neck and knocked her head against the wooden post in a precise and effective blow that seems practiced.

"My boy says you spit in his face," the woman says. "That true?"

Mother, she realizes. *This is the mother he mentioned in the truck, and here I was hoping for a skeleton in a dress.*

Dread so total moves through Zoey's body that her sob comes out more like a wail. She feels cold all over, realizes it's the wooden post she's tied to. She thought she was already hugging the thing, but apparently she'd been resisting her confines more than she realized, and now the leveling effect of realizing this woman is not her rescuer has drained every last bit of energy from her body.

"Screaming fight in the mall, then you spit in my boy's face. What's wrong with you, girl? Go ahead and answer. I won't hit you if you answer truthful."

Zoey didn't say anything about her fight with Jerald in the mall. Her abductor must have told this woman, and hearing it mentioned now makes her dizzy. It seems like a moment from a previous life, and the idea that anything might bridge the two other than her memory makes this place all the more horrible.

"Why?" Zoey asks.

"Why what?"

"Why did he . . . why is he doing this?"

"Oh, well isn't that a damn fool question. You draw all kinds of attention to yourself and then you cry when someone answers the call? That's rich, girlie. Let me guess. You were expecting a knight in shining armor? Well, he'd turn into a monster, too, after having to listen to your screams."

"Why are *you* doing this?"

The woman grabs the back of Zoey's head, gathering her hair in her fist, hard enough to pull at the roots. "Because women like you make me ashamed, that's why. Ashamed of your ignorance and your selfishness. You refuse to see what you do with your careless words. And if I can't wipe women like you from the earth, maybe I can teach you a lesson before you go. Maybe you'll come back smarter. In a new life. Because you're not keeping this one, little girl. All you can do is decide how you want to leave it."

"A fight . . ."

"What?"

Zoey's scanning their surroundings, trying to look dazed and confused so the woman doesn't realize what she's doing. She wants to keep her talking, but she's having trouble forming questions.

"He picked me because I had a fight with my boyfriend?"

Dirt walls, at least ten feet high. A patch of lofty ceiling high above the opening to this narrow pit. Maybe a barn or some other type structure. Could someone of Zoey's size climb the surrounding walls, or would the dirt start to come lose under her clawing hands and feet? It looks dry, but clumpy. This hideous Mother took a ladder down, but no doubt they'll pull it up as soon as she climbs out. If the woman climbs out.

If I live to see her climb out.

"He could hear what's inside of you," she whispers. "He could hear the destruction in it. And that's how he knew you were another foul, warped woman who tries to break men down into something she can keep in a drawer like jewelry. Because you don't understand them and you don't deserve them. The world loses everything they could be because of women like you. Because you bully and assault them with your hysteria and your abuse of your voice. And no one protects them. No one. Except for me. I can't save them all. Just my boys. But I can sure as hell get rid of you."

Zoey Long has never been this close to death. She's never been in a bad car accident; never come close to drowning in a swimming pool; never gone home with a guy who tried to prevent her from leaving the moment she wanted to. For every hour that she spent in that psycho's truck, the prospect of death was pushed a little further away. But now it's here, pressing in all around her on the dirt walls of this pit, riding each of this insane woman's hate-filled words.

Her new captor smiles faintly, and Zoey thinks she must be pleased by whatever expression despair and defeat have brought to Zoey's face.

"There you go," the woman whispers, "you're getting it. Silence is your friend. Silence is your strength."

Some people might call what Zoey does next a scream. Zoey wants it to be a roar, a monstrous, deafening roar that comes from deep inside of her, from a place uncovered by the knowledge that she won't escape this. That she won't live to see another dawn. She takes a few deep breaths, then unleashes another so loud the woman stumbles backward and actually grabs the dirt wall behind her with one hand to steady herself. It's not high pitched or piercing, the sounds Zoey is making in this moment; it's a symphony of anger and rage.

Her throat burning, she runs out of breath and feels the threat of sobs. Releasing all her anger has left her with nothing to fight her despair. In this moment, at least.

"Save your breath," the woman says. "You're going to need it if you want to decide how you're going to die."

The woman climbs the ladder. When she reaches the top, the killer who drove Zoey here helps her up by one arm before pulling the ladder out of the pit.

Her abductor and his crazy mother vanish from sight. Then a second later, some sort of plastic tube is placed right at the edge of the pit's opening, inspiring memories of rats and snakes and the terrifying prospect of what this pit might soon be filled with.

36

From this distance, downtown Amarillo looks like it has about two substantial high-rises in its skyline. There's a lit-up logo atop the tallest one. Charlotte thinks it's for Chase Bank, but she's too far away to be sure. Still, anyone familiar with the city should be able to recognize its familiar profile from this view, so Luke and Charley wheel Mattingly's gurney through the divider, then turn it sideways so he can see through the open cargo area door and across the empty field toward the small, sparkling city on the dark horizon.

With one hand, Luke turns Mattingly's head, trying to give him a better look. But the leather strap across their captive's forehead pulls back hard. Charley would help, but although Cole has remotely injected her with a dose of Zypraxon, she's not triggered yet and doesn't want to disabuse Mattingly of the notion that her hands are always strong enough to break rocks.

Luke removes his Glock, places the barrel against Mattingly's slightly upturned temple, then undoes the forehead strap with his other hand. Eyes closed, his lips tremble from the threat of tears.

"Open your eyes, Cyrus," Charley says.

Instead of obeying, he whispers the lyrics to "The Sound of Silence" under his breath like it's a life-giving mantra. She steps forward, crouches down where Mattingly can't see her, and whispers into his ear. "Open your fucking eyes or when I find your crazy family, I'll tear them limb from limb while you watch."

Another minute goes by, then another. It's late and the field's empty, but it would be reckless to keep sitting practically out in the open like this while Cyrus takes his sweet time deciding whether to give them the address of Mother's hell house. She pats Luke on the shoulder, gestures to the divider door. He holsters his Glock, refastens Mattingly's head strap, then lowers the cargo area door.

They step into the rear compartment formerly occupied by the gurney, standing where they've both got Mattingly in sight.

"Get the Thunder Derm," she says.

"One strike will kill him."

"You're not using it on him."

Getting her meaning, Luke meets her eyes. "I thought we were saving your trigger window for when we really needed it."

"We need it."

"There's a risk of the trigger gap not being—"

"Luke, I did it with a bear trap six months ago. The Thunder Derm will work."

"Yeah, but *I'll* have to do it."

"That's correct."

"And then we're racing against the clock again."

"Luke," she whispers, taking his arm, "there are two women out there in trucks like this, headed for we don't know what kind of hell. We're *already* racing against the clock."

"You're right. And I hate it."

She can't blame him. The memory of her last trigger window closing is still fresh and painful.

"It could kill you," he says, but he's studying Mattingly, wincing a little at the man's continued perversion of the haunting Simon and Garfunkel classic.

"No, it won't."

"How can you be sure? I mean, what if my aim's off?"

"For one, you have great aim. Two, you won't have time to kill me before I trigger. You'd have to sever a nerve that controlled my breathing, and I'd have to be deprived of oxygen long enough to go brain dead. Just don't fire into my neck or anywhere above my waist, for that matter."

"Yeah, but you've got arteries all over."

"You won't be able to drain me of enough blood to kill me before I trigger."

"And if you don't trigger?"

"Realizing I'm not triggering will be enough to trigger me. Luke, I have thought this through. There's no other way. The only thing that's worked on this crazy son of a bitch is watching me snap metal. And if this phone call doesn't work, that's the only way we'll get this woman's location."

And I'm sorry but this is part of the job you signed up for, she wants to add, *an important part.* But that might be more than necessary.

Luke grunts like a ten-year-old being told he has to do his homework before screen time. "Fine."

The Thunder Derm's inside its case, resting against the wall not too far from where Mattingly lies bound and singing under his breath. As Luke carefully removes it, Charley listens to Mattingly's crazed voice, wondering with increasing dread if the man's truly lost what mind he had. She pushes the thought away as Luke approaches, giant Thunder Derm awkwardly in one hand. For an instant, it seems as if the goofy-looking weapon—it's not a weapon, she reminds herself; it's a medical device that only works on her—is the size of a regular gun and somehow Luke has shrunk before her eyes. She laughs.

"I'm glad you think this is funny," he says once they're nose to nose.

"It's not. I'm sorry. Just . . ."

"What?"

"Never mind. Let's do this."

"What if you imagined it?" he asks.

"Imagined what?"

"The remote dose. Maybe you were just so upset that you wanted to believe it but it was just a headache from the stress or—"

"Luke!"

Startled by the sharpness in her tone, he looks right into her eyes. While she's got his attention, she reaches down, grabs the Thunder Derm's barrel, presses it to her right knee.

"Do it," she whispers.

"Fine," he whispers back.

He sinks to the floor on one knee, the other leg bent, bracing himself for impact from the device's significant recoil.

Once again, the tennis ball–cannon sound makes Mattingly yelp, but this time it also sends an arc of pain up her body so white-hot it feels like her scalp's going to blow off. She can't remember the last time she's really screamed, but she's screaming now. And then comes the miracle that changed her life. It's like a bucket of ice water poured over fire, as muscle, skin, veins, and damaged nerves heal in a miraculous instant. The pain is doused as quickly as it conquered every nerve in her body, replaced by a hallelujah chorus of tingles throughout her right leg, flights of tiny angels working miracles within.

Now that she can breathe again, she looks down, sees Luke's been knocked on his ass and is staring up at her goggle-eyed, as if not fully convinced she's triggered. When she sees the splashes of blood on his face and hands, she wonders if she hasn't actually triggered, if she's just in shock. But when she looks down at her leg, she sees the bullet-size wound healing through the hole the Thunder Derm blew in her jeans.

It worked just like they hoped it would, only they forgot one thing: all the vials they left in the SUV, full of her paradrenaline-filled blood. Which means there isn't one inside the Thunder Derm, so what blood the device did manage to yank from her body before she triggered just spurted all over Luke.

"Sorry," she mutters.

Luke's so relieved she's not bleeding to death he hasn't even noticed how badly he's been slimed.

Most importantly, Cyrus Mattingly, psycho of the open road, has stopped singing under his breath. Maybe it was the sound of the Thunder Derm that did it.

"Showtime," Charley says.

37

When Marjorie went down the ladder into the silencing pit, Jonah and Wally were setting up the cement mixer, but the bellowing of that pathetic sow brought them to the pit's edge, and that was a good thing because she needed help ascending the ladder's last rungs.

Now that Jonah's laid the tube right next to the opening, he asks, "Should we start?"

"Not till Cyrus gets here," she says.

"When did he call?" Jonah asks.

"He hasn't yet."

Jonah's tempted to say something cutting about his brother, she can tell.

"Don't you go casting suspicion on him just 'cause your ride didn't go as planned," she says.

Instantly ashamed, Jonah says, "Yes, Mother."

You could argue that what Marjorie just said to Wally's seedling wasn't entirely truthful. A seedling can't choose how she dies, just the length of time it will take. She can live for as long as she can scream; the minute she falls silent, the cement mixer starts disgorging its thick, wet contents into the pit all around her. If she marshals enough strength to start screaming again, they shut the mixer off, buying her a little more time for her to reflect on how she's abused her voice throughout the years. But in the end, the seedlings realize there's no point, that they're just delaying the inevitable. In the end, they all die in breathless silence, which is exactly what they deserve.

"Is there food?" Wally asks.

"Casserole needs another few minutes. Show me what you brought."

She's excited to see Wally's gifts. Wally, her sweetheart, remembered how much she hates watercolors, and he ribbed Jonah plenty about bringing her one. But their teasing seemed as innocent and playful as a game of hide-and-seek. The bond between them is as strong as ever, despite their having been apart a year. She has herself to thank for this, she's sure.

"Watch the pit," Marjorie says to Jonah before she and Wally step out the barn's back door.

Just then the phone rings.

"That'll be Cyrus," she says. "You boys stay put and mind the seedling."

They agree with quick nods, and then she's striding toward the house.

The phone's still ringing by the time she enters the kitchen. Good thing the call drew her back. Another few minutes and the casseroles would burn.

"Hello?" she answers.

"Good evening, ma'am."

At the sound of Cyrus's voice—his straining for calm, slightly phlegmy voice—all the muscles in Marjorie's upper back instantly tense with enough strength to send little flames of pain up into her neck. Something's wrong. So wrong she's pretty damn sure he's not about to give their official thumbs-up code by asking for the mythical Sheryl Peterson.

"Hello . . ." Marjorie repeats because it's the only thing she can think of to say.

"Is Patricia Whitney there?"

Marjorie feels as if a dart's been fired at the center of her chest, and for a second or two, she's convinced cardiac arrest is on its way.

The name Patricia Whitney is part of no code they've agreed to, good or bad. But she is the name of one of the most violent seedlings they ever captured. She was Jonah's girl from a few years back, snatched outside Albuquerque. A real fighter, and the only seedling to ever slip her confines and require a bit of chasing before they managed to get her into the silencing pit. She's also long dead, and Cyrus can only be going off book now because something on his end has gone very, very wrong. Catastrophically wrong, the kind of wrong for which they've got no agreed-upon code.

Her hand trembling, Marjorie goes to hang up the phone when the voice of a woman she doesn't recognize says, "Hang up on me and Cyrus dies. Slowly."

38

Charlotte was sure her captive would warn his beloved Mother no matter what he promised, so why not use that to her advantage? It would ensure he called the right person. Then Charlotte would have a chance to butt in and speak to the supposed architect of this nightmare.

When she first pulled the phone away from Mattingly's ear, their captive tried to get off a few warning shouts, but just then Luke shoved the barrel of his Glock into the man's open mouth. Too late, Mattingly went to close his lips, ending up kissing the gun before he opened his mouth wide to avoid the taste of the gun's metal.

His mouth's still wide, teeth bared, but he's gone silent. So has the woman on the other end of the phone, save for her strained breathing.

Charlotte speaks fast, delivering words she rehearsed in her head a thousand times during the last hour of the drive. The worst outcome in this moment will be if the woman hangs up before Charlotte can make an impact. "I'm not the cops and I'm not the FBI. I'm not any kind of law enforcement. You probably won't be able to understand what I am and what I'm capable of, so try to understand this instead. What I want is very simple. You're going to release the two women you're holding captive into my care, and then I'll let you have your boy Cyrus back."

"I don't know who this is and I don't know what you're talking about, but you seem very disturbed. I have to go now."

"You go and I will be at your ranch in five minutes and I will rescue those women from those pits myself and anyone who gets in my way will die."

A total lie, given she still doesn't know where the ranch is, but the woman on the other end doesn't know that. But the detail about the pits has silenced her, probably has her frantically wondering what other facts her beloved Cyrus has revealed.

"I'm tempted to call you crazy, but that's a very strong word and I'm a kind person."

"Well, I'm not. Crazy is what Cyrus will be after I break every bone in his body and leave him to scream himself to death under a great big Texas sky. Kind of like what you're about to do with those women, right? Now, are you going to be a real mother to this boy or not? Let's figure this out; then we can call it a night and go our separate ways."

Not for one minute is this lunatic going to agree to a hostage trade. But Charlotte's after something very different.

"I see," the woman finally says.

Not a denial. Maybe Charlotte's getting somewhere.

"Do you?" Charlotte asks gently.

"You think I'm capable of terrible things, I guess," the woman says softly.

"Your son says so."

There's brittle silence in response, and that's good. That's what Charlotte was hoping for.

"You want to know how I got your boy, ma'am?"

"I'm growing concerned for your mental well-being, so if it helps you to talk to me . . ."

Yeah, right. Charlotte laughs under her breath. She's not about to reveal the digital mechanics of the Red Tier and how a man like Cyrus ends up on it. But in this instance, a neat summary should suffice.

"Every few months your boy buys the kinds of chemicals you need to help a human body decompose down to nothing in about no time flat, and he's got no other use for them. Now if everything he's said about this little family game of yours is true, you don't need him to get rid of anybody. You bury your victims under a bunch of concrete. So if he's buying this stuff on his own, that means he's doing a little killing on the side. And to hear him tell it, the whole point of your sick little game is to help him purge all those instincts under your supervision. Because you're his 'mother.' And so it's your job to make sure he only kills once a year. And the way you want him to. Well, news flash. Your little game ain't workin', Momma."

Silence from the other end.

"Thanks for letting me get that off my chest," Charlotte says. "I feel saner now. Do you?"

There's no telling exactly what the silence on the other end means. But the woman hasn't hung up; that's the important thing. Has this revelation loosened the thread between her and Mattingly as much as Charlotte hopes it did? The next few seconds will tell.

"Why do you think I wouldn't be able to understand what you are?" the woman asks.

"Most people don't."

"Why's that?"

She's not about to define her powers for this woman over the phone. Much better to fill her with the fear of the unknown.

"Because I'm from some place you don't understand," Charlotte says.

"I see. Well, if you came from hell, you shouldn't have any trouble going back now, should you, missy?"

The call ends, just as Charlotte predicted it would.

At her signal, Luke pulls the Glock's barrel from Mattingly's drooling, half-open mouth. The man lets out a wail like an abandoned calf.

"You told her . . . How could you . . . You told . . ." It's not the same question trying to take different forms, she realizes. It's two questions fighting to get out at once. One, how did Charlotte know about the murders he committed on the side? Two, why did she tell his mother about them? Charlotte doesn't plan on answering either one. But it was her plan to expose Mattingly to the terrible realization that when push came to shove, his beloved mother would cut him loose without a second thought. Maybe it was a lucky guess on her part, but only a self-obsessed psychopath would be foolish enough to believe an entire family of psychos could maintain a unified front under the slightest external pressure. She saw living proof of this in how quickly Daniel and Abigail Banning turned on each other after their arrest.

"Sorry, sweetheart. Your mother just dropped you like deadweight." Charlotte crouches down next to the gurney. Avoiding the piss stain that stretches from his crotch to his right thigh, she runs one hand gently down Mattingly's right shin. "Guess you're going to have to find a new family. If I let you."

Brow furrowed, lips clenched, Mattingly's attempts to hold back his despair are failing fast.

Now that she's split the bond between Mattingly and his mother, it's possible the woman's cutting and running. If she's panicking, it won't be easy for her to erase all evidence of what she's done. And that's exactly what Charlotte hopes she's created on the other end of the line—an all-out panic. True, chaos could endanger the lives of the captives, but if the other option was letting this family's terrible ritual play out unimpeded, was there any better choice?

If, in the end, the best thing she can do is lead whatever team Cole's been forced to send after them right to this crazy woman's doorstep, then so be it. She doubts they'll suddenly stand down when they're within sight of whatever horrors lie on this woman's ranch. Unless Bailey pulled a miracle, her blood trackers have been broadcasting their location every minute since she destroyed their TruGlass feed.

"I've had my own experience with mothers," she says quietly. "They can be very disappointing."

Especially if they kill your real mother and pretend to be yours, she thinks. *Which is kind of your speed, shithead.*

"Fuck you," Cyrus Mattingly whispers.

"Or fuck *her*. I mean, she's the one who just picked your brothers over you, isn't she? How hard would it have been to set up a meet and then come at me with guns blazing? But apparently, you weren't worth the risk. So what do you think she loves more than you? Planting seedlings, or your brothers?"

"Fuck you." This time it's a whisper riding the threat of a sob.

Charlotte gives him a second to catch his breath, during which she places a gentle grip on his right shinbone, a reminder of her strength. Which, she realizes, is probably not going to help him catch his breath. But that's OK.

"I need an address and directions, Cyrus, and I need them now."

Eyes screwed shut and spitting tears, Mattingly shakes his head like a defiant little boy.

She looks into Luke's eyes.

He stares back. She knows the expression well. Jaw slightly clenched, eyes wide and unblinking and seemingly disconnected from the rest of the tension in his face. It's the look he gives her when he's biting his tongue, tamping down on an acute need because he knows expressing it forcefully will distract from a decision that's hers to make. Sometimes it's the look of desire he gives in the bedroom, when he's horned up but not sure it's the right moment to instigate. Sometimes it's the look he gives her when he knows she's forgotten something from the grocery store that he needs for the recipe he's cooking that very moment, but he doesn't want to jump down her throat because she was doing him a favor by running to the store at the last minute anyway.

She knows what he wants now. He wants an enhanced interrogation, the kind only she can administer.

But will he really be able to stomach it? The last time he saw her unleash relentless violence against other humans, his life was at stake.

This time's different.

Lives are at stake here, too. Two of them, apparently. Just not his.

Luke nods. It's almost imperceptible. Maybe he was fighting the urge and then gave in. But he made the gesture nonetheless, and that's all she needed to see.

With a simple twist of one hand, she breaks Mattingly's right shin.

By the time she breaks his left foot, Cyrus Mattingly is adding information to his screams.

Marjorie races for the barn, seeing fleeting shadows out of the corner of her eye. Shadows of ghosts. One ghost, in particular. Her wicked mother, brought forth from the beyond by the hateful words of that woman on the phone. *Killing on the side . . .*

Her boy. Her boy Cyrus betrayed her, betrayed all of them. She sees him luring back-alley whores into some dirty pickup truck, fondling their breasts after they're dead like a bargain-basement serial killer. After all she'd built for him, all she'd given him over the years, rescuing him from orphanhood at Caden Ranch, teaching him to focus and channel his dark impulses, he'd been killing on the side all this time and somehow it had landed him in the clutches of whoever that evil woman was.

It's like her mother's racing alongside her as she runs for the barn, hissing that strange woman's words. *Your little game ain't workin', Momma.*

When she explodes into the barn, the boys are still filling the cement mixer and they whirl at the sound of her entry.

"Get her out of the pit and into the truck now," she says.

"What?" Jonah says.

"Someone's got Cyrus and it's bad, real bad."

"They're coming?" Wally asks.

"I don't know."

"Well, we can't just up and leave and—"

"We have to. Now! Get her in your truck and put the Head Slayer on her and quit arguing with me. Jonah drives. You stay in back with her."

They're standing atop dozens of concrete-encased graves, and they all know it. Jonah looks to the ground briefly as he approaches, arm out. "Momma, you gotta calm—"

"Don't you fucking get it?" The hysteria in her voice has amped her words to a pitch that's terrifyingly near to one of her mother's fatal screams. "He broke the rules! He was killing on the side and someone got to him 'cause of it."

The shock of this seems to wash over them in a second wave. Or maybe they're noticing the way she's flinched at what looks like a flash of motion past the barn's half-open back door; a flash of motion she's sure is wearing one of her mother's old floral-print housedresses.

"We put everything that's for killing in one of the trucks and we go. Now. Get her out of the pit!"

Without another word of protest, her boys get to work. The boys she has left anyway.

Zoey can barely make out the words. But the terror in the crazy old woman's voice has stirred something in her she was on the verge of losing.

Hope.

Then the ladder drops down into the pit once more and down it come two men, her abductor and one she doesn't recognize. Both descend with a determination that brings the chill of dread back to every bone in her body. And the one she doesn't recognize is holding something strange. At first, she thinks it might be another hideous contraption like what they gagged her with. But it's more ordinary than that.

It's the harness they used to lower her into this pit. No sooner has she noticed it than the man she's never seen before is putting her blindfold back in place.

A few yards from the entrance to the ranch Cyrus Mattingly directed them to, Charlotte sees something in the truck's headlights: deep, fresh tire tracks cutting through the last section of the ranch's dirt road before vanishing into the blacktop of the road they're traveling. She thinks she can see which direction they headed, but she's not sure.

She cries out for Luke to stop and he does, but she's jumped from the passenger-side door before the truck stops moving, and the run of skipping steps she takes as soon as her feet hit the road would probably have broken the ankles of a normal person.

Behind her, the truck groans to a halt, brakes squealing, as she bends down and studies the tire tracks in the headlights.

Luke starts toward her, Glock out, shooting glances up the dark road. There's a gentle swell in the earth that keeps the ranch house hidden from here, and if Mattingly told the truth about everything, it's a good ways up the dirt road.

"They ran," Charlotte says.

"Canadian River's that way," Luke says.

By the time she'd made her way up to his wrists, Mattingly told them that if Mother and his brothers made a run for it, they'd probably use back roads heading north of the property, through the isolated landscape where a few creeks intersect with the Canadian River's east–west passage above town. The reform school where she'd first recruited all three boys had been close to this area before it burned down, and all the boys have experience hiking and horseback riding through its small, dusty canyons. None of the canyons are very deep, but they were the few hiding places amid a landscape that was mostly flat.

"Is it one truck or two?" Luke asks.

"Looks like one."

"Go."

"What?"

"Take the truck and go. See if you can catch up with them. I'll check out the ranch."

"Isn't this the part in the horror movie where everyone splits up and the audience screams?"

"In the horror movie, the hero can't break the killer's neck with one hand. Go, Charley. If they ran, they ran with those women. No chance they'll leave them behind so they can tell everything they know."

"And if they did?"

"That's why I'm going to secure the ranch."

"Luke . . ."

"Charley, take the truck and go. Give it thirty minutes. If you don't catch up with them, come back and we'll search everything together."

He's got a point, but leaving Luke to search the ranch alone turns her stomach. But it won't be much longer before the team following them descends out of the sky in a blaze of military-issue lights. If that wasn't the case, she'd never leave him alone here in a million years. She doesn't care how good his training is.

"Charley, go. You're their only hope."

You, not us.

If she lingers on this moment, regret will slow her down even further. So she just nods and walks past Luke and carefully steps up into the driver's seat of the truck. Only once she's pulled the door shut does she remember she's still got Cyrus Mattingly in the back. She's not going to dump him now. That would give Luke a distraction as he searches the ranch alone. And besides, the guy's got two broken feet and he's strapped down like a shrink-wrapped chicken breast.

The first time she drove while triggered, she almost broke the gas pedal.

This time, she's had practice.

And that's good.

Because she plans to go fast.

39

"Turn the headlights off," Marjorie says.

"I can't, Momma. It's too twisty."

"Do what I'm—"

"Momma, there's no moon; we'll go off the road!" Jonah's voice sounds as frightened as hers did back in the barn. Maybe it was a mistake to have him drive given his recent failure. Wally's always been a cooler operator. But Wally's seedling is Wally's responsibility; he's been with her for hours, knows all the tricks she might try if she sees their flight as an opportunity. As for Jonah's panic, it can only mean her mother's ghost is doing far more than just dancing at the edges of Marjorie's vision. She's infecting their minds, their souls. And it's all Cyrus's fault. His betrayal has weakened them, cast cracks through all the majesty and meaning of what she built for her boys over the years.

She's once more riding beneath the Texas skies her father taught her to love, but she's never felt more distant from him. Because her mother's back, and she's not just screaming. She's filling Marjorie's mind with hateful curses she's fine-tuned during the years she's spent in hell. *Your game ain't workin', Momma.*

On the camera linked to the truck's cargo area, he can see Wally holding on to the wall next to him to stay balanced, loaded shotgun in one hand. A few feet away, his seedling's strapped to the gurney and gagged once more, staring at the ceiling overhead. Something's wrong with the look in her eyes, and Marjorie realizes there's not enough fear there. There's hardly any at all.

"She knows something. She's in on it."

"Who?" Jonah asks.

"Wally's seedling. Look at her. She *knows* something. This whole thing, it's some kind of trap. We've got to question her. Find out what she knows."

"We will. Let's just get some distance between us and the ranch; then we can find a highway and keep going. I can take us all the way back to my place in Albuquerque—"

"No, no. They might know about all of us. None of us can go home."

"Where do we go, then?"

"We just drive."

Jonah shoots her a look. She doesn't look back because she doesn't want to see whatever's in his eyes—the fear, the confusion, the disappointment. It's sinking in. They're homeless now. Who knows how much Cyrus told? Cyrus failed them, but that means she failed them, because Cyrus was her boy.

"Forget it," Marjorie says.

"Forget what?"

"I don't give a damn what the little bitch knows. We kill her and dump her and the other one in Chicken Creek. Then we keep going. If we don't know where we're stopping, I'm not towing all that evidence along with us."

"That's just fi—"

But Jonah never gets a chance to finish the sentence because just then headlights flash in the side-view mirrors, briefly blinding them both. It's a box truck about the size of theirs, and it's gaining on them fast.

Cyrus's truck, she realizes, *but is Cyrus driving it?*

Marjorie's first cry drowns out the sound of the first few strikes Jonah levels against the metal wall behind him. That's Wally's cue to get ready to fire back at their pursuer.

Charlotte almost missed them. She was heading due north on the paved county road when she saw what looked like tiny lights moving through the dark off to her right, like tea candles floating atop a vast lake. At first she thought they were security lights atop the gate of a distant property. But then they winked out briefly, and when they came back they were farther to her right than they should have been if they weren't on the move themselves.

She hit the brakes, turned the truck around as fast as she could without tipping the thing over. She and Luke had both trained on vehicles of this size as prep for this operation, but she'd never once thought things would escalate to the point where she'd actually have to drive one.

Now, she kills the headlights, but it's way too dark to drive without them. Maybe if the dirt road wasn't so narrow and serpentine. The landscape's not mountainous, but it's not perfectly flat, either, the kind of arid stretch that was carved by eons-old bodies of water that have long since dried up.

Maybe she's got the wrong truck, but she doubts it. There's nothing out here except the prospect of concealment and escape. And while she hasn't been able to get a good look at the truck's length, the cargo door looks about the same size as the one on the truck she's driving now, and the metal's also dilapidated and rust splattered. Maybe it's a bigger truck overall. From this angle, she's not sure. But like Cyrus's, it looks anonymous, easily disposed of once it's served its purpose. Both of them bought for cash so the purchase wasn't traceable.

Any doubt she's honing in on the right target vanishes when the cargo area door in front of her suddenly rises, followed by a shotgun's blast. She braces for impact or for the windshield to explode. Instead, the truck's hood dents upward from shrapnel flying inside the truck's nose. The guy shot straight through the grille, and the impact just sent a shudder through the vehicle's carriage that she feels in the steering wheel, even though she's gripping it lightly to keep from accidentally tearing the thing in half.

Another blast. Sustained, grinding noises follow, telling her this shot did real damage to the engine's moving parts. It's a smart strategy. The front of the truck is a big, reliable target, unlike her shadow behind the windshield.

She releases the steering wheel, turns to face the passenger side, then straightens her left arm like a baseball bat before striking it against the windshield. The glass shatters.

By the time she crawls headfirst through the broken windshield, black smoke is streaming from underneath the edges of the truck's hood. But the man standing in the half-open cargo area door can still see her through the twin clouds. His shock is evident in his paralysis. He's holding the door up with one hand, but it seems he's forgotten he's holding his shotgun in the other.

The vehicle under her is losing power and speed, but she's on all fours on the hood now. When the distance between them starts to widen, she leaps.

In the shooter's scramble to pull the cargo door shut in her face, he drops the shotgun. It spins away from his feet, then out into the night.

By then, she's airborne.

The pure sensations of what comes next are what she imagines it feels like to dip your upper body in wet concrete. Her vision blacks out as she hits the door; then in widening tendrils, she can see what must be the inside of the truck's cargo area: a divider door just like the one that walled her in, a metal floor. Someone's howling like an injured wolf, and she's sure it's the shooter. If she hasn't injured him, he's losing his mind. The metal that's molded around her head and neck starts to yield in various spots like some quick-drying substance that's now cracking and flaking. There's cool air on her right arm, making it feel exposed. It must have punched straight through the cargo door on impact, while her left arm feels like it's coated in some-thing vaguely molten but also very cold. Because it seems like the quickest and most efficient thing to do, she shakes her upper body like a dog trying to dry itself and hears what must be a dozen pieces of metal clunk to the floor around her. The man's screams intensify to the level of madness.

Standing now and freed from her metallic shroud, Charlotte sees the shooter. He's curled up against one wall as if he thinks he might be able to crawl through it and away from her. Jaw trembling and nostrils flaring, he's watching what must be dozens of cuts instantly healing along her face and arms.

What she does next seems to be too much for him to bear.

She looks him in the eye.

Without a second thought, he crawls to the hole in the cargo door and jumps out into the night. She spins just in time to see him hit the road legs first. In his delirium, he must have thought the truck's speed would give him a running start. Instead the momentum breaks both his legs and sends his body into a grotesque series of somer-saults before the shadows swallow him. For the first time, she sees the truck—her truck, *Mattingly's* truck—is long gone, careened off the side of the road and into the dark night somewhere.

Behind the divider, she finds a terrified, wild-eyed woman strapped to a gurney just like the one she was tethered to for hours on end. The woman hasn't seen any of what she just did to the cargo door or the final choice her captor just made, but no doubt, she's heard all of it. Charlotte expects a frightened struggle when she starts tearing the leather straps free, releasing the woman's forehead and then her ankles. But the woman goes limp and numb, as if she realizes instantly that no one who wanted to hurt her would try to free her. Not right now. Once she can, the woman sits up, starts pulling on the gag. Charlotte's afraid this process will require more precision than can be managed in the bouncing cargo area of a speeding truck, but if it's what the woman wants, who is she to stop her? After what she's been through, she deserves any release she can get.

Hacking and coughing and clawing at it with her now free hands, the woman spits the gag out; then Charlotte pulls it from her lap and casts it aside so she won't have to look at the hideous thing anymore. That's when she sees the body. The other woman is lying in a fetal position on the floor against the metal wall; the gag's slid across the floor and is now resting against her back. Her lifeless arm is milk pale, and she jostles from the cargo area's movements with unmistakable deadweight.

Charlotte wants to scream, but instead she runs Luke's words back and forth through her head until she can breathe again. *We'll do what we can with what we've got.*

"Are you hurt?" she asks the woman before her, the one she can still save.

"Hurt . . ."

"Injured. Are you physically injured? Can you move?"

The woman shakes her head and swings one leg to the floor as if to prove it.

"What did you do to him?" the woman asks. "He was screaming so loud."

"He's gone. He jumped."

"Are they gonna stop?" Hours of agony are preparing to split the woman's sanity in two. "Are they *ever* going to stop?" she wails.

A clanging sound, like a giant rock has hit the underside of the truck. Then another—the clanging of something very large underneath the cargo area. Metal engaging with metal?

Or disengaging?

They're trying to uncouple from the cargo area, she thinks. *They're trying to cut us loose.*

On a major highway, being in a loose trailer would be dangerous because of other traffic, but there'd be enough roadway to recover if they didn't get struck. Out here on this narrow, winding road, they'll go plummeting into a ravine, and the only way to protect the woman she came here to save would be to throw her arms around her. Which could also crush her.

Charlotte throws herself against the wall between the cargo area and the passenger cab and drives one arm through it. If she can manage to grab the back of the cab and hold it for a few minutes, she can release it at a time of her choosing, maybe keep the cargo area steady. At the very least, whoever's driving will realize he can't cut the cargo area loose so easily. Maybe then they'll resort to pumping the damn brakes and trying to bail on foot. That'll give the woman behind her time to recover and the truck time to slow to a stop.

But when she punches her arm through the metal wall, she doesn't feel open air on the other side like she expected. Instead she feels something slick and warm. She was wrong about how the truck's built, wrong about her belief that the cargo area was about to be released. There's no gap between the cargo area's back wall and the passenger cab at all. She didn't see the truck from the front as she approached it, and the violent sounds of rocks impacting the underside of the cargo area tricked her into believing it was a different style of truck from the one Cyrus put her in. Thanks to this misunderstanding, she's just driven her arm straight through someone sitting inside the passenger cab.

She withdraws her arm. It's covered in thick black blood turning deep red as oxygen hits it. What at first looks like tufts of fabric are actually splinters of human bone pulverized by the quick passage of her fist.

Agonized howls pour through the bloody hole she just left in the metal wall. A man and a woman's screams combining in a terrible harmony. Both are so piercing it's impossible to tell which one of them she just injured. One thing's for sure. If they're both screaming this badly, the one who's driving won't have control of the wheel for much longer.

"Get down on the floor in a ball," Charlotte shouts.

"*What?*" the woman she just freed screams.

"Do it! I'm trying to save your life. We're about to—"

Before the rest of the sentence can leave her mouth, the cargo area's floor starts wobbling like a ship at sea. Either one of the tires has blown out or the driver's losing control.

Wide-eyed, the woman hits the floor and curls into a ball, right in the corner the divider makes with the cargo area's side wall. Knowing she'll crush the poor girl if she throws herself on top of her, Charlotte drops to her knees next to her instead. There's nothing to grab on to so Charlotte punches one fist through the cargo area's sidewall, then another through the divider, and does her best to hang on to the resulting holes as if they're grips without pulling on them. But it's a useless effort. When their world turns upside down, the woman's thrown into Charlotte's chest, and Charlotte has no choice but to close her arms around her as they both go flying, praying she doesn't break the woman in half while trying to save her life.

40

In the darkness, it's possible to believe it was all a nightmare.

In the dark, she can convince herself she didn't really see an arm come bursting through Jonah's chest as he drove. Didn't hear his keening, throaty screams as he spit blood and tried to stare down at the impossible eruption of gore his own torso had become.

In the dark, she's her daddy's girl again, poised on the edge of her bed after dusk, waiting for him to bring her a moon pie, a sign they're about to go stargazing.

In the dark, Marjorie Payne realizes she's chewing dirt.

Blindly, desperately, she unbuckles the seat belt that's twisted up around her like a tentacle. A mistake; she drops sideways against Jonah, whose body's been half consumed by the twisted remains of the cab's driver side, which, she now realizes, struck earth first after they went off the road. The only mercy in his awful posture is that his horribly bent limbs conceal the wound in his chest.

But she can't get out unless she pushes herself away from his corpse, then steps on his soft limbs. That's the only way she can reach the upturned passenger-side window so she can pull herself free of the cab. Ignoring the shards of glass slicing into her hands, she gets her chest free, flops up and onto the door like a fish leaving water, then manages to swing one leg free, then the other. When she lets herself drop to the wet dirt, it's as if all her energy has been exhausted and suddenly her age makes itself known in every bone in her body.

She crawls. It's the only thing she can do that will take her farther from the truck and the terrible noises coming from inside it. There are no screams now, just a deep, persistent scratching that reminds her of the time a rat got stuck in the wall behind her oven. Only bigger.

If she hasn't knocked out several teeth, she's jostled a bunch of them loose, and she's afraid to lift her face from the mud and find out just how many. But she does, and that's when she sees her blood running through the stubborn rivulets of creek that haven't gone dry yet.

She can't go any farther, and so she rolls over onto her back because she'd rather see what's coming for her than sob facedown on the ground.

She refuses to believe what she sees next: two hands, a woman's hands, it looks like, pressing against the narrow lip of what remains of the windshield, pushing outward from within a space too small and mangled for a human to fit. A living one, at least. But what else besides life could be animating the arms that just shoved the large spiderwebbed piece of glass from where it's been clinging perilously to its bent frame?

The hands look spotted, but they're moving without any hesitation or fatigue that would indicate injury. The spots, she realizes, aren't exactly round. They're misshapen. They're bloody openings in the woman's skin. Marjorie blinks what must be a hundred times before she can accept what her eyes are telling her—they're all changing size; they're each getting smaller. Healing.

The hands reach out, grab the edges of the windshield's bent frame, and pull.

One eye stares wildly, and Marjorie realizes it looks that way because the skin's separated above and below it, revealing glimpses of white skull underneath. The woman's hair looks like it's been pulled back because her entire scalp has been pulled back, revealing a blood-spotted patch of skull where her forehead should be. But that terrible wound is healing, too. And as she pulls herself out from the truck's demolished front cab, yanking one leg free of the wreckage at an angle perfectly parallel with the rest of her body, so parallel it should break her hip, Marjorie sees the eye looks normal now.

And then the woman is standing beside the truck that should have crushed her to death. She looks healthy and vital in the fractured halo of the one headlight that's still illuminated. That's when Marjorie wonders if she's dead and if this is how death plays out for everyone—you pick up from where you left but in a realm where all things are suddenly possible.

The woman's footsteps splash through the water as she approaches. Her expression is rageful. If this is death, if angels are real, then the young woman standing over her might be an angel of judgment.

"Who are you?"

It's a stupid, useless question. Marjorie knows it's the woman on the phone, the woman who broke Cyrus.

She crouches down, gazing into Marjorie's eyes.

"I am your mother, returned from the storm," she answers.

And that's when Marjorie breaks the promise she just made to herself.

She screams.

"How many?" Charlotte asks.

The woman's old age, her pathetic sobs, her mangled broken state; none of these things inspire pity or sympathy, and Charlotte wonders if she's gradually losing those emotions altogether or if she's heard and seen enough on this long, terrible night to keep her focused on what this woman truly is.

"How many bodies are on your ranch?" Charlotte asks.

When the woman doesn't answer, Charlotte gently rests one hand atop her throat. The woman's eyes go wide, but her sobs don't stop.

"I will make you hurt a lot worse than you do now unless you tell me where to find every body of every woman you killed."

"*I* didn't kill anyone—"

"You did. You're a murderer just like your boys."

"I made them . . ."

"What? You made them what?"

"Better. Once a year. They . . . they only had to do it once a year because of *me*. That was the rule . . . I gave them *rules*."

"You found them when they were teenagers. Cyrus had only killed animals. You made it easy for him. You taught him how to kill people."

Women like your mother, she wants to add, but it's possible this vile woman really does believe Charlotte is her mother reborn and that's why she's so talkative. Charlotte's not going to steal the illusion from her. Yet. And it looks like the old woman isn't hearing what Charlotte does: the low approach of a large helicopter, massive rotary blades chopping air.

"The barn," the woman whispers. "They're in the barn. Under it. Planted. Silenced. Where they belong."

"How many?"

The old woman stares into her eyes with a coldness and a focus that seem to laser through whatever physical pain she's in.

"Not enough," she says.

Before Charlotte realizes what she's done, the woman's head is twisted to one side; her right ear where her face just was, her glassy eyes staring at the slope the truck went over. It was a slap, that's all. Just a reflexive, sudden slap, the kind someone might unleash in the heat of the moment and either atone for or regret for the rest of their lives. But this one snapped the old woman's neck like a doll's, the force of it leaving her right cheek misshapen.

The helicopter's closer now; it's probably the Black Hawk. But there's another sound, softer. Footsteps. Halting, slow.

After the truck had landed and once it was clear the woman she'd tried to protect hadn't broken any bones, Charlotte told her to flee out the back of the cargo area. She didn't want her to see what Charlotte might have to do to the people in the cab. But the woman obviously wasn't content to wait. Maybe she sensed a life being snuffed out in the blink of an eye.

It's too dark for Charlotte to make out her expression, so there's no telling if the woman saw her kill Marjorie Payne.

"Are you for real?" the woman finally asks.

"Yes."

"Well . . . shit."

She's in shock, Charlotte can tell.

Slowly, Charlotte moves to her, fully expecting her to scream and run. How else would anyone respond after everything she's been through, after everything she's seen Charlotte do? But instead the woman stays put, swaying slightly, backlit by the truck's headlight.

"What's your name?" Charlotte asks.

They're a few feet apart now.

The woman doesn't look like she's about to bolt, but now that they're close, Charlotte can see her trembling lips and her flaring nostrils, her failing attempt to fight tears. Despite the terrible jostling she endured when the truck went off the road, her long mane of raven hair is still matted in the shape left by the gag's hood and the gurney. And once Charlotte's close enough to see her big, tear-filled brown eyes, she's overwhelmed by the pain in them. Hours and hours of degradation bubbling up inside of her. And Charlotte knows it's shortsighted, but it suddenly feels as if the goal of saving this woman was a selfish thing, because now the woman will have to endure the pain of being a survivor.

"Thank you," she whispers.

All the usual responses seem unbearably inappropriate. *You're welcome. Don't mention it.* None of those will suffice, not in this moment.

Before she can pause to consider all she's revealed to this woman and the potential consequences, she offers her something else. "My name's Charlotte. Charlotte Rowe."

"Zoey," she answers through the first sob, as if saying her name out loud again after all she's been through is a brave and defiant act, her first move to begin collecting all her abductors tried to take from her.

When Zoey starts to sob, Charlotte offers comfort with the same hands she just used for murder.

41

In the first light of dawn, the Black Hawk looks wildly out of place where it landed not far from the barn in the middle of the isolated and desolate property that from the air looks like a patchwork of desert. If you were flying overhead and didn't have any idea of the events that had led up to this moment, you would think the chopper had made an emergency landing here while on its way to take part in some elaborate military exercise.

But as his own helicopter—an Airbus H155 with a leather-padded passenger compartment housing him, Noah, and Scott Durham—swoops low over the property, Cole spots the other evidence of the small battle that took place here.

The pilot lands them close to the barn's entrance.

They've already given him a rough list of the dead—the owner of the property, Marjorie Payne, dead. Jonah Polk, one of the other drivers, dead, remains collected from inside the cab of his truck. Wally Shore, killed by a botched attempt to escape from the getaway truck.

But still, the response team's refusing to provide a total body count. "Not until you see the barn, sir," was their response when Cole asked why. As for his super-secret ground team, he ordered them to fall back as soon as the Black Hawk caught up with the getaway truck. So for now, Charley and Luke have no idea armed mercenaries were waiting to assist once they pinpointed Cyrus Mattingly's intended destination. When the stand-down order came, the ground team had been closing in on Marjorie Payne's ranch as Luke cased the place by himself. As soon as Cole can clear Charley and Luke out of here, he'll have the ground team enter the scene to help with the cleanup. Which sounds like it's going to be a nightmare.

Dreading the surprise in store, Cole steps from the helicopter. There's a hand on his shoulder before his second foot hits the ground. He brought Noah because he thought they could use his combat skills. But the fight's over, and now his presence might cause more problems than it solves.

"Just wait here," Cole says.

Clearly stung, Noah averts his eyes and sinks back against the leather bench seat.

Two response team members advance as soon as they see Cole approaching the barn. One's strapped with an assault rifle he never got the chance to use, the other a Glock in a hip holster clearly visible under his windbreaker.

They start to explain what's waiting for him inside, but he holds up a single hand and they go silent. He's too busy observing what he can already see. It's a large concrete mixer, or what's left of it. The damn thing's the size of a small car, and there's a large plastic tube wrapped in its wreckage. Grooves in the earth between the barn's half-open double doors suggest the machine was dragged to its current position by a giant. That makes sense. Charlotte's actions often look like a Titan's handiwork.

"Watch your step inside," the guy with the assault rifle says.

Cole walks through the double doors and into the barn.

There are no horse stalls or interior structures of any kind, and Cole wonders if there were previously and Charley tore them all to pieces. He doesn't see any piles of splintered wood, however. No, what she's torn to pieces is the ground itself, and that ground, it turns out, is mostly concrete. Evenly spaced squares of concrete that travel the entire length of the barn; multiple rows of them, about three rows in all, but it's hard to tell because what mostly fills the barn are piles of large concrete chunks. With the strength of a god, Charlotte has managed to dig down into most of them.

As he walks carefully between the concrete piles, he sees that each hole reveals something stomach churning. In some, there are mummified arms. In others, desiccated heads. It's a gallery of bodies entombed beneath the barn's floor. The awful scene reminds him of those death casts from Pompeii, but those were created by pouring plaster into the cavities once occupied by bodies long since decomposed. What he sees here are actual corpses unearthed for the first time by the impossible strength of Charlotte Rowe's hands.

Then he sees Charlotte. She's rocking back and forth, her arms looped around her bent knees, powdered head to toe with concrete dust. Her second trigger window closed a few minutes ago, and he wonders if that's the only reason she stopped.

"Charley?"

She doesn't even look at him. It's quiet enough for her to hear him, he's sure. His helicopter's blades have powered down, and the only sound is a gentle huff of wind that blows through the half-open barn doors, lifting little twisters of concrete dust into the threads of early-morning sunlight pouring through the slats in the barn's roof.

"Charley?"

I have broken her, Cole thinks before he can stop himself. *Broken her as surely as she tried to break these long-buried bodies free.*

He approaches her until only a few feet separate them. She doesn't look up, doesn't recognize his presence, and—worst of all—doesn't stop rocking gently back and forth.

"Charley?"

No response. He scans their surroundings again, sees a few untouched squares of concrete in the barn's floor she hasn't gotten to yet. Will she ever?

Will they?

He says her name a few more times. The results are the same. She's never gone into shock before. But during their last operation an unexpected explosion caused her to lose consciousness while her entire body regenerated from burns that would have instantly killed a normal person. Maybe this silence, this retreat inside of herself, is a part of her process now.

Or I've pushed her too far.

Charlotte dug until the concrete wouldn't give underneath her clawing hands anymore. When she crawled her way up out of the last hole she'd dug, her fresh scratches didn't heal right away, and her fingers were bleeding like a normal person's. She told herself she just needed a minute to regroup, to recover, to catch her breath with lungs that were no longer superpowered. But as soon as she gazed into the middle distance, her vision went misty, and when people spoke to her thereafter, she heard them and even formulated answers to their questions, but those answers got stuck on a tape loop inside her mind.

It's her fault she ran out of time. Once she realized she wouldn't be able to remove the bodies from their concrete graves intact, that her incredible strength was ill suited to such a delicate and intricate task, the sheer volume of the dead she was uncovering started to overwhelm her. She had no idea what condition they'd be in when she started to dig. She's not a chemist. She'd hoped for something close to preservation. While there were some variations to their conditions, for the most part they were mummies. Some badly decomposed, whole body parts missing.

If she couldn't extract them, she would reveal them. That's what she'd decided. The crown of a skull or a bent arm. A distress flag, no matter how grotesque. Something to say *I am here and I will not be forgotten or erased by the madness that took root on this property.*

"Charley?"

Cole's here. As usual, he looks like a menswear model amid the horror.

"Zoey," she says.

"What?"

"The woman I saved. Her name's Zoey Long. We take care of her. We figure it out."

Cole nods.

"That means we don't drug her and leave her on the side of the road and make the world think she's crazy."

"I get it," Cole says.

Steadying her voice as much as she can, she points one dusty finger toward the expanse of pits before them. "We learn their names, too. Every last one. And we let their families know. Or so help me God I'm never doing this again."

Cole turns to survey the awful sweep of the barn's freshly opened floor.

He's hesitating.

She's waiting. She'll wait for hours if she has to.

"Deal," he finally whispers.

The men standing guard outside the barn part before her like she's the president, clearing a path to the Black Hawk, where Luke stands waiting for her next to the open door. Zoey Long's already inside, wrapped in a blanket, watching her approach. She looks alert, present inside her skin, and that fills Charlotte with relief.

Cole wants them airborne as soon as possible. She can hear him giving orders to the response team members behind her, telling them to scrub all evidence they've been there, including removing the third truck they found left on the property, the one in which the slain victim presumably died. Luke's helping her into the Black Hawk when she hears one of the ground team guys ask Cole, "What's the cover story?"

Cole says, "This time we're not using one."

For a second, she thinks that means Graydon Pharmaceuticals is about to out itself to the world as a freelance hunter of serial killers. But that can't be it, and she's too tired to figure out what else it might be. Inside the helicopter, she settles onto the bench seat. Luke sits down next to her as the door slides shut next to him. He slips her headphones on, puts on a set himself. He's explaining how they're going to make a refueling stop on the way back to Kansas Command, but she's not paying much attention. She's just spotted something outside.

The Black Hawk is lifting off above the parched landscape of Marjorie Payne's ranch when their angle shifts and the bright-orange sunlight reflecting off the windows of Cole's personal helicopter leaves the glass. Now she can see inside the passenger compartment, where a familiar face is watching the Black Hawk rise into the dawn.

It's been six months since she's heard his voice, even longer since she's laid eyes on him. Once she called him Dr. Thorpe; then, when they became more comfortable with each other, Dylan. Then, after he tricked her into taking a drug that could have killed her, he became a nameless monster until his real name was revealed to her. Noah Turlington.

Luke falls silent when he realizes what she's seen.

When she looks to him for an explanation, he says, "Yeah, there's also that."

And Charley realizes she might not be too tired for anger after all.

42

Lebanon, Kansas

"Sit," Charlotte says.

Noah Turlington obeys.

Leave it to Cole to lace the grounds around his top-secret command center with paved walking trails and little clusters of benches shaded by sycamore trees like the one she's sitting under now. While most of the vast farmland next to the airstrip is just empty fields, these landscape ornamentations around the hangar and the main house will mislead unwanted visitors into believing this place is a corporate retreat dropped in the middle of America's rural heart. Although with Cole's levels of security, she has trouble imagining unwanted visitors getting anywhere near here.

Noah's windbreaker is more suited to the cool breeze kissing the property than the heavy woolen blanket Charlotte wears over her shoulders. But ever since they finished her examination in the infirmary, she's been clutching it for security, not warmth.

Luke offered to attend this uncomfortable sit-down with her, and while she appreciated the gesture, she needs to do this one alone.

"He says you helped," she finally says.

"Cole said this?"

"No, Santa Claus."

"I see. So we're going to do sarcasm."

"Dr. Turlington, it will be a very long time before I'm interested in what you think of my tone."

Noah bows his head and clears his throat. What he cleared it for, she's not quite sure, because he doesn't say anything further. Maybe he realizes he overstepped and got this meeting off on the wrong foot.

"You weren't supposed to be here," she finally says. "Ever. That was the deal I made with him."

"With Santa Claus, you mean."

When she glares at him, he gives her a smile that's probably earned him far too many things he doesn't deserve. Fine. She'd prefer charm over condescending superiority. If it's a choice between one or the other. But does it have to be? She's the one who called this meeting, after all.

"Well, he's kind of like that for us, isn't he?" Noah asks. "The man who makes all our dreams come true."

"I'm not sure I'd call this a dream."

"I didn't say it was a *pleasant* dream. It's just beyond the realm of the everyday, that's all."

"Sure, OK."

"Charley, can we . . ."

"Can we what?"

"Can we maybe agree on some sort of suitable punishment I can go through? Some benchmark I can meet that will satisfy you in some way? I mean, unless we're all going to find some way to call it quits, which I don't recommend, we're going to have to work together somehow."

"I didn't agree to work with *you*. You were supposed to be off in some lab trying to turn your drug into something Cole could actually sell to the world. I was working with him, not you."

"Because he's a saint and I'm not?" Noah asks.

"Because he didn't almost kill me in Arizona. You did."

"I understand."

"Do you?"

"You can't forgive me for lying to you, and I don't expect you to."

"That sounds about right."

"Good. Then in light of that, maybe you can stop asking me to apologize since you're never going to accept any apology I give."

"I don't need an apology."

"What, then?" he asks.

"Answers."

"Fine."

"The woman you tested Zypraxon on before me, after you left Graydon."

"I didn't leave Graydon. I was forced out."

"You weren't. Cole didn't fire you. He just shut down your labs."

"That's Cole's version."

"Stop deflecting. The woman you tested it on before me. Who was she?"

"I'd rather not discuss this." He's staring right at her when he says this, a poor attempt to make it seem like some empowered assertion of selfhood rather than a curt dismissal.

"I bet you wouldn't. There's a lot I wouldn't have discussed with you back in Arizona if I'd known who you really were."

"That's fair, I guess."

"You guess? You spent months picking my brain, trying to find anything that could let you manipulate me into taking your drug. And now you're going to stonewall me?"

"Here's the answer you want." The charm's gone. So's any pretense of cold remove. There's an intensity in his eyes that seems genuine. "I didn't know you'd live. I'd love to make up a story about how I'd fine-tuned Zypraxon to the point where I was sure it wouldn't be a risk. But that would be a lie, and I've told you enough lies.

"I had a theory, a theory that was mostly conjecture. Every test subject until then, every one, including the woman before you, had experienced violent physical trauma throughout their lives. It was the one thing every failed test had in common, and it suggested their neural pathways might have been altered in similar obstructive ways. You hadn't. You'd been near violence, but it had been hidden from you. You were never the direct victim of it. But none of that was enough to make me confident you'd survive the test. That's not why I picked you."

"Then why?" she asks.

"I picked you because of what it would mean if you did survive. Not just because the drug had finally worked, but because of who you were. I knew you'd see the potential. You'd be my ally, and together we would change the world. And I was almost right."

"Is that what we're doing?" she asks. "Changing the world?"

"Ask Zoey Long."

He's given her some version of these answers before, but up until now he's always overstated how confident he was she'd survive her first dose. Should she count that admission as a victory? Is there ever going to be any such thing as a victory when it comes to Noah Turlington?

"If you're going to change the world with someone, you should ask them first," she says.

"Noted," he says with a nod.

"Cole should have asked me before he brought you here."

"I think he could benefit from hearing that."

"He did. In no uncertain terms."

"Good."

"So what were you doing while we were out there anyway? Lecturing him on my brain? Trying to predict my next move?"

"That was just his pretense for bringing me here."

"What was the real reason?" she asks.

"His business partners are turning on him, and he needed to see where my loyalties lie."

"And where do they lie?"

"With you. And after what I saw him do on your behalf, with him."

"I see. So it's going to be like this from now on?"

"Like what?"

"You're going to be more involved."

"I think so. But that doesn't mean you have to forgive me. It just means you'll have to be able to stand the sight of me now and then without retching."

"Thanks for clearing that up."

"I should get back. We've got a lot to review. Not the least of which are your test results."

She doesn't protest, and mercifully, he doesn't pat her on the back or the head or give her some other physical gesture of farewell she isn't ready to receive.

He's a few paces from the bench when she says, "His business partners."

Noah turns but says nothing, his face a fixed, blank mask.

"What did they do? Aside from telling me to stand down."

"There was an attack on your remote dosing system," he answers.

"An attack?"

"An attempted hack. They were either trying to lock us out of the system so we couldn't re-dose you or they were . . ."

"Trying to give me a double dose."

"Perhaps."

"That could have killed me."

"We know. That's why we stopped it."

Her mouth feels dry, and her heartbeat feels like it's reduced to a dull patter. She's always seen Cole's mysterious business partners as a potential obstruction but never as a direct threat to her life.

"Well, are we going to find out which one it was?" she asks, her voice reedy.

"We think it was two of them."

"That's not what I mean."

"I'm listening."

"Are we going to find out if they were trying to stop me or kill me?"

"That's actually become my job," Noah says with a smile.

"I see. And if the answer is . . . the latter?"

"Then they're both going to die."

There's not a trace of hesitation in his voice and not a hint of it in his steady stare. As if he's grown satisfied she's impressed by this promise, he turns and starts back toward the main house. She's still watching him depart when suddenly he stops.

"Charley?" He hasn't turned around.

"Yes?"

At the sound of her voice, he looks back over his shoulder. "My sister."

Her expression must betray her confusion. Almost a year ago she was given a file on his background. Though it contained some information about the father who'd whisked him out of the country after his mother was murdered by the Bannings, she can't remember anything about a sister.

"The woman I tested it on before you. She was my sister."

She realizes her mistake. By letting him know which answers she still wants from him, she's given him something to bait her with.

"She knew the risks," he adds.

"Lucky her."

"No. I'm afraid she wasn't."

He wants her to ask more questions, she's sure of it. Wants her to ask him back to the bench after he made the pretense of politely excusing himself in the interest of getting more valuable, world-changing work done.

She's not ready to give in.

Not yet.

"See you around, Dr. Turlington," she says.

Then she turns and makes a show of staring up at the sycamore's breeze-rustled leaves until she can no longer hear his departing footsteps.

IV

43

La Jolla, California

Cole can't remember the last time Julia Crispin was in his house. Maybe for a holiday party, but it's been years since he's had one of those, primarily because they obligate him to rub shoulders with his mother's dreadful friends. He's certainly never hosted her for anything as intimate as brunch for three on his glass and steel terrace overlooking La Jolla Bay. But that's what they're doing now. Dining on crabmeat salad in the sparkling Southern California sun just a few weeks after exposing the horrors of Marjorie Payne's ranch to the world.

He's shared meals with her before, however, and knows that she's not moving her latest potential bite of crabmeat around her plate because she's nervous. She's just the type of person who assesses every bite of food before she deigns to let it pass her lips.

"I still think it was a bold call," she says for the third time. "We could have just wiped the farm off the face of the earth, and nobody would have been the wiser."

"It's a ranch, and that would have meant wiping the victims off the face of the earth. Their families would have gone the rest of their lives without knowing what happened to them."

"Still, perhaps we could have concocted some sort of cover story rather than turning it into one of America's greatest unsolved mysteries."

"I'm telling you, the condition of the bodies didn't allow for a good cover story. How many car wrecks do you want me to fake?"

"Which bodies? The victims?"

"No, the killers."

"We could have vanished them."

"Then the families of the victims wouldn't have had the slightest sense of who was responsible. The only thing worse than knowing your loved one's been buried in a pit of concrete is not knowing what happened to the people who did it."

"Still."

"If you're worried about someone figuring out what actually happened, forget it. People love a mystery. They love it so much they'll speculate their way past the truth at a hundred miles per hour. A story full of holes invites everyone to fill in the blanks with their absolutely bullshit explanations."

He leaves out that his own digital services team is currently flooding Reddit threads and any other public forum they can find with nonsense conspiracy theories designed to throw true crime junkies far off the scent of anything truthful.

"I'm seeing stuff online about helicopters in the area that night," Julia says.

"Men in black. Even better!"

"Cole, be serious."

"I'm very serious. We've honored Charley's wishes. The remains are being excavated and identified by actual law enforcement agencies, and so far it doesn't look like we left behind a single shred of evidence that any of us were there."

Cole lifts his wineglass, and he's surprised when Julia toasts him back.

Two sets of footsteps approach across the expansive terrace. Scott Durham and just behind him, Noah, looking unexpectedly dapper in a hunter-green polo shirt and beige jeans. Noah takes a seat at the place that's been set for him, pours himself a glass of wine.

When he sees Scott lingering, Cole waves him away. "Thank you, Mr. Durham. But move along now. Plausible deniability and all that."

"That's supposed to apply to the person in charge," he says with a smile. But he's gone in a few seconds, and suddenly the three of them are alone for the first time ever.

Nobody says anything for a bit. Cole knows exactly where Noah's been, and he's looking for evidence of his time there in his expression. There isn't any.

"Soon it will just be the three of us," Julia finally says, "and I'll be the one who's outnumbered."

"Well," Cole says, "I thought the whole point of moving in this direction was that we were the ones with common ground."

"Which is?" she asks.

"None of us wants Charlotte in a lab."

"Charley," Noah says.

"Excuse me?" Julia asks.

"She actually likes it," he says. "She likes being called Charley."

Cole's tempted to ask Noah when Charley had the chance to mention it to him, then realizes it must be something she told him back in Arizona.

"I'll make a note of that," Julia says, as if she won't, probably because it's a concern for people who actually plan on being in Charley's presence, and Julia doesn't. Not anytime soon.

"Easy, stallion," Cole says to Noah. "She hasn't been your patient for a long time."

Noah seems to realize the folly of chastising the two of them over details he learned when he was deceiving Charlotte Rowe under an assumed name.

"Apologies," he says. "I do have a tendency to get . . . committed."

"That's one way of putting it," Julia says. "And it manifests as a tendency to do things entirely on your own."

"Indeed," he says; then he reaches into his pocket and drops something in the middle of the glass table. A silver Saint Christopher's medal Stephen Drucker used to wear around his neck.

From the pinched expression on Julia's face, it's clear she recognizes it.

"I see," she says quietly. "I was aware the job was being done, but I wasn't aware you were doing it yourself."

"Both jobs," he says.

This is news to Cole, but not too much of a surprise.

"I was able to go through his phone thanks to Bailey." Noah forks a bite of crab salad into his mouth and chews carefully. "I learned two things. One, he was absolutely working with Philip. And two, the plan wasn't to stop us from remote dosing Charley. The plan was to overdose her."

"To kill her," Julia says. "Well, then, so they didn't just want to confine her to a lab."

Noah nods, takes another bite of food. Of course he can relay this news casually. Killing the men responsible allowed him to purge his ill will toward them.

"And paradron?" Cole asks.

"I think their code name for it was Pay Dirt. I downloaded the texts onto a flash drive. I'm sure they'll be helpful."

Pay Dirt . . . paradron. So there it was. Noah was right. Stephen had decided to blow apart The Consortium because he and his scientists had discovered something within the molecular structure of the supercharged cancer strain paradrenaline created, something Cole and his scientists must have missed. For reasons they'd have to uncover, Stephen thought paradron wasn't just an effective poison; it was something far more significant. Something that could produce benefits to him and Philip more profitable than anything they could harvest from paradrenaline alone or from the mysteries of Charlotte Rowe's blood. *Pay Dirt.*

But what was the dirt, and who was going to get paid?

"We have to make a move on his lab," Cole says.

"Easy, Cole," Julia says. "Build a surveillance file first like we agreed. Let's see what Bailey can turn up. I'm at my massive-cover-up threshold for the month."

The discovery that Noah's theory was right, that Cole's hasty surrender of paradron was the cause of so much of their recent troubles, is easier to accept now that Noah's sitting right next to him, quietly eating lunch. There's also the simple fact that Julia's decided not to rake his ass over the coals for it, either.

"A toast," Julia says, raising her glass. "To whatever it is we are now."

"An investment opportunity."

"There's that," Julia says, "or Dr. Brains here could make a breakthrough that we could actually reveal to the world without upending it. Something that would give a veneer of legitimacy to the project. Then we could direct funds to it through proper aboveboard channels."

"You're talking about making it a project of Graydon Pharmaceuticals?" Cole asks.

"Perhaps, yes," she says.

"Where does that put you and your stake?"

"I don't know. I've always thought I'd be quite at home on the board of Graydon Pharmaceuticals."

"I'm not sure that would work, Julia."

"You don't want me on your board?"

"I don't think my mother does, given you had an affair with her husband."

"Oh, I'll work on her. It's a new chapter in both our lives. And there's one thing that's more important to your mother than any sense of fairness or justice."

"Me?"

"I wish I could say differently, but no. Money and connections. And I have plenty of both."

"Good luck with that charm offensive. You're on your own."

"Good to know. I'll leave you to find the few billionaires in the world who are into developing secret weapons and will also happen to share your great affection for letting Charlotte Rowe enjoy small-town life."

"*Our* affection. I was under the impression neither one of us wants to make her a prisoner."

"That's correct, but I can't say I'm a big fan of her town. I had them drive me through when I went to visit friends in Carmel. It's sort of dreadful, if you ask me."

"I don't think anyone in Altamira did," Cole says.

"Very well, then. I don't have to live there. She does. That said, allow me to say, even though it was presented as more of an announcement than anything else, I am very happy that Dr. Turlington will be absorbing the paradrenaline studies into his lab. While I was a big fan of Dr. Chen's demeanor and presentations, her actual progress left a lot to be desired."

Julia rises to her feet, picks up her purse from where it's hanging on the back of her wrought-iron chair. "All right, I'll leave you boys to do whatever it is you two do to each other."

"We haven't had the entrée yet," Cole says.

"Oh, that's so dear of you, but I've got to run. I'm having drinks with a Saudi prince who is a huge fan of my new microdrones."

"Ask him if he hates serial killers," Noah says in between chews.

"No, thank you. I'm not jumping into that pool again feetfirst. Even if we do have to get creative with our financing for a while.

Goodbye, gentlemen." She's at the sliding deck door when she turns as if a thought's struck her. "And Noah?"

"Yes?"

"Thank you for killing Stephen and Philip. I hope they burn in hell for what they tried to do to Charley." Then, as if she did little more than compliment them both on the menu, she smiles, waves, and leaves.

"News flash," Cole says. "Julia Crispin believes in hell."

Cole sips his wine and reminds himself that the expansive view from his terrace is one he should never take for granted. Kayakers make bright dots on the sparkling blue water, and the cliffs on the northern side of the bay are gaining definition as the sun travels west. Noah appears to be enjoying it, but there's no telling unless Cole asks. His glazed eyes could mean he's lost in thought.

"She's not giving me a hard time about everything because she wants on my board," Cole says.

"Ah, the perils of being a master of the universe."

"Cynical," Cole says.

"Sarcastic," Noah responds. "There's a difference."

"I see. Was it quick?"

Startled by this abrupt subject change, Noah looks into his eyes. But he doesn't stop eating.

"Stephen, yes. Philip, no. He saw it coming sooner and had a lot to say."

"Like what?" Cole asks.

"Something about the greatest scientific breakthrough in history being in the hands of a spoiled, incompetent little fag and his inexplicable affection for a mouthy white-trash girl from nowhere."

"Charming."

"We can't all go out in a blaze of elegance."

"Do you agree with him?"

"Of course not. Why do you think I killed him?"

"Because we told you to," Cole says.

Noah takes the last bite of his salad, chews it thoughtfully.

"And I owed it to you," he finally says.

"How's that?"

"You were right. I had no idea what I was asking when I told you to activate The Consortium again. I didn't know them well enough, and I didn't stop to consider how they'd react when they learned we had one living test subject. But the truth is, I only had to ask because I never expected her to run."

"Charlotte?"

He nods. "I thought once she realized what I'd really slipped her, she'd be grateful. And we'd end up working together. That was my weakness, I guess."

"Arrogance," Cole offers.

"I was going to say optimism, but OK."

"Were you in love with her?" Cole asks.

The question seems to startle Noah, and that was exactly Cole's intention. He reaches for his wineglass and takes a sip. But he doesn't break the eye contact, and so the moment starts to feel like a stare down.

"I hated her. Before I met her. I thought she'd exploited everything about what happened to our mothers. And then I learned the real story and . . ."

"And what?" Cole asks, his heart racing.

"She became like a sister to me."

The question's at the tip of his tongue, but he can't bring himself to ask it. *Were you in love with me?*

"Scott told me my flight's scheduled for tonight at ten," Noah says.

"Correct."

"I'd like you to push it until tomorrow night."

"Why?"

"So I have time to fuck you. A lot."

What startles Cole isn't Noah's choice of words but the unaffected tone with which he's just delivered them, without any of the leering flirtatiousness he's used to tease Cole on this subject in the recent past. As if Cole—or his body, at least—is something he's decided to acquire after careful consideration.

"Murder turns you on, does it?" Cole asks.

"Thinking of all the ways we might change the world turns me on."

"I see."

"Do you?"

"You know you're not obligated, right?" Cole says.

"For Christ's sake, Cole. It's not like I'm going to make a complaint to HR."

"OK. Well, I'm not sure the way we used to is going to work anymore."

"We can do it any way you want." Noah stands, sets down the wineglass he just emptied in one long swallow. "Within limits," he says. Then he steps through the sliding door into the living room.

"I guess no one's eating lunch, then," Cole says to himself, then he sets his fork down and his napkin on his chair and gets to his feet.

At the base of the stairs, Cole finds Noah's crumpled polo shirt. At the top, his beige jeans. And by the time Cole enters the bedroom, Noah is naked and on all fours atop the bedspread, head bowed, a human coffee table of muscle and unexpected submission. He probably thinks Cole's special box of toys—handcuffs, restraints, and other implements that were once the only things capable of reducing him to wordless and thoughtless surrender in the arms of another—is still tucked under the bed. But it isn't. Cole hasn't used those things in forever. Because he wasn't lying. Something in his desire had shifted. Maybe it's evolved or grown, or maybe those words for it are too charged with value. Maybe killing a man has given him a taste for exerting power in the bedroom.

All he knows is that he doesn't want to be tied up, and he doesn't want Noah tied up. He wants Noah to look into his eyes, and that's what he does now as Cole rolls him onto his back atop the still fully made bed with its metallic-silver bedspread and night tables that look like steel cubes. His home is such a nest of sharp angles that at present Noah, for all his hard muscle and battle scars, seems like the softest thing in it. There's more stubble across Noah's chest than in years past, but all the traces of old combat wounds Cole used to caress and gently nibble are still there in flowery patterns along his waist and stomach.

Noah sits up, reaches for the hem of Cole's shirt. Every graze of his fingers against Cole's stomach sends gooseflesh racing up his chest. But untucking Cole's shirt causes him to break eye contact, which is the last thing Cole wants. He cups Noah's chin, raises it until they're looking at each other again.

"I wish I knew who you really were," he says.

"You do," Noah says. "You just haven't accepted it yet."

Then he's pulling him to the bed, and in another few minutes Cole is naked and on his back beneath the man's delicious, welcome weight, absorbing the studied hunger of his kisses, and too late, he realizes he's whispering Noah's former name, the name he went by the last time he was inside more than just Cole's mind.

44

Cambria, California

Luke suggested some recovery time at a cabin in the mountains, and as much as seclusion sounded tempting, Charlotte knew it was the last thing she needed. She needed people, life, the bright energy of a world where the Bannings and the Paynes were wolves stalking the forest shadows but the sidewalks were full of the kind of decent human being who stops to let others pass or dodges in front of a stroller with a hand up in case an oncoming car didn't see it.

So they settled on Cambria, a charming seafront village about an hour's drive south from their home in Altamira.

In Cambria, the shore was open and welcoming, nothing like Altamira's little crescent of beach, sandwiched between soaring cliffs and accessed only by a steep and treacherous staircase. In Cambria, wooden walkways traversed the crowns of low oceanfront bluffs, and when fog didn't shroud the coast—which was often, no matter the season—there were views for miles, mostly of golden mountains plunging to the sea, dappled with oaks. Hearst Castle sat atop one. When they both realized they'd never been, which seemed absurd given they'd grown up so near to it, they booked tickets. But as soon as they laid eyes on the bus they would have had to take up the mountain, they both went very still. Luke looked to Charley and Charley just shook her head. Its long, boxy shape, its giant hissing tires, the diesel fumes wafting from its tailpipe, invoked too many memories all at once. And so they lingered in the large gift shop, sat for a while outside the snack bar, watched the silly movie with all its dramatic reenactments from the life of William Randolph Hearst, and made jokes under their breath about whether a similar hagiography would ever be made about Cole Graydon or his late father.

They watched life. Children evading parents, only to be caught and lifted skyward in their mother or father's arms, giggling hysterically or wailing in protest or doing all the things that children do without regret. Then they drove south to Morro Bay, walked along the seafood restaurant–lined Embarcadero and out to the giant haystack rock that sits at the entrance to the harbor like an ancient monolithic temple from a lost religion. They smiled and nodded at the people they passed—tourist couples, families, college students from Cal Poly San Luis Obispo who'd made the short drive to the coast to ride some waves with their surfboards.

And occasionally as she and Luke sat quietly on benches and at outdoor tables at restaurants, she thought, *We are strangers here. We have seen more darkness than anyone else on this sidewalk or at this restaurant or possibly in this tiny, quaint town, and that means we don't belong.* But it was a lie. They belonged. How could she bring light to the darkness if she cut herself off from light altogether? And who's to know what seas of darkness lay in any stranger's memories? How many war veterans had she passed on the street in her lifetime who were locked in a near constant struggle with their painful memories of combat? How many criminals whose crimes were still undiscovered?

This is who I fight for, she reminded herself. *Not just the woman traveling alone. I fight for the right of a family to remain unbroken by the perversions of a human monster. I fight for the ones who stay vulnerable by risking connections with other humans, and so I can never withdraw from them again, no matter how tempting.*

Their bed-and-breakfast is one of many that line Moonstone Beach. They are on the second floor, and each night they've opened the double doors to let the cool ocean air blow through their cozy little room. Tonight is no different, with the exception that they've made love for the first time since leaving Texas. They'd made the agreement before the operation started that their first time after they got back she'd have to initiate. And something about the sight of Luke shaving in the mirror ignited a hungry urge. She thinks it was the combination of the boyish furrow in his brow as he studied his reflection and the slow military precision with which he drew the razor across his shaving cream–covered jaw. It wasn't the first time she'd seen him do this. Luke shaved as if the ceiling of the Sistine Chapel were at stake in his every razor stroke. Most nights it made her laugh, but tonight it was something else. It was familiar. Something from before that had easily survived all they'd been through. Cyrus Mattingly's truck, Marjorie's last wheezing breath, her unexpected reunion with Noah. Something as untouched by those things as the happy children they'd spotted on the street outside Linn's Café that day.

She'd slid up behind him, crossing her arms over his chest, surprising him into sudden stillness. Then she grabbed the nearest rag and used it to wipe the remaining shaving cream from his face before pulling him to the bed. It wasn't the right moment for his best alpha routine, not after the hours of confinement she'd recently suffered. He realized this as she mounted him, taking him inside. As she pressed their foreheads together, he gripped her waist firmly and forcefully, his eyes working to meet hers as he let her maintain control. By the time she finished, he'd risen to a seated position, his arms wrapped around her. When the sound of her release tore from her in a cathartic, unguarded cry, she felt something beyond the physical unclench.

Life. More life.

Now they're in their bathrobes, sitting on the small balcony of their room, watching wind-wiped fog blow through the branches of the bent Monterey pines lining the shore, listening to the roar of the ocean waves, sipping wine like something out of a commercial featuring people who've never killed anyone. Somewhere out there, Graydon security guards are monitoring their every move, possibly even staying at this bed-and-breakfast. She spotted a few that afternoon on Main Street. But that, like so many other strange and extraordinary things, is a fact of their lives now. And security's probably a good thing, given the feud Cole's decided to start with his business partners over her defiance. More importantly, just for the length of this trip, she and Luke have agreed. No shoptalk.

Shoptalk. That's how they've encircled and walled off the horrors they witnessed a few weeks before. *Let's see how long that works.*

"I feel bad for your grandmother," Luke finally says.

"That's the thought sex leaves you with?"

"No, silly. Wine. We're drinking wine."

"Oh, 'cause she was sober?"

"She never got to do this."

"She could do this; she just couldn't do the wine part."

"I know, but it's probably not the same."

"You know what she used to say to me?"

"Stay away from that Luke kid 'cause he's dog shit."

"She didn't have to say that. We all hated you when I was in high school."

"So I've heard."

"And confessed. Anyway, she said to me that after she first quit drinking, she'd look at somebody having a glass of wine in a restaurant and she'd kind of feel . . . I don't know, like, she'd grieve it for a second. Then she'd realize, I never had a glass of wine the way that person's having one right now. Just one nice, pleasant glass of wine. She'd say, if I had one, I'd have ten and wake up the next morning with no memory of what happened. So when I looked at the woman having a glass of wine in the restaurant and mourned for it, I was really mourning for something I'd never had at all. So I stopped."

"Profound."

"She could be that, for sure," she says.

"So, um, not sure that was the best lead-in, but I brought a bottle of your favorite Cakebread Cellars. It's in that canvas tote bag from the Copper Pot."

"Yeah, what a lead-in. You want to open it now?"

"Yeah, this one's empty." Luke upends the open bottle and pours so much into his glass it fills almost to the rim.

"Well, it is now," she says.

"Just get the Cakebread. I don't feel like going out. If we get hungry, I'll go grab us something."

"Fine."

Even though she could swear she didn't see it earlier, the canvas tote bag he just mentioned is on top of the television. When she goes to grab the neck of the bottle, she notices something off about the shape. That's when she sees the ring box taped to the outside of the bottle's neck, right below the cork. Her heart is racing as she tears it free. When she looks up, she sees Luke is on his feet, standing in the deck door, his eyes as wide and alert as when he first stepped into the back of Cyrus Mattingly's truck.

"What a lead-in, right?" he asks.

But there's piano-wire tension in his voice, and he's watching her every move as if he's afraid she's going to bolt from the room.

"Luke . . ."

"Open it."

She does, and the ring that glints back at her is simple and elegant. Is it the engagement ring of her dreams? There's no telling because she's never allowed herself the dream of even being engaged, not until recently, and so she's never rehearsed this moment in her head, never expected it. And suddenly all the negative voices she's held at bay during the course of this little vacation are on her in an instant, and they're insisting her suspicions are right: she's not meant to walk among the normal, the living. This is a gift for a normal girl who confines herself to a normal world.

"Now, though?" she asks.

It's all she can manage to say, and when she sees Luke's face fall, her heart lurches and she actually brings one hand to her mouth, as if her words have left a stain there she should wipe way.

"When?" he asks softly. Her response knocked the wind out of him. "When we retire? When we have a normal life again? We didn't pick normal, did we? That's kind of why I picked you. I've never wanted normal. I've always wanted a fight, as long as it's a good fight."

"So I'm a fight?" she asks, voice trembling.

"No. We fight the dark together. Always. And I'll go wherever the fight takes us, as long as I get to go with you, Charlotte Rowe."

"Luke . . ."

He moves to her, hesitantly at first. Then when she starts to cry, he takes her in his arms gently, and she knows as she says his name again and again that what she's really saying is *life*, because that's what he is and that's what this proposal is, and that's why she has no choice but to say yes.

45

Tulsa, Oklahoma

Zoey Long passes her sister's phone back so she can swipe through the photos from her vacation and Zoey can hide how badly her hands are shaking by clenching them between her knees under the table. Only once since returning home has she taken one of the pills her new friends have given her for moments like these. She speaks to the psychiatrist they've provided for her every night, a gentle, patient woman who's warned her that for the foreseeable future even basic uncomfortable emotions will feel coated in a layer of tremor-inducing anxiety.

No wonder her hands are shaking. She's been lying to her sister. Yes, she actually is leaving town on a plane later tonight, but the reason she gave for the trip is a fiction.

For the time being, she can only pretend to be enamored by Rachel's Paris photos. The truth is, the story Rachel tells for each picture goes in one of Zoey's ears and out the other.

She brings her bottle to her mouth. A mistake. Rachel looks up from her phone and goes still. Her hand must have shaken visibly enough for her sister to see.

"Oh, honey, is it the producer? Are you nervous?"

"Kinda, yeah. I feel bad."

"About what?"

"Quitting on Dr. Keables the way I did."

"Aw, fuck that, gurl. You got an opportunity. Jump on that shit. I don't want to see my little sister working in a dentist's office for the rest of her life. Not when she's as talented as you."

On the television above the bar, she glimpses the helicopter footage of Marjorie Payne's ranch that's now familiar to just about everyone in the country. Zoey closes her eyes, looks to the high-top table between them.

"Are you following this shit?" Rachel says. "My friend Tom is all about the Reddit thread on this one, and he thinks the woman felt so guilty one day she went out there and tried to dig up all the bodies herself and realized she couldn't do it, so she invited the guys over who helped her and killed them all. Me, I think they did it together, like as a suicide pact or something."

They definitely died together, Zoey thinks. And everything inside of her wants to tell her sister how close she came to being one of those bodies they discovered partially encased in concrete, but her new friends would hate that.

And her new friends are scary.

"Sorry," Rachel says when she sees the expression on her face. "I thought you were all about that true crime stuff."

"I'm kind of losing my taste for it, to be honest."

"You're not going to watch *Dateline* with me anymore?"

"Rachel, I will watch anything you want."

"OK, good. Don't go soft on me just 'cause you're writing a bunch of romance now. How long are you going to be out there anyway?"

"A couple weeks, at first. But I'll be back and forth. We're going to work on putting a pilot script together and then a treatment for a whole series. So he wants me to stay out there until the materials are ready to go to studios and networks. Then we'll probably have a bunch of pitch meetings, maybe meet with showrunners. So it's going to be a while."

"And you're sure this guy's not creepy? Hollywood seems creepy right now."

Not the kind of creepy you're thinking of, sis.

"Listen, Rachel, there's something I really want to say to you."

"Sure."

"Do you remember that day at the mall when we were little and that guy dressed up as a security guard—"

"Oh, Zoey, you really got to stop beating yourself up about that. We were—"

"I know, I know. I mean, I know every time I bring it up I say that . . . But I had a moment of thinking about it recently . . ." Several tears slip free before she's even aware they've filled her eyes. *A moment when I thought I'd never see you again.*

"Honey, are you OK?"

"I'm fine. I just . . . I'm having a moment, you know. The TV thing, it's really exciting. And it's just got me reflecting about a lot of stuff. And I started thinking about what you did at the mall that day, and I just thought it was so important. What you did. The way you spoke up. And it occurred to me that I'd never said what I should really say about it."

"What's that?"

"Thank you."

Rachel's not a big crier, but for some reason this little moment brings tears to her eyes as well, and Zoey thinks, *Good. She'll just think her sister's being a big softie. And I am, but she's got no idea why.* The fact that an old photograph of Marjorie Payne has just filled the television hanging over the bar only makes it all the more surreal. That and the Graydon security guard who followed them here. He's studying Zoey from across the bar with a concerned look. Sure, there's probably sympathy in it, but she's willing to bet he's more concerned she might be spilling secrets about what she really went through while her sister was gallivanting down the Champs-Élysées with her husband.

Shedding a few tears was apparently the tension release she needed. For the rest of Rachel's Paris stories she manages to act like the sister she was before Rachel left.

And suddenly, just sitting there, listening to Rachel talk fills her with gratitude so total she's afraid she'll start crying again. She'd lost her faith in that pit, came to believe that a horrible, violent death was only minutes away. And now, here she is. Every giggle and joke and curse word out of her sister's mouth is a gift. And why should it end with Rachel? Colors. Smells. Music. All of it is a gift; she came so close to having it all pulled away.

And maybe this realization will help her accept the fact that while she wasn't exactly thrilled by the prospect of going back to work, her new friends didn't suggest that she quit her job; they instructed her to. And a producer isn't flying her to the West Coast, even though he has an amazing website complete with a dummy phone number and contact email addresses, all of which appeared overnight. And she didn't ask for the security guards that have been following her ever since she left Marjorie Payne's ranch; they just never left.

Zoey hugs her sister long and hard as they wait for their Ubers outside the bar. But Rachel's got no idea where Zoey's really headed once she steps into hers. It's not Tulsa International like she said. Instead, after she picks up her bags and her cat from her apartment, she'll head to a private airfield—and then from there to a destination that seems shrouded in mystery even though she's heard the name a million times before.

46

San Diego, California

Maybe it was the time she spent with her sister, or maybe it was the fact that the inevitable trip was finally underway and there was nothing else to plan or prepare for, but Zoey passed out cold the minute she sank into the Gulfstream's comfy leather seat. She didn't wake until the wheels touched down and she heard Boris the Destroyer meowing inside the cat carrier, probably from the change in pressure.

Now they're taxiing across a small private airfield that looks similar to the one she took off from in Tulsa. Three Chevy Suburbans with heavily tinted windows are waiting for her like she's the president or something. She doesn't recognize any of the people standing next to the cars. There are a few security types who look and are dressed similar to the guys on board with her. But these guys are younger. The one standing in front has really thick sandy-blond hair, and he's dressed in ratty jeans and a T-shirt for some band that looks like it hasn't put out an album in years. His face seems vaguely familiar, but she can't quite place him.

The stairs descend, and the guards gesture for her to go first, one of them taking her suitcase. Before she reaches the bottom, the kid in the T-shirt is coming toward her, taking the cat carrier out of her hands.

"Hey, I'm Bailey. Is there a cat in here?"

"Yes."

"I'm allergic, but I'll carry him anyway because you're probably kind of freaked out right now."

"I'm glad someone said it."

"Excited about your new job?"

"I wasn't really looking for a new job, but they gave me some options and this sounded like the best one."

"Yeah, that seems like their style. By the way, Luke's my brother. The guy who helped rescue you."

He must be referring to the guy who was waiting for her and Charley back on the ranch. Now she realizes why the guy before her looks familiar. "I remember him. So this is, like, a family business?"

"Sort of. Maybe. I mean, sure."

They reach the first Suburban and Bailey places the cat carrier in the cargo bay. The guards follow suit with her bags. Well, at least she's being treated well. But Bailey's stopped with his hand on the door handle to the back seat, studying her closely. She's about to break the silence by asking him if she'd said something wrong when he says, "Have they told you what you're going to be doing?"

"Basically, yeah."

"It's disturbing. Like really disturbing, especially considering what you just went through. I mean, I can go basically anywhere on the internet I want. I have to go to dark places and I collect massive amounts of data, but I can't go through it all myself, and sometimes we need actual human intelligence to interpret it. That's what you'd be doing if you go this route."

"If I can do anything to stop someone else from going through what I went through, I'll do it." They're unrehearsed, these words, and come out of her with a strength that convinces her that maybe she really did pick the best option. Maybe this is the best way to let her new employers ensure she remain silent about every impossible thing she's witnessed.

Bailey nods, then smiles. "All right, then. Let's hunt some monsters."

As she steps into the Suburban, Zoey wonders for the first time if the inevitable result of mortgaging your life to write books about magic is that you'll eventually cross paths with someone who seems to practice it.

GLOSSARY OF TERMS

ZYPRAXON. An experimental drug invented by Dr. Noah Turlington that produces bursts of incredible physical strength and nearly instantaneous healing in animal test subjects, but only when the drug is triggered by a stimulus that terrifies the subject. All attempts to replicate the results of animal tests in human subjects caused the human subject's swift and gruesome death. With one notable exception—Charlotte Rowe.

PARADRENALINE. Partially resembling a hormone, paradrenaline is believed responsible for the bursts of incredible strength and rapid healing Zypraxon causes. It is a never-before-seen chemical compound found only in the bodies of those in whom Zypraxon has been triggered. For paradrenaline to remain active and extractable from the subject, the subject must survive well after the trigger event. The medical implications of paradrenaline are vast and extend far beyond its connection to Zypraxon.

TRIGGER EVENT. An event or stimulus of any kind that produces an acute sense of panic and terror on the part of the human subject. Only events of this magnitude are capable of causing Zypraxon to trigger the synthesis of paradrenaline in the subject's bloodstream. Typically, subjects must feel as if their lives are in immediate and mortal jeopardy or experience intense and almost debilitating physical pain.

TRIGGER WINDOW. Following a trigger event, the subject experiences incredible physical strength and nearly instantaneous healing for a period of three hours. The window is slightly shorter in nonhuman subjects.

THE CONSORTIUM. An alliance of several defense industry contractors and the CEO of Graydon Pharmaceuticals. It has been convened only twice. Once, when Dr. Noah Turlington, then an employee of Graydon Pharmaceuticals, first brought Zypraxon's implications to the attention of its CEO, Cole Graydon. And second, after a covert and unsanctioned field test determined Charlotte Rowe was the only human test subject in which Zypraxon functioned effectively. The Consortium's goal is to ensure absolute secrecy around all tests of both Zypraxon and paradrenaline, while also providing the vast funding required for the experiments in a manner that does not raise red flags on the accounting ledgers of their individual companies. In exchange, members are allowed to exploit the benefits of Zypraxon and paradrenaline that prove relevant to their specific industries.

PROJECT BLUEBIRD 1.0. First initiated to discover if Zypraxon could be used in humans, it was hastily terminated by Cole Graydon after all four volunteer test subjects went lycan. The test subjects were all male with backgrounds in military special operations.

GOING LYCAN. The phrase used to describe the gruesome acts of self-mutilation the majority of human test subjects performed when Zypraxon was triggered in their bloodstream. The majority of these acts culminate in the human subject targeting their own head in a fatally destructive manner.

PROJECT BLUEBIRD 2.0. Initiated after it was discovered that Charlotte Rowe was the only human in whom Zypraxon seemed to work properly. In exchange for the opportunity to conduct field tests that generate extractable paradrenaline in Rowe's bloodstream, The Consortium finances and provides the logistical support for Rowe to hunt serial killers, posing as a potential victim to ensure abduction to their kill sites so that she might use the resulting trigger events to overpower them and leave them exposed to the arrival of law enforcement.

THE HUNT LIST. A database listing individuals worldwide who regularly purchase chemicals that can be used to aid the rapid decomposition or complete destruction of a human body and who have no legitimate personal or professional reason to do so. This database is compiled through a sophisticated series of computer hacks of both public and private records that are arguably unethical and entirely illegal. The fifteen individuals on the list who make qualifying purchases most frequently occupy what is called "The Red Tier."

ACKNOWLEDGMENTS

Creative inspiration for this novel along with invaluable research insights came from the book *Encyclopedia of the Great Plains*, and I thank its editor, David J. Wishart, along with all the other writers who took part in this cooperative project from the Center for Great Plains Studies at the University of Nebraska.

The massive tornado that struck Lubbock, Texas, on May 11, 1970, is a real event that changed meteorology forever, but the Payne family as well as the Plains Rapist are complete fictions. A big thank-you to authors Pamela Brink and Cindy Martin for their wonderful picture book, *Lubbock*, which is part of the Images of America series.

Charley's third outing was gifted with the same great editors as her first two, Liz Pearsons and Caitlin Alexander, and the same great agent, Lynn Nesbit. Also to Thomas & Mercer, major gratitude for the continued support from Grace Doyle, editorial director, publicity director Dennelle Catlett, and marketing director Lindsey Bragg. And for making Texas a state I don't have to research as much as many others, thanks to all my family there, who keep me connected to the state's uniqueness and colloquialisms and who I can say, much to their delight, appear nowhere in these pages. Much gratitude to Elizabeth Newman, formerly of CAA and now of Fox 21, and my fantastic attorney, Christine Cuddy.

I also have to give thanks to a very special group of people who enlightened me and educated me in ways they might not have realized while I was writing this novel: Dee Johnson, Paul Keables, Rebecca Kirsch, Emily Bensinger, Terry McGrath, Henry Thomas, and Evan Kralj-Johnson. I miss our special Fridays.

And, of course, profound gratitude to my *bestest* of best friends and my partner in the TDPS podcast and video network (www. thedinnerpartyshow.com), Eric Shaw Quinn. Launching our new podcast *TDPS Presents Christopher & Eric* with you has been a gift . . . even though you might quit when you find out I wrote another scary book with snakes in it. You're the only dude I'd ever do Christopher & Eric's True Crime TV Club with. Thanks also to our TDPS support team, Brandon Griffith and Brett Churnin. And a massive thanks across the board to our amazing web team at the Unreal Agency, specifically Cathy Dipierro and Christine Bocchiaro.

And last, but certainly not least, thanks and love to my mother, Anne Rice, and my beloved aunt, Karen O'Brien, both of whom taught me the redemptive power of justice fantasies. And by justice, I mean revenge. Sometimes.

ABOUT THE AUTHOR

Photo © 2016 Cathryn Farnsworth

Christopher Rice is an Amazon Charts bestselling author whose works include *Bone Music* and *Blood Echo* in the Burning Girl series; the *New York Times* bestseller *A Density of Souls*; and the Bram Stoker Award finalists *The Heavens Rise* and *The Vines*. He is an executive producer of *The Vampire Chronicles*, a television show based on the bestselling novels by his mother, Anne Rice. Together they penned *Ramses the Damned: The Passion of Cleopatra*. With his best friend and producing partner, *New York Times* bestselling novelist Eric Shaw Quinn, he runs the podcast and video network TDPS, which you can find at www.TheDinnerPartyShow.com. Visit him at www.christopherricebooks.com.